W9-AYD-034

STONEWALL INN EDITIONS
Keith Kahla, General Editor

Buddies by Ethan Mordden

Joseph and the Old Man
by Christopher Davis

Blackbird by Larry Duplechan

Gay Priest by Malcolm Boyd

Privates by Gene Horowitz

Taking Care of Mrs. Carroll
by Paul Monette

Conversations with My Elders
by Boze Hadleigh

Epidemic of Courage
by Lon Nungesser

One Last Waltz by Ethan Mordden

Gay Spirit by Mark Thompson, ed.

As If After Sex by Joseph Torchia

The Mayor of Castro Street
by Randy Shilts

Nocturnes for the King of Naples
by Edmund White

Alienated Affections
by Seymour Kleinberg

God of Ecstasy by Arthur Evans

Valley of the Shadow
by Christopher Davis

Love Alone by Paul Monette

The Boys and Their Baby
by Larry Wolff

On Being Gay by Brian McNaught

Parisian Lives by Samuel M. Steward

Living the Spirit by Will Roscoe, ed.

Everybody Loves You
by Ethan Mordden

Untold Decades by Robert Patrick

Gay & Lesbian Poetry in Our Time
by Carl Morse & Joan Larkin, eds.

Personal Dispatches
by John Preston, ed.

Tangled Up in Blue
by Larry Duplechan

How to Go to the Movies
by Quentin Crisp

Just Say No by Larry Kramer

The Prospect of Detachment
by Lindsley Cameron

*The Body and Its Dangers and Other
Stories* by Allen Barnett

Dancing on Tisha B'av
by Lev Raphael

Arena of Masculinity
by Brian Pronger

Boys Like Us by Peter McGehee

Don't Be Afraid Anymore
by Reverend Troy D. Perry
with Thomas L.P. Swicegood

The Death of Donna-May Dean
by Joey Manley

Sudden Strangers
by Aaron Fricke and Walter Fricke

Profiles in Gay & Lesbian Courage
by Reverend Troy D. Perry
and Thomas L.P. Swicegood

Latin Moon in Manhattan
by Jaime Manrique

On Ships at Sea by Madelyn Arnold

The Dream Life by Bo Huston

Sweetheart by Peter McGehee

Show Me the Way to Go Home
by Simmons Jones

Winter Eyes by Lev Raphael

Boys on the Rock by John Fox

Dark Wind by John Jiler

End of the Empire by Denise Ohio

The Listener by Bo Huston

Labour of Love by Doug Wilson

Tom of Finland
by F. Valentine Hooven III

Reports from the holocaust,
revised ed. by Larry Kramer

The Gay Militants by Donn Teal

Created Equal by Michael Nava and
Robert Dawidoff

Gay Issues in the Workplace
by Brian McNaught

Sportsdykes by Susan Fox Rogers, ed.

Long Road to Freedom by Mark
Thompson, ed.

Sacred Lips of the Bronx
by Douglas Sadownick

The Violet Quill Reader
by David Bergman, ed.

West of Yesterday, East of Summer
by Paul Monette

Love Songs of Phoenix Bay
by Nisa Donnelly

The Love Songs of Phoenix Bay

Also by Nisa Donnelly

The Bar Stories:
A Novel After All

THE LOVE SONGS

OF PHOENIX BAY

Nisa Donnelly

St. Martin's Press / New York

While San Francisco and Marion, Illinois, are real locations, the characters, businesses, addresses, and events depicted in this work are fictional. Any relation to actual persons, businesses, addresses, and events is purely coincidental. Peru is considered to have possibly the largest collection of excavated and unexcavated archaeological sites in the world. The archaeologists and university sponsorships depicted in this work are fictional. However, many archaeologists have been leaving Peru because of the civil war there, which continues.

THE LOVE SONGS OF PHOENIX BAY. Copyright © 1994 by Nisa Donnelly. *All rights reserved. Printed in the United States of America. No part of this book may be used or reproduced in any manner whatsoever without written permission except in the case of brief quotations embodied in critical articles or reviews. For information, address St. Martin's Press, 175 Fifth Avenue, New York, N.Y. 10010.*

Library of Congress Cataloging-in-Publication Data

Donnelly, Nisa.
The love songs of Phoenix Bay / Nisa Donnelly.
    p.   cm. — (Stonewall Inn editions)
ISBN 0-312-13561-0 (paperback)
1. AIDS (Disease)—Patients—California—San Francisco—Fiction.
2. Friendship—California—San Francisco—Fiction.   3. Lesbians—
California—San Francisco—Fiction.   4. Sisters—California—San
Francisco—Fiction.   5. Women—California—San Francisco—Fiction.
6. San Francisco (Calif.)—Fiction.   I. Title.   II. Series.
PS3554.0532L68   1995
813'.54—dc20
                                                    95-31675
                                                      CIP

First published by St. Martin's Press

First Stonewall Inn Edition: November 1995
10 9 8 7 6 5 4 3 2 1

For Ellyn for always being there

Acknowledgments

Every book belongs to many people. This one belongs especially to my best friend and surrogate sister, Ellyn Ford, who has been saving me from myself for longer than I care to admit, and who provided a safe home where I could heal and write. Without her, this truly would not have been possible. It also belongs to my editor, Michael Denneny, who saw a statue beneath the rubble and had the patience and skill to help me find it; my mentor, Judy Grahn, who believed in me even when I no longer believed in myself, and who remains my beacon and my rock; my best critics, Kris Brandenburger and Theresa Corrigan, who kept me honest and on track; my publicist, Michele Karlsberg, whose tenacity amazes me and whose wit always makes me smile; and my long-time friends Bob Anderson and Franco Sisneros, who took me in, taught me the fog game, and planted the seeds for this project. It also would not have been possible without the words, work, lives, courage, and support of these truly remarkable gay men, who helped me become a responsible tourist in their reality: Fred Banuelos, the late Allen Barnett, Steven Corbin, Allan Gidley, Patrick Hoctel, the late Bo Huston, the late Joel Johnson, Jeff Kahn, Richard Labonte, Paul Monette, and the late John Preston.

Oh hell yes! I stand,
have stood, will stand;
my feet are killing me!
—JUDY GRAHN
Helen you always were
the factory: Annie Lee

The Love Songs of Phoenix Bay

"When I was three years old, I wanted to see my mother's cunt. Does that shock you? It shocked her, to wake up and find her youngest child's head under the sheets, between her legs, staring. That was the first time she slapped me. Looking back, I think I wasn't so much curious as I wanted to go back in. Maybe even then, I sensed what was out here waiting for me. It's the first clear memory I have of my mother." She drops the curtain and turns, half smiling. The psychiatrist meets her gaze, unblinking. Cats. Do this. The idea skits, then disappears. She turns back to the window.

"Mama named me Phoenix for the city in Arizona. It's a family tradition, naming people for places, which isn't all that strange considering the number of places named for people. We take our names from where we've never been and have no real interest in going. It started with my great-grandmother TaTa Hassee—for the city in Florida. Her daddy liked the sound of it. Tallahassee. She named my grandmother Cicero for the same reason, I suppose. The only place she ever went was crazy. That would've been shortly after she named my mother Villanova for, you know, Pennsylvania. She's never been west of the Mississippi River, unless you count St. Louis. I don't. My sister Savannah spends her winters in Arizona—Scottsdale, which isn't all that far from Phoenix. I, on the other hand, have no interest in deserts, but once spent a long and rainy February in the arms of a redheaded woman from Georgia—Atlanta, as I recall. We were in college. We weren't in love."

On the street below, a bus lumbers toward its stop. She could fade out the door, down the stairs, across the street, and then disappear. The bus will wind through classy neighborhoods and shabby. She would get off in the Tenderloin, stumble on a broken curb. She will catch herself on a bent and rusted sign: NO STOPPING, NO STANDING. She will climb stairs, thinly carpeted, nails exposed like seeds. A small man, with mute and rheumy eyes, will rent her a room by the week. She will speak to no one, and no one will speak to her. She will buy a blue plastic transistor radio from one of the cut-rate electronics stores on upper Market. When the batteries wear down, she will buy more at the corner liquor store, run by a man who sits on a high stool behind a cage, doling out half-pints and single cigarettes. "Dime," he says, "dime each." He is a gray man, very fat; no one dares ask his name. Like the others, she will approach his throne carefully, holding out crumpled dollar bills, her hand trembling, anxious for change. Two dimes and three pennies. She will take a job in a diner two doors down from the hotel and wear a pink polyester apron and a pencil behind her right ear. Her name tag will say, HELLO, MY NAME IS BETSY or DOLLY or MARGE; it will have been left behind by the woman who had the job the week before. She will have found it on the counter under the cash register. She will let them believe it is fate that she has the same name. Her universe will constrict to one small block, two sides of the street, where you can have your hair cut, your fortune told, your belly filled, or your wildest fantasies stoked for a negotiable price. The past will not reach there. Eventually she will forget her own name. She will forget how to cry. Again. She will have no use for such things, where she is going.

The bus shudders and moves on.

"Phoenix?" Turning at the sound of her name, she drops the curtain, refocusing on the psychiatrist, framed by sunlight, shades of brown rimmed with gold. Teddy Grayson is like that, too: an elegant, nutmeg-colored woman, with solid-gold bangles that never jangle, marching up her arms. Insured insanity pays well. "You were telling me about your family's names. What are your thoughts about your name?"

"That Mama could have done better than Arizona. The only truly interesting thing about that place has to be the immortalists. Two men and a woman. I've seen their pictures; they must be fifty years old or so by now. They're planning to live forever; same bodies, same brains, just cranking on and on, out of fear I suppose, or some private version of hell, or maybe even salvation. I don't envy them. I keep coming back to the same question: If this is all there is, why bother?"

Beyond this window, The City languishes cold and easy, an overpriced whore still living on her looks, but not for much longer, hoping the strangers won't notice her flaws, and the regulars will remember enough of how she used to be to forgive what she's become. The City. The newspapers here always print it that way, with capital letters, as if the only city in the world were San Francisco. People here believe it's true. It's not.

Here for the better part of a decade, a long time by California standards, Phoenix Bay has grown blind to it all. Houses like colored barnacles cling to the sides of the hills; people dressed in rags cling to the sidewalks. If you live here long enough, you don't notice, until someone points them out, the barnacles or the beggars. She moved here to be with a woman, of course. Jinx. Wasn't a woman always behind the worst and the best decisions of her life? She's moved a dozen times for love, in and out of cities and houses and lives. She can't remember all the addresses she's had in the last seventeen years; she can't forget the names or the faces of the women she's shared them with. Or wanted to. And now she's moving again. Rennie Johnson, her only friend left in the world, told her "We need each other." Maybe so. All that's left of her old life is in the back of the Jeep parked in the bus zone across the street: three boxes; a Hefty Steel Sack garbage bag holding a pair of matched dwarf sinsemilla marijuana plants, both female, the strain perfected for indoor growing; and a small hydroponics system. Hydroponics is the savior of urban dope growers. Like her,

3

the plants are alive but not much more. Nearly everything else went to Mr. Rizzo, the junk dealer. She told him she was moving to Mauritius because it was the only place that came to mind. He gave her sixteen fifty-dollar bills. Not enough for a whole life, she told him; he'd shrugged. Not enough.

Phoenix Bay's life gapes with not enough. Not good enough. Not smart enough. Not pretty enough. Not enough of a real lesbian, whatever the hell that means. The angry young women she knew when she was first out as a lesbian, out of her mother's house, out into the world, used to accuse her of that. Enough of a lesbian to have your lover in my bed, Phoenix would think, but never dared say. Well, she was always good enough for that. Even Jinx said so that last night, hanging her head like a pup: "The sex was wonderful, Phoenix, but it wasn't enough." Then after "Jeopardy," Jinx dropped her house keys on the kitchen table and ran off to Sonoma County into the arms of a woman whose name Phoenix can never quite remember. Pansy? Patsy? Something like that. Not that it matters. Now Phoenix is running, too. Some things never change.

In the darkening glass, a woman, huge eyes sunken into shadows, regards her, scowling. Loser. She stares, fascinated by the sight of her own collarbone glaring, hard and hungry, her shirt hanging in loose folds. She imagines she is losing her skin. This is how it happens, this is how you disappear. Last week, she thought she was dying; a cancer, perhaps, or an exotic tropical disease borne by spiders with sharp infected jaws. But there is no cancer growing in her and she has not been to the tropics; there are no such spiders here. The doctor, a sweet-faced woman named Madonna for the mother of God, not the rock star, looked on Phoenix with pity, perhaps, or compassion. Impossible to say which. "What have you been eating?" Fumé blanc and Oreo cookies was not the right answer. The doctor scowled; the rock star wouldn't have cared; the mother of God is gone the way of dead angels.

"What's the matter with that tree? It looks dead."

Teddy Grayson sighs, almost imperceptibly, but not quite. Phoenix hears her rise from the tufted green leather chair, where the buttons are perfect, untouched, unlike the couch where the clients are supposed to sit, its buttons worked loose, its leather folds free of dust. Too many frantically busy fingers there. "Which tree, Phoenix?" Teddy Grayson even smells expensive. She leans close to look out the narrow, paned window. Paned to keep the unruly or truly desperate from flying away, out into the middle of California Street, where cable cars sing and shriek, tourists clinging like grinning snails. "A tree of heaven and it's not dead. Deceptive, isn't it? How it looks lifeless in winter? In another month, you'll start to see it come back. By summer, they're barely recognizable. The change is very rapid and actually quite amazing."

Phoenix turns and regards the psychiatrist carefully. "Is that supposed to be a metaphor?"

"I didn't mean it to be, no."

She smiles a little. "Good, because it wasn't a very polished one. I used to be an English teacher, you know. Of course, I probably wasn't very good at that, either."

"Do you want to tell me about that, Phoenix?"

She looks beyond Teddy Grayson's questioning eyes into the faces of three African masks hanging on the opposite wall, where they share space with gilt-framed diplomas that Phoenix has never bothered to read. The masks are more interesting, how the empty eyes seem to follow, the expressions changing with the light. They always look a little superior, as if the secrets they've heard are nothing compared to what they in their hundred years or more have witnessed. "Nothing to tell, really. Monday afternoon, I couldn't remember what class I was teaching. *Hamlet* wound up in *A Midsummer Night's Dream.* I honestly don't think any of the students would have noticed if it hadn't been for Sue Lin. She's my best student." Sue Lin will name her daughters Ophelia or Desdemona. Or she will not. "She ran to get the department chair when I couldn't stop crying." Phoenix wonders if Teddy Grayson suspects that she's lying. She was not crying; she was weeping the way Ophelia wept, and Gran Cicero; wringing her hands and crying to the heavens for salvation. Instead, she got the department chair, a man with an irrational fear of lesbians, a condition caused less by Phoenix than by his Gothic novelist wife, who had moved her secretary, a charming butch with black eyes, into first their

5

house and then their bed. The department chair apparently had neither the good sense nor the pride to leave; instead he moved into the guest room that overlooked the novelist's prize rose bushes, which he ceremoniously pissed on every night before retiring.

"Being a teacher is the only respectable thing I've managed to accomplish in my entire life, at least as far as my mother is concerned. What am I supposed to tell her now? That I don't eat? Can't sleep? That I wake up screaming?"

Turning away from the window, Phoenix regards Teddy Grayson, motionless, fingers making little pyramids, face perfectly composed, showing less emotion than the masks on the wall. She is a patient woman (you need patience in this line of work) and carefully beautiful, the way seasoned, successful women so often are. The face of a list maker, of a woman who understands priorities. Phoenix has no use for priorities. She does not understand the kinds of women who do.

"How often has this happened, Phoenix, that you've awakened screaming?"

Awakened screaming? Put that way, it sounds less terrifying. Probably something Teddy learned at one of those universities responsible for the diplomas on the wall. Phoenix shrugs, caught. She hadn't meant to step so close to the psychoanalytic trap. "This week? Two or three times. And then again this morning. Before that? I don't know. A few times, I guess. The night Daddy left. And Jinx. It's a pretty fair indicator of when you've actually hit bottom." Phoenix Bay looks up and smiles, quick, insincere, then studies her hands: long fingers, ragged nails, a cuticle chewed bloody. She used to be proud of her hands, rubbed thick cream into them every night. Jinx used to love her hands. But then Jinx had loved a lot about Phoenix before she slipped and started to slide down, not the kind of down where dreams rip like silk—making that perfect, high-pitched whine—but further, where everything becomes clear because nothing is left: pride, shame, joy, hope, most of all hope. All that's left is a crystal vision of what is and what can never be again. There should be some comfort in that, but there's not.

"Funny, I always thought bottom would look . . . I don't

know . . . different somehow, more grotesque, like hell in a cheap horror movie. But it's just like the rest of life, only picked clean." Bleached bones on the desert floor. Shades of black and white. Great photographers see the world this way, stripping away the seductive colors down to bare shapes and emotions. Photographers and blues singers. "Do you suppose Bessie Smith ever woke up screaming? Probably not. Seems more like a Janis Joplin kind of thing. Maybe it's one of those baby-boomer phenomena. Well, why not after the bill of goods we've been sold? Disneyland. Fucking happily-ever-after. Pretty little Snow White and her seven eunuchs. Hi-ho my ass.

"I once had a religious experience at Disneyland. Of course, I was still drinking then. It was the weekend Daddy died and I found Jinx in a West Hollywood bar. Freud probably would've made more of that than there was. Daddy always promised he'd take me there—to Disneyland, not a gay bar in West Hollywood—'Just the two of us,' he'd say, 'but you've got to be good.' I guess I wasn't ever good enough. And nobody ever loves you enough. And that's just the lay of the play. Daddy used to say that, too: 'The lay of the play.' I always did wonder what he meant by that. I guess I should've asked. I should've asked him a lot of things, like how he could walk out on a seven-year-old kid and leave her to grow up in a house full of crazy women. Well, too late to worry about that now. He's dead and I'm living out my legacy."

Crossing to the couch, Phoenix balances on its wide arm, her legs stretched out. She has strong legs, not especially long, and more powerful than shapely. She is an intense woman with huge indigo eyes, full lips almost too large for her face, and brindle hair—blond and taupe streaks and shadings on a field of brown, as if the sun had settled there—which leave her with a look more sweet than sultry. Although lovers and the occasional stranger have insisted Phoenix is beautiful, hers is an accidental kind of beauty, the kind so often seen in the backwater parts of the country. All those years gone, and still she wears the look of it, carries the sound of it on her tongue, in her ears. Nothing from that hated place ever was, ever could be, beautiful. Locking her hands behind her, she leans back and stares at the ceiling. Little patterns

7

try to push through the plaster. She is a kid, picking out faces in the clouds. There, a rooster. There, a chariot. There, the eye of God.

"My mother called at six o'clock this morning. She likes to get in on the cheap rates. And since I don't have anyplace else to be, she doesn't get the answering machine, the message with Jinx saying: 'We can't come to the phone right now; we're in search of the perfect orgasm.' You wouldn't believe some of the messages people leave. Left, I mean. You know, Jinx and I weren't good at a lot of things, but we were damned good at fucking. As a matter of fact, we were terrific. Fortunately, it never occurred to me until after she was gone—and I doubt if she knows it yet—looking for the perfect orgasm is like looking for the perfect high. I mean, what do you do once you've found it? Put it in a frame? Invite the neighbors over to take a look? It's not like you can even describe it. Compared to sex, pain is easy to describe: The bitch tore my heart out. That you can relate to; it says something. But passion? No, passion just tangles and sways. Still, everyone is out there looking for that one perfect, ultimate, blow-your-brains-out body rush. But what if you've already had it? Do you say, 'Sorry, babe, let's just go for coffee?' Of course you don't. Or what if it only gets worse or stays the same? No one ever thinks of that. We're all just emotional masochists out there looking for one more high, sure the next one will be better than the last, even if it's not, even if it can't be. And every woman in the world is sure it'll be the next one or the one after that; all we have to do is find it. What I want to know is: What difference does it make when we do?"

Pacing to the window and back, she rummages through the pockets of Jinx's tattered leather jacket—the one with the broken zipper that Jinx always meant to fix but never did, the one she left behind stuffed in the back of a hall closet (Phoenix had cried for joy the night she found it). Pulling out a cigarette, the last in a crumpled pack, she smoothes the white paper, then slowly inserts it again, shrugs out of the jacket, and drapes it across her shoulders, like one of her great-grandmother's lone-star quilts, frayed now, and faded. The jeans are Jinx's, too, once tight but now so loose she can take them off without unbuttoning them. She used to unbutton Jinx's jeans with her teeth. No use in thinking about that

8

now. Time enough to think later, when sleep won't come, when peace is as elusive as fog.

Whoever said the first casualty of depression is memory was wrong. The first casualty is sleep. Every morning at three-seventeen, Phoenix Bay wakes up, as if a gong has sounded inside her head. Three-seventeen and twenty-four seconds, according to the digital dial on the clock radio that she chucked into the wall the night Jinx left. There's a big dent where it hit. The clock never lost a second. Not bad for $14.95 from Kmart. "When Mama called, I was making a list for Mr. Rizzo of all the junk Jinx left behind, what she calls my *assets*." Phoenix punctuates the word with a staccato sting. "Well, the sum total of my *assets* are a college education and a teaching certificate, both worth very little considering what's happened; a used Jeep Cherokee, grudgingly given me by my father's third wife the afternoon we buried him—it's okay, though, we didn't really know each other well enough for a new car; a pair of solid gold rings in my cunt, one for Molly, the first woman I ever really loved, and the other for Jinx, the last; and my hands, which are terrific." She draws the words out slowly, almost tenderly and smiles, leaving Teddy Grayson no room to misinterpret.

"Now, Jinx might include the tigress she tattooed on my belly. She always said I was her best work. Some of the most famous lesbians in the world wear her tattoos, but her lovers—ex-lovers, I should say—we have the best. We could all get together and do an exhibit. Now wouldn't *that* just send the NEA over the edge? But I don't really consider the tigress an asset; mostly it's just there, like my twenty-seven gray hairs and my eleven wrinkles and my tits sagging. Life scars its survivors. I know all about that, being a survivor; it's the one thing I'm really good at. Anyway, Jinx left me a piece of art I can't get rid of and a bunch of used furniture to unload. I'm not complaining, that's just how it happened. She left me the bed; said she wanted to start fresh. I guess you can start fresh with an old couch, but not an old bed."

From the window, she watches madness stumble through the streets of the city in the shape of a man; his face, like his palm, upturned. He mumbles a language only he understands. He is looking for God; God cannot find him here. Quarters, but not grace, fall into his open palm. No one looks him in the eye, asks him how he happens to be here in a field of gray, where only glass and steel and concrete grow. He slumps into a doorway on the corner by the spot where the blind girl plays her guitar. She twines roses, pink and red and lavender, through her hair. Her clothes are gauzy rainbows, billowing in the wind that runs wild and hard down concrete and asphalt. She sings simple love songs in a soft soprano; a voice fit for a choir of sweet-voiced angels. Her fingers are strong and thick with calluses from guitar strings. She sings the songs she likes to hear. Men in pinstripe suits and women who carry briefcases—no room for babies, here, in the late-afternoon rush from the city's core—tap-tap past, dropping quarters and more often dollars into her basket, which is tied with pink and red and lavender and a few yellow ribbons. No one gives the old man dollars. To them he is dangerous—muttering, muttering, and cursing sometimes, at the demons only he can see. The men in pinstripe suits and the women with briefcases do not see demons. The blind singer sees nothing at all.

"A thousand times a day, maybe more, I ask myself what went wrong. How could Jinx just run off to Sonoma County with . . . What *is* that woman's name? Polly? Patty? Something like that. No, Perry, that's it. I wonder what tattoo Jinx is burning into her skin? That's what we do, isn't it? Scar our lovers. Maybe some don't, the lucky ones. Some women are lucky at love. I wouldn't know. It's not in my genes. Mama wasn't good at it, either, or Gran Cicero, or even TaTa Hassee. And my sister's track record is even worse than mine, once you factor in being queer, which is probably three lovers to each husband. Or at least it used to be.

"My sister is recently perfect, thanks to her new husband, Floyd. He has more money than God, thanks to hog bellies—he's a genius at commodities trading—and looks like Santa Claus. An odd combination. Mama says Savannah married well. She's the first in our family, and it took her only three tries. Unfortunately, I take after Gran Cicero. She didn't marry well, either, but she was the first bona fide madwoman and unsuccessful suicide. The county committed her after she tried to hang herself in the barn. Twice. Too bad she didn't make it. But I'm not suicidal; I don't have the energy to try."

The first time Phoenix Bay tried to kill herself, she was ten.

She wrapped her mother's pink silk scarf, which smelled of cheap perfume and rain, around her neck and pulled in opposite directions. Pulled until the room started to spin, until the lights over her bed shot small crystals across her eyes and she was floating, the pressure on her throat a dull ache, the gentle smell of her mother rocking her toward eternity. She didn't know that once she lost consciousness, she wouldn't be able to pull anymore. She cried when she came to, because she was still alive, because no one had found her. She never told anyone. When she was seventeen, she read in her high school biology book that air injected into a vein is lethal. A girl who worked in the nursing home gave her a used needle and syringe. The needle slid into her arm easily, the ache slow and steady as Phoenix found the vein. It was so blue. And she pushed the plunger, waiting for peace. But Phoenix wasn't good with needles and pushed it through the vein. She wore a bruise the size of her fist for a week. No one asked what it was from. In college, she swallowed pills: pink ones and black ones and tiny white ones, washing them down with cheap wine. She could have died then, the young doctor who pumped her stomach at the Student Health Service told her. She switched to Southern Comfort. At twenty-two, on a night that hung cold and empty, she stopped turning the steering wheel as her car flew down a curving road that opened onto a bridge over the Mississippi River. The car hit the bridge railing and spun once, twice, three times, maybe more. That's what she told the state trooper who found her sitting on the railing. The car had bounced, side to side, as it spun across. Bounced against, but not through, not over. After that, she stopped counting.

"My mama is a self-appointed authority on madwomen. Of course, because of the way she was raised, she considers anything short of stark-raving mad as sane. If you don't talk to people no one else can see, or walk downtown naked at noon, or climb out the window to sit on the roof at midnight, you're sane. I've never had the courage to tell her I do all those things, or have. The naked part was for Jinx."

Wearing only a trench coat bought at the Salvation Army for eight dollars and a pair of black patent stiletto heels, Phoenix could feel the coat's tattered lining tickling like slow and easy fingers across the backs of her naked thighs, as she walked along Folsom Street one afternoon. Jinx was waiting in the back of one of the men's bars, shooting pool and laughing—she seldom laughed. When Phoenix approached, she'd raised her hand, stopping the game, and beckoned Phoenix closer with a slow and steady smile. Jinx pushed back the coat with the end of the cue and ran the smooth rubbed wood along the inside of Phoenix's thighs. Slow. Phoenix trembled, but held her ground, even when Jinx raised the coat, then pushed it back to show off the tigress stalking through the private jungle of Phoenix Bay's belly. "My best work," she told the man closest to Phoenix, who stepped closer to inspect the jungle vines trailing down her thighs, the amaryllis and hibiscus and orchids along her side, the tiger's green eyes. "Orchids are the most erotic flower there is; she asked me for them, said they remind her of cunts." Jinx's voice was low and steady; she was the artist displaying a canvas, making a sale. Phoenix blushed, then, unable to look at him or at Jinx. The others were laughing, maybe at her, maybe not, she never knew. The music was so loud the floor shook and it was only lunchtime. Later, Jinx would tell her the man wanted a tattoo, a large one, thanks to Phoenix. She hadn't disappointed Jinx that afternoon; the disappointment had come later.

"Damn her for leaving me! For taking the smell and feel of her, the taste and need of her, the lies and then the passion, and leaving me naked . . . and alone . . . and oh, my God, afraid. I can't stand . . . the reality . . . of my life." Her voice has descended to little more than a whisper. The psychiatrist nods; her fingers rise into a tiny pyramid, the kind of finger games children play. This is the house, here is the chimney, open the door and inside's the family. The house of Phoenix Bay's childhood was plain and clapboard, with a long front porch, its only real architectural feature a small summer porch off the front bedroom, where Villanova slept alone. On summer nights, lightning bugs winked like tiny stars, and Phoenix in her white cotton nightgown would twirl across the front lawn, a ballerina on a stage. Peggy Lee, scratchy and a little warped on Savannah's old record player, sang down the moon. Tollie Pengrove would hang her head out the screen door from the house next door, "Turn that damned thing down before I call the cops!" Villanova would angle her backside in the direction of

in her cell. Miracles happen when you least expect them. Like when you hear Peggy Lee singing "Is That All There Is?" on a scratchy record player and refuse to let it pull you back. For the first time. Like when you wake up screaming and know the worst that's going to happen already has, and there's nowhere left to go but up.

 The Great Highway stretches like a rubber band between the ocean and San Francisco. In truth, very little is great about it, hardly even a highway. Still, Rennie Johnson found happiness, if not greatness, here in a white stucco house built fifty years ago to have an ocean view. That was possible then. Now, the house, like its neighbors, looks out onto a high and occasionally green levee, which Rennie refuses to call a dike out of principle, or so he says. Built to protect the houses from the inevitable sand and tides which never seem to reach that far, the levee blocks the view of the ocean from all but the top stories. The houses on this block squat, as most do here by the sea, on top of a garage, so that the first story is actually a good dozen feet above the pavement. Front windows like large, unblinking eyes gaze onto the levee bank, giving the houses an almost subterranean feel. The strangeness of space is compounded by the dog walkers and power walkers and bicyclists and joggers—all wearing the same determined look as if they were going somewhere important—who seem to glide along the levee's crest, so that any time of the day, and even night, a parade of torsoless legs and feet move along the top of the living room window. Ducks in a shooting gallery, Carson said.

Poor Carson, dead since the holidays. Poor Rennie, left a widow. Widower? Whatever. In the box at her feet Phoenix Bay has a black lace merry widow. Funny name. Nothing merry about what's been going on here. Leaning into the doorbell, which is embedded into the wrought-iron gate at the bottom of the gray and pink marble stairs, she peers inside. No wonder Carson loved this place. Wrought iron and marble and stained-glass windows— some of it original to the house, the rest scavenged from his development projects. There are some advantages to being an architect. He and Rennie had lived well here, maybe even happily, although it's hard to tell who's happy and who isn't. Looking in from the outside at the Sanchez Street flat, even she and Jinx had looked happy, right up to the end. All their friends thought so. Little lies. It had mattered at the time.

Through the open door at the top of the stairs, from deep inside the house, comes a steady, escalating wail, as if hell itself were grieving. Phoenix shudders. Rennie's taste in music is nothing if not eclectic. But then very little about him is predictable. Shockingly handsome when they'd first met in college, his face has since relaxed into the mellowness and grace that sometimes comes with age. Easily six feet tall and always determinedly thin, he is the kind of man that women describe as elegant, and men as sophisticated. He is probably both, although she doesn't think of him that way, at least not often.

Just as she rings again, a long shadow appears at the top of the stairs, then materializes into Rennie, glowering. "You're early. I wasn't expecting you until six." It is nearly seven o'clock. "I was working and didn't hear the bell. Have you been out there long?" The gate buzzes under his hand; the stereo shrieks again. She climbs the stairs slowly, the backpack thump-thumping a stair at a time behind her. She's tired, and sleep, when it comes, is erratic. She suspects it's starting to show. Although she wouldn't really know; Phoenix stopped looking in mirrors months ago, afraid of what she'd find.

"Forever. And I'm not early, I'm late." Practically shouting to be heard over the stereo, she lowers her voice only when she reaches the top of the stairs.

Perplexed, he looks at his right wrist where Carson's watch hangs. "Oh? So you are. Well, then I really am sorry." His face warms as he plants a dry, almost enthusiastic kiss near her lips. She recoils automatically at being touched, and Rennie, misunderstanding, scowls. How do you explain to a man who is constantly on guard for signs from the healthy that he is not, that every human touch is painful? Maybe they've been friends long enough that he'll forgive her.

"I think I'm catching cold," she says. Hoping he'll believe her lie, she sniffs for effect. Taking anything for granted is dangerous. Rennie nods. The floor throbs. Thirteen thousand dollars worth of customized stereo equipment installed in every conceivable crevice of this house sends chattering demons out from the corners, down from the ceilings, along the baseboard. "What *is* that on the stereo?"

"Plague Mass."

"It sounds like hell."

"You don't like it?"

She shakes her head. "No, I mean really. Like hell. Or what I always figured hell would sound like."

"I think that's the point. The man at the music store says it's supposed to make you feel . . . Angry, I think is what he said. I don't really need a CD to accomplish that, however." Phoenix follows him into the living room, where he picks up a remote control and in a moment the house sighs in silence. "Did you know there's actually a town called that in Norway . . . or is it Finland? Anyway, up by the Arctic Circle. It's a tremendous tourist attraction, everybody sending postcards with the inevitable message: Wish you were here." He grins.

Phoenix considers this, then smiles. "I can think of a few people—one in particular—who would deserve that. Or I could just send her a one-way ticket there. What do you think a trip to Hell would cost?"

"More than she's worth, I dare say. So, I take it that you've just come from happy hour with the good Doctor Grayson. Detailing the shortcomings of Jinx Sloan, again? Or should I say *still?"*

"No," Phoenix says, suddenly sobering, the light draining from her face as quickly as it had come a moment before. "My own."

A tiny scowl flashes across his face. "Too bad. You really should get over that, Phoenix. She's the villain in this little melodrama. You've got it all turned around. Or, as my father used to say, 'The horse is dead, girl, get off it!' Of course, he wouldn't have said 'girl.' Or maybe he would have. Manny did have an ugly streak." He's teasing, trying to pull her back. "So, would you like to listen to something else? More upbeat?"

"Could we not . . . listen to anything? I mean not right now." Her voice is pleading, on the edge of tears, and hearing that, Rennie turns, looking at her closely. "It makes me nervous . . . music, I mean. It makes me remember. Things I'd rather not. Sometimes. You know?" He nods. Illness has made him cautious, too.

"Sounds like Teddy's happy pills have lost their zing."

Phoenix leans against the doorjamb, her hands flat on either side as if she were bracing for an earthquake. She won't look him in the eye. "Sometimes . . . they don't seem to make any difference."

"Yeah, mine either." He means the AZT. "But I figure what the hell, how much worse can it get? The danger is, of course, that if the fates hear you say that, they'll show you." He's thinking of Carson, she realizes.

"Looks like you're going to Mexico just in time," she says, changing the subject, "you're pale as a ghost." Poor choice of words, with Carson barely a ghost himself, but Rennie lets it slide. Pushing back a lock of curling black hair, which is just beginning to gray at the temples, he steps over three suitcases lined up like sentries by the door and takes the box Phoenix hands him, filled with lace underwear and Jinx's old love letters. Keeping the letters was an afterthought; it made sense this afternoon. Now, she's not so sure.

Draping his arm around the box, he pulls the pack onto his shoulder and starts down the hall, then stops and turns, looking a little surprised that she's following him. "Why don't you bring up the rest of your stuff? I can handle this."

"This is it," she admits, suddenly feeling guilty. "Except for the plants. No point in bringing them up. I'll just unload them when I put the Jeep in the garage."

"But, Phoenix . . . Where are all your things? Your clothes? Or am I not supposed to ask?" He is looking at her closely, trying

18

to find some sign of lunacy, she supposes. How many bags and boxes do you need to prove you're sane? She doesn't know.

Phoenix shrugs. No point in lying. "You can ask. I sold it."

"Everything?" He raises his eyebrows, surprised.

She nods eagerly. "Gone. Sold. Clothes out of the closet, pictures off the wall. Mr. Rizzo gave me eight hundred dollars for it. Want to see?"

He shakes his head sadly and starts up the spiral staircase to the second floor of the house. As the stairway turns, Rennie pauses and looks down at her, "Do you want to tell me why you did that?" He means the clothes.

"Does it matter?" She looks up into his brown eyes magnified by the thick glasses he wears when he travels. The glasses give him a look of perpetual surprise. How can she tell him that the clothes were like loose skin, that the furniture belonged to a woman she had grown to pity if not hate, that the pictures on the walls, the dishes in the cupboards, all of it, belonged to a stranger, and that pitiable stranger is her? "You're surprised."

"No." His voice is dry, not exasperated, not impassioned, just tired. "Nothing you do lately surprises me. I just would like for you to get beyond it, back to normal."

The thing about teetering on the edge of madness is how those on the outside assume it is a perpetual state, like blindness or deafness, or any number of other not fatal but highly inconvenient afflictions. Only those on the inside know how it comes and goes, masking itself like perfect sanity, depending on the situation. This is one of those times, and for that, at least, she is grateful. In better days, house-sitting would be an adventure, masked as a favor for an old friend. But in better days, Phoenix would have had a home to go back to and Rennie wouldn't be leaving for Mexico alone.

"You're sure you're up to staying here by yourself while I'm gone?" Rennie drops the bag and the box on the king-size bed. How can she tell him she won't go crazy and set fire to this magnificent room, huge and open, decorated with polished wood and antique brass from a junked yacht? That she won't destroy his memories of Carson? The imprint of Carson Cole is everywhere in this house, but no more so than in this room that takes up the entire top floor. It would be easy to be happy in a house like this. No wonder Rennie loves it. She opens the door that leads onto the front deck, letting the evening wind sweep through. Shaking her head, as if to clear it, she steps onto the deck and inhales. This close to the sea, you can taste the salt on your tongue. The ocean growls loudly a few hundred yards away. In daylight, the view is nearly uninterrupted blue, if you overlook the stream of traffic on the highway and joggers on the dike. Here by the ocean, maybe she'll be able to think at last.

"It'll do me good, being out here. Negative ions or something." She's heard about negative ions; they sound important, even if she can't quite remember what they do. But in a room like this, anything is possible. All her life, Phoenix Bay has looked on new rooms, empty apartments, vacant houses as possibilities. Sometimes she even dreams of discovering rooms in houses where she's lived for a very long time. None of the rooms were ever as beautiful as this. "By the time you get back, I'll have my own place. Get myself a new lease on life. Something like that." She sounds like a television commercial. No wonder Gran Cicero was always so enraged when they interrupted her diet of game shows.

"Don't," Rennie says, his voice rough. He smiles, then softens. "I want you to stay . . . as long as you need to . . . want to, I mean. It's a big house, with Carson gone."

She understands how a house can rattle and moan under the weight of people who used to be there. When she was still considering keeping the Sanchez Street flat, Phoenix even got so far as writing a newspaper ad: *Lesbian roomie for large, furnished flat; share phone.* That was what had stopped her, the idea of sharing the phone. What if Jinx were to call, to figure out she'd been reduced to living with strangers? She never considered that Jinx might think she'd been replaced as easily as Phoenix, herself, had been replaced. Instead, Phoenix had decided to let Rennie take care of her and she, in turn, would take care of him. A marriage of convenience Mama would say if it were a marriage or convenient. "It's just . . ." Just what? She can't remember what she was going to say. She blushes and looks at her hands, grateful for the darkness that hides her cheeks. What would Rennie think, if he knew how thoughts sometimes flutter against her like untended birds, then fly away, leaving her confused and afraid?

"What's that, Phoenix?" His voice is kind, patient. Maybe he does know.

"Nothing," she lies. "I just wish you weren't going, or I could go with you."

Rennie grins and shakes his head, leans out over the railing, clasping his hands in front of him, then looks back over his shoulder. "So come along. What's stopping you?"

She shakes her head. "I need time to think. Besides, who would take care of Marcel Proust? That's why I'm here, isn't it?"

"Partly. By the way, the pet store delivered his feed this afternoon—it's inside the back door." Following him back inside, she rubs her hands together, trying to warm them. Engrossed in his list, Rennie doesn't notice. "Towels and sheets are in the cupboard by the bed, and I've cleared out space in Carson's closet, which wasn't easy as you might imagine, clothes horse that he was—by the way, could you do something about that while I'm gone? I haven't had the stomach for it, to tell the truth. Is this really all you've got left?" Phoenix nods, ashamed. "Well, then, you've got nothing to worry about. And you remember, of course, about the retractable skylight from hell."

"Yeah, I know. Open at your own risk." She recites the words he's drummed into her. For a writer, he's not very creative about that instruction. Those exact words are on a card inside the control panel by the bed.

"I'm serious, Phoenix, it's defective. Carson was always meaning to get it fixed, but you know how that goes. Anyway, you'll do fine. This place will seem like home in no time. Just better memories." He means Jinx. He never really liked her and no longer bothers to pretend otherwise.

Her eyes flit around the room, and she has the sensation that she doesn't belong. "Rennie, are you sure you want me to stay up here? I mean, the guest room downstairs would be fine. I really don't want to turn you out."

"You're not turning me out of anything," he says too quickly, as if he'd expected her to say just that and had been rehearsing his reply. "And so far as this room goes, I haven't slept up here since . . ." He pauses, then smiles almost delicately. "Well, for a long time. Besides, to insist on sleeping downstairs *would* be turning me out. Not to be indelicate, Phoenix, but so long as the crapper is on the first floor, so am I. Humpty Dumpty impressions don't show my best side." He means the spiral staircase, as beautiful as it is deadly, she imagines. "I seem to be falling apart at an alarming rate." Only a year older than Phoenix, he seems . . . very old. It's not his age, but the disease, she reminds herself. Damn. "Besides, when Cecelie comes, this can be the girls' dorm. The couch turns into a bed. Unless you still have designs on my sister?" He wiggles his eyebrows. "I haven't forgotten that summer in New York. You really were shameless, you know."

Phoenix smiles. So, Cecelie really is coming. She hasn't thought of Cecelie Johnson in—how long?—years maybe. "I thought she never left Peru."

"Occasionally. I'm letting her think she's doing it for me. Well, you know Cecelie." Yes, Phoenix does know Cecelie. If a good fairy had one day materialized in front of Phoenix Bay, promising her one wish, it would have been to be Cecelie Johnson. Stunning Cecelie, a mirror of her brother except for her magnificent breasts, the same eyes, quick and dark and missing nothing, golden skin, and a seemingly untamable mass of dark, curling hair that was always hopelessly, almost endearingly tangled. What Phoenix would have given for golden skin, black curling hair, and huge, dark eyes. When they'd first known each other, Phoenix would measure herself against Cecelie. Each time, she'd come up short: her face too pale, her hair too straight, her eyes too close-set, her skin too sensitive to the sun. Is Cecelie still striking, or have all those years of digging up the past somehow eroded her? So many questions, but Phoenix settles for one: "When is she coming?"

"Early June, or so she says as of a couple days ago. Rumor has it the university may pull out because of the war. Not that she seems to consider that a reason to leave." He shakes his head, disgusted. "But I'll be home long before then." Rennie is struggling with the heavy glass door that opens onto the back deck. "Damned thing always sticks. There's some WD-40 in the workroom; you might want to give this a few shots. UCLA's

22

bringing her back for the winter." Phoenix looks at him, baffled. "You know, our summer, their winter. Everything gets fucked up once you cross the equator. She has this wild idea that I need her."

"Now, why would she think that?" Phoenix is trying to keep the conversation light.

He turns and looks at Phoenix, his voice low and serious. "Because that's what I told her. And even if she won't admit it, she needs us. She's not doing all that well since she lost Mala. I think she blames herself."

Mala was Cecelie's adopted daughter and Rennie's only niece, the one he described as "the toughest six year old outside of Brooklyn." The little girl died of spinal meningitis in January and Cecelie didn't call her brother until it was over. And then, he was the one who'd cried, his sobs reaching Peru on a connection as scratchy as an old 78 RPM record. He gives the door a final shove. "Cecelie is tough; she always was. I'll give Mona credit for that, if nothing else: She made my sister a survivor. I always told Cecelie an archaeological site was no place to raise a kid. But she was determined. When my sister wants something . . . You know, I think she's the most tenacious woman I've ever known. And that's saying something. I know you. But you, at least, have the good sense not to live in a shack in a graveyard."

Phoenix smiles, used to Rennie's theatrics. Fallout from having a bad actress for a mother. "Oh, Rennie, it can't be all that bad."

He snorts. "Hell, Phoenix. She's sent pictures. Take a look for yourself if you don't believe me—they're on the photo wheel by the TV. My sister has a fucking doctorate and she lives in a shed with a tin roof. Her backyard consists of pits. She digs up skeletons for a living, spends all her time rooting around in the past. Not even *her* past. What business does she have in Peru? Do you know what she tells me? That she feels safe there, that she's trying to sort out her life. You know what I think? That she went there to hide and it just got to be habit. Then, after Mala died . . . I don't know, Phoenix, it changed her. Or maybe just having Mala changed her. Cecelie's easier, I think. At least she *sounds* easier. I think the kid actually taught my sister to be spontaneous."

"But how did you get her to agree to come?"

"Oh, I told her I'm dying, of course. Soon, I mean." Phoenix inhales sharply, her stomach grabs and then her throat, before she realizes Rennie is only being dramatic. He smiles. "You'll see. Once she's here, she'll stay. We'll win her over."

Phoenix isn't so sure. Cecelie away from her work for long seems beyond comprehension. "What makes you think that?"

Rennie is still smiling, but the smile, like his skin, has grown taut and pale. "Perhaps her unflinching sense of duty, or maybe because she loves me a little, or maybe because she needs us but doesn't know it yet." In the distance, a woman cries for help. Phoenix turns toward the sound, her eyes wide. Rennie laughs. Then she remembers the peacock, Marcel Proust. "You'll get used to it," he says. "Marcel Proust takes nightfall personally. I think we misnamed him." Marcel Proust is the only peacock that Phoenix has ever seen outside a zoo. Poor thing. Screaming at the indignity of darkness. Hasn't she screamed at the beach when it was dark and no one could see, when she imagined no one was around to hear, didn't care if anyone did?

The back deck looks down over a sparse and sandy yard, with a large but scraggly Monterey pine in a far corner near a streetlight. Through heavy green shadows, the sparkling blue of the peacock's tail shines. "Carson used to say that bird has a direct line to God," Rennie says, watching the grand bird strut through his backyard kingdom. Phoenix remembers. It was one of Carson's favorite stories, how in the 1950s an apparition at a small convent near the Lost Coast appeared three nights in a row. On the fourth night, nothing. The nuns—there were only a dozen, maybe less—waited all night. In the morning, when they came out of their chapel, there was a flock of peacocks. The nonbelievers in town said a bird dealer's truck must have stopped, a flat tire perhaps, and some of the exotic cargo had escaped. But the others, the believers, protected the birds, which they came to believe really were blessed, because they had to believe in something. By the time the church sold the old convent to Cole Development more than thirty years later, it was overrun with peacocks. The church had closed the convent years before—all the nuns had died or retired by then—and supposedly a zoo had taken the peacocks then, but they obviously had missed a few. Carson called a bird dealer from L.A., who paid him two hundred dollars for each breeding pair, and another fifty apiece for a half dozen juvenile birds. "Two grand of pure peacock profit," he liked to say. The bird dealer made two passes through the property to make sure he'd rounded them all up. And he had, except for Marcel Proust, secreted in the depths of a Monterey pine—as it would happen, his only trick. The peacock didn't come down for two days. With the bird dealer long gone, Carson brought him home. "It was either that or leave him to die lonely," Carson liked to say. The great bird had loved Carson, fanning his glorious tail whenever he approached.

"I always figured a peacock with a mainline to Heaven would bring us luck," Rennie says, his voice bitter. "Unfortunately, I was wrong."

Phoenix watches the bird lift itself, gracelessly, into the pine, which closes up around him. "Do you think maybe he could be blessed?" Embarrassed by the foolishness of such an idea taking form but unable to stop the words, her voice is soft.

"Honey, if I thought that, I'd be out there under that pine tree praying twice a day. No, Phoenix, I do not think Marcel Proust is God, although I once had a professor who did. A different Marcel Proust, of course." He chuckles at his own small joke, then turns somber. "But I have discovered, very much to my surprise, that in these last few months I've developed a profound faith in two things: God and my own abilities. God is a fairly new addition to the mix."

"That's two more than most of us."

"Still not a believer, Phoenix Bay?"

"Sure." Trying for cocky, she leans against the doorjamb and smiles. "I believe things work out the way they're supposed to, even if it's not the way you think they should at the time. These last six months, it's about the only thing that's kept me going."

"Some would call that a belief in God."

"Well, some would be wrong." Pushing herself upright, she stalks back inside.

Irritated, Rennie closes the door harder than he'd intended, so hard the glass rattles, but she doesn't look up and he refuses to apologize. After a long minute, he finally asks, "So, what else do you need to know before I fly away? The peacock eats once a day. You can expect Mrs. Chin from next door to drop by at least twice a week to complain about something, usually Marcel Proust. If she doesn't show up by Thursday afternoon, call the police because it probably means she's over there dead and nobody's found the body. If Marcel Proust doesn't show up, call the police because it probably means she's got him boiling in a pot on her stove." He grins.

Phoenix turns to him and smiles, their small storm already forgotten. "That's awful!"

He winks. "So, unfortunately, is Mrs. Chin. I personally think that's what happened to Mr. Chin—nobody's seen him in years. Oh, and the answering machine's in my office. Any phone numbers you might need are in the Rolodex. Instructions on how to get through to Cecelie—you have to go through radio operators—are in the top desk drawer. The ocean's across the street. The park's twelve blocks north, as you no doubt know. If you were male, I'd tell you that the big cruising area's by the old windmill, but I don't think you would find it very interesting." Rennie is growing almost buoyant, probably at the thought of traveling, even though it will be his first real trip in years without Carson. "There's a passable breakfast restaurant three blocks down and that charming health-food restaurant around the corner has the best sweet rolls this side of hell. We have a standing order. Am I forgetting anything?"

Me, she wants to say, take me with you. Instead, she shakes her head. "Everything will be fine." He looks skeptical, so she adds, "Really."

Smiling, he touches her cheek gently. "I hope so, Phoenix, I really do. But if anything catastrophic happens, the number in Mexico is on the phone." He means if there's an earthquake or the house burns down, or if she goes stark-raving mad. Did he tell Mrs. Chin to check on her, as well? That she might pop Marcel Proust into a pot on the stove? That nobody's seen Jinx in a long time, either?

"Okay, but I won't need it." There's that look again, as if he is already bracing himself for disaster. "Promise." She raises her right hand, a child taking a pledge, and grins. "No disasters." Jinx was the one who was always so afraid of disaster. A natural pessimist, she kept a map of the major earthquake fault lines on the closet door, a stash of peanut butter and crackers in the freezer, a flashlight on the windowsill next to the bed. Just in case, she always said. And Phoenix, more pragmatist than optimist, laughed. No wonder she wasn't prepared for the end. Jinx gone in such a rush, no apologies, no regrets, damned few tears. Maybe Jinx was right; you do have to prepare for disaster, it comes too quickly, even when the warnings are there.

"And, Phoenix, if you're planning on falling in love while I'm gone . . ."

"I'm not." The words come too sharply. Embarrassed, her cheeks flush. "Besides, aren't you the one who's always telling me what lousy taste I have in women?"

"Only because it's true. With you, my dear, love is not only blind, it's also proven to be deaf and incredibly stupid." Rennie has patiently pieced her back together after more than one shattered love affair, always admonishing her to take more care next time, not to lose herself so easily. But losing herself in women has become habit, so much so that when she says, as she so often had with Jinx, "I don't know where you begin and I end," it is true. Lovers say things like that all the time, but with Phoenix it is more than whispered lies of passion. When the affair ended, as it inevitably had to, she was left hollow as a mannequin. Once, she read about an amputee whose absent leg still throbbed. Phantom pain. She understood. Lately, she's begun to suspect that the older she grows, the deeper the pain, the longer it takes to heal. She can't take that risk again.

Rennie sighs, frustrated, but only a little. "What I started to say, before you so rudely cut me off, is you'll find another set of house keys in the utility drawer in the kitchen."

Embarrassed, she smiles, blushes. "Oh."

"Or, if you're smart, you could wait for my sister." He wiggles his eyebrows. "As our dear mother used to say, sex keeps you young. She spent most of her life trying to prove that theory. Unfortunately, Cecelie seems to be nothing like our dear, departed Mona. Thank God." Mona Morgan, a small-time sometimes actress, is alternately described by her son as a slut and an emotional terrorist; the greatest regret of his life is that his sister was

27

raised by such a woman. "Maybe in Mexico, I'll write one of those made-for-television movies about her. But she'd probably come back to haunt me for writing the perfect part for her when she's not around to play it."

"Rennie, you're terrible!"

"No, my dear, actually, I'm very, very good. Ask anyone. Well, almost anyone." He grins, an aging, gangly imp. From the driveway, a horn honks twice, a door slams, the buzzer rings. "My ride," Rennie says, kissing her lightly on the cheek. "Hang over the balcony and tell him I'm on my way down." He descends the steps gingerly, one at a time, clutching the railing with both hands. She watches as a young man, bodybuilder probably, effort-lessly hoists the three suitcases into the back of an airport shuttle van, hears the door slam as Rennie settles inside. Rennie doesn't look up or acknowledge her wave, but the bodybuilder nods before ducking inside. She watches the taillights from the van, until it turns onto the highway.

With Rennie gone, Phoenix prowls the house like a careful bur-glar, opening drawers, peering behind doors. The house reminds her of something out of a magazine spread: casually perfect, but as if nobody actually lives here. No personal pictures clutter the mantel or end tables; no piece of bad art, bought on a whim, worth more in sentiment than dollars, hangs on the walls; no tacky throw pillow made by great-aunt somebody, sits on the sofa. Except for Rennie's office, a jumble of books and papers and memorabilia that seems to stretch all the way back to his childhood, the place is as pristine as a hotel, and about as welcoming. For the first time, she's beginning to think she's made a mistake. How can she live in a house that has so little need of people?

At the far end of the mantel is a classic, eighteen-inch-tall cube of ebony, with a silver inlay in a stylized rendition of a sparse forest that rises up from a silver oval, obviously intended as a nameplate, but not yet engraved. Leaning in for a closer look, she realizes it is apparently seamless. How did they get Carson's ashes in there? She considers picking it up to investigate, but that seems irreverent. Instead, she settles for polishing one of the silver trees with her shirttail. Is Carson lonely? Afraid? She wonders, and a wave of sorrow rises like bile up from her belly, turns to tears in her throat. "She left me, Carson," Phoenix whispers. "She left me, and I lost it all piece by piece; I don't even know how. There's no place left for me. Can you understand that? Rennie asked me to come here. He's lonely. You know that, I suppose. And I'm . . . so awfully scared. Do you know that, too? Do you know everything now, or nothing?" The silver forest gleams. She smiles. "When I was a kid, we used to say, 'We ain't much, but we're all we've got.' Do you suppose kids still say that? Yeah, I don't know, either. Anyway, we'll take care of each other. I just wanted to tell you that, so you wouldn't . . . worry." With the shirttail, she wipes at her eyes. Crazy, she tells herself. Talking to a wood box as if she expects an answer. What's next? Levitation? Seances?

Running her fingers along the cool black marble of the fireplace, she is surprised when they come up dirty. Looking more closely, she sees the place is covered with a fine layer of dust. Pots where huge plants once bloomed stand almost empty, except for a few scrappy diehards. The windows are streaked and grimy with salt. Months must have passed since someone cleaned, probably not since Carson's family was here while he was still in the hospital, maybe even before. At least this will give her something to do.

Playing with the light switch, she finds one that illuminates a pedestal in the far corner of the room. Marble she decides, then on closer inspection discovers it's really just wood painted to look that way. Under a large and well-lighted Plexiglas box is a small pot, obviously ancient. Probably a gift from Cecelie. Peering into the lighted dome, she tries to make out the figures etched into the clay. On the top level are plumed dancers, and beneath them a row of tiny figures, depicted with their hands tied behind their backs, faces contorted, but no more so than the faces of the dancing figures. One of the bound figures kneels in front of a dancer with a long knife. She walks around the pot, then recoils in horror. A plumed dancer, wielding a long knife, is slitting the bound figure's throat, while another dancer catches the blood in a goblet. She shakes off a quick chill. "Goose walked over your grave," TaTa Hassee used to say. What kind of people would make such a thing? What sort of person would give it as a gift? Cecelie, of course.

Funny, she hasn't thought of Rennie's sister in a long time, and they were all so close once. All these years and she's still an archaeologist. And why not? Rennie is still a writer. Phoenix is the only one of the three who doesn't know what she is anymore, if she ever did. She can't even hold on to a lover. A woman like Cecelie wouldn't worry about that. And Rennie? He'll find someone else soon enough, all that talk about his constricted timetable. By now, there should at least have been a new woman to take Jinx's place. But a new woman would want to draw too close, and Phoenix isn't sure she could stand that. Her flesh is still too raw. All Rennie's talk about extra sets of keys, and she wasn't able to tell him, or even Teddy Grayson, the truth: She can't stand being touched, couldn't even before Jinx left. Maybe that was what had finally driven her away. Sex was what had brought them together, was what had sustained them all those years, and then, one morning, without even knowing why, Phoenix couldn't stand to have the woman she loved touch her. Jinx had to have known, although they never talked about it. Of course, they never really talked about anything. Always before, sex had done the talking for them. And when that was gone, they were lost. Later, she would see the list of ten symptoms of depression and there toward the top would be loss of sexual appetite. Would it have mattered if she'd known before? Probably not.

Rooting out Jinx has been hard, harder than Phoenix would ever have imagined, considering their beginnings. Phoenix found her one Saturday night in L.A., both of them looking for a free bed and a Hollywood angel to wrap her arms around, and coming up with each other instead. Each of them just passing through: Jinx on her way back to The City from Nicaragua, where she'd been picking coffee beans for six weeks; Phoenix on her way back to Chicago in the Jeep, which was almost new then, after burying the stranger she called Daddy. Her father's third wife, Veronica, a tiny ex-cheerleader of a woman with very tall blond hair who called herself Ronnie—"Just like in the comic strip, honey"— had pressed the Jeep on Phoenix the day of her father's funeral in Escondido. Phoenix, in honor of the occasion, had gotten drunk.

In those days, almost any occasion or none at all was a good enough reason to get drunk, and a father's funeral was one hell of an excuse.

By the time her stepmother beckoned Phoenix into the family room, which Ronnie called a den, they were both drunk and a little too sentimental. Ronnie's den reminded Phoenix of the basement recreation rooms of her childhood: a long, plaid sectional parked in front of a console television set, and over the couch, pictures of waterfalls and mountains that seemed to glow from some unseen source, giving the water the impression of actual movement. "Your father wants you to have one of the cars," the woman had whispered, as if it were some special secret between them. Phoenix thought it unlikely that Hank Long wanted anything at all, at least nothing to do with this world. Yet, she'd felt a wave of pity for that tiny woman, all alone in her overpriced house with its second mortgage and garish furniture and pictures of waterfalls and snow-capped mountains that she thought were art.

Both her father's wives since her mother had been remarkably alike: tiny, birdlike women, whose heads always seemed too small for the mass of hair they wore; whose faces were always a little too colorful for their frozen smiles; whose skin was always a little too brown, as if they spent long afternoons working on their tans, to hell with the wrinkles. That's what beauty cream and plastic surgeons are for. Their manicures came from shops with huge fingernails over the door and signs in the window advertising Full French or Silkwrap. To Phoenix, the signs always sound like something to try on a lonely Saturday night: "A full, French silkwrap, honey," and beautiful women with skin like satin would take it from there.

Villanova had been the aberration, the girl Hank Long had married out of Dahl's Sporting Goods, where she was the bookkeeper: a year older than he and an unwed mother, as they were still called in those days, living with her grandmother in a small and ugly house on Carbon Street. Phoenix likes to think he loved her mother in those days, had loved her, too. But if he'd loved them, where was he all those years? No, Hank Long had massaged his conscience with an occasional card and a check at Christmas every few years and, less often, presents that generally arrived after her birthday, rarely on it, never before. The women her father had preferred in the end were soft dolls who drove sports cars, laughed a lot through red lips, and called everybody "Honey." Good-time girls. Villanova never knew how to have a good time.

But Ronnie knew. The same way she'd instinctively known to dress her dead husband in a gray suit with a red tie, a power tie they were called that year. Red is the color of life. Not such a bad color to meet death in. The Jeep is red, too. A lark, Ronnie had called it, laughing, with tales of how Hank made grand and foolish plans to go fishing in the Baja every year. He always took her to Las Vegas instead. Her stepmother had laughed as if the idea of Hank Long fishing was as funny as a comedy routine.

Hank used to fish, Phoenix remembered. The memory had washed over her suddenly, pulled her down. Even now when she thinks of it, her stomach clenches and she has to swallow hard, gulping air like the fish he brought home in a bucket. Her father coming in the back door, jeans low-slung and muddy, smiling, smelling of fish and whiskey and smoke. Pulling her up onto his shoulder, rubbing his whiskers into her face. How old must she have been? Three? Four? "A mess for my baby." He kissed Villanova, smearing her face with sweat and mud. "And one for your kitty." He opened a silver-colored bait bucket; a tiny fish, no longer than Phoenix's hand, thrashed in the water. The cat came without being called, reached her powerful paws into the water. Quick. Flipping the tiny fish onto the linoleum. All the while, her father was laughing, the sound warming the kitchen. "Nobody can say I don't take care of my girls and their pussy." Even Villanova laughed. Phoenix watched the fish, gasping under the cat's paw.

If it hadn't been for Ronnie and her dead father's Jeep, Phoenix would never have decided to drive up the coast to San Francisco, then east to Chicago, never would have stopped in L.A., never would have met Jinx. If she could go back to that afternoon, would she still turn north? But she had—and not a damned thing in the world could have stopped her. Hank had loaded the Jeep shamelessly, the way car dealers do. The sound system was good, excellent, in fact, and the engine powerful. It was midsummer; school didn't start for another six weeks— Phoenix was teaching high school English then—and she was between women. No one back in Chicago was expecting her and even if they were, who could say how long it would take to bury a father, even one like Hank Long? Plenty of time, all the time in the world.

It was dark but still early when Phoenix stepped into the gloom and glitter of the bar, still in the black dress, a little too tight and too short for a funeral in Chicago but not for Southern California. She'd long since shed her stockings—too hot—and her shoes dangled in her left hand. "Put your shoes on, doll," the sleek blond bodybuilder at the door whispered, "the health department." She winked, extending her forearm to Phoenix for balance. "Nice." Her eyes dropped Phoenix's breasts as she bent over to stuff her feet back into the shoes. Phoenix, still feeling a little giddy from the drive and the promises of the night, winked back. Later, her look promised, if nothing better turns up. Being in a strange city made Phoenix feel reckless, bad and beautiful; no familiar eyes to answer to.

You can tell a lot about a woman by the way she stands when her back is to you, when she isn't aware she's being watched. At the end of the bar, alone because it was still early or she was a stranger or both, stood a woman. Hard and sure and easy. She turned, for no reason, really, and looked back over her shoulder. The words *grimly beautiful* flashed across Phoenix's mind. That is how she would always think of Jinx: grimly beautiful. Phoenix stood a dozen feet behind her, willing her to turn, to look, to step into her life. Phoenix Bay had never considered herself brazen, but she was that night, slipping into the space between the grimly beautiful stranger and the bar, and when the woman had finally looked up, Phoenix was waiting. But she'd misjudged, and fell into a pair of pleading eyes.

"Jinx?" she would ask later on the dance floor. "Is that a name or a character reference?" The grimly beautiful woman had smiled, leaning close, whispering against Phoenix's neck, "Baby, it's whatever you want it to be." In heels, Phoenix was a good three inches taller than Jinx, so shed the shoes and buried herself in the arms of this woman, who smelled of beer, cigarette smoke, and sweat, memorized the little creases in her neck, the taste of salt, the tight muscles. Patterns of blue and green and red on her chest showed at the open white shirt that glowed against the permanent dusk of the bar. At a tiny table on the edge of the dance floor, Jinx leaned close, listening to Phoenix talk, rolling up her sleeves absently, exposing her forearms, the right one colored in dark patterns. The tail of something, sliding down and wrapping around her wrist where a watch might have been on another woman, ended in a point just below the knuckle of her right middle finger. Phoenix stared, then pushed the shirt sleeve up a little higher, struck by how her fingers looked against this woman's skin.

Jinx was watching her closely, still smiling. Curling her hand into a fist, she flexed her fingers; the skin on her forearm rippled like the hide of a strange and exotic animal. Phoenix took her hand back a little too slowly. "What do you think, Chicago?" There it was again, that loose, worldly, and just-left-of-arrogant grin. Jinx locked her hands behind her head and stretched her legs on either side of Phoenix's chair. Phoenix had the sudden impulse to slide up this woman's leg like a snake, licking against the soft leather, tearing at it with her teeth. Instead, she shuddered and leaned forward, tucking her feet back into the shoes. The bar was only slightly more full than when Phoenix had first arrived. Obviously, the Hollywood angels were all somewhere else. Not that it mattered; she'd found what she wanted.

"Phoenix," she corrected, almost automatically. "I'm from Chicago."

"I know." Jinx was still smiling. "So, what do you think, *Phoenix*?"

Pushing the chair back and standing, Phoenix listed a little. "I think it's time to go home." But home was two thousand miles away and nothing more than a couple of cats and a roommate, who spent her evenings sprawled on the couch, an MTV junkie. She would find a hotel, then decide what to do in the morning; in the morning she would regret not having made love to a grimly beautiful woman with a lizard crawling up her arm.

Jinx, taking Phoenix's statement as an invitation, shrugged and hauled herself upright. "Have you ever been to Disneyland?" Phoenix shook her head. Intense as only a drunk can be, Jinx brought her face close to Phoenix's. "You should go. You want to do that tomorrow?"

"Why not tonight?" Phoenix said, catching the hand with the lizard's tail in her own and stepping into the night.

"It's a long drive."

"I'm in no hurry."

The motel Jinx picked was pink and in the shadow of Disneyland. Phoenix remembers that, but not the name. Something about candy. A small, graying man, his eyes rimmed in red, had looked at Phoenix suspiciously through a Plexiglas plate in the office door as she dropped her credit card into the security drawer, the kind gas stations use.

"We're going to Fantasyland," Phoenix offered, although he hadn't asked.

The man in the booth smiled. "Well, then, you'll want to get there early, lines are hell this time of year." A key with a large pink plastic room number clattered through the security drawer. Room 316 was a gritty pink, trimmed in red, like candy canes. The Candy Cane Motel, was that the name of the place? How could she have forgotten? Funny, the things you remember, even funnier the things you forget.

Over the years, Phoenix would forget the name of the song Jinx hummed that night, all night it seemed at the time, but she could never forget that missing tile, the three patches of glue against the dirty-white ceiling. Just as she could never forget Jinx, the way she looked as the neon changed outside their window, blue and red streaking across her chest, where a wild, winged lizard dipped its tongue around her left nipple.

It wasn't the first time Phoenix had opened herself to the arms and tongue and hands of a stranger. But that night she was brazen and wanton and selfish, and nothing in the world mattered except the woman beside her, the flash of heat rising through her belly, the prickle of cold air against bare flesh, the salty taste of her skin. Jinx was clean, the way morning is clean, without traces of the past.

Jinx had called her beautiful that night, and Phoenix believed it was true. So much seemed true with Jinx, who could raise sparks from her very touch. And when Jinx pulled Phoenix to her feet, stripped away the dress, the scraps of nylon and lace, Phoenix had the feeling she was at last free. Jinx was perfect, with magnificent breasts and a snake that slithered from her navel toward a brown and curling jungle, then out again and down her thigh. Phoenix swallowed the snake, felt the lizard grow hard and angry under her tongue, its head in her mouth. Its tail disappeared between her own legs, pushed the breath out of her, until the room twirled and tilted, until Phoenix Bay was no longer able to tell where she ended and this grimly beautiful woman began. The lizard moaned when Phoenix sunk her teeth into its flank and Jinx tightened against her, the lizard smooth and slick, not like a real lizard at all. Inside Jinx was warm and slick, too, Phoenix's fingers exploring a strange and beautiful terrain. So much flesh to master, a mountain, sweet and slick, and all of it at Phoenix Bay's command, all brought down to that one burning core. They fell through the night that way, into a place where flying lizards beat their tails in deep pools.

They lost most of the next day to that small room and didn't make it across the street to Disneyland until just before closing. In an orange sky tram that rocked slowly, high above the flying elephants and the twirling teacups, Jinx taught her that maybe they truly were in the happiest place on earth, like the sign says. Maybe so, maybe so. They were happy then. Giddy with freedom and new love and possibilities.

The first time Phoenix Bay saw San Francisco, the streets seemed to open like a promise. Jinx's studio was in a loft on a sidestreet in an area clustered with warehouses. In front of the few clapboard and shingled houses, straggling flowers fought for sun. In the three weeks she was there, Phoenix never saw any neighbors, never saw anyone come and go from the houses with the valiant geraniums. For all she knew, it might have been a movie set. Over the years, various inhabitants of the loft had added thin walls and dividers, until it was a crazy quilt of strange angles and open spaces. A large door opened onto a fire escape that looked down on a patch of broken concrete and asphalt, where half a dozen cats played in the moonlight. Every morning Jinx fed the cats, talking in a guttural monotone of what she must have imagined to be feline. The most brazen of the cats would stretch up around her, front paws on her thighs; the others would wait for her to come to them. Once, when Phoenix was left alone, she had ventured into the back lot, her hand outstretched. "Here, kitty-kitty." But the half-wild creatures had eyed her with distrust; finally she'd slunk back into the building, feeling curiously betrayed.

Jinx's studio was creaking plank floors and thick glass windows, embedded with chicken wire, so that the sun was always filtered. Nothing like the lofts in the movies or the ones that now dot San Francisco. Trucks came and went from the first floor, huge and rumbling, so the whole place shook every morning at four o'clock and again, when they returned at eight or nine or ten o'clock at night. Jinx had settled into one of the strange small rooms, a futon on the floor, the walls hung with her maps and threadbare tapestries. Tiny, blue Christmas-tree lights were strung across the ceiling, so it always looked as if the sky had suddenly given birth to blue stars. It was where they fell in love—or what they called love.

"Why do you teach English?" Jinx asked one night, when the blue lights had finally settled back and the trucks were quiet. Phoenix could hear the cats calling to each other, plaintive sounds. What could she say? The truth hurt. English was safe, safer than the girls she'd taught, years before, girls who came with broken spirits and battered lives. She was supposed to lead them back, but she was too weak. She couldn't save them, couldn't even save herself. So she'd quit. Walked away like the coward she'd always known herself to be. She'd seen herself in them and the reflection was terrifying. But she told Jinx none of that. Instead, she had taken Jinx's nipple into her mouth, teasing back and forth through her teeth until the question was forgotten, or until they pretended it was. She would rather Jinx think her noble, trying to save young minds or at least to open them. She answered with a question: "What's with the neon? I thought you did tattoos." On the workbench in the next room, Jinx was making a large pair of flashing red neon lips that puckered, then smiled. Already on the north wall of the studio was a green and blue neon that winked out the message *No Moleste* followed by *Art Zone*. The neon delighted Phoenix, lights glowing like promises.

"I do everything." Jinx always seemed so strong and sure in those days, the kind of woman Phoenix could lose herself in for a long time. Phoenix breathed deeply, inhaling Jinx's essence, the way animals must, locking her arms around this woman she knew so intimately and so little. Already, she was slipping away from herself, and she had no regrets, not one.

Later, when the warehouse was dark and silent, the night slow and heavy, she'd felt Jinx watching her. Turning, Phoenix opened her arms automatically. Jinx smiled and kissed her lightly, smoothed her hair, kissed her eyes, as Phoenix had moved under her, pulling her down for a long moment, before Jinx leaned back on her knees, balancing herself on Phoenix's thighs. The neon outside the room shone blue and red and green across their skin. The lizard watched as Jinx's right hand moved lightly across Phoenix's breasts, down her ribs, then on to the fine down of her belly. Raising her eyes, Phoenix had expected to see her new lover smile. But Jinx's eyes were on the pale skin of Phoenix's belly, looking at her the way artists look at a blank canvas. "What?" Phoenix asked, sure she'd disappointed this woman.

Jinx smiled then—a look Phoenix would remember long after she'd forgotten everything else. "I was just thinking." Her fingers were tracing small circles on Phoenix's belly, making her back arch, her eyes close, as she relaxed. This is the way a cat must feel, she thought, trembling a little. "You are like a cat," Jinx said, reading Phoenix's thoughts. "A tigress." Yes, Phoenix would like being a tigress, strong and sure, determined, beautiful, deadly. "Here." Jinx placed her hand at an angle against Phoenix's waist, so that the fingers pointed toward the tangle of light brown hair. "A green-eyed tigress stalks." Jinx's eyes were green. And slowly, Phoenix realized she was talking about a tattoo. Jinx had gained no small amount of fame for her tattoos. Was Phoenix only one more blank canvas?

"Yes." The answer came sure and without hesitation, "There." Jinx pulled herself off Phoenix; her feet shuffling lightly against the raw boards, as she padded out into her studio. The night prickled against Phoenix's flesh, but they hadn't bothered with blankets or sheets. Rising on her elbow, she stretched to watch and was disappointed when Jinx pulled on jeans and a T-shirt—black, the sleeves ripped out, the lizard peeking through a tear. Coming back to the bed, Jinx wrapped Phoenix in a frayed blue silk kimono, the fabric colder against her skin than the night. Jinx kissed her lightly, then led Phoenix into the studio and sat cross-legged on a futon under a pair of bright lights.

"I've been working on this for days." Jinx unrolled a drawing of a tiger prowling through a magical jungle. She'd just started coloring it in, and then only a pink amaryllis. The drawing was intricate but not delicate, like the woman who had made it. Her eyes were suddenly shy.

The tiger's shoulder gleamed under the light. "It's beautiful," Phoenix whispered. She had never seen any of Jinx's drawings before, except for the quick sketches she sometimes made at breakfast or after dinner, when she was explaining an idea or trying to remember one. But those were nothing like this. Perhaps Jinx would finish it, color it in, send it away with her. Phoenix would frame it and keep it over her bed in Chicago, and when Jinx came to visit, she would see it there and smile, remembering. Phoenix watched their reflections in the chrome light reflectors. Floating. This is what passion is, she thought, as Jinx opened the kimono and kissed the skin there. Phoenix held Jinx's head against her belly, her cheek warm like her breath against the skin that already was cooling from the night. She could no longer remember what her skin felt like without Jinx's hand there.

"How much do you trust me?" An odd question, Phoenix would think later, much later. She knew this woman so little, they were hardly more than intimate strangers. Yet, in those first weeks, Jinx already had made all the other women of Phoenix Bay's life, even Molly, seem like nothing more than a dress rehearsal for this moment, for this woman.

"Enough."

Phoenix Bay had never connected the idea of pain, hot and insistent, with tattoos. No one mentions that. Or the blood. Only how they were drunk or foolish or both, or worse; or how the final result is worth any pain. Prickling, some call it. Over the years, as Jinx worked on the tattoo, Phoenix became accustomed to the pain, sometimes anticipating it, other times understanding it, but never, ever slighting it. That night, when the needle first pierced her skin, Phoenix had trembled until she was sure she would vomit. Pride was all that had kept her from it, from running, pride and then Jinx's voice, "You're doing fine. It's always worse at first. You're fine." Those words became a lullaby. In the window, their reflections watched, and she watched shadows, until tears washed away even those, until she was somehow above the pain, no longer part of it. Make me feel, she remembers thinking, before floating away from it all. And when Phoenix returned, there were the beginnings of a pink amaryllis on her belly. Jinx worked relentlessly: first on the picture and then on the tattoo. By August, the flower was pink and perfect, the jungle growing, and a shadowy tiger beginning to prowl.

They called it a vacation, but did none of the things tourists usually do, except for her last Wednesday morning there when they took the ferry to Angel Island. They carried sandwiches in their backpacks and hiked across to the deserted far side of the island, where the ferries never dock. The island was all but empty because it was a workday and overcast. She'd pulled Jinx into the trees and then laughed at how Jinx jumped back, her eyes wide, every time the wind rustled. Not such a renegade after all, Phoenix chided, as she stripped off her shirt and ran half-naked along the beach. Pulling Jinx down into the sand, "You're crazy, Phoenix! Somebody will see." And then Jinx forgot to look over her shoulder. "There's nobody but us," Phoenix told her. "There's nobody else in the world. Only us." And for years, it was enough, even if it wasn't true.

Arching her back over the ancient wrought-iron grating that rims the front deck of the beach house, Phoenix Bay has a clear if upside-down view of the sea: winking silver, already angry as it slams into the shore. Like the stained-glass window in the dining room and the peacock in the backyard, Carson had salvaged the railing from the old convent. Our Lady of the Peacocks, he called it, or at least the notes attached to the plans over Rennie's desk do. The village of weekend homes he'd planned for the kinds of people who imagine they need such things would be maybe half done by now, if construction had started on time, or if Carson had lived. Small, perfectly detailed peacocks, drawn with an architect's sense of precision, strut through casual gardens, fenced with replicas of the railing here on his beach house: curlicues, with tiny Gothic crosses, swirled into an intricate pattern, the kind so often used on Victorian widow's walks. Funny name, considering the place was once a convent. No widows there, just professional virgins, lesbians, and runaway wives, who found God to be a better husband than the ones they'd left behind. On the master plans is the large redwood and gilt sign EMANIA, maybe for the Celts' land of the moon where lost souls go, maybe because Carson just liked the name. No Emania, now or ever.

Stretching out her arms, Phoenix Bay has the sensation of rising: the same feeling as when she's running, as if something magnificent and as yet unnamed is waiting for her. All she has to do is get there first. Winning is important in a world of losers. She hasn't thought of herself often as a winner, but she still remembers what it feels like, felt like, might feel like again.

A curious gull hovers low, wings cupped to the wind, feet dangling loose, then turns, heading toward the gray horizon, streaked with shades of sunset gold. What must it be like to fly, really fly, free of the constraints of airliners and strangers who inhale sharply at that moment when the engines pull back, starting their descent, welcoming the certainty of land? That feeling of excitement tinged with dread. The last time she'd flown alone was to come to California and home to Jinx. Four hours from Chicago to San Francisco and none of it mattered except that last crucial half hour when the plane made its approach. Smiling as much at the sensation as at the thought of Jinx, lounging against the post at the airport gate. Jinx. Afraid to fly, more afraid strangers would see the fear etched on her handsome features. Afraid of everything, really: the landing gear suddenly freezing; the plane tumbling over itself, turning into an exploding fireball. So much worse can happen, Phoenix would tell her. So much worse had.

Hugging Jinx's worn leather jacket more tightly around her

against the spring wind, she turns to go back inside. The jacket doesn't fit anymore. Maybe she should trade it for one of Carson's. Certainly better leather. And linen and silk and cashmere, all matched by color and style. Carson Cole was a man of infinite taste. Only slightly taller than Phoenix, certainly shorter than Rennie, but solid where Rennie is gaunt, Carson wasn't so much beautiful as assured. The sweet scent of pipe smoke greets her each time she opens the door to his closet. Carson's scent. Has Rennie ever sat in this closet, eyes closed, just breathing, the way she had in the closets in the Sanchez Street flat after Jinx was first gone? The small closets still smelled of her then, and the sheets that Phoenix refused to change for weeks, until her own scent was all she could find. Had Rennie loved Carson that much? No, not loved, but needed—had he *needed* Carson the way she needed Jinx? Unlikely. Rennie Johnson isn't the kind of man who ever really needs anybody, no matter what he's told her or his sister.

Rennie was always the golden boy, first at Northwestern University and then, later, in New York publishing circles. "We're expecting great things from you, Rennie," the professors would say, "don't disappoint us." And he hadn't, at least at first, when he was still living out their dreams. No one ever told Phoenix that they were expecting great things from her. No point in lying; she was just one of a thousand drudges in the English department. At least she hadn't disappointed them in the end, unlike their golden boy. A few beautiful and promising volumes, turned to larger, more predictable, more marketable books, then, a couple years ago, he'd started writing pornography to support himself and because it was fun and maybe because he was tired of being the great gay literary hope. So much for expectations. "Always expect the worst," Villanova used to say. But Rennie had always expected the best, had assumed the party would go on forever. Mostly it had.

She and Rennie have floated through each other's lives for most of two decades, losing track and then reconnecting, the years in between lost. Nobody's fault, just the way life turns. When he had surfaced in San Francisco six years ago after suffering the seasons of New York one winter too many, it was expected, in a way. The East Coast had grown intolerable. He needed California's freedom, its forgiveness, its cultural amnesia. The critics were starting to turn on him, saying that unlike his earlier books, the new work had a hurried quality. Words like "rough" and "unpolished" became common in his reviews. How could they not understand? He had a great deal of work to do and he was running out of time. Phoenix could feel it in the words. Then one slow and sunny afternoon, Jinx had pointed out his picture in a newspaper: "Here's your buddy, the writer. Says he's living out here now." Phoenix had studied the picture carefully: older, of course, and wearing one of those then-fashionable three-day beard growths, but more than that, he looked relaxed, almost happy. Rennie Johnson was known for writing about rage and death and desperation and survival, but his face was clear of pain. Even though he never smiled for cameras, as if smiling would somehow make the words rearrange themselves on the page, strip them of their meaning, Phoenix could see he was contentedly, ripely happy, as only a man secure in his choices is. By then, of course, Phoenix was playing at happy, too.

At the bookstore where he was reading and signing his latest book, she waited with the others, men mostly, composing the few words she'd have time to say when he signed the book she was holding. But what is there to say after so many years? Would he take her hand, pull her aside? They would remind each other of who they'd been; she didn't know if she could face that. The bookstore was small, and R.J. was a popular author. Phoenix had arrived early and, still, there was nowhere to sit, except on a table with a book display. She'd balanced herself precariously. When R.J. had come in and started to read, there was a hush. He'd been on the road a long time promoting the new book, and tired lines around his eyes, which she suspected had been airbrushed out of the photographs, were showing. But his teeth were the same. Funny to remember somebody's teeth. When he raised his eyes, taking in the audience like a deep breath, he smiled at Phoenix, and said, "I'm so glad you came. It's been a long time." A titter of applause rippled through the audience, each imagining the words were for them all. She knew better; nodded, smiled, her hands folded carefully in her lap so that they wouldn't betray her. The man sharing a corner of her table looked at her with what? Envy, maybe? Curiosity? It didn't matter.

When they first met, there was all the time in the world, enough to weave a blanket to wrap around the sun. Phoenix was charmed by the handsome young man who had no interest in politics, who read Milton even when it wasn't assigned, and who quoted Chaucer, his voice rich with the strange cadence of the language. Not only was Rennie easily the smartest boy she'd ever known, he was the first to call himself a poet. In her world of strip mines and cornfields, no man ever admitted to so much as reading a poem, much less the desire to write one. She considered that, alone, a sign of consummate bravery. With astonishingly slender hands and huge eyes, which Phoenix imagined were signs of great intelligence, Rennie already looked the part. He'd spent much of his childhood in Mexico with his filmmaker father and the rest of the time banished to private schools called ranches. He smoked marijuana and dropped acid and mescaline. To a girl who had never left Illinois, he was worldly.

One spring afternoon, he brought Cecelie to the pilings on the Lake Michigan shore, where Phoenix had spent the morning composing a poem about unrequited love, sentimental and foolishly graphic with the clitoris as a rosebud. Lesbians who weren't quite sure they wanted to be lesbians, who still thought there was an option, did things like that then. *Waiting, the passion of the lonely,* was the first line. The years have blessedly flushed the rest from her memory. She hadn't heard Rennie approach—usually he called out to her, mostly to hear the sound of her name, or so he said—but wasn't surprised when he flopped onto the shelf of rock next to her. "Phoenix, I've brought you a new friend. My sister Cecelie is visiting from UCLA. Entertain her." He was delighted. Cecelie was shy. Phoenix was overcome by this woman who looked enough like Rennie to be his twin. Rennie plucked the new poem from the open sheaf of papers by her side and frowned. "Sappy." Wadding up the paper, he tossed it into the water, where it trembled for a moment before bobbing away. He was smiling.

"Anybody who waits for passion deserves to be lonely. Consider that."

Rennie never waited for passion, but still he's lonely. The by-product of the plague years. The doctors call him lucky. He has lived with it long enough to become a slight curiosity, although not an aberration, like the man who lived well beyond a decade, so long he came to believe he was invincible. (He'd died, rumor had it, growling.) "If you'd asked me five years ago, I would have honestly told you that I would never see this day," he said as part of a strange and rambling toast to Carson's fiftieth birthday last year. Those there had understood: Rennie was the one who'd been sick for so long; he obviously would go first. Carson, smiling, had raised his glass and kissed Rennie lightly. Who could have known that all those tiny microbes were already preparing to wage war in Carson's brain? First his arm hadn't worked right, when he was up at Emania. Then the headaches had started. Too much work, they'd told each other, probably nothing serious. And finally the diagnosis: PML. How can you die from something that sounds like a foreign airline? But Carson had, and quickly, too, so quickly that a pair of jeans still hangs on a hook inside the closet door waiting for their owner.

Phoenix has been slowly working her way through the closet, making piles: Keep, Toss, and Give Away, by far the largest pile. All the shoes go there. Lots of bad karma sloughed off through the soles of the feet. A barefoot woman who lived under a freeway told her that once. And Phoenix, accustomed to listening to the rantings of crazy women, had paid attention. "Darlin', " the woman had beckoned with swollen hands, "listen to what I'm tellin' you, darlin'. " Phoenix drew closer, fascinated; no one had ever called her darling before. So many lost women huddle in San Francisco's doorways or in parking lots under the freeway overpasses. You see them often after six o'clock, when the commuters have taken their cars and streamed back across the bridges. Cut through the parking lots and you find yourself apologizing, as Phoenix Bay had that night, as if you've strayed into a stranger's living room. Cautious eyes watch, but they make no pleas for spare change. You are the intruder; they, too, are done working for the day. But wouldn't it be better to risk what little bad karma Carson might have had—

and how could a man so happy have ever had much?—than to go barefoot in San Francisco in winter? She doesn't know but adds more shoes to the pile. And boots and socks and underwear and suspenders and the entire contents of a drawer labeled Work Clothes. What kind of man labels the drawers of his closet? The same kind that fills the drawer with custom-made shirts, perfect except for a small frayed spot on one cuff or a tiny stain on the collar. Carson.

The Keep and Toss piles are harder, now that Phoenix has discovered she can wear Carson's clothes. Many of his clothes look ridiculous on her, but some, like the smooth white linen suit, make her seem, if not beautiful, then at least sophisticated, almost elegant. Slipping on the jacket, she assesses her reflection. Not bad. Odd, that these clothes would fit. Carson always seemed compact to her looseness. Looking in the mirror, she sees no difference in how she looked six months ago, but there must be, the way Jinx's clothes, once too tight on her, now hang. Carson's clothes make her look hard and cold, she decides; she would like to be hard and cold. Regarding herself in the mirror, pushing her hair up under one of his hats, she considers the possibilities. She looks foolish. No, not foolish, femme. Even a man's suit doesn't mask that. And the butches love it, even the ones who pretend they don't. Being femme is the hardest damned thing in the world, even if the world accepts such things a little more than it did when she was first coming out. Still, though, there's that little underlying current of shame, but shame makes women stronger and nobody knows that better than lesbians. Weak femmes are the great myth of lesbianism. Femmes have to be tough to survive. The butches look tough, but femmes *are* tough. The butches know it, too, the way the femmes know their soft spots. That's the beauty of it. And white linen suits don't change a damned thing.

"Nothing changes," Jinx used to say, "no matter how they look from the outside; people are what they are." She actually considered that to be an original thought. "A rose by any other name," Phoenix replied. All those years of teaching Shakespeare sometimes paid off. "What else *would* you call a rose?" Jinx asked, playing dumb, unwilling to give up.

Molly, Phoenix Bay's first real lover, was fond of unoriginal platitudes, too, although Phoenix didn't know they were unoriginal at the time. "Change comes one day at a time, in either direction," was Molly's favorite. If Molly wasn't the smartest or most original of the women Phoenix Bay ever loved, she was certainly the first. She was older, no older than Phoenix is now, of course, but sure of herself, more self-assured than Phoenix imagines she ever will be. And because Molly was her first real love, Phoenix thought she was the most beautiful, desirable, and magical woman in the world. Now, Molly is with her still, on the first gold ring through her left labia, caught with a black onyx stone. Jinx was always fascinated by that ring and the stone, so round and perfect. It had seemed natural enough to take one of the lapis earrings Jinx had given her to the piercer. The two women she's loved best in her life, reduced to gold wires and small stones. Black and blue. What would Molly think of that? She always did have all the answers— an irritating trait at the time, but one Phoenix would welcome now. Phoenix is tired of looking for answers and coming up empty. All those years of almost getting it right, all those years of believing everyone else understood the rules, only to find out there are no rules.

Phoenix Bay watches night come alive in stages as it does so close to the sea: first the blue haze; then the satin-black sky; finally the stars, coming on in a rush, warriors called to battle. The days are growing subtly longer. Every evening, Marcel Proust's calls come a little later. The peacock, too, is welcoming spring. Sometimes, just before nightfall, he fans his tail in a final salute to the day, before disappearing into his tree. She uses his calls as a timer for her evening visits to the basement.

Rennie's darkroom has turned out to be the perfect grow room for her marijuana plants. Already hung with electric outlets and deep troughlike sinks, the room glows with the clear, too-white light that seems to suck the pigment from skin. Phoenix is happiest here, where the plants are thick and lush. She loves the soft, feathery leaves, the pungent odor, the too-green color, enhanced by their artificial, nearly endless sun. Too sweet and beautiful to be dangerous, no matter what the government says. She's spent years perfecting this strain and now she's growing them for Rennie as much as for herself.

On the wall over the sink, she's taped newspaper clippings about Brownie Mary, a grandmotherly sort who puts reefer in her baked goods that she takes to the AIDS patients. A fine tradition, when you think about it. Gertrude's Alice would have done as much. Brownie Mary is doing well in court. Apparently it's hard to convict a grandmother with good intentions. At least she's not like that one in Sacramento who killed off her boarders to get their Social Security checks, and would have got away with it, too, if she'd buried them deeply enough. Turned out she was too feeble to dig a good grave. The rainy season did her in: a hand here, a foot there, surfacing unannounced in her garden. Even at that the press didn't call her the first female serial killer; they saved that for some poor dyke in Florida. Grandmotherly types apparently can get away with more. The dyke's girlfriend turned her in, said she still loved her, though. Maybe so.

Next to the newspaper clippings are photographs of Rennie and Carson: arms draped over each other's shoulders; walking along a beach maybe in Hawaii, she guesses from the background; sitting on stairs like a totem, Rennie on the lower step, smiling up at Carson. The men in the pictures look not so much happy as content, not so much in love as comfortable. Maybe that's what love is supposed to look like. She wouldn't know.

Night flows, unrelenting, closer to dawn than to midnight. Phoenix Bay lets her mind close and begins to float away, clear-cutting the past to make it less damning. All the tricks Teddy Grayson has taught her don't come even close to those crucial few she's learned on her own, like how to hold the demons at bay when they come whispering in your dreams, and how to fly away when the world is closing in on you too hard and too fast, and most of all, how to appear normal in a world better suited for chaos. Night is the hardest. Defenseless, her dreams take her into rooms where Jinx is waiting, but not for her; where women are laughing; where her own voice taunts her, reminding her of what might have been, should have been, can never be again. Waking from a fitful sleep, unpleasant memories threaten to pull her back if she'll let them.

She dresses quickly and creeps out of the house and across the dark and deserted highway to the beach where the surf rolls, relentless, unforgiving. There is a kind of peace here. Across the water, a fog horn lows. One clear note gives birth to an idea, pure as truth: "Let go. Let go and you'll never have to think ever again." It's the devil's best lie: "Let go, and everything will be all right." But Gran Cicero had let go and all the Thorazine and shock treatments in the world couldn't bring her back. Phoenix Bay steps into the surf, shockingly cold, so that her mind must focus on her ankles, freezing, on her feet, numbing, on anything but the wispy voices disguised as wind. Gran Cicero must have believed the seductive lies. How long, Phoenix wonders, until she does the same? How long until she slips? How long until she can't find her way back? Villanova likes to say things are never as bad as you think. Most people say, "Bad as they seem." Villanova knows the difference; women raised in the company of madwomen do. But what can be worse than this, this fear that sticks to thighs like wet sand?

Run. Impossible to run at night, so many treacherous mounds and holes. More impossible to not. Run. Until Phoenix Bay's chest heaves like a racehorse, breath clouding in front of her. Run. Until she can hear nothing but the pulse of blood beating through her brain. Run. Until she trips and falls, bruising her hands on the damp-packed sand, hard as concrete, the surf washing against her, cold as the strip of gray lighting the sky, while she prays. Every morning the prayer is the same: Please, God, let me die.

The wind laughs behind her. Wiping her hands on soaked jeans, she kneels in the surf, turns her head toward the sound. Of laughter. A large yellow dog, a retriever of some sort, hard to tell exactly in this pale half-light, tumbles across the sand toward her, mistaking her for a playmate. His tongue lolls out, pink and friendly. He sniffs, sniffs again, as she tries to rise. Stiff. Her feet prickle from the cold; the wet has seeped into her joints. How is that possible? A man's voice, too loud for so early in the morning, laughs again. "Ranger! Down, boy! She's not playing." Then, mistaking her hesitation for fear, he turns serious. "Don't worry, miss, he won't hurt you. Will you, old boy?" The dog turns and gallops up the beach, then back toward the man with the laughing voice. "Ranger! You devil! Stick, Ranger, stick!" Ranger turns, eager, something pleasurable registering deep in his simple doggy brain, and bounds away after a black stick, flying through the air. She should have buried her face in the warm doggy neck, let the soft pink tongue wash away the salt, part tears, part ocean; she might have found comfort there. Should've, could've, didn't.

Ranger skirts the surf, then dives, and the ocean is blank. Blank. The laughing man, serious now, paces the edge of the sand where dog tracks lead to the water, as the surf fills them, one by one, washing them smooth. Phoenix shudders. The dog is dead, washed out to sea, all from trying to please that selfish bastard with the stick. Grief wells inside her for the pink tongue and yellow eyes—they were yellow, weren't they? All he wanted was to please. How could that bastard let this happen? Hatred for the man rises in her throat like bile. He will get another dog, maybe this same day, and another, and another after that. What does he know of Ranger struggling out there in the cold, black water, trying to hang on with all his might, only to be swept away? What does he care? And no one will blame him, that's the worst part. "It couldn't be helped," they'll say. "How could you have known it would end this way? Don't blame yourself, it wasn't anybody's fault. These things happen." She's heard it all before. But then Ranger's head bobs up on the surf and he is swimming toward shore, the stick, or at least *a* stick, clutched in his massive jaws. Betrayed, she turns and starts back across the sand, pushing back the tears that spilled for a stranger's dog.

Wiping her eyes with the back of her hand, she squints, hoping the laughing man will think the salt wind brought them. Never ever let anyone see you cry, she knows that as well as she knows her own name. They look for weaknesses, for the slightest deviations, the finest imperfections. One slip is forgivable, unless they see the cracks; they do not forgive cracks. Cracked pots. Her mother's cupboards were lined with them, cracked teapots, so badly broken they could no longer hold water. Villanova said you couldn't see the cracks, but you could. Gran Cicero had broken them all during one fit or another. Crackpot. Her mother bought them at auctions, one at a time, called them her "pretties." After they were broken, she would piece them back together with a special clear glue. What was it called? That glue in the yellow tube? Does it matter that she can't remember? She can't remember Gran Cicero breaking the teapots, either, only that it had happened, only that she would find Villanova sitting at the kitchen table with a box of toothpicks and that glue, piecing, piecing, and then holding up the pot: "See, good as new." Smiling as if she believed it. "Why, if you didn't know the cracks were there, you'd never see them at all." But they knew, they all knew, they would have to have been blind not to see.

One step at a time. She is an actress. One more step and one after that. Important to keep moving. Crazy women stand too long in one place. Straighten the back, swing the arms a little, back to front, back to front, take long steps. Crazy women hold their arms close to their sides and mince their steps. Zip the jacket. Crazy women clutch their clothes around them. Think of something to say. "Nice dog," she calls before Ranger and the laughing man are completely out of earshot. Crazy women talk to themselves, don't notice when they aren't alone. The man waves, smiles, throws the stick. Wave back. Smile. Keep walking. She is playing the role of a lifetime. She knows what happens when you forget your lines.

Funny how everyone except Rennie had blamed Jinx's leaving for pushing Phoenix over the edge. He knew better; he'd seen it before. That spring when she'd turned up unannounced on his doorstep in New York, he hadn't asked why; he could see it in her eyes, how they flitted from one point in the room to another, never focusing for more than a minute, never looking another living being directly in the eye. Gone more than he was home, she was content to cower in his bedroom in the shabby apartment he was sharing with two other beautiful young men, who were home even less. Licking her wounds, he told the others, excusing her antisocial behavior. Not that they cared. And by the time she'd finally ventured out, imagining she was somehow magically healed, summer had draped itself across the city. Long, hot nights led into longer, hotter days. He found her a job teaching English to new immigrants. Out there still are women who probably add "r" to *wash,* place the accent hard on the first syllable of *insurance,* and drop the final "g" from almost any word ending in *ing* because Phoenix hadn't yet tamed her country accent; that wouldn't come until later. Cecelie was in New York that summer, too. Now whenever Phoenix thinks of her, it's with a wash of warm sun in the background. Cecelie had just won a Fulbright and was preparing for the trip that would take her to Peru for a dozen years. They were twenty-four years old and thought they understood politics and passion and love.

To the amusement of the men who slipped through the apartment like evening shadows, dropping by to change clothes before going out again, Phoenix and Cecelie courted each other with a kind of formal, but determined fatalism. It was understood that Cecelie would go to Peru, no matter what happened between them; she had a doctorate to finish, after all. But it was summer, and New York spilled out before them; October seemed a lifetime away. Phoenix didn't cry when Cecelie left, although she couldn't shake the feeling of loss that clung to her for weeks. She charged it off to the shortening of the days, as winter approached. After all, she told herself, she hadn't lost herself in Cecelie, although she would have if Cecelie had allowed it. At the time, though, she told herself she was being careful.

Careful. Filled with care. Every action, every moment. Before these last few months, she could not imagine paying attention to all the routines of living: shopping or eating or fucking or dressing or undressing, either, for that matter; or showering, shitting, brushing her teeth. Then slowly the routines themselves had become overwhelming, not so much the acts themselves, as having to repeat them over and over again, and never getting better at it or worse, just the same pointed motion. Sometimes she thinks it was the dreadful routine of the unending maintenance that had dragged down the corners of her mouth, clouded her eyes, and finally driven her over the edge, leaving her motionless in bed for hours at a time, not sleeping, but unable to move. And now she's begun to inch back, a tightrope walker on the wire again after a bad fall. She can't shake the sensation that if she slips again, she won't be able to climb back up again. Carelessness, she imagines, has cost her everything, sucked her into a swamp of quicksand and sinkholes.

When she was a child, she'd watched her best friend, David, a boy her age but small as a girl, slip into quicksand by the creek. She'd run then, back across the fields that still lined the edge of town. Hot-baked earth, hard as chipped concrete, tore at her bare feet, threatening to throw her off-balance before she reached the big green tractors on the far side of the field. Heat burned her sides, dust caked her throat, and still she ran, waving her little-girl arms back and forth at the men on the tractors: "David's stuck in the quicksand!" She thought they would want her to lead them back, but the men left her there, in the dirt, on the far side of the field where she'd fallen.

By the time she got back to the creek, only David's thin arms and shoulders were free of the mire; when Phoenix had left him, it wasn't even up to his knees. Hadn't they been warned about playing in that creek during dry spells? Why hadn't they listened? She had; but why hadn't David? A tall man was tossing a rope out to the boy, who tried to catch it. She squatted in the sand at the edge of the bog. The man with the rope leaned over her, "You go on over there and stay out of the way, honey; this here's serious." David caught the rope finally, wrapped it around his forearm, like his father commanded. "Move slow, boy, like you're swimming. Now, don't make no sudden moves, just slow and steady. That's right, son, you're doin' just fine—ain't he, boys?"

The rescue seemed to take a long time, although it was probably only minutes before David's father could reach him. Phoenix remembers how the man's back arched, the way the sun played on his hair, the satisfied suck the quicksand made when it finally gave up the boy. "You done good, boy. You okay?" David's father had a meaty hand on each of his son's bony shoulders. Trembling, the boy had nodded, struck dumb by fear. "That's all I wanted to hear." Phoenix heard the crack of his father's fist against David's face, more than she had seen it. What she saw was the boy drop onto the dirt, covering his head with his bony arms, his body curling into it-self, as huge hands reached down and lifted the limp boy, stood him up, and knocked him down again. David never made a sound. From deep inside a hollow maple, a squirrel scolded, then another.

"Come on, girlie, this here's between the boy and his pa." The man with the rope was pulling her along, out of the woods, across the field toward the gravel road and home. This time, she'd remembered her shoes. She didn't see David much after that. When she called to him on Saturday afternoons at the movies or out on the square in front of the five-and-dime, he would tuck his head against his shoulder and turn the other way. After awhile, she didn't call to him anymore.

4

The Bucerias sun, so comforting when Rennie Johnson first arrived, has turned oppressive with the arrival of May. Moving carefully onto his stiff back, he strains upright, his face toward the path, shielding his eyes with his right hand as if watching for someone coming up the road, where late-morning shadows play through heavy jungle green. In the distance, a bird cries; no answer comes and the trees fall silent again, except for a faint rustling in the undergrowth.

Two months here and he has grown used to the ghosts who walk these paths so easily: Carson smiling and bearing flowers and wine from the Puerto Vallarta market; Mala riding on her mother's shoulders, small black eyes on the lookout for parrots and snakes hanging from branches in the trees. Most often, though, he feels his father: good-natured enough, except when he was drinking, his arm slung easily over the shoulder of a woman, always a different woman, younger but no more or less beautiful than the one before. Rennie was never here long enough to really get to know them—his father or the women—hardly here at all except for vacations from the schools in Colorado or New Mexico or one year godforsaken Texas, wherever Manny Johnson had decided to send him in attempt to turn the boy he despised into a man. All the horses and roundups and lock-step marching in the world couldn't have stopped Rennie from becoming the kind of man his father feared, the kind he could never let himself love. In the end, their sameness, not their differences had driven them apart.

The last days of his life, Manny Johnson had sat here on this balcony that looks out toward the sea. Frail in the way only the dying are frail, Rennie had seen his father's face turn, almost eager but still closed, toward the sound of his son's footsteps on the path. Rennie supposes he himself must look much the same now, that same guarded expectation, veiled, in case someone is there to see. In truth, though, he is waiting for someone this morning, the real estate agent, with an offer to sell this place and its memories. If he were a sentimental man, he would keep it, but the night sweats and constant bouts with nausea and, finally, Carson's death have stripped him of sentiment and left him impoverished. He needs the money or, to be precise, the doctors in San Francisco will need the money. It will buy him not time—if he were a dreamer, he would believe that, but his dreams died with Carson—nor dignity, but perhaps comfort and peace of mind. For a time.

Herman and May Schwartz, a couple from Santa Barbara, are interested in the villa, although this is not so much a villa as a rambling house, larger than some, less grand than many. The Schwartzes have stayed here before, many times over the last sixteen years, celebrating anniversaries and important private holidays. Here Mr. Schwartz—Rennie finds it impossible to think of a man he's never met by his first name—has become a fine fisherman. Sailfish. Bonitos. Jacks. Now he wants to retire here, in this house that they call their second home. Hard to imagine a couple named Schwartz finding happiness in Bucerias.

Rennie Johnson knows this about the Schwartzes from the guest diaries left on the tiny table by the front door. The guests, who are not really guests but temporary tenants renting the house out by the week or the month, carefully record bits of their lives: sunsets watched, pineapples bought, iguanas cited, bonitos caught and cooked and eaten, sailfish that got away, sunburns and rashes and home remedies discovered. Constant streams of middle-aged Americans with their children, who grow into parents and bring their own children, the occasional honeymooners, and less often, same-sex groups that he hopes are gay, flow through. These strangers, who have lived more in his father's house than he ever could, don't seem like real people so much as character sketches. And now a pair of them are buying his house, "lock, stock, and barrel," he'd told the agent, and a small cloud had crossed her face. American idioms confuse her. "Furnished," he'd amended quickly. She'd smiled, relieved. The Schwartzes have had a standing offer on the place for years, he knows this from the notes in the book, from the letters they send him every eight months or so. "If you ever decide to sell . . . the happiest times of our lives . . . must mean a great deal to you, as it does to us . . . the greatest respect for your fond memories."

Had they hugged each other when he'd finally responded, their heads bowed over his letter, typed because his penmanship is so erratic, incredulous at their good fortune? Or had the letter come at a bad time, just when they'd made an offer on another house? Apparently not, for they had called the agent a few days later. Yes, their offer stood. Not a great offer, no more than he could get if he were to put the place on the market, but no less, really, considering time lost and the inconvenience of strangers who would want God-knows-what improvements. The Schwartzes were easy. It was time.

He watches the real estate agent picking her way up the path, her high heels sinking into the soft earth. Silly shoes. But the vanity of women has always fascinated him, the way he was fascinated by his mother, or at least by her image—the real woman repulsed him. A Kewpie doll with razor edges is how he always thought of her, thinks of her even now, more than two years after her death, when he thinks of her at all. Her scent was of stale cigarette smoke and expensive perfume. Long, red fingernails dug into his arm for any indiscretion, real or imagined. The brush of eyelashes tickled his cheek on those rare occasions when she bent to kiss him, her lips, red, wet, as if a painter had just finished the portrait of her face and it hadn't yet had time to dry. But on screen, Mona Morgan was perfect, with her high breasts, tiny waist, and that irritatingly mincing walk, a simple effect of physics created by tight skirts and too-high heels. Huge eyes, with their feigned innocence, gave her face an almost angelic look. No wonder his father, the only son of an ill-matched marriage between a Merchant Marine from Wisconsin and a *cargador*'s daughter from San Blas, had fallen in love with or at least had married Mona Morgan, the daughter of a Bakersfield, California, truck driver. The marriage lasted five years, and when it was over, Manny took his son and moved here, to his mother's house. Mona, though, had kept Cecelie, for what reason Rennie never really knew. Maybe she really did believe the line from the song that promised a boy for you and a girl for me. Or perhaps Manny really didn't believe Cecelie was his child (as he'd said often enough while drunk, and he was drunk often) no matter the stark family resemblance. Both children had inherited their grandfather's long Wisconsin build and their grandmother's dark good looks—a striking combination that Rennie mercilessly exploits and Cecelie ignores.

Cecelie. The one regret of Rennie Johnson's life, or at least the one he thinks of at this particular moment, is not knowing his sister better. He likes the idea of having a sister, even one as elusive and preoccupied as Cecelie. But the realities of her remain a mystery. Just when she'd draw close, just as he was growing comfortable with her, she would slip away again. (She is the only archaeologist he's ever known, and this, alone, fascinates him.) Then she would surface, a few years later, bearing strange and beautiful gifts from South America: pots and bangles from peoples he could only barely imagine. Once, instead of an artifact, she brought him a writer from *National Geographic*, an intense young man who was documenting Peru with a photographer, a gangly, hard-edged woman that Cecelie called her lover. They'd spent a long week here, at the Bucerias house, the photographer intent on exploring the jungle and the beaches alone. Rennie had dragged the writer along on every expedition and errand to avoid the inevitable lapses he'd come to expect with Cecelie. When they were all together, though, he couldn't help but notice that the photographer and his sister acted less like lovers than casual acquaintances: no long, stolen looks; no finishing sentences one for the other; no disappearances in the last rays of the afternoon light to watch the sunset from the beach. In fact, Cecelie had seemed genuinely surprised when the photographer—Rennie has long since forgotten the woman's name, the writer's too, for that matter—said she had grown up not far from where Rennie was then living in New York. A year or two later in Los Angeles, when he and Carson had made the trip down from San Francisco during one of

Cecelie's rare and obligatory trips to UCLA, Rennie had asked about the photographer. His sister had looked at him blankly. "From *National Geographic,*" he'd prompted. "Oh," she'd replied in her irritating, preoccupied way, "she finished the story, I suppose." It was that "I suppose" which had bothered him.

He and Carson had promised themselves they would go to Peru. Someday. But Rennie was terrified of its strangeness: the thin air rumored to fell even the hardiest travelers; revolutionaries and government troops who seem to be everywhere and nowhere at once; cocaine traffickers; bandits along the highways; armed guards at the airports; and untamable, exotic germs, waiting to stage their own invasion. If Cecelie had known of his fears, would she have laughed or turned her head away, as is her way, so he couldn't see the disappointment in her face, so much like his own, so much like their father's? Instead, he'd convinced her to come here. Even that had taken nearly a year—all those problems with getting a birth certificate for Mala, the little girl his sister had un-officially adopted. He'd finally wired his sister a thousand dollars and Carson's curt message in English: "For God's sake, *buy* the damned thing!" Carson had imagined, not incorrectly, that anything as simple as a piece of paper was for sale and probably for much less than a thousand American dollars.

Mala, he would discover during that visit, was four, going on sixty. Cecelie had sat here, in this same spot, whispering in English—Mala didn't speak English well, but who could say what she understood? Those huge eyes seemed to know everything. Her Senderista mother, disappeared. Her father, along with three hundred other prisoners, dead in the 1986 mutiny in the notorious Castro Castro jail. The Senderos had already surrendered, his sister told him, but the guards kept on firing, until the stones inside the prison ran with blood. And what about Mala's future? he'd pressed. Surely she couldn't grow up at an archaeological site. What kind of life would that be for a child? No, Cecelie should come to California, take an appointment at one of the universities, put the little girl in school there. Carson was rich, he'd told her with the assurance of a man well taken care of, there would be money for private schools. "She'll forget who she is," Cecelie had protested. "Would that be so damned terrible C.C.?" His voice had carried down to the garden where the little girl was playing with a kitten, a gift from Carson. So like Carson, not thinking of how the child could take a kitten back to Peru or how they could get it to San Francisco. "It's a rental," Carson had whispered finally. "When it's time to leave, back it goes to Señora Rivera. I gave her twenty dollars for the week. Do you think that's too much?" Smiling, always smiling. Twenty dollars to rent a kitten. A thousand for a birth certificate. Carson had approached life as if it were one long business negotiation, as if time could be bought and the money would never run out. It had.

"The kid's parents pawned her off to the first *gringa* they could find." Rennie's voice had been louder than he'd intended. "Would forgetting all that be such a damned crime?" The little girl had looked up at the sound of his voice, shamed, the way children so easily are when they hear harsh words about themselves. Of course she understood English; how could he have been so stupid? She must hear it at the site all the time. He'd cursed himself for his insensitivity. He would make it up to her, this little round-eyed doll-like creature, make her forget, let her go back to crooning a lullaby in a language he didn't understand to a rented kitten with yellow stripes and white whiskers. He didn't have to wait for Cecelie's reply; she was already on her way down to her child.

In the end it didn't matter. The child would forgive him, of course. It was his sister who looked on him with guarded eyes. "Forgive me," he'd asked finally that night when Carson was putting the little girl to bed, telling her wild stories of growing up in Arizona, which, according to him, was a great deal like where she lived in Peru. Places neither of them had ever been or would, as it turned out, ever go.

"You don't know me at all, Rennie. You never did." Cecelie's words were more observation than accusation. "I won't give up everything just because you think it would be convenient. I can't take my daughter away from her country, her people. She needs to know where she belongs. She deserves a home."

"But what about *your* country, *your* people? Where you belong, your home?"

She'd looked at him oddly. In the lantern light, there by the window, he could see their father in her face, the way she pursed her lips before speaking, the angle of her head, tilted slightly to the left, as if ideas were pooling there. "I don't belong anywhere, Rennie."

"Here . . ." he'd started to say, but something dangerous in her eyes stopped him.

She'd exhaled slowly. "I've been here five times in my life. Thirteen weeks out of thirty-two years isn't a home, it's a recurring holiday. Besides, Manny left it all to you."

"Well, what about L.A.?" He'd known it was a ridiculous statement even as he said it, and his sister had laughed, a cruel, hollow sound.

"Mona and I moved twenty-three times in seventeen years. Which one of those addresses is home? And can you honestly imagine Mona Morgan as anybody's grandmother?"

"At the rate she's going, she'll soon be younger than either one of us." An ugly little joke, but true. They'd both laughed. Mona was still alive then. Alive and living in a house in Van Nuys with a white leather couch and a rather large bird, with a clown's face in its beautiful feathers. She was at the height of her career in dog-food commercials that year. Their mother was fifty-three years old. Her publicity statements said she was in her midforties. She'd sent a Christmas card to Rennie and Carson in San Francisco: *A White Christmas with Mona Morgan* was printed in gold script. The extent of her personal message was her signature, also in gilt. Even as that holiday picture was being snapped, aberrant cells on her cervix were dividing, mutating, but she didn't know it that Christmas.

Mona lasted only another year after that ridiculous card. Rennie had to track down a shortwave radio operator to call his sister at the site. "Mona's dead," he'd said, too abruptly, because the connection was filled with static. "The sheriff's office says it was an accident. Too many pills."

There was a long pause, then Cecelie's voice: "Pain kills."

And because it had sounded too philosophical for the sister he knew so little, he'd shouted "What?" into the microphone.

"Pain killers. For the cancer." Long pause. His sister was waiting, he had to think of something to say.

"I didn't know, honest to God." But Cecelie had known; she had always known everything: that they were orphans even when their mother was alive, that the real reason their father left Rennie the house was to avenge their mother. There appeared to be very little of their mother in either of them; still too much, Cecelie would say.

Their last night in the Bucerias house, Rennie had sat on the balcony with his sister. Through the window to the bedroom where the little girl was supposed to be sleeping, Mala and Carson were singing. The little girl, in her child's determination to fight sleep, was making up songs about a kitten in the jungle, her voice high but not excited. And then Carson would answer in a low growl, impersonating animals, Rennie guessed from the snatches he could hear. Carson would have made someone, some never-to-be-conceived someone, a wonderful father, if life had been different, if there had been time. *Tío*, the child called him. Uncle. And Carson would smile, repeating the word, teasing, as if he didn't understand even the most common of the Spanish words. He called her *gatita*. Kitten.

The next morning Carson and Mala had taken the kitten—the child had named it something, but Rennie can no longer remember what—back to Señora Rivera. Rennie and Cecelie had watched them walk down the path, Carson's handsome, graying head bowed to hear Mala's observations on Mexico and jungles and kittens and life. When they came back, Rennie, at least, had expected tears, but Mala was smiling with tales of the kitten being welcomed back, his brothers and sisters tumbling across each other to bring him into their games. "How did you do it," Rennie had asked Carson later, "get her to give up the kitten so easily?" Carson had smiled as if Rennie knew nothing about children. "I told her the truth; if he stayed here, the snakes would get him. That it was time for everybody to go home." Rennie wonders whatever became of that kitten. He knows what happened to Mala and Carson.

The real estate agent is smiling as she settles gingerly on the edge of the vacant chair next to the flowered chaise, where Rennie spends his mornings. She is a pretty woman, competent, and, by reputation at least, successful. Unusual profession for a woman here. He wonders if he should ask how she came to do this, might make an interesting anecdote for Phoenix, but then decides he really isn't all that interested. The ice in her glass tinkles each time she raises it. A bead of ice sweat hovers on the glass, then drips onto the lap of her white, very white, suit. Carson wore white suits down here, too. Rennie, with less appreciation for the customs and concerns of fashion, dresses here much as he does in the States: black jeans and T-shirts, and for more formal occasions, a black shirt and black tie. He imagines it makes him look like the angry young writer he used to be. But for the real estate agent, he has settled on a long, striped robe pulled over his otherwise naked frame. Dressing reminds him of how thin he is becoming, the jeans bagging again and, so soon, the shirts hanging lank and listless, as if there will never again be enough flesh to fill them.

The Schwartzes' offer is solid, she tells him in Spanish. She often uses that word, *sólido,* he's noticed: solid, firm, unshakable. Her English is good, better than his Spanish, which lately sometimes stumbles on his tongue. The language had come so easily when he was a child. What had happened? It's as if his grandfather's Wisconsin blood has risen up and claimed him, leaving him too tall, too gangly, and now too verbally inept to belong in this world his father occupied so easily. The real estate agent tries not to look directly at him at all, probably in deference to his health. He can see it in her face: He looks ill to her, probably fragile and pale, even under the skin that tans so easily. He promises to be out by the end of the month. She smiles. The Schwartzes do not wish to wait any longer, should not have to, once their money is transferred to his account. He watches her walk down the path, sees her stop, glance back toward the house, and, imagining he cannot see her or perhaps no longer caring if he does, bends down and steps out of the shoes.

Rennie Johnson picks up the small stack of mail left on the table next to the chaise. Letters, long overdue, have chased him down here from The City. No wonder, he was supposed to be back weeks ago. On top is a letter from Phoenix Bay. Poor Phoenix, slipped off the edge and landed in his house. Once, sometimes twice a week she writes to him: details about the progress of her marijuana plants; the peacock; who has called and who hasn't; and always, the new batch of his manuscript pages freshly word processed, with her comments in what must be her school-teacher's script. Lately, she has taken to printing the pages out in a larger-than-normal type, deference to his eyesight, he imagines. Fortunately, it was always bad, not a by-product of the disease, an odd thing in which to take comfort. He shuffles her letter to the back of the pile and picks out a large, creamy envelope with his name handwritten in an elegant script, the embossed return address under the single word *Rico.*

Pursing his mouth, he runs a long index finger under the thick paper, no doubt an invitation to one of those frantic, overdone affairs in Puerto Vallarta that Rico is famous for. The parties are elegant. Only the most beautiful, the most tanned, the most carefree of the American tourists down for a holiday make the invitation list, which is inevitably filled in with the few transient locals, like himself, and a very few real locals. Rico likes to surround himself with people who play at life. They float through dinners with too much wine and cocaine and beautiful young men, and too little conversation; Rico laughing and prancing like a young proud colt, shamelessly spending his inheritance, which some say is drug money. Rennie doesn't know and has never cared enough to ask. He'd met Carson at one of Rico's parties. Carson had seemed slightly displaced, as if he'd accidentally stumbled in and then wasn't sure how to excuse himself. Maybe that was what had attracted Rennie to him, the benevolent innocence seemed so out of touch with the material world which that dreadful singer Madonna was always huffing about. As it turned out, Carson knew a great deal about the real material world.

The expensive paper puckers, then tears into little ruffles. All that rag content. Snapping his finger against the card inside, heavy and thick and smooth, to hear the dull echo, Rennie focuses on the message: A memorial service for Ricardo Barroso will be at three o'clock in the afternoon on May 13, in the Dominican Rose Gardens, Santa Monica, California. A small, square paper, thin as

63

tissue but with a vague pattern of leaves, flutters into his lap. A map. Rennie swallows hard, surprised at the ache in his chest. He and Rico weren't friends, exactly. He'd always found his bad-boy routine irritating. But still. Checking the date on his watch, Rennie wonders at how slowly time passes here and yet how quickly it has gone. May 15. Two days late. Would he have gone, even if he'd known? Unlikely, he decides, still grateful for the reprieve.

Lighting what's left of this morning's joint, he considers the rest of the day. Two o'clock. Usually he's started his afternoon writing by now, but the last few days have left him exhausted. Some days he feels as if there are not enough words to say all that must be said; other days, the words well up inside him, spilling out, until the sheer volume alone is maddening. At times like those, the writing comes with, or oddly enough, without him—or at least without his conscious attention.

Picking up the tiny tape recorder, a gift two Christmases ago from Carson, he tries to get back to where he left off at four o'clock this morning. He's stumbling. If he were the sort of man who pampered himself, he would pour himself a drink, call his attempts what they are: writer's block. But that is a luxury left for men who have time, or who think that they do. He had always imagined that when he knew time was truly short, all the words that had ever eluded him would come. Instead, he sits. And smokes.

The marijuana helps, keeping his bowels quiet and his appetite alive and his dreams soft, more like memories than night terrors. Rennie Johnson inhales deeply, closes his eyes. Already he has added Rico's image to the album in his mind. He is writing about them all: George and Wayne and Franz and the boy with the scar under his left eye, whose name he's forgotten (he hates it when he forgets) and Alan and Rex and Joel (sweet beautiful Joel) and Paul and Russ and Chris. And of course, Carson. Yes, never forget Carson. And now Rico, poor bastard.

Who was left for him in the end? There must have been somebody who cared enough to go through his address book, to write all those names on all those creamy envelopes, to enclose the tiny map with its patterns of leaves so faint, hardly more than tissue-paper shadows. Some well-intentioned friend, a sister perhaps?

No mention of family, though, not that it matters. You get to a certain age, a certain position, and all those blood ties strain from distance. Strangers connected by birth; that's all most of us have, he decides. That's all he has, although Carson had more; Carson had him. At least he was there for Carson, right up to the end, which came too quickly. Three months, almost four. It should take longer. Why wasn't Carson luckier? But it has nothing to do with luck, of course. Rennie's infections have been treatable . . . so far. Mornings still stretch out in front of him like one more thin promise. And he's grateful, damn it! Grateful that it isn't him in some hospital bed, that it isn't Cecelie hugging the shadows, waiting.

Benign vultures, that's what Carson's family had felt like those last days, perched around the hospital room. Not a one of them talking, their mouths opening and closing like mute marionettes. They were the intruders, but they'd pushed him out, as if he didn't belong, as if he hadn't been there all along, watching Carson turn into a stranger.

At least he hadn't run, like so many do; he's grateful for that. Not that he didn't try, would have succeeded, too, if it hadn't been for Phoenix. The Friday night before Christmas and the hospital was decorated with red lights and green, and construction-paper Christmas trees from some grade-school class. A florist had brought tiny pine trees with gold and silver ornaments, no larger than marbles, for each of the patients. The one by Carson's bed had a red-feathered bird no bigger than a thumbnail nesting in the branches. In all the places he's lived, Rennie can only remember seeing cardinals in Illinois, when he was at Northwestern. There was one nesting in the big Scotch pine outside the English department. The bird's feathers would flash like blood against the snow, which was always so perfect and white at first, until it turned to gray slush. But during those first hours, it was beautiful. He'd tried to write a poem about that, but the fragility of the scene had always eluded him.

That night in the hospital, rain had begun to fall halfheartedly, a last chance for the Christmas-party revelers to start home before the inevitable downpour that would follow. Nine o'clock. The family, Carson's family, had gone to dinner and then back to the house. They'd claimed the house so easily and wrongly, without meaning to: pouring coffee into Rennie's favorite mug or Carson's; putting the glasses on the left side of the cupboard instead of the right where they belonged; storing the frying pans in the oven instead of in the drawer under the stove; folding the towels in thirds instead of quarters. Little things. Trying to be helpful, trying to be the perfect guests, and none of it right. God, make them go back to Arizona; don't let them stay for Christmas. But they would stay, all of them, together: Rennie, and Carson's brother and sister-in-law, and the tiny sad-eyed mother, gathering around Carson. Rennie didn't want anything to do with Christmas then or ever again. Looking out the window on the hospital garden, he was surprised to see his own face washed with tears. He'd learned to cry there. What would Carson think . . . if he'd known . . . if he'd seen? But Carson knew very little by then and saw nothing at all. Not even the valiant little Christmas tree with its red-feathered bird. The stupid thing reminded Rennie of the last year he spent in Chicago. Old Mayor Daley was dead, leaving a string of inept impostors to jostle for the throne. One of the mayors, a woman, Jane Somebody, was afflicted with a romanticized view of poverty. Her first Christmas in office she had the city workers distribute candy canes and plastic Christmas trees to the people living in the projects. The old mayor had always sent food baskets. The television news cameras cranked out the scene: All those women, mostly, and kids waiting in line for turkeys and bread, being handed candy canes and plastic Christmas trees. "I don't mean to seem ungrateful," a woman with only a few of her front teeth told the reporter, "but I got nothing to put on a tree and nothing to put under it." I don't mean to seem ungrateful.

Rennie Johnson was supposed to be grateful for the rain that was easing the drought, but he wasn't. Grateful that Carson wasn't suffering, but he wasn't grateful for that, either. Grateful that Carson's family had come and that he hadn't been sick himself, really, in months. Grateful. I don't mean to seem ungrateful. And that's when he'd run, following the twinkling red lights down the hall, down the stairs, out into the night and the rain. He could take Carson's credit card—who knew? maybe it still worked—and buy a one-way ticket to Mexico. No, too many ghosts. Or Hawaii. He and Carson always planned to retire there. He would watch the sun rise over the ocean. That would be nice. Watch the sky being painted pink and gold with promises. He'd already seen too many spectacular sunsets in his life.

He started walking. Around the block. Then one block turned into two, then a mile, then two, stumbling past the restaurants and bars, where the company Christmas parties were just letting out, the men in their pinstripe suits, ties loosened, the women in suits, too, for once not wearing those running shoes the way they do when they're on their way to work. Somewhere along the way, he'd stopped for coffee and was still holding the Styrofoam cup, empty except for a few drops, when he realized he'd forgotten his watch on Carson's nightstand. What time must it be? "Excuse me," he'd said, approaching one of the men in a knot of drunken revelers, "Excuse me, sir." The man in a gray pinstripe suit and a red Christmas tie had turned and, without speaking, without even really looking at Rennie, dropped a quarter into the cup. The woman he was with cluck-clucked, "It's Christmas, Tony, don't be such an asshole, give the poor man some real money." Red Tie then produced a five-dollar bill, waved it so the others could see, and grandiosely pushed it into the cup. "Merry Christmas," the woman offered, in what sounded almost like an apology. "Poor bastard, out on a night like this," Rennie heard as he retreated. "Could have at least said thank you."

Eventually, he ended up in the Castro, the familiar rise and fall of the streets he knew so well, the music and the lights pushing back the night, inviting him inside. But he didn't belong there, either. Finally, he found himself at Phoenix Bay's door. Past midnight. The flat was dark, but he rang the bell anyway, the old-fashioned kind that screams. Too late. He hadn't considered calling first or that Phoenix might be asleep, hadn't considered Jinx at all, until he'd rung the bell, until the window over the door slid open and Phoenix's head poked out. The rain whipped her hair away from her head, then across her face like a veil. She would wear it long like that for only a couple more weeks. After Jinx left, she would cut off her hair and flush it down the toilet. There was so much, she would tell Rennie after she'd done it, the toilet had backed up and she had to use the plunger to make it go away. She would think the story was very funny, telling it over and over again, the way a child might.

He'd offered to go, although he didn't mean it, and she let him in, of course, fed him herb tea and brownies laced with her marijuana—Phoenix always kept a plant or two, had as long as he'd known her—and held his hand while he cried. She made him a bed on the couch, covered with crisp white sheets that smelled of bleach and faintly female scents, as if some of her and Jinx defied being washed away, as if they left their marks on everything they touched. Jinx wasn't home, she rarely was by then, and he fell asleep listening to the rain and traffic. He stayed there for four days, checking in with the hospital by phone—the nurses liked him, said they understood, said Carson was the same, said they would call if there was any change, "significant change," they called it. Except to go down for the morning newspaper and what seemed like endless packs of cigarettes, he never left the apartment; the hospital might call, he said. The truth was that the world outside the flat terrified him. Every night, Phoenix put a fresh sheet on the couch because he'd told her how nice the crisp newness of it felt that first night. Jinx passed through like a bitter shadow. Having him there wasn't her idea, and she'd never forgotten how Rennie had told Phoenix that she deserved better. But even Jinx didn't ask him to leave.

The last night he was there, he awoke to find Phoenix at the window seat, watching the occasional car pass, then a lone dog—Rennie could hear its nails scritch-scratching against the pavement, claiming the sidewalk for his own. She turned toward him, the streetlight illuminating only the side of her face, dark shadows hiding her eyes. "I've been thinking about how things used to be, Rennie, with you and me and Cecelie. Were we happy?" It was an odd question for three o'clock in the morning.

"Sure," he lied; at least it felt like a lie. One he wanted to believe.

"I think you were. Probably Cecelie. I wasn't. At least not after she left. I wanted to be a poet and to see the world, all those big dreams, do you remember?"

He didn't remember, probably hadn't listened at the time; he'd been so engrossed in his own life, everyone else seemed superfluous. "That's what we all wanted. We were, what? Twenty-three? Twenty-four?"

"And do you remember what you told me, the day before I left New York: 'The revolution doesn't need another mediocre poet.' "

He smiled a little; that, he remembered. He and Phoenix were sitting in a bar where she was a cocktail waitress, assigned a ridiculous costume that was supposed to make her, all of the waitresses, look like Revolutionary wenches. Desperate for money, she was a little ashamed of the job. He was the only one who knew where she went every afternoon before her English classes started at night. Shame, although he wouldn't have called it that at the time. "I'm sorry."

"Don't be; you were right. I *was* a mediocre poet. You're the poet and Cecelie gets to see the world and I get to teach English at a community college. The revolution didn't need an English teacher, either, but it's what I do." She lit a cigarette, inhaled deeply, held the smoke in for a long moment, before sending a blue plume out the window. "I've been thinking, Rennie, it's time for you to go."

A chill, as sharp as a slap, shot through him. "Just because I told you more than ten years ago that you were a lousy poet?" A small joke and not very funny. But she smiled.

"No. Because you can't run away from what's going on with Carson . . . forever." But "forever" didn't sound like the word she'd started to say. Still, he took it, grateful he didn't have to hear the alternatives, the unspoken obvious.

"He won't know if I'm there or not." Defensive. His mother's whine slipped into his voice and he hated himself for it.

"Maybe not, but *you* know. Promise me you won't run out on Carson. That's the worst thing in the world that can happen—to have someone you love run out on you when you're sick. Promise me you won't do that." Rennie had promised; what else could he do? The only place he had ever felt he belonged was in San Francisco those years with Carson. Good years. Not perfect, but good enough. Probably better than he deserved, certainly better than some had. The next morning he was back at the hospital, where nothing had changed: the red bird was still nested in the tiny tree, the red lights still winked in the hall when he passed, and Carson smiled until the end.

When they'd first met, Carson Cole was the beautiful athlete gone to seed, his once-magnificent muscles softened under flesh that had settled a little too easily across his not-too-tall frame. Older and successful, established, *sólido*—as the real estate agent would say—in the way writers never seem to be, Carson was not the kind of man Rennie Johnson considered generally interesting. Still, there was something about him, the way he smiled as if he and fate were involved in some complicated but terribly funny practical joke. He had, Rennie would think later, charisma. No one was immune: not the clients who had made him a rich man, not waiters or cabdrivers, nor the construction workers on his sites, and certainly not Rennie. It was as if Carson knew from the beginning that Rennie would, of course, take him to dinner the next night at Fonda Las Amapas, where they would eat iguana. And why not? He wasn't the most handsome man Rennie Johnson had ever seen or slept with, or the richest, but he was the most charming, and that was as seductive and terrifying as it was comforting.

"And you?" Carson had asked that first night over a late dinner. They'd left Rico's party, and Puerto Vallarta was frantic, as it always is in February, with the tourists from the cheap cruises and package tours. Outside the restaurant, which was across from one of the popular discos that catered to Americans, the sidewalk was filling with revelers.

"On the lam." It was Rennie's third week down and he was deeply tanned and unshaven as an outlaw; he thought of himself that way in those days. The virus was still a dreadful question he didn't want to know the answer to. In Bucerias he was hiding out the persistent notices that he must either buy or vacate his apartment in New York. He didn't have the money to buy the place, which never felt much like home, but that wasn't the point. New York had grown tiresome, not small and routine, which is never possible there, but draining. He'd lived there most of a decade—

had gone there to write—then one day had the revelation that he could write anywhere, except possibly Mexico. Too much tequila caused him to laugh at his own joke and Carson had laughed too, as if he understood. Maybe it was time to try California, Rennie had found himself saying. He was surprised, a little, to give the idea voice, more surprised when Carson took his arm and laughed, as if it were a wonderful joke.

"Do it!" Carson's palm came down flat and full-force on the table, making the wine glasses jump; red-eyed tourists at the next table looked at them suspiciously. "California is the ultimate cure for boredom." And Rennie, who hadn't really been aware of it until then, realized what Carson said was true: He was bored and a little afraid and very, very tired. He hadn't really planned to see Carson after that night, but found himself drawing a map to the house in Bucerias, not so very far from the resort development that Carson was going to "look over for a friend."

Carson's life, Rennie would discover, was filled with such friends, land developers mostly, who created fantasies in paradise with a little help from architects like Carson. Cole Development, the company Carson owned with his brother, had netted them a small fortune. The rest of Carson's time was devoted to what he called "my little rehab in San Francisco," a 1940s house with a little more style and space than those on either side of it, built originally to overlook the ocean, although a levee installed years later interrupted the view from the first floor. Carson was fixing that by installing a new second story, nearly half of it windows, even a skylight that would open more than a third of the roof. He was doing the work himself, knocking down walls and tearing out ceilings. The main floor was done, and on the second floor the skylight was already in. "It'll be just like sleeping outdoors, only without the aggravation." Carson, Rennie would discover, disliked the wildness of nature, believing architecture was a way to impose order.

Rennie Johnson had come to love that house: the easy way the rooms link, the windows that open to face the sea, the fog teasing across the highway. They spent summer evenings on the top front deck that overlooks the sea, drinking wine, making bets on when

71

the fog would roll in. Weekend mornings, Carson would pull on a yellow wet suit, tuck his surfboard under his right arm, and climb across the levee to the beach, hailing his friends, mostly kids half Carson's age, that they called the "surfer fraternity." The wet suit still hangs inside the basement, where Carson left it last fall. Rennie gave the board away to a boy who'd come to visit Carson in the hospital. "Thanks, man," the boy kept saying, "I mean really."

Rennie has done some of his finest work in the little office off the downstairs guest bedroom, where he'd started sleeping when Carson could no longer climb the spiral stairs, the better to hear Carson in the guest room. Would he have moved to his office so easily if he'd known he would never again want to, much less be able to easily negotiate the spiral stairs to the beautiful room, where you can watch the stars chase overhead? Probably. Without Carson, the room was too much space waiting to be filled. The office, so small and cluttered, is easier. It's the kind of room that writers and old men keep, Rennie had told Carson when he'd claimed it. Carson had laughed: "If it makes you happy." All of it had made Rennie happy. Now he's terrified of it: empty and too full of Carson. And nothing to do but go back and try to move on. Alone.

5

"Give up, Phoenix. It's all over."

"What?" The sun has dulled Phoenix. She turns toward Rennie and smiles slowly, her eyes dreamy, her thoughts floating on a cloud of marijuana smoke.

"Pay attention. I'm taking six-fifteen for five. By my calculations that leaves you with"—Rennie squints at the bank of white fluff creeping over the ocean, blue and gray—"damn near nothing."

"So, what else is new?"

"My, my, look who's turned into a sore loser." He jiggles a half dozen loose dimes in his left hand, before stacking four carefully on the last available square between now and six-thirty. "I'm absolutely in control."

"Nothing new about that, either." She raises her eyebrows quickly, teasing, and puts a pair of dimes on a dark square, black streaked with ochre and flecks of gold. The board is more interesting than the game. Originally designed to be a chessboard, the inlaid Italian tiles have long since been relegated to bets on when the fog will come in. Carson, seduced by the romantic reputation of chess, had insisted Rennie teach him to play but lacked the necessary patience, and Phoenix has never bothered to learn. Not that it matters to Rennie, chess takes too much concentration. Lately, he finds it hard to concentrate. Phoenix drums her fingers slowly in a silent piano exercise. Side-by-side, bare legs dangling loosely over the edge of the deck, a jar of dimes between them, they are like bored children, making up rules as they go along. "You want six-twenty?" She shrugs and reaches for the jar. As if on cue, the fog moves toward shore. Rennie is winning. He always does.

Scooping up the dimes, he leans back and squints west, where the light, gray but very bright, hurts his eyes, but he doesn't turn away. "You were right, Phoenix."

"I'm always right. Or perhaps you were referring to something specific?"

Grinning, he leans back on his elbows. "I was thinking about when you said how it hurts most to see things the way they really are, not the way they should be." She frowns. When had she told Rennie that? Not that it isn't true. "That's why we bet on the fog, Phoenix—fog leaves room for deception. There's a great need for deception in life. Reality exhausts me."

"It exhausts us all, Rennie."

Not acknowledging her, he watches the fog, a blanket being pulled across the water, slow and steady. "I've learned things in the last year that I never wanted to know. Horrible things. That's what I hate about all of this. AIDS. Being sick. It makes you see things about yourself, about death. It burns off the fog." He means those last horrible months with Carson. Not horrible, he'd often enough insisted. Not good, she'd said. No, not good, but not horrible, either. Rennie pulls himself back, puts a pair of dimes on six forty-five. "Match," he commands, and Phoenix does, if halfheartedly. Nothing left to do but bet on when the fog will hit the beach, then cross the highway. But she's become bored with the game, which was more fun with Carson and Jinx, shouting encouragement to the fog as if they were at the racetrack. "Yo, baby! Bring it on in for Mama!" Rennie checks his watch. Carson's Rolex, that hangs too loose and seems oddly formal on his wrist.

The fog has passed the midpoint, hiding much of the ocean. "Do you always lose so badly, Phoenix, or are you taking pity on me?"

"I'm a lousy gambler, Rennie, you know that. Now if Carson were here—" The words are out before she realizes. "I'm sorry . . . I didn't mean . . ."

He waves her silent. "Don't be. I think of him every time I come up here. I'm just glad there's someone else to play the game with. He thought it up, you know. And betting against yourself is a drag. The urge to cheat is too great."

"I miss him." Phoenix draws her knees up under her chin, wishing there would be a good sunset, one that would paint the sky with streaks of peach and silver and purple, instead of this inevitable fog.

"I know." Rennie leans into the railing, his dark hair falling in loose curls over his eyes, giving him an almost rakish air. "I always thought it would be . . . I don't know . . . different than this . . . more melodramatic or something. Instead it's just one day and then the next. The pain doesn't go away, but you do get more used to it. When Carson was dying, I thought I was losing my mind. Nothing seemed real. But by the time we got to the end . . . Phoenix, the very end is absolutely real." He leans close, eyes shining. She blinks under the intensity of his gaze. "Did you know that it took Carson eleven hours to die?" She did, but makes no sign. He looks away, then down, studying his hands. "Actively dying, it's called. The ultimate irony. By then, nothing is active. I remember waiting, thinking, *Now*. Phoenix, I wanted it to end and I wanted it to never end and I wanted to wake up back in New

York with it never started." He glances at her and tries to smile. "Pretty crazy, huh?"

She covers his hand with her own. Cold. His hands frighten her, how thin they've become, like an old man's with so little separating skin from bone. "Not so crazy. Just sad. But then, that's a lot of what crazy is." At least the crazy she's known: sad and lonely and scared.

Turning up his hand so that his fingers curl around hers, he asks, "Do you remember that play, *No Exit*?" She nods. "And how at the end, the stage is so full of characters you can't keep track anymore? It's like that. Death. All these strangers keep coming. And you let them because you can't stand to let anyone else near you. There was one. George. One of those volunteers the hospitals keep around to help people die. Not that, exactly, but you know what I mean." Rennie looks at her hopefully and although she doesn't know, she nods encouragingly. "He gave me cigarettes. When Carson got sick I started smoking again. After twelve years. Now I can't seem to quit. Worrying about lung cancer isn't exactly a priority with me anymore. Anyway, George said he'd stay with me, with us, until it was . . . over. I found out later the people at the hospital call him an angel, because of how he sort of appears and goes through this with you. He's supposed to be there for the ones who are dying alone, but he found us. I am not a religious man, you know that, but it was . . . remarkable. He was remarkable. Almost made me believe in angels." Phoenix wishes she could believe . . . in something. Maybe angels are easier. She squeezes Rennie's hand.

"I told him, sometime during that night, or maybe it was the next morning—it's hard to remember—that George was a pretty funny name for an angel." Rennie smiles, a sort of crooked half grin. "You know what he told me? That he'd put in for Gabriel, but it was already taken." Rennie untangles his hand, takes a drink of the lemonade, and checks his watch, then rearranges his dimes. Some nights the fog moves too slowly. "All the time he was there, while Carson was . . . dying . . . I kept trying to keep track of every minute. I wanted to remember it all. I have to remember—only I can't. Phoenix, it was strange. Surreal. That must be what it feels like to be in a foxhole during a battle. Or living in a Harold Pinter play. Or maybe a Harold Pinter play about being in a foxhole. It was bizarre. I've tried to think of a better word, but I keep coming back to that. Time distorted, so that sometimes a minute would stretch out—and then you'd look at the clock again and two hours had passed and you never noticed.

"I found out that night that no one knows about death. The doctors sweep in and then move on; they can't be bothered. It terrifies them, all that Hippocratic oath stuff. Carson's doctor was royally pissed—he pretended he wasn't, but doctors are lousy actors—as if Carson was doing this just to be belligerent. And the nurses come and go. They try, but they're more concerned with the living. And so that left me. And George. Up until it happened, I thought it really would be like the last scene in *Camille*. How's that for the classic old queen's response? God, Phoenix, I didn't know what to do, what it would be like. I'd run through it a thousand times in my mind and when it happened, it was all wrong. Not just for me, but for Carson. I expected it to be . . . neat. But it isn't. Not at all. It's not neat and tragic. It's terrible and beautiful and overwhelming. And I didn't know what to do." He inhales sharply and looks toward the darkening sky. In the distance, the peacock cries his evening song.

"It was the hardest, most personal thing I've ever been through in my life and it made me feel . . . insignificant. No, that's not the right word. I don't even know what the right word is. I didn't think I could survive. I remember asking George how he could stand it, all that death. You know what he told me?" He glances at Phoenix, although he expects no reply. "He said death isn't the enemy, it's the friend that takes away the pain. Then . . . when Carson finally . . . died, it was . . . not good, but over. Finished. And I had survived. Sometimes, even now, I'm so fucking scared that I feel like I'm going to puke or that my brain is going to explode. I don't know what I'm going to do. I only know that I don't know how to do this." Embarrassed, he wipes the backs of his hands across his eyes. She pretends not to notice. "I wanted to tell you because I knew you'd understand."

He means the suicide attempts, of course, her occasional descents into a darkness so deep that death becomes the light on the surface. As a child, she used to swim in the strip-mine lakes, deep and foreboding. One night in a dive, her foot was caught, probably a branch or a line, and she'd panicked. No light glimmered to guide her to the surface. She never forgot how it felt not knowing the way toward the light. "I guess there are lots of things worse than death," she says, finally. The free-falling fast slide toward nothingness, never knowing how long until you'll hit bottom, never knowing what will be waiting for you down there, is worse. But she doesn't tell Rennie that; instead she puts a dime on an impossible number and smiles.

"You're a born loser, Phoenix Bay." Rennie gathers up the dimes and tosses them into the pot. They'll use the same dimes tomorrow night and the night after. No one ever wins but no one ever really loses, either. "Carson used to tell me that to win this game, you've got to remember that you're just buying time." Buying time. The endless barter with an ever-silent god. One more day, God. Then one more hour. Until there is no more time left to barter away. He's right; she does understand endings. Time, look what you've done to me.

Time has been kind to Simon and Garfunkel, though, or at least to one of them. You don't hear much about Art Garfunkel anymore. They'd parted on bad terms, but reunite every decade or so for some megacause, even if they can't stand each other. Maybe they think they owe it to someone—maybe to the fans, more likely to themselves—to prove they can, once more, capture time even if it doesn't matter. The few times she'd seen Jinx were like that: careful, brittle. Intimate strangers. When they'd had all the time in the world or imagined that they did, they'd gotten sloppy, careless; only when it was too late did they finally become careful. All the tiptoeing had made her nervous. "Simply pretend." Like that song. Something, something, then "build them again." Build what again? She can't remember the rest of the words, not that it matters. Simon and Garfunkel. R.J. and Carson. Jinx. Cecelie and Mala. All of them floating out there, torn apart by something out of their control and no way to get it back again.

The clear, too-white light of the grow room seems to suck the pigment from Rennie's skin, giving him an almost ghostly appearance.

"Casper," he observes, studying his reflection.

"As in The Friendly Ghost?"

"No, Weinberger. I always did think he looked a little other-worldly. Other than that, horticulture suits me, don't you think?" Most evenings, sometimes long into the night, he's here. "Look how well Greta and Mona are doing. Must be that new fertilizer." Mona is named for his mother; the larger and more beautiful plant is Greta Garbo. "Do you think what they said about her is true?"

"What?" Preoccupied, Phoenix is inspecting the underside of Greta's leaves, looking for mites.

"Well, if you don't know, I guess it's not worth discussing. Mona's growing quite fat, don't you think?" He leans close to the plant and mock-whispers. "Keep it up, love. You can do it. If any-one deserves to burn, it's you." Phoenix smiles and climbs onto a stool, at the opposite end of the long sink. "My mother's greatest fear was fat. Unfortunately, she made my sister's life a living hell because of it. I've no doubt that Mona is already burning, or know-ing her, she's probably seducing the devil himself. Serves her right. Payback for telling Cecelie it didn't matter if she's a dyke, since no man would ever want her anyway." Phoenix winces. "So, what do you think, Phoenix, six weeks until the harvest?"

Phoenix shakes her head. "Eight, if we're really lucky." A pungent odor fills the room already. Rennie coughs twice, gasps then coughs again. How will his fragile lungs ever handle a har-vest? One more thing to worry about. Later.

Disappointment clouds his face, purses his lips. "Let's get lucky, Phoenix." Brightening, he climbs onto the stool next to hers and crosses his legs, and leans forward, chin on hand, the same pose used in his publicity shots. "Carson would have loved our lit-tle guerrilla garden. You wouldn't have known, but in his own way, he was a warrior. And I was the outlaw. But unlike us out-laws, warriors have conviction."

"You have conviction, Rennie."

"Oh, yeah." The way he says it, though, sounds like a curse. "I'll be lucky if I don't end up *with* a conviction. What's the penalty for dope growing in the basement? Five to ten? After all, the feds can't have a bunch of dying fags turning into potheads."

The plants are too sweet and beautiful to be dangerous, but they are. "Rennie, you need to know that. If they bust us, you'll lose everything."

Turning toward her, he clasps both hands between his legs. For a moment, she's afraid he is going to cry. "Look at me, Phoenix." She raises her eyes to his. Each word comes slowly, almost painfully. "There is nothing left to lose." On the wall behind him, Carson, his arm looped easily around Rennie's waist, smiles out from a test print on which someone has printed in neat block letters: BURN, DODGE, BURN.

Settling into a chair near the window of Hamburger Mary's, Phoenix waits for Rennie. "A late lunch date," he'd promised, adding, "my treat." A rare treat at that, both of them broke, the way they were back in college. Some things never change. They come here because it reminds them of Four Squares, a cluttered hole-in-the-wall just across the line in Chicago. Easy enough to imagine that no time has passed.

The street is alive with summer. Phoenix Bay loves this city in summer, every city really, but this one most of all: the way the fog slips in, turning the streets cool and damp and hazy, so much better than the feckless heat that weighs down most cities between June and September. Here, girls wear summer dresses early in the spring and late into the fall; wide flowered skirts and low-cut bodices show off the gentle rise of perfumed breasts. Little girls and teenaged ones and women older than Phoenix. Old enough to know better, her mother would say. The fashions this year are the same as the year Phoenix first kissed Jayne Walker in the locker room after track practice. That was a good year: light and colorful. Sweet. The air that spring was thick with honeysuckle and lilies. A young woman, hopelessly straight, wearing a look heavy with promises, the kind that men cling to or would like to, slides by, pelvis leading, the way models walk on the runway: clothes lead; woman follows. Her skirt, the color of summer sunsets, rides two feet above her knees, grazing the tops of her thighs—on her way back to work, judging by the hour, a secretary perhaps or maybe a clerk in one of the big department stores. She is not an executive; no one takes you seriously with your crotch showing.

All those years of feminism, a generation of rage and rejection, so that women can wear orange miniskirts and call it freedom. Freedom sometimes wears dangerous masks. What would it be like to be coming out now, with everything so easy and so available? Not just women—there were always women—but the rest? How easy it must be to have the choices, the options, to know that you're not alone. But is there still the rush when you find out an unknown world is waiting. Is that still true? That's what she misses most, the exhilaration of having discovered the thrill of the life, before all the petty grievances set in, the sense of discovery, then trying to sort it out. It was so easy, once, to make up the rules as you went along, only to change them when they didn't work anymore. Exciting. The way a new lover is exciting and wet with possibilities and promises. Phoenix, all of them, had believed they could change the world—and they had, too—they just didn't expect how much they would change in the process. That wasn't part of the plan. In the end, they'd learned that life is nothing like the dyke comic books, confined to neat frames and spaces, that camouflage won't always protect you.

Her camouflage lately has been the clothes of a dead man. At first, Rennie was unnerved. Seeing Phoenix in Carson's clothes hadn't bothered him as much as the clothes themselves lying about—a jacket over the back of a chair, a tie left carelessly on the coffee table—as if their real owner were only in the next room or down the hall, on the phone perhaps, waiting to make a late and apologetic entrance. But better the clothes go to Phoenix than to the Salvation Army. The way she wears the clothes amuses him: Carson's best white dress shirts, with the monogrammed French cuffs, tied recklessly just above her navel; pinstripe shirts half-buttoned, showing off a flash of skin and breasts; the double-breasted, white linen jacket and loosely pleated trousers worn with black patent leather stilettos and, so far as he can tell, nothing else. The effect is striking; even he has to admit that. Whatever she did to herself while he was in Mexico has turned her into a beautiful woman. The brindle hair—natural, though stylists make a fortune trying to imitate the streaks and flecks of pale gold—is short and tousled. Her eyes shine, seemingly always near the verge of tears, but a stranger wouldn't notice that so easily. All have coalesced into a kind of sophistication he's never before noticed. Or maybe it is just the clothes. This afternoon she is wearing one of Carson's suits, a pinstripe, and very high heels, which make her nearly as tall as Rennie. Easier than hemming trousers, she insists. He tells her the clothes make her look a bit more like the women in the offices, even though it's not true.

"Well, if it isn't the late Rennie Johnson." Phoenix smiles as he drops into the chair across from her. "I was beginning to think I'd been stood up for some beautiful Polk Street boy. Or work." Work is more likely. Rennie spends his mornings dictating into a small tape recorder, and she transcribes the tapes every evening. Some nights the work is strong and flowing, some nights scattered, like so many dried leaves. On nights when the work has gone poorly, he writes pornography: three hundred dollars a story; the plot doesn't matter, just gray matter to wrap around the pictures. Not unlike the human brain, he told her once. The story never really changes, only the names and the setting. Porn is easy, no heart there.

He folds his hands, settling his chin on them, the perfect author pose. "I've spent the morning on the phone trying to convince a man I barely know and like considerably less, that I'm still a poet, contrary to popular belief. There's a writer's camp in Oregon—a 'colony' this idiot keeps calling it. Anyway, the poetry teacher they'd lined up is too sick to make the trip, and he suggested that the director call me. The director, by the way, is an ass as well as an idiot. He had the audacity to say, 'I'm desperate, can you suggest anyone, anyone at all?' " Rennie flutters his fingers and raises his voice in a vicious impersonation of the director. Phoenix laughs. "What am I, a booking agency for out-of-work poets? So, the upshot is now I'm a poet again—at least for the next two weeks. The only catch is he wants me to bring new work to read. Inspire the students and all that."

"Well, there's always *Hard-On Harry*. Or maybe they'd prefer the *Truck Stop Jock*?" The two stories have become the foundation for a dozen others. Sometimes, Harry is Hank or Hunk, and the Truck Stop Jock just last week moved out of the desert to take a city job.

Rennie scowls. He dislikes being teased about his work, even the porn. "New stuff, old stuff; what difference does it make? Besides, for a thousand bucks, I'd take my dick out and wave it at them."

"Probably for considerably less."

He smiles benignly and raises his glass. "Touché. Or as you used to say 'touché.'" He pronounces it like "ouch."

"Only when I was drinking."

"Then touché, again." This time he pronounces the word correctly. "Anyway, they've got me on a flight day after tomorrow. Will you take me to the airport?" Phoenix nods, sucking on a piece of ice, wishing, and not for the first time, that there were something stronger than iced tea in her glass. Too bad Teddy Grayson's pills don't mix well with alcohol. "You'll miss a morning at Ad Agency from Yuppie Hell." He's referring to her assignment this week by the temporary employment service.

"No loss." She runs her fingers down the side of the glass, watching little rivers form. "They think I'm Secretary from Lesbian Hell. But the faggots there love me."

"I'm sure they do. Are they beautiful, any of them? Or at least a respectable selection from which to choose?"

"Some. I hear the senior partner's queer, although I've never seen him."

"Good, maybe I'll walk you back to work. Apply for a job as a copywriter or something. Anyway, as I was saying, the workshop doesn't actually start until Sunday, when the next crop of literary novitiates arrives, but I have orientation on Saturday, whatever the hell that is. Which presents another slight problem. I've finally heard from Cecelie. She's coming late next week or early the week after; she's not sure what day. Apparently, getting out of Peru is more complicated than one would imagine." His face closes a little. Every morning he searches the newspaper for stories about

Peru, but the war there isn't big news in San Francisco, and the stories, when any appear, are usually small and sketchy. Every night at six, he watches the news on the Spanish-language channel. Bombings in El Salvador compete for airtime with captured drug lords in Colombia and fires in The City's Mission District. Television's usual view of the world. Often, though, a few seconds of pictures and soundbites from Lima flash across the screen. Those rare nights when there is nothing on television or in the newspaper leave him morose and withdrawn. Angry. The longer it takes for Cecelie to leave, the more convinced he is that she will never come back. "She says she's not quite ready."

"What's the matter? Did she dig up some thousand-year-old pot that can't wait?"

R.J. glances at the menu, scowls, then sets it aside. "The university may close down the site. She says that she can't understand why. They're in the middle of a damned civil war and a bunch of archaeologists are acting as if it's a personal inconvenience. You know what she told me today? 'There have always been civil wars here, look at the Mochica.' Who the hell are the Mochica?"

"The ones who ate the hearts of their enemies." Phoenix has fallen into bed every night with a book on Peru, one she found on the bookshelves. She wants to have something to talk about with Cecelie, if she ever gets here. *When* she gets here, Phoenix reminds herself.

"Oh, terrific. Well, that certainly explains a lot, they no doubt remind her of life with Mona. She should've stuck with the cat people. I always thought they sounded a little more . . . I don't know . . . friendly. You know, meow and all that."

He means the Chavins, who worshipped fanged and dangerous feline gods. "I doubt it. Don't you read your own library?"

"Not mine," he says, leaning back until the chair balances on its back legs, and taking a long drink of Coca-Cola. A droplet of moisture from the glass disappears into his black T-shirt. "Carson's. I don't give a damn about that country. If you want to know the truth, it's always scared the bejesus out of me. The most civilized place is Lima, and that's only if you consider energy blackouts and starving kids and cholera civilized. I've never understood what Cecelie sees in it, but then I understand very little about my sister. She should have come home before this."

"Maybe Peru is her home."

"Don't be ridiculous." He drops the chair with a loud clunk. "Peru is . . . well, I don't know what it is, but it is certainly *not* her home." He is silent for a long moment, then takes another drink. Finally, he smiles, obviously having decided to veer toward safer ground. "She'll be disappointed you've cut your hair. She always did say it was your best feature."

Phoenix's hands move automatically to her hair. When she'd first known Cecelie, Phoenix was still wearing her hair long—a daring act in itself in those days when such things actually mattered. She never imagined Cecelie would remember something so simple. "But once she's out of there, she'll be fine," he continues, "Cecelie is more grounded in reality than any woman—or man, for that matter—that I've ever known." Rennie is balancing the chair on the back legs again. "She has Mona to thank for that. I honestly think that the only person in the world my sister ever romanticized was our father, which is certainly forgivable. He could be very charming, and the few times she saw him, everybody acted like they were at a job interview." Phoenix understands; she'd romanticized her father, too. "She used to say that Manny was 'real.' If only she had known the real Manny, I doubt she would have found him so delightful. Of course, nothing about Mona was ever real. I suppose when you're raised in fantasy, reality becomes seductive."

"But only in small doses."

"Not true, Phoenix. You don't understand how lucky you are to have been raised in the muck and mire of reality. That leaves you with fantasy."

Phoenix shakes her head. So like Rennie to covet the intolerable. "Everybody's reality is dreadful, Rennie. The challenge is to get beyond it and start over. Lessons learned and all that."

"Is that what your overpriced Nob Hill psychiatrist is teaching you? Whatever happened to simply inventing something better?" He smiles. "You taught me that. That and the fact that I should always try to stay sober because I'm such a damned lousy drunk. And you know me, I can't stand being thought of as lousy at anything."

Phoenix shrugs. "I don't remember. I was probably drunk at the time."

"It was good advice. My father drank himself to death; did you know that? Nothing proud or noble about it, although Cecelie might like to believe otherwise. Mona always said his 'decline,' as she liked to call it, began at the time of the McCarthy hearings. Her timing was right, but my father was of no interest to Joe McCarthy, or frankly almost anybody else famous." Shaking his head slightly, he sighs. "Pure coincidence became the stuff of tragedy. It made a much better story than the truth: that he was a plain, old-fashioned drunk, who somehow managed to get by. Mona couldn't admit that any more than she could admit that dog-food commercials were her personal best. Unfortunately Cecelie got the worst of it. Given the options, Manny and Mexico weren't bad."

At the next table a boy and a girl are debating the pros and cons of an iguana as a pet. "It'll grow to be as big as this table," the boy says, thumping the octagonal, scarred surface. He is grinning loosely, showing too many teeth, bulging out his eyes, until the girl laughs and reaches for his hands. Rennie watches them closely, perhaps seeing something in the tilt of the boy's head, the hair falling across his forehead, the hands long and lovely. Something that the girl doesn't see. The boy glances toward Rennie and smiles, a questioning greeting, then turns away. Rennie keeps on looking, until the boy glances up, pushes back a lock of hair, and shifts slightly, uncomfortably in his seat. Satisfied, Rennie smiles and turns back to Phoenix.

"In Mexico, when I was a kid, people kept iguanas tied to the porches before fiestas. Fattening them up. In fact, Manny's big brush with stardom came about as the result of an iguana. My father had the great good fortune, to hear him tell it, to arrange for that very famous iguana which was carried up from the beach. Not just any iguana, mind you, but *the* iguana. And then, he and Richard Burton got drunk. Quite a career, huh? He'd say, 'Boy! Richard Burton and I got drunk at this very table when we were on *Night of the Iguana*. He was a gentleman and a star—and he could hold his liquor.' " Rennie slaps the table hard with his open palm. The boy and girl at the next table look up, startled. This time, it is the boy who stares and Rennie who doesn't respond. "I should write to the Schwartzes, don't you think, and tell them they are now the proud owners of a table at which the famous Richard Burton once got drunk?" His voice is bitter. He exhales slowly. "My father was determined that I master three things: how to ride horses, which I despise; how to drink, which I can no longer tolerate; and how to fuck, which I still occasionally have the energy for. To Manny, those were the primary components of manhood. I was never sure quite what he wanted from me, but I always suspected it was something more . . . than what he got, I mean."

"And how to speak Spanish," Phoenix prods, trying to lighten the conversation, "he taught you that."

"Yes, well, even that isn't what it used to be. Besides, it came with the territory."

"Like tying iguanas to the porch."

Rennie laughs, *heh-heh-heh*, a dryly irritating sound, as if Phoenix is making a joke but not a very funny one. "Oh, no, not us. My father kept women. Tied to him, of course, not the porch. He was an eloquent man, and women fall easily in love with liars. The lies that bind and all."

The vision sickens Phoenix, but fascinates her, too, conjuring images of Jinx: "Do you want some of this, baby? How much? Show me how much."

"Women put too much stock in words. It's the general failing of the gender, if you ask me," Rennie is saying. "How do you stand it when two of you get together? That's what I've never understood. All those words, all that sorting and sifting. Too much talking and too little doing."

Phoenix pushes away the flash of Jinx. "It's a lot like panning for gold. Sometimes you get lucky; mostly you don't. Sometimes you find your fortune on the bathroom floor. I found one this morning." Digging in her pocket, Phoenix produces a scrap of paper, the kind used in fortune cookies, that she'd found sticking to one of the green tiles in the ladies' room in the building where she works. *Your love life will be happy and harmonious.* She imagined it was a sign. She still isn't convinced that it's not, although she won't tell Rennie that; he has so little patience with superstition. She passes it across the table.

Rennie takes the little paper, glances at it, wads it into a tiny ball, and flicks it into the ashtray with his middle finger. He shakes his head and shrugs. "Well, why not?" Why not, indeed?

6 The streetcar, empty when Phoenix first boarded, is filling with morning commuters. Huddled into her seat by the door, she is trying to disappear. Her eyes toy with the lines in the book on her lap, *Inside Peru, A Traveler's Perspective.* In the margin next to a long, and to her mind dull, description of an ancient irrigation system, Carson has written in his architect's lettering: "Yes! Why?" Why, what? Rennie has the same habit, cramped script spilling down the margins, unfinished thoughts sometimes in Spanish, sometimes in code. His letters to her from Mexico were like that; some half-formed, half-decipherable encoded message would inevitably send her to the Spanish/English dictionary only to discover he'd been using the margins of the letter for a shopping list.

Jerking to a stop, the streetcar sighs and moans as another dozen passengers press on board. A woman in very high heels and a white crocheted dress balances herself next to Phoenix Bay's left shoulder. Delicate hands with long fingers and dark red nail polish clutch the overhead bar. Full hips sway, keeping time with the train. The dress, loose, but not quite modest, stretches more than its owner probably imagines over naked flesh. Phoenix smiles at the woman's secret, at the flash of skin and the deep shadows where her legs end, at the promise of what the lace could reveal. The bronzed woman leans low across Phoenix Bay, to pull the stop cord, showing a flash of bare breast where the dress separates. Her skin would taste of salt and bitters, warm and slick. Black eyes fringed in thick lashes look down on Phoenix. The woman smiles, slow and easy.

"Trust me," the eyes whisper, and she opens her legs, straddling Phoenix Bay's naked thigh, where the vines twine, kneading the tigress who prowls her private jungle. Breasts, brown as toast, nipples puckered, graze the tiger's back, until the creature trembles, then purrs, a low, almost painful throb that Phoenix thought she had lost. How long since she's wanted a woman this way? How long since her skin has prickled and flushed? Too long. Phoenix closes her eyes and lets her mind rock into the woman, who tastes of salt and sin, who has magic hands. Too little magic left in the world. They're good together. Too good, almost, for strangers. Only the flesh, not the face, is familiar. Phoenix doesn't care. This woman wants her the way no woman has in too long. This is the woman who will bring Phoenix to her knees. Warm and sweet against bare flesh, Phoenix buries her face in the woman's damp neck as the train jerks to a stop.

The woman whispers something Phoenix can't quite hear. Smiling, she raises her eyes. "I'm sorry. What did you say?"

The bronzed woman is not smiling. "I asked if this is the Civic Center stop."

Phoenix nods and pulls closer to the wall, as the woman evaporates out the door. She strains to see if the dress will part again, show one last flash of breast, a shadow of thigh. It doesn't. The streetcar jerks back to life. A fat man, smelling of sweat and garlic and Old Spice, crowds into the space vacated by the woman in the crocheted dress. Phoenix Bay turns to the window, feigning sudden fascination with the gray slabs of concrete that line the tunnel, her reflection watching. If she were a man, would she have followed the woman off the train, making ridiculous stabs at conversation that inevitably begin with "Hey, baby!" No. She would follow silently. Up the escalator. Stop to buy one perfect, blood-red rose from the one-eyed flower vendor on the corner. The woman in the white dress would turn, once only, look over her shoulder to assure herself that Phoenix was still there. They would go to a hotel, maybe, or one of those tiny apartments on O'Farrell

Street, the kind where the FOR RENT signs always hang. The woman in the crocheted dress would live alone. Taking the rose, she would prick her finger on a thorn. Phoenix would lick the blood drop clean. Wordless. Phoenix would call herself Suzanne. The woman in the crocheted dress would lie, too. They would not fall in love; they would never see each other again.

She'll break the hearts of a hundred women—well, a couple dozen anyway—and never fall in love again. She won't listen to promises they can't keep or won't. No matter, they'll both know the score. She'll kiss them hard and say, "I don't do love." And they'll understand and ask for nothing more. Love makes you blind, like you've been looking too long into the sun. She wants a woman who will blot out the sun. Women are like mirrors, cluttered with memories, painted in light and shadow, singing with the echoes of what was and what might have been. The mirrors hold reflections of their mothers' eyes and their own, the eyes of all the women they've ever known blend, rippling under old, smoky glass, where the silver backing is crackled and fading. Looking into another woman's naked eyes is the most wonderful and terrifying moment she has ever known. Love junkies move fearlessly into each other. Phoenix Bay comes from a long line of fearless women. Lately, she has learned to be afraid.

The escalator from the underground MUNI station to the street is broken as usual and she begins to climb the stairs, behind a rumpled suit, probably a salesman from the looks of the shoes and the briefcase, who pauses every three steps to wheeze. Poor jerk will probably keel over on these very stairs one morning on his way to work. She steps to the left sharply, feeling strangely buoyant, and pushes past; the man doesn't even glance her way. Half a block east on Market, she turns left on Sansome. Pass the wall where the bike messengers wait, trading jokes and getting high (the telltale smell of marijuana smoke filters up to the sidewalk from the steps below). Smile. The young woman with the heavy German accent is setting out pink roses at her flower stand on the corner. Cross the street (watch for the cars that are supposed to give pedestrians the right of way but rarely do). Drop a quarter into the cat woman's plastic cup (two cats doze on her lap, a third peeks out from beneath her sooty tweed coat). Then finally, step into the third building, a stylish old dowager of a structure, with long narrow windows and real marble in the lobby, and an elevator with a brass grate that protects the blackened wood door. She drums her fingers against the inlaid wood. The elevator doors sigh when they open.

The ancient cage jerks, then sways a little before finally opening the door to the sixth floor where a narrow, old-fashioned marble hall gleams like dirty ice. Carnelian Tours, one of the other tenants, has hung the wall with posters. YOUR SUNSPERT SPECIALISTS, says one. A grinning, eight-foot-tall woman, with huge golden breasts barely contained by a sky-blue bikini top, rises out of the foaming sea. Venus without her shell. Water sheets off bronzed skin, eyes squint against the sun and salt water. WE BRING YOU THE WORLD, says the next. The same woman, still squinting, still grinning, wearing this time a very tight, very short, and very red dress, has her head thrown back, supposedly in awe, at the modern wonders of the world that are flying through an indigo sky. Phoenix likes the idea of somebody bringing her the world, especially if it's a world different from this one. She notices that The Sunspert Specialists have a new poster this morning. This time the larger-than-life woman reclines on a white-sand beach, with an orchid lei covering her bare breasts. Foot-tall letters bleed sunset red across a process-blue, cloudless sky: HEAVEN IS HAWAII. Well, why not? Heaven must be somewhere, why not Hawaii? And this presumably is one of the angels. So much for George, Rennie's itinerant angel. Phoenix Bay has never been to Hawaii, but she imagines her chances of getting there are considerably better than getting to Heaven.

Still thinking about Heaven and Hawaii, she opens the door to the ad agency, where she's been the sometimes secretary, occasional copywriter, and frequent editor for the past three weeks. "A permanent temporary assignment" the employment agency calls it. Whatever the hell that means. The ad agency is currently working on a campaign to sell the services of a very large accounting firm, complete with tax lawyers, to the wealthy. A lethal combination, she thinks. The slogan is "Real Experience for the Real World." As if there's any other kind. She picks up the Styrofoam coffee cup she's been using for the past three days and goes to the coffee maker, which is in a cubicle next to the art department.

Marty, the graphic artist, looks up from her drafting table and smiles. "Phoenix! Greetings!" Leaning against the doorjamb, Phoenix considers Marty's hair and grins. Burgundy. Just yesterday, it was black with streaks of bright blue.

"Fell in love on the streetcar, but she was probably straight."

"Pity," Marty says, although she doesn't sound especially surprised. She leans back in her chair and pushes a shock of hair out of her eyes, which are magnified by thick, horn-rimmed glasses that seem almost too large for her narrow face. "C'mere and take a look at this. Tell me what you think."

Stretching up to look over Marty's shoulder at roughs of the real-world ads, Phoenix shrugs. "I don't know. Don't they have focus groups for this sort of thing?"

"Oh, sure, sure . . . that will come. But right now, I want to bounce this off you. What do you think? Be honest."

"To tell the truth, I don't get it."

Marty snorts softly, one quick, exasperated breath. "Yeah. Me either. 'Real Experience for the Real World.' Like what experience isn't real? That's what I want to know."

"And how many other worlds are there?"

"Now on that, I would definitely have to say the jury is still out." Marty winks and picks up one of the largest coffee mugs Phoenix has ever seen, takes a sip, probably cold from the face she makes, and lights a long, filtered cigarette. "Open that window, will you? Richard will have a cow if he catches me smoking again." Richard, the youngest of the agency's partners, who wears Brooks Brothers suits and smiles too much, is the man behind the real-world campaign. "God, for the good old days." Marty exhales in the general direction of the window, then fans her hand in an attempt to dislodge the blue haze that hangs over the office. "The first place I ever worked, we got high all the time. 'Course they went bankrupt. Too bad. We turned out some great stuff there. So, tell me about the streetcar woman. I could use a little morning titillation."

"What's to tell? I'm reduced to fantasizing about strangers."

"Personally, I've always found them more interesting to fantasize about than lovers. Sex is easy. Easier to get the hang of than bridge and not as boring. Cheaper than a night at the movies. It doesn't make you fat. And if you're careful, it doesn't even make a mess on the couch. It cures cramps and headaches, gives you an excuse not to call your mother, and makes you late for work. Personally, I've been here since six. Lynette's still in Tulsa waiting for her sister to pop that kid. Sometimes, being married's the pits."

"Beats not being married."

"Yeah, I suppose so." Marty frowns a little. "You two were together for a long time, too—like six years or something, right?"

"Seven. It was our anniversary. She said she knew the timing was bad."

Marty lets out a long, low whistle. "Did that like appeal to her sense of symmetry or something, only one major date to remember? Jesus. So, if you don't mind my asking, what did you do?"

"Went nuts. Lost my job. Sold all my stuff to a junk dealer. Went nuts again. Then Rennie figured somebody had better save me from myself before I ended up being number nine-hundred-thirty-six—or whatever it's up to now—to take the big dive off the Golden Gate Bridge. So here we are, living happily ever after. More or less." She hopes she sounds more buoyant than crazy.

"Wow," Marty says softly. She looks at Phoenix for a long moment, then asks the inevitable, "So, are you, like . . . okay now?"

Phoenix smiles a little and nods. She's gotten used to the question, and the answer is automatic. "About as well as can be expected." Marty's brows knit. Phoenix has seen the look before, has worn it herself, around the women love has abandoned. Circling the wagons, she's come to think of it. "Really. Some days are okay. Some are . . . well, less than okay. Today is okay. I fell in love on the streetcar, so there's hope."

Marty nods, considering this. "Cool," she says at last, "that's great, really." Next she will say she has to get back to work, Phoenix thinks, turning to leave before she has the humiliation of being dismissed. But Marty looks up from her drafting table and asks, "So you want to have dinner tonight or maybe go out or something this weekend? Not like a date or anything," she adds quickly, "just, you know, good company?"

Before Phoenix has time to answer, Richard James comes to the door. "Phoenix. Here you are." He sounds surprised to see her, as always. "Could you drop by my office for a minute? Now's good for me. And Marty, how many times do I have to ask you not to smoke in the office?"

"I guess once more than you already have. And good morning to you, too, Richard." Snubbing out the cigarette, she winks at Phoenix.

He scowls. Damned dykes. They could be beautiful if it weren't for— What? He can't put his finger on it. Something about how they look at him. Cold. No, not cold; dismissive, as if he just doesn't matter. They didn't cover women like this in his organizational management classes at the Harvard Business School. Come to think of it, they didn't cover much of anything he's needed to know in the last seven years.

"I'll call you," Phoenix mouths, following Richard James down the hall and back to his office, with its antique mahogany desk and leather chairs. The best advice his father ever gave him was never to appear trendy at work, leave the glass and chrome to the upstarts. "Phoenix, please," he indicates one of the two leather wingback chairs across from his desk; she sits, he takes the other, wearing his best smile. Perching on the edge of the chair, as if flight might be necessary at any moment, Phoenix regards him cautiously. No openings there, no smiles of gratitude. She probably thinks I'm going to fire her, he thinks, and he finds the idea pleasing. If it were up to him, he would send her back to the temporary agency. If only Dylan Brenner weren't so taken with her: "Watching her work," he'd said, ". . . a natural gift for getting to the heart of a message . . ." and then the kicker: "Don't let this one get away." Well, that much they did teach at Harvard: Cover your own ass first. Richard leans casually into the desk, hands folded in front of him, and smiles. "So, Phoenix," he says, looking at her directly, his gaze, like his voice, conveying no emotion, "I like to check in with my people every so often, just to find out how things are going. You're a teacher or something aren't you?"

She smiles, the same cool, sardonic smile she saves for work and men like Richard James. "Was. I *was* a teacher."

He makes no sign that he's heard. "You know, Phoenix, I've been watching your work. I'd say that you have a natural gift for getting to the heart of the message. And I don't mind telling you that, frankly, I'm impressed." She glances at him suspiciously. Men like Richard James are rarely impressed with women like her. "I said the same thing to Dylan Brenner just yesterday—that we shouldn't let you get away. I told him I'd like to see if we can find a fit. A good fit, if you know what I mean." He stands up and moves to the front of the desk, still smiling.

Confused, she nods and tries to smile. "Thanks." He looks expectant, so she adds, "I guess I don't know what to say." She wonders if he's planning to sit on the edge of his desk, one of his many irritating habits.

Pushing a file folder out of the way, he drops onto the desk and leans forward. "You know, Phoenix, Dylan and I run a pretty good little team here—I'm sure you've noticed." He pauses. Dylan Brenner is the controlling partner; she's supposed to be impressed. She isn't, but Richard James, the man cursed with two first names, obviously is—enough for both of them. "I like to think that Dylan and I are the quarterbacks, but as you know a quarterback is only as good as the men behind him. And women, too, of course." He chuckles nervously, annoyed at the slip. "So the bottom line is, Dylan and I want to know what it would take to get you suited up."

Suited up? What does that mean? She looks at Richard James in his charcoal pinstripe suit and burgundy tie, perched on the edge of his desk, smiling the same smile he wears for clients: a warm, beneficent look designed to exude trust. Does he wear this look when he's trying to con his wife, too, that preppy, peppy woman with expensively styled hair who smiles out from the picture in the silver frame? What *is* her name? Heather? Bonnie? Something perky and slightly Scottish. Phoenix even met her once, when she came by to collect Richie—one of the drawbacks of marrying someone who actually knew you at fifteen is they seem to insist on using those stupid childhood names. "I . . . really don't know. I never considered . . . anything like this."

"Actually, Phoenix, the timing couldn't be better, now that Marina's decided to put her career on hold for a while." His voice has turned confiding. "You know how it is with these first-time mothers—want to stay home during the baby's formative years and all. Bonnie's been doing the same thing." Bonnie, so she was right about his wife's name. And while she's never met Marina, who went on maternity leave about the time Hamlet had that little run-in with Puck in English 120 last winter, a pang of jealousy tweaks her. Staying home with a baby would be nice. "Now I know what you're thinking, Phoenix. You're saying to yourself, 'What do *I* know about advertising? What can somebody with my background bring to the table?'" That isn't what she's thinking at all, but she doesn't bother to correct him. "Well, I'm here to tell you that you're a bright woman with a real gift. Brenner agrees. Like I told him, what is advertising but communication, and what is English but . . ." He pauses, looks at her expectantly.

"Communication?"

He snaps his fingers and points at her. "Bingo! English. Advertising. Not all that far apart when you think about it. And I personally want to take you under my wing, teach you what I know. You see, I'm convinced that with the right cultivation . . ." His voice drops to that confiding, pseudo-whisper again, "Well, just between us, I told Dylan that I believe we can expect great things from you." Richard James hasn't stopped smiling yet. This must be what he calls The Big Pitch. Often, coming back from a successful meeting, he struts from desk to desk: "I gave them The Big Pitch. Wind up, deliver. They never even knew what hit 'em!"

"Great things," she echoes. "It's just . . . well, I haven't really decided . . . I might want to go back to teaching."

"Teaching?" He cluck-clucks and shakes his head. "No one respects educators more than I." He draws out each word. "But frankly, Phoenix, is that what you *really* want to do? For the rest of your life, I mean? We're talking opportunity here. And I don't mind telling you that there are good people, hungry people, talented people out there who would, quite frankly, kill for this kind of chance. It's tough out there, Phoenix. Good jobs are hard to come by. But it's up to you, of course. We don't have to decide this minute. Our offer's on the table. I want you to think about it. You can let me know Monday." He grins and eases himself off the desk, pauses, then snaps his fingers, as if a great idea has just come. "Tell you what. It's nearly noon, right?"

"It's ten o'clock in the morning, Richard."

He ignores her. "No matter. We're looking at a slow afternoon. Why don't you take the rest of the day off. Go home, think about our offer, then on Monday we'll be playing a whole new ball game. How's that sound?"

"Fine, I suppose. But, Richard, I don't even know what you'd expect me to do. Or what the job pays. Or anything." She finishes feebly.

"You'd be an account exec, of course. As far as the rest . . . Well, let me just say that we're really *very* flexible."

"Yes, but why?"

"Because we've found that in our business, any business really, flexibility is the true foundation of success." A tiny beeping is coming from somewhere under his coat. He reaches under his shirt sleeve to silence his watch. "That's me," he says. "You know what they say, no rest for the wicked." He chuckles. "Now remember what I said and promise you'll think about it. And remember, I never take no for an answer." He is dismissing her, his right hand already extended to seal the deal, his smile warm. If she didn't know better, she might believe he actually likes her.

She takes his hand and shakes it, a little surprised at its strength, more surprised at its roughness. "I . . . well, I just want to say thanks. For your vote of confidence, I mean."

Cocking his right thumb and index finger like a gun, he winks. Of all his irritating gestures, this may be his most irritating, she decides. Although desk-sitting is definitely close. "Until Monday."

Phoenix pauses at Marina's empty, darkened office, looks around to make sure no one is watching, and steps inside. "A natural gift" Richard had said. Natural gift for what, though? For knowing what doesn't make sense? She doesn't feel naturally gifted; she feels nervous. She wonders if this office is part of the deal. Is that what "flexible" means? She's never had an office of

96

her own before, just one desk in a shared faculty room where three or sometimes even four teachers are crowded together. Maybe she'll get a plant, something tropical, with big leaves. She'd like that. And a picture for the wall across from her desk. Rennie must have a dozen paintings in the storeroom, from that pre-Carson artist boyfriend in New York. Maybe the man went on to fame and fortune. But if that were true, Rennie would have sold off his paintings by now. She hasn't even taken the job yet and already she's redecorating the office. And why not? The money can't be worse than what she's been making doing temp work, and Richard said they're flexible; of course, Richard James is a pompous ass, but he does seem to know advertising; and Brenner wants her, that could be a plus; but then she might want to go back to teaching, it's not as if she's absolutely decided against that; but maybe it is time for a change; still, what if she blows this, too? But who's to say that would happen; there must be some reason they made the offer; of course, she really wasn't looking for this; but why not? Why not, indeed? And without telling Richard James, yes, she accepts his offer. She doubts he'll be surprised.

Jumbled thoughts dog Phoenix as she prepares to leave the office. She wants to call somebody to share her news, but who? Jinx wouldn't care, and even if she did, that woman she lives with might answer the phone. No point in risking that. And Marty, her only real friend here, has disappeared. She dials Rennie's number automatically before she remembers he's still in Oregon. Too late, the machine picks up on the first ring, a sure sign there's a message waiting. Maybe Rennie calling. Phoenix punches in the access code: 3-4-5. Couldn't the answering machine people come up with something a little less obvious? As if a hacker wouldn't think to try that. The machine grinds and whirs the tape back to the beginning. The first message is from a bill collector calling for Carson (persistent bastards)—well, good luck trying to collect from a dead man. The second is from Carson's dentist saying it's time for his annual checkup; Rennie must have forgotten to call. She jots down the number as the machine rolls to the next message. After a long pause, a woman's voice: "Rennie, this is

97

Cecelie. The plane was late. Customs was no problem, but I missed the connecting flight. They've put me on the next one. I still have the keys Carson gave me, so you don't have to meet me at the airport. I'll see you tonight." Smiling, she sets the receiver down gently. Richard James, on his way to his meeting, passes her desk and, mistaking her smile for him, turns and winks just as the door closes. Let him think what he will, it doesn't matter. Cecelie is home, at last.

 A pair of waterfalls, persistent but tiny, trickle from Cecelie Johnson's breasts onto her belly, wide and firm. A nice belly, but too pale, she decides, like the underside of that alligator she saw once, a pitiable, half-tame creature sentenced to performing in a sideshow on a Trujillo street. So old some of its teeth were missing, its belly was exposed, as if the core of the beast were there, just beneath the surface waiting to be scratched open, set free. What was an alligator doing on a Trujillo side street, so far from its element? It was like one of those knock-knock jokes children tell: "Knock-knock." "Who's there?" "Alligator in Trujillo, that's who!" Mala loved knock-knock jokes. Too bad Cecelie didn't think of this one until now.

A bit of soap strays into her eyes making them tear. Wash away the memories, watch them swirl down the drain with the years of grime that seems to have permeated her pores. Hot water. White soap. Thick towels. The States are full of such luxuries. Three different kinds of toothpaste, sweet as candy. Here, in her brother's house, will she be able to put away the past, finally? There is no past in California. No one bothers to remember in this land of promises and forgetfulness. They are all snakes shedding their skins.

For the first time in her life, Cecelie Johnson does not believe the past holds the key. All those years, she'd imagined there was peace to be found in the past, some ancient wisdom. But if it was there, she missed it, even with all her years of searching. Now she wants only to know that which is new and brash and unquestioning. Her daughter is dead, her country is exploding, and she ran like a terrified rabbit as the horror closed around her. It was all she could think to do. She couldn't save her child and that country isn't really hers. She turns the shower handle all the way to the left, waiting for the shock of hot water. When it touches her skin, she begins to cry. She cries only in the shower, one of her mother's indelible lessons: tears are for suckers and cry babies. And Mona Morgan tolerated neither. Mona took baths, long rituals of oil and perfume, the way the great queens bathed. She regretted not being a queen, but then Mona Morgan regretted many things, or should have. Should have, but probably didn't. Cecelie can't remember her mother ever apologizing for anything.

Their mother was proud, and there was so little to be proud of: leading roles in three grade-B movies, not even bad enough to become fashionably camp; parts in a few television westerns and, later, a couple of sitcoms, but she was losing her looks by then; and finally a string of dog-food commercials. Mona's most memorable role, as it turned out, was as a dog-loving housewife. After all those years of Cecelie begging for a dog, Mona had ended her career surrounded by dogs, and ugly ones at that. Mutts. How often had she called Cecelie that? "I gave up everything for you, Cecelie. I could have sent you down to your father, but I didn't. I knew what you needed." Cecelie had put the phone on the bed in Rennie's apartment in New York and continued packing while her mother, drunk and scared and full of herself, ranted into a pillow. Occasionally, she would pick up the receiver, say, "I'm sorry, Mother," before laying it back down again. "I'll be forty in a few years. Do you know how hard that's going to be on me? How can you run off and leave me? After all my sacrifices . . ." Cecelie was twenty-four years old, which made her mother forty-four. A Hollywood publicist had once subtracted a decade, which would have made Mona nine years old when Rennie was born, not that she ever mentioned him or Cecelie in her publicity. Lies, all lies. Eventually the telephone receiver was quiet; Mona had passed out or hung up, it didn't much matter which. The next day Cecelie Johnson would be on a plane bound for Lima, Peru; by the end of the week, she would be at the university at Ayacucho, working on her doctorate. But that night, she had fallen across her bed, not bothering to reset the receiver in its cradle. "I know I wasn't a good mother, Cecelie, but I did the best I could. I love you." If only Mona had said that. Cecelie Johnson promised herself she would be a better mother—no, the perfect mother—if she ever got the chance. Mala was her chance, there won't be another.

Cecelie's skin has grown used to the hot water, the way she'd grown used to the Peruvian heat and colors, which she was sure would consume her when she'd first arrived, and which made, which still make the rest of the world seem stark and colorless by comparison. Stepping out of the shower, she shivers. How could she have forgotten how pale, how cold California can be? Is.

Four days ago Cecelie turned her back on the past, hoisted her pack onto a mule, and started down the path, so slowly at first that the animal occasionally had turned, eyeing her questioningly, and then when she could no longer see the site, faster. She had declined Gerlof's offer for one of the Jeeps or to call a plane to the landing strip. She needed to walk out, needed to feel the country under her feet, needed to remember. While she was preparing the mule, Gerlof had kissed her hand, a formal, old-fashioned gesture. "We will miss you," he told her. "When you are ready to return, we'll be here waiting." She had the sense he meant the dead as well as the living.

A small ghost walked the trail to Lambayeque with her. Pictures of Mala during those last frantic days flashed: Gerlof running down the dirt path toward the landing strip, with Mala flushed and feverish in his arms; the flight to Lima, and then all of them running again across the tarmac at the airstrip—never mind the armed guards—to the waiting ambulance. The crowds on the street outside the Clínica Angloamericana had parted in front of the huge gringos running ahead of the stretcher. Privilege. But all the privilege the American university could buy for one of its own and her child wasn't enough. For two days, Cecelie and sometimes Gerlof stood guard over Mala. Through the curtain that shielded them from the old woman in the next bed, incantations rose and fell. *"La hermana es una bruja,"* a nurse had hastened to explain in a low whisper, in case Cecelie thought the hospital put more stock in magic than modern medicine. In the end, the Western drugs made no more magic for Mala than the *bruja* had for the old woman. The doctor had touched Cecelie's hand. "Nothing you could have done," he said in English, "nothing anyone could have done."

The site was curious and quiet when she and Gerlof returned. He and his wife cried; they had lost a child once, too, a boy, many years before, attacked by a pack of wild dogs in the mountains outside a site in the far south. "A death more horrible than any sane person could even imagine," Gerlof whispered. They did not say there would be other children; there had been no more for them, either. "You must cry, then go on," they told her. But Cecelie couldn't cry and didn't know how she could ever go on. By night, she roamed the site, listening to ghosts wail on the wind; by day, she worked, constantly and painstakingly. She left no room for her mind to wander, only room enough for the recriminations that come after dark when you walk alone.

The path that led to Lambayeque and Luz, her anthropologist friend, took eight hours to walk. Into the evening, the two women had sat under a tree, drinking warm pisco and listening to the *ambulantes* on the street hawking their sweetcakes: *"King-Kong! King-Kong!"* When Cecelie had first heard their call years before, she'd laughed out loud remembering that silly old movie which had sometimes played on Sunday afternoon television when she was a child. What would an oversized gorilla do in Peru, with no Empire State Building to climb? Be happy, she decides.

Mala loved those cakes, would beg Cecelie for them whenever she returned from Lambayeque, her eyes shiny with a child's hope and anticipation. And Cecelie would tease: *"King-Kong? No sé."* Then she would laugh and pull the package out of her pack, watching her daughter's delight, her tiny pink tongue darting out in search of the crumbs that clung to her pouty, doll-like mouth, sweet as the cakes themselves.

By the time she left Luz, Cecelie's head was aching from too much pisco and unsteady dreams. A *colectivo* passing through Chiclayo left her at the Hotel Royal, a badly misnamed establishment that caters to traveling locals and the few determined tourists who make it so far north—She was neither, but no less displaced. The other guests watched the big *gringa* curiously. She was not one of them, yet she navigated the streets and the language with familiarity. They did not ask her business, whether out of politeness or disdain she did not know, and she did not volunteer.

As Cecelie crossed the Plaza de Armas to El Cordano, the afternoon sun was already setting long shadows across the square, the light clear and almost too pure against the cathedral. Summer was long over. She walked quickly to the Avenida José Balta and the *mercado central,* where the women sit all but hidden among the strings of the *guitarra,* drying rayfish that wave like so many shirts in the breeze. A small girl peeked out from between cages of parrots. No wild fox cubs today, her mother told Cecelie, although she hadn't asked. Cecelie can never look the foxes in the eye, too sad; Mala had once cried at the sight. Why hadn't Cecelie bought the poor creature? They could have taken it into the hills and set it free. Instead, she'd swung Mala onto her shoulder and pushed through the crowd, imagining if she carried her away quickly enough, Mala would forget the horror. Cecelie never took her there again.

Pajarito, the *curandero,* was in his stall in the *mercado,* as Cecelie had known he would be. Squatting beneath the weather-beaten tarp, eyes half-closed, he listened: of the child's death, which had bruised the mother's heart; of her fear of leaving the home that is not a home; and, finally, of the brother, with the strange wasting disease that weakens the lungs and twists the bowels. Pajarito sat, quiet as a stone, long after she was finished. Thinking, perhaps, or praying, she couldn't tell. Then he motioned her close, whispering in Quechua, the language of the mountain people. Sitting cross-legged, she watched as the *curandero,* his mouth moving quickly and silently in separate incantations, filled four small glass vials with pieces of bone and dried bugs, some seeds and herbs, the claw of a large lizard, and small beads she recognized as Moche. Good magic, Pajarito promised, handing her the final ampoule; the contents were especially strong, cured for many seasons on his *mesa.* But would it help Rennie? Pajarito had shrugged, lifting his thin shoulders up high near his ears, and answered loudly in Spanish so those passing by would not wonder what he was doing with the American, *"Nunca se sabe lo que puede pasar."* She wanted more than speculation. He drew up on the balls of his feet, close to her face; his breath was sour, his eyes rheumy from age and smoke. He would pray, he whispered and so must she. Cecelie didn't tell him her prayers would be as impotent as dust. Mala took God with her when she died.

Three young Canadian archaeologists, trying to hide their excitement with the forced formality of students, were waiting for her the next afternoon when she finally arrived at the Instituto Nacional de Cultura in Trujillo. So young and eager—she could remember feeling that way, once, long ago—they had pressed her about the sites to the north. "Had she actually seen Cerro Chepén?" "How long until it can be excavated?" "In your opinion, doctor . . ." they always added, using the word the way only those who possess very new doctorates seem to. *Doctor.* She is not a doctor; if she were, her child would not be dead. She is a scavenger. They'll learn, soon, how well the past guards its secrets.

Long into the night, they'd huddled around a table at the Costa Azul, laughing sometimes, their faces clouding only slightly when the conversation turned to the Sendero Luminosa and the archaeologists who were leaving the interior, moving down to the coast or on to Ecuador, where it was safer. Peru's long, ungainly, and unpredictable guerrilla war promised to drive them all away or mad before it was over. They didn't believe her; she could tell by the looks they exchanged. She had been here too long, their eyes said; she should go to the classroom, let them get on with the real work. Drunk, she'd said good-night and staggered back to the Hotel Americano. The next morning, without saying good-bye to the Canadians, she boarded a plane for Lima.

Even before Mala's death, Lima had seemed to Cecelie what hell must be like: crowded and dark and fogged with fear. Displaced women roam the street, begging, their hands outstretched, their eyes pleading, Save me, save my child. The stench from the *pueblos jovenes,* constant reminders of the shantytowns' open sewers, rises between cardboard *chozas;* children play in piles of garbage that line streets of sand. Glittering high-rises look down with blind, shuttered eyes on the heart of the city, promising a future for some, just as the well-protected mansions had a century before. Always frightening, since Mala's death the city had become intolerable for Cecelie. She did not venture in from the airport for one last look; instead she'd waited patiently for hours for her flight to California. *Home.* How strangely empty that word sounded.

On the plane, Cecelie watched the light change, green to blue to gold, as the mist burned away. When the plane finally lifted its belly into blue sky, before plunging through the clouds, she was struck by how peaceful it all looked: green and yellow splashed thickly against blue. Like a child on her first flight, she pressed her face against the Plexiglas window, trying to see it all, to memorize it, the shape of the land she had come to love, the outline of the mountains. She must not forget. Ever. Then the plane had turned, showing nothing but blue.

The towels in her brother's bathroom are the same blue, pale and deep, wide and soft—another minor luxury, like ice cream and endless hot water and classical music on the radio, instead of cassette tapes scratchy from humidity's abuse. Draping a towel over her shoulders, Cecelie steps into the hall, still dripping, tracks marking her brother's hardwood floors, so carefully refinished by Carson, she assumes. Carson was different and yet so much the same as the other men in her brother's life, or what she's known of the men in her brother's life. Older, perhaps, and certainly better established, Carson was strong; her brother gathers strength from those around him, as if he might somehow syphon it to protect his more obvious and, she imagines, now well-hated fragility. Unlike her brother, Cecelie was never fragile. Nearly as tall—a giant compared even to the men in Peru—she is hard and solid. Mona often mourned her daughter's appearance. "Now look what you've done," Mona would wail, "what man is ever going to want you like this?" as if Cecelie had grown to just under six feet out of spite.

The telephone in R.J.'s study is ringing and Cecelie pads toward the sound. The machine beats her. Nothing clever about the message: no background music, no special effects, just Rennie sounding impatient and a little bored, reciting the number. A good invention, answering machines; eventually technology will eliminate all requirements for human interaction, from test tube to cryogenic cylinder, a whole life untouched. Vibrators to make us come. Walkmen to teach us French. Elevators to carry us into the sky in silence. At the airport, on the moving sidewalk, a subliminal voice under the music urged her to keep to the right, to keep walking. And she had. The caller hangs up without leaving a message.

A twenty-year-old version of herself smiles down from the top of the bookcase by the phone. There is something harsh about the girl in the picture: young and cocky, looking out on the world through already-wise eyes that are framed by a tangle of wild black curls. Cecelie pushes down the temptation to look at the image too long. She has spent as many years burying her own past as she has unearthing the past of others. The girl she was is no longer recognizable. The woman in the mirror is what matters now: full and solid, hardened muscles line strong arms; small wrinkles crease the skin around her eyes, still wise, but no more so than those of other women her age; her hair has lost its tight ringlets; gray streaks her temples. There is nothing shadowy about her now. From behind the door, Mona smiles winningly; a pair of darts are wedged in her shadowy cleavage. Cecelie pulls the darts free and carefully replaces them in the cork near the rim. No point in adding to Mona's indignity; she always managed that well enough on her own.

The top level of the house is as casual and open as the first floor is formal and closed. Cecelie is drawn here, to the big room with its captain's quarters' warmth. But how much of it is Phoenix Bay? Not much, she decides. Women claim their spaces differently, and there are few traces of a woman here. But the secrets of a live Phoenix Bay may defy the simple rules of archaeology.

Sliding open the large glass door, she steps onto the back deck overlooking the yard below, neat and blooming with lilies and roses; a peacock struts, dragging his magnificent tail through dusty grass. What is her brother doing with a peacock in the backyard? Maybe it's the latest thing; she wouldn't know. Rennie was never much of a slave to fashion, or so she's assumed from his letters: humorous commentaries on work, domestic life, and Carson. She misses Carson more than she should. He was hardly more than a stranger. Still . . . Every year he and Rennie promised to make the trip to Peru, and every year they canceled. Maybe she should have tried harder to get them to come, or made more of an effort to get up to Mexico. "Next year," they always promised, "when we have more time." But Carson and Mala had run out of time. And now Rennie, too. Pajarito's ampoules are in her pack; but can magic save the unbelievers?

Following the sun across the room to the front deck overlooking the ocean, she drapes her towel on the grating, stretches, then drops naked into a chaise lounge to wait. The first rule of archaeology: all secrets reveal themselves, given enough time. Sun spills easy, hot, and too soon across Cecelie, lulling her. Summer, lazy and unexpectedly warm, has come to Northern California. A tease of ocean air prickles her skin, like a woman's breath, cool, forced through pursed lips. Lately there has been so little opportunity or time for women or for passion. Now it seems as if the few she's known are melding together into one woman whispering against her breasts and her belly, breath cool and sweet, a woman of contradictions and surprises. She could love a woman like that.

The house is quiet as dust when Phoenix Bay climbs the spiral stairs to the bedroom. Through the open deck door, a sea breeze blows, leaving the room smelling sweet and salty and fresh. Crossing to the deck door to close it, she starts when she sees the naked woman sleeping there. Cecelie. How little she's changed in all these years, older of course, but still striking. The only naked woman she's seen in months has been herself in the mirror. No surprises there. Phoenix Bay has forgotten—is that possible?— the curves and depth of any woman's flesh other than her own. And now Cecelie, warm and toast brown, stretches out full and perfect, her skin gilded from the dark brown of her legs, then progressively more pale up to the nipples, pink and smoothly un-puckered, almost innocent from the sun's warmth. Two steps for-ward and Phoenix could drop to her knees and take one of the sleeping nipples under her tongue, awaken the thin flesh. What would Cecelie say? Or had she forgotten that night in New York: a frantic, sad, almost obligatory coupling that left them more strangers than lovers. There was so little time. A summer of teas-ing, temptations, and false starts had ended like a firecracker with a damp wick. But what if Cecelie hadn't been leaving? Phoenix doesn't dare start down that path with its twists and turns of ad-dresses and lovers. Too many years gone and too many women in between. Better to store up those memories like a bit of string added to a twine ball. Still, here is the past, sleeping on her deck and looking enough like the future to be interesting. And to make sure she doesn't have to wait much longer, Phoenix lets her feet clang heavily on the stairs as she descends to the kitchen.

Rennie's kitchen is bright, not like the kitchen of Phoenix's child-hood that was always streaked in shadows, especially in winter when the sun hung low, as if even it were cold. Summer wasn't much better: shades drawn against the afternoon, light filtered by the elm tree. Thick heat still found its way inside. Soft light and shadows, that's what she remembers of her mother's kitchen.

Phoenix chews her lower lip and considers her options. She isn't good in a kitchen; Jinx was the cook. Unwrapping the pack-ages of shrimp, fat and slick in their shells, and the scallops, too white, Phoenix scowls. She should have picked one or the other but couldn't decide and finally in desperation had ordered a pound of each. There went the twenty dollars Rennie had pressed on her to make everything perfect for Cecelie's first night home. Lunch money for the next week went to artichokes and flowers and a bottle of so-so fumé blanc. She fills a pot with water and sets it to boil on the stove, puts the shellfish in a colander to wash, stores the wine in the refrigerator, and unwraps the flowers. The florist, a round Russian woman with a very large mole on her left jowl, had laughed as Phoenix examined each stem of the lilies and daisies and mums crowded into buckets lined up just inside the shop door. "For my friend; we haven't seen each other in years." Phoenix felt obliged to explain. "Ahhh," the woman had drawn out the word, then motioned Phoenix into the tiny back room. "These come just today. Go on, you take." Phoenix bought irises and roses and tiger lilies, their buds like tight angry little mouths, still wrapped in the telltale newspaper from the Flower Market.

Rennie's newspaper from days ago is still on the kitchen table, open to the page where he'd been reading, before his inevitable rush to the airport. She drops the flowers onto the newspaper, covering the face of a woman, not much more than a child really, holding a starving baby on her lap. The mother is all knees and legs, and the baby has the empty look photojournalists love for their pity pictures of people dying from drought or famine or war, as if pictures can make any difference. Phoenix is always a little fascinated by people who actually want to take in the horrors of the world over their morning coffee. Rennie reads the paper patiently, as if through all that precision some sense can be made, some answers found, instead of the world being a constant puzzle. Phoenix dislikes the uncertainty; better to wait, then you can look back and see how so many divergent events fell into place to become the inevitable. History. While it's happening, it's far too easy to become embroiled in the whirl and shake of the moment, so there's never time to really look. She picks up one long-stemmed rose. Snip. Snip. Then another. Until green leaves and slightly bruised petals cover first the woman, then the child.

"Rennie said you haven't changed, and he's right. I'd know you anywhere." Phoenix starts at the voice behind her. She turns, a tiger lily still in her hand, smiling, a little disappointed to see Cecelie dressed. But why wouldn't she be?

"Cecelie! It's been forever, but I'd know you anywhere, too." The image of naked Cecelie sleeping flashes across her mind, and Phoenix blushes. Opening her arms for an obligatory hug, Phoenix is surprised that they don't feel familiar; she'd imagined they would. But the touch doesn't make her recoil, either, the first time that's happened in months. She clings a little too long, until she feels Cecelie stiffen. Only then does she pull back, embarrassed.

"You look good, Phoenix, really. But I remember you used to have all this hair," Cecelie's hands flutter around Phoenix's short-cropped head.

"I flushed it."

"What?" Cecelie draws out the word, the funny way she has of talking that piles meaning into tiny spaces.

"My hair." Phoenix blushes. "It's . . . well, kind of a long story," she chuckles at the accidental pun. "I got pissed one night and cut it off and flushed it. By now it's probably halfway to China, depending on the ocean currents. You might have passed it on your way here."

Cecelie laughs, but not much. "Well, you still look good. I ran across the girl I used to be in Rennie's study. Now *that* is a scary sight. He's got to get rid of that picture. By the way, where is he?" Cecelie crosses to the sink where the shrimp are still awaiting an inspiration from Phoenix that seems slow in coming. "You need help with these?"

Phoenix nods, hoping this is an indication that Cecelie knows what to do with shrimp. "He's at camp." She hands Cecelie a knife. "Didn't he tell you?"

Cecelie seems to consider this as she picks up a shrimp and the knife and, with one smooth motion, pops the meat from its gray, papery shell. "I really don't remember. Isn't he a little old to be playing Boy Scout?" Another motion and the vein is out. She dips the shrimp in the boiling water, then pops it into her mouth.

"Writing camp. They call it a colony, even though it's just a bunch of cabins in the Oregon wilderness. The poetry teacher backed out at the last minute, so Rennie's filling in. He needs the money." Phoenix doesn't know why she added that small dig at how well she knows Rennie, maybe to make up for the way Cecelie stiffened when she was hugged.

Cecelie shrugs, letting the comment about money pass. "My brother, the colonist," she says, as if she's trying to fix a picture of Rennie in the woods in her mind. She pops another shrimp, slides the knife along the vein, and drops it into the colander. "So, what am I cleaning these for?"

Phoenix flushes. Not an unreasonable question, unless you

don't have a suitable answer. A wok, she decides, Jinx was always making things in the wok. How hard can it be? "I thought stir fry."

"Stir-fried artichokes?" Cecelie's eyes go to the pair of green thistles on the counter. "Is that some new California thing? I know I've been gone a long time, but it really doesn't sound too appetizing."

Phoenix blushes deeply. "No. I mean, I thought I'd stir-fry the shrimp and steam the artichokes. You taught me how to eat artichokes."

"Did I? I don't remember." Cecelie pulls herself up onto the counter and continues her assault on the shrimp. Surveying the damage in the kitchen, the table filled with flowers, the pitiful scallops half-unwrapped and nearly forgotten, the array of pans and not one of them a wok, she asks not unkindly, "Do you have any idea what you're doing here, Phoenix?"

"I . . . just . . . I'm house-sitting for Rennie."

Cecelie chuckles. "I don't mean *that;* I was referring to dinner."

"Oh. Well, actually, no," Phoenix admits, her eyes on the newspaper as if she might find some miracle recipe there, beneath the petals and leaves. "Do you?"

"I do." Cecelie dips another shrimp into the water for a second then pops the nearly raw thing into her mouth. Phoenix winces. "Perfect." Cecelie smiles. Little lines crinkle around her eyes. "I'll make ceviche. Do you know ceviche?" Phoenix shakes her head. "You'll love it, a true delicacy that you can eat without fear only in California. It will make coming to the States truly worthwhile."

A flash of disappointment washes over Phoenix, who had grown so used to the idea of Cecelie coming she had forgotten the real reasons behind the trip. "Why?"

"Why, what?" Cecelie is reaching for another shrimp. "Oh, about the ceviche?" Phoenix nods, grateful Cecelie has misunderstood, more grateful the tremor in her voice didn't betray her. "Because of the cholera. Now, it's in the shellfish. Don't you read the newspapers?"

"There isn't much in the newspapers about Peru."

If Cecelie is disappointed, it doesn't show. "Well, that doesn't surprise me. So, we need a couple of onions—you do have onions, don't you?" Phoenix nods. "And some chilies. If I know my brother, and mind you I'm not necessarily saying that I do, he probably has chilies around here somewhere. You couldn't grow up with our father and not. Then some of those limes there, and a little of that cilantro you've got growing in that window box on the back porch and . . . by the way, what's the peacock doing in the backyard?"

"Oh, my God! Marcel Proust. I forgot to feed him. He's Rennie's pet. I always feed him as soon as I get home from work, but this evening I . . . forgot." No need to tell Cecelie why.

"So, you go feed the peacock Proust and pick some cilantro while you're at it and I'll get things started in here. Deal?"

Phoenix smiles, relieved. "Whatever you want, Cecelie."

"You *must* remember, Cecelie, it was that summer in New York, right before you went to Peru . . . Rennie was living in that awful old apartment house that always smelled like garbage." Dinner over, they've turned to reminiscences, or at least Phoenix has. But Cecelie, who can remember every detail about a tribe that lived two thousand years ago, is having trouble dredging up anything other than the most obvious of those times. Phoenix has been talking about one of Rennie's roommates, Gary, the waiter who practiced for opera auditions in the apartment's only bathroom because the acoustics were better. "How can you have forgotten those arias at midnight? They nearly drove us all nuts."

"There were so many people in and out all the time," Cecelie says, finally, toying with her fork. "And it was such a long time ago. I just really don't remember." She looks up and smiles apologetically.

"I remember everything about that time." And you, Phoenix thinks, but doesn't dare say.

Cecelie flushes a little, or maybe it's only the candlelight, the way it reflects across her skin, turning her cheeks rosy. They are sitting at the dining-room table, the flowers between them, the remnants of dinner turning sour. "Well, your memory is better than mine," Cecelie says at last. Phoenix rises and gathers up the plates to carry to the kitchen. "Let me help," Cecelie offers.

"No, please," Phoenix says, too quickly. "It's your first night here. I can manage. Really." She stacks the dishes along one arm, collecting flatware with her free hand. Her short career as a waitress left her adept at bussing tables, even if she can't cook a decent meal. "In the mirrored box by the flowers, there's some reefer and papers . . . if you want some, I mean."

Cecelie laughs, a short, disquieting burst of sound. "You really haven't changed at all. Yes, don't mind if I do. Might take the edge off this headache, so I can get some sleep." She doesn't tell Phoenix she hasn't slept well in months.

When Phoenix comes back into the room, Cecelie is leaning across one of the candles, lighting the joint. She holds the smoke in a long time before exhaling a blue plume. "Yours?"

Phoenix nods. "It's all that's left from my last harvest. I . . . well, I sort of had some problems this winter and the crop wasn't . . . anything really. I don't like buying it, though, you never know what chemicals they've dumped on it. I keep this out for Rennie, he says it helps his appetite."

"I can imagine. It's always helped mine, not that mine ever needed much help." Grinning, Cecelie passes Phoenix the joint and leans back into the chair. High-tech and designed more for looks than comfort, the chair has an overly tall back that narrows to a rather lethal-looking point. Cecelie rearranges herself, trying unsuccessfully to find a hospitable position. When Phoenix and Rennie have dinner here, he always sits in a nest of pillows. "So, how is he?"

"The same, I guess." Phoenix passes the deteriorating joint back to Cecelie. "Brilliant, beautiful, bereaved. Losing Carson was hard, harder than he wants anyone to know. He's writing again, though." Cecelie cocks her eyebrow, questioningly. "He was blocked for . . . well, for a while. When he went to Mexico, he left me some notebooks and tapes to transcribe, things he'd done while he was at the hospital with Carson . . . and after. I can show you later, if you'd like. I don't think he would mind. He works on a tape recorder a lot. So I help out, transcribe his tapes, do a little editing, just comments, of course. He says it's helpful, but I don't know."

"Writing about Carson or collaborating?"

Phoenix flushes. Rennie was always the undisputed talent, the thought of being his collaborator is presumptuous, but Cecelie, not being a writer, never wanting to be, wouldn't understand. "Both, I suppose. I wouldn't call it collaboration, though."

"What would you call it?" Cecelie snubs out the roach in a small and very stylized ceramic dish, part of Carson's collection that she's mistaken for an ashtray. Phoenix blanches. "What you and Rennie are doing . . . you said you wouldn't call it collaboration, so what is it?" Cecelie's intense black eyes shine.

"Oh, just helping out, being a friend," Phoenix says absently. She seldom smokes with Rennie. The steady rise of a marijuana high became increasingly uncomfortable in the months just before Jinx left and even worse after. Dissociation, Teddy Grayson calls the feeling Phoenix has of pulling out of her skin, of being afraid that one day she will float away and never find her way back. Phoenix grips the edge of the table, waiting for the room to settle. If she holds on to something solid, she won't fly away. God, don't let Cecelie notice.

But Cecelie is in the kitchen, rummaging through the refrigerator, looking for the homemade sweet rolls Phoenix had planned for dessert. A pair of aging Armenian sisters bake the rolls in their kitchen and the health-food store takes orders. Carson had a standing order for a dozen every week. Easy to understand why. The rolls taste like home: coarse and sweet, with pieces of seed that stick to your teeth.

Cecelie returns with a plate of four rolls still warm from the microwave. Phoenix relaxes her grip on the table and inhales slowly. TaTa Hassee used to bake bread, too, filling the house with an aroma, so thick it smelled as if the air itself could be cut. Warm, like love. All those girls who think love smells like wet cunts are wrong. These rolls are full of poppy seeds. Something new the Armenian sisters have added. Phoenix has heard if you eat poppy seeds, you test positive for drugs, even if you're clean. It doesn't seem fair. There are too many false positives in the world: women who look like somebody you know until you get close and realize that was ten years ago and a thousand miles away. But Cecelie hasn't changed: older, but the same. Clear, unflinching eyes take in too much all at once, the voice, just a little more rusty than Phoenix remembers. She could have loved this woman; she's never stopped loving what they were and might have been.

Are they the women they wanted to become? Cecelie was always safe and solid, but strangely unpredictable, too. Like going to Peru. None of the rest of them had the courage to do anything like that. And Phoenix? What does Cecelie see when she looks at her: the girl she was, or the woman she's become? How different are they, really?

They've fallen onto one of the long, deadly silences that come when small talk is exhausted and real conversation is too dangerous or too much trouble. Cecelie looks at Phoenix and smiles. She should ask about Peru, Cecelie probably expects that, but at this particular moment Phoenix doesn't want to know about a country where she's never been, or archaeology that she knows nothing about, or a little dead girl she never met. And her own miserable stabs at success seem shallow. She should have taken Cecelie as her lover years ago, should have seduced her long before that last night. What had stopped them? Not Phoenix, she was willing, not even Cecelie, really. Time. There just wasn't enough time.

"Cecelie, do you ever think about that summer, I mean what might have happened . . . with us?" Phoenix turns, watching the light flicker and fall in a golden haze across Cecelie's face. She can't read her eyes, but presses on, too late to stop or maybe too foolish; it suddenly feels the same. Phoenix continues in a rush, "Sometimes, I wouldn't think of you . . . for months, years even, and then I'd get a card with some exotic stamp and it would all come back to me. I guess I always was in love with you . . . and you never even knew."

Cecelie puts down a roll and looks at Phoenix closely, considering. "I knew."

"But you never let on. Why?"

"It was too much, Phoenix. I'd just won the Fulbright and I was sure something would happen that would take it away—that I'd, I don't know, get a letter saying they'd made a mistake, that I had to give it back. One wrong step and it would all be gone. And you were . . . dangerous, I suppose. My mother always lamented blowing her one big chance. Well, I thought that Fulbright was my one big chance. I couldn't risk getting lost with you, with wanting too much. I guess it sounds pretty silly now."

Phoenix shakes her head. "No, if you'd been right, you would have hated me."

Cecelie looks at her oddly. "Do you really believe that?"

Phoenix nods. She and Jinx hate each other, or say they do—Phoenix isn't really sure, such a fine line between love and hate, the ultimate emotions—and she hasn't heard from Molly in years. You get too close to people and then, when it's over, there's no way to go back to a safe middle ground, even if you want to. Cecelie is sucking the poppy seeds out from under her fingernails. Jinx used to do that, too. Such an odd thing to remember, like the trees that summer in New York, how they hung heavy and almost too green, and how the nights were too long and too hot, until the whole world smelled like sweat and shampoo and cheap whiskey. She remembers Rennie grabbing both their hands, pulling them down the street under those trees, singing some silly song—something about "faggots and dykes, oh my." Life was easy then; they had only imagined it was hard. What had happened? "But now it's a whole new summer." Phoenix leans across the table, her cheek so close to the candle its heat makes her eyes tear.

"So it is." Cecelie rises from the chair and bends down to kiss Phoenix Bay lightly. "And I think this time that it might be very easy to get lost with you."

8

Cecelie's words, "easy to get lost with you," follow Phoenix Bay to the grow room, where an eternal electrified sun shines. The plants are doing well enough for a Labor Day harvest, if nothing goes wrong. A lot can happen in two months: bugs, mold, water rationing, which the Water Department threatens every summer. The sound of water gushing rolls through the walls. Cecelie must be doing the dishes, trying to be the perfect houseguest. Is sleeping with the hostess part of the plan? Not that Phoenix is the hostess, really; still, the idea leaves her a little breathless. Easy to get lost with you. Well, she's had worse offers, if it was indeed an offer. Hard to tell when you're so many years out of practice, and lately she's run like a rabbit whenever a stranger approaches. But Cecelie isn't a stranger. Cecelie is . . . what? Beautiful in that butch-dyke way that the straight world never quite appreciates, let alone understands. And smart. That goes without saying. And what was it Rennie called her? Solid? Something like that.

Phoenix washes her hands, carefully, running the towel under her fingernails. Her hands, with their long fingers, smooth knuckles, sweet little half-moons, are a small source of pride. She used to wear rings, sometimes two on one finger, to draw attention to them, until Jinx said the rings made her nervous. After that, Phoenix grew her fingernails long, painting them violent shades of red. It had taken weeks to convince Jinx that the polish wouldn't come off in her cunt—she'd read something about red nail polish causing cancer. "I don't think that's what it means," Phoenix had said and laughed. Jinx, who never saw anything funny about her irrational fears, had sulked. "You don't know that, Phoenix." So Phoenix had relented. With Jinx gone, there was no reason not to wear rings, not to paint her nails, but habits die hard.

Pulling the steel door on the grow room shut, Phoenix locks the dead bolt carefully. Such elaborate precautions to protect a simple darkroom—she sometimes wonders if the room isn't back to its intended purpose. Rennie says no, but how would he know, really? Carson didn't change the ground level of the house, leaving it part garage and part storage and, of course, this room, larger than she would imagine a darkroom needs to be, with heavy-duty wiring and, of course, the steel door. Maybe Rennie is right, the previous owner was a serious photographer. Still, you never know. Houses hold a lot of secrets.

Far above her, the house growls. Pausing on the steps, Phoenix listens, then takes them two at a time until she reaches the spiral staircase, where the sound reverberates. Impossible to run up a spiral staircase, so she shouts from the bottom, "Cecelie! No!" as the unmistakable sound of the skylight opening stops, followed by "What the hell?" from Cecelie. Too late, Phoenix finds Cecelie gazing, mouth agape, at the open roof. Unlike some architects, Carson Cole was generally unimpressed with the high-tech toys available for houses, except for the self-lighting fireplace and the retractable skylight. Operating on the same principle as a garage-door opener, but persistently less reliable, the skylight came to be called "Carson's folly" for how easily it glides open but, depending on humidity or maybe whim (Rennie insists the thing is possessed), refuses to close.

"Welcome to California." Phoenix steps into the room and looks up. "I should have warned you, the skylight opens. Obviously."

"I've never seen anything like it." Cecelie looks puzzled. "I tried to stop it, but it just . . . kept going." She spreads her hands.

Hoping to look more confident than she feels, Phoenix smiles. "No problem. All we have to do is wait a minute for it to reset and then it will close." No point in telling her that the last time it was open, it took the man who'd invented the thing to finally get it closed. "Don't worry," Phoenix adds, as if having an open roof were an everyday occurrence. About a third of the skylight is closed. Could be a good sign, Phoenix decides. She's never actually seen it open, so maybe this is as far as it goes. She turns the dial, winks over her shoulder at Cecelie, and pushes the switch in. Cecelie, kneeling on the bed next to the control panel, nods encouragingly. They both look toward the ceiling. Nothing. No comforting whir of motors, no grinding of gears.

"Maybe it blew a fuse," Cecelie offers, although that seems unlikely; all the lights are still on. "Where's the box?"

"In that closet behind you."

Climbing across the bed, Cecelie casts a wary eye at the ceiling, opens the closet door, and leans inside. Her satisfied "Ah-ha!" is followed by the reassuring clunk of a circuit breaker switch. Smiling, she emerges and watches Phoenix go through the motions again. They both look up hopefully as a motor grumbles deep in the wall. Slowly, the skylight begins to move.

"Well, will you look at that? And Rennie said it would never close once it's open. He thinks it's possessed." Looking back over her shoulder, her hand still on the dial, Phoenix follows Cecelie's gaze toward the ceiling where the skylight is moving, but slowly. Very slowly.

"It opens much faster," Cecelie offers. As if on cue, still a good six feet shy of closing, the movement stops. "Oh damn, damn, damn!"

"I'll just reset it . . . again," Phoenix says, although it's harder to sound confident. The room is already starting to chill as a night wind from the ocean rustles through the hole gaping in the roof.

"Maybe it's stuck on something." Although Cecelie doesn't sound too confident, either, she volunteers, "There's a stepladder in the closet. I'll climb up there and help it along."

Not a bad idea, Phoenix decides. Cecelie is nearly six feet tall, on a ladder she could certainly reach the thing. Maybe. But Rennie is taller than Cecelie, not much, but taller; wouldn't he and Carson have tried that, too? "I guess it's worth a try." Phoenix tries to sound optimistic, as Cecelie positions the ladder under the skylight and climbs to the top, a flashlight stuck in her belt. Always anxious about heights, Phoenix cringes, but Cecelie, standing with her head poking through the roof, seems unfazed. Maybe climbing up to look at a skylight isn't all that different, when you think about it, than climbing down into somebody's tomb. Less creepy, in fact.

"Whoa! Great view from up here." Cecelie ducks her head back through the ceiling. "Want to come up and take a look?" Phoenix shakes her head and Cecelie shrugs, one of those suit-yourself gestures, then braces her hands on the skylight, apparently preparing to pull. "Let's do it!" She sounds almost exuberant, as Phoenix pushes the switch for the third time. In the wall the motor churns. As Cecelie pulls, the ladder sways like a drunken rodeo bull. Cecelie will pitch off the ladder, down the spiral staircase, and die; how will Phoenix ever explain that to the police? Or Rennie? God, then what will she do? "Don't fall!"

"Wasn't planning to," Cecelie calls down. The skylight moves an inch, then another. As it begins creeping forward again, Cecelie loosens her grip. "Damned thing weighs a ton," she shouts over the roar of the motor, which is growing increasingly loud and seems to have developed a whine that Phoenix hadn't noticed earlier. "But it's okay now."

"I don't think so," Phoenix says under her breath, as the motor sputters and, with a decisive clang, dies. The skylight rolls back to where it was before Cecelie had started pulling. "Well, shit." Phoenix takes her hand from the knob. With the motor silenced, the room is painfully quiet. Phoenix sinks onto the bottom step of the ladder. "Shit," she repeats. "What do we do now?" She raises her eyes toward the woman perched atop the stepladder. Cecelie looks down at her for a long moment and shrugs, then she starts to chuckle.

"What's so funny?"

"I broke the damned roof." Cecelie starts to laugh.

"That you did."

"Most of my roof catastrophes are under a ton of silt. Occupational hazard." As the stepladder sways, she lets out a surprised "Whoa!" Phoenix steadies the ladder as Cecelie drops to the floor, inhales sharply from the impact, then starts to laugh again. "You push one lousy button and the damned roof just . . . opens up. Does this hellish invention have a name?"

"The Light Walker. It's a retractable skylight. Carson's idea."

"Obviously," Cecelie says, folding up the ladder and carrying it back to the closet. Phoenix can't decide if she means obviously it's a retractable skylight or obviously it was Carson's idea. "So, what's next?"

Sitting cross-legged on the bed, Phoenix shakes her head. "The last time it took three days to get it closed. They had to call in the inventor. But he was on vacation or something, and then it started to rain. By the time he got here, they were so pissed, they shot him and buried the evidence in the backyard. That's why the roses are doing so well."

"You're kidding."

"Yeah, but only about shooting the inventor."

"So, what's his name? Where's this guy's number?"

"Don't know. Even if I did, it's ten o'clock on a Friday night. We'd never get anybody out here to fix it. We could call Rennie; he was here the last time this happened."

Obviously skeptical, Cecelie shakes her head. "Have you

ever known him to fix anything? If Carson had to call in someone, what's R.J. going to do? He gets back, what, Monday or Tuesday? So, if it's fixed by then, fine. If not, he'll have his little temper tantrum—I'm assuming he still does that?"

"Not much. He's mellowed."

"Really?" Cecelie seems surprised. "Well, that's something. Either way, the roof will eventually close. Is it supposed to rain?"

Phoenix shakes her head. "We're having a drought. Eight years and counting. Heavy mist off the ocean is about the worst of it."

"So we camp out under the stars. Could be fun, like Girl Scouts or something."

"I was never in the Girl Scouts."

"Me either, unless you count Sharon Harper. She was my best friend in junior high school." Cecelie raises her eyebrows and grins.

"You *seduced* a Girl Scout? How old were you?"

"Fourteen. I think it was the uniform. Or the cookies. She was great at building fires. I wonder what ever happened to her? We could use her right now."

"If you're cold, we could go downstairs." And do what, Phoenix isn't sure. With the exception of Rennie's office, the main floor is about as welcoming as a hotel lobby. Her eyes sweep the room and settle on the fireplace. "Or light a fire. That's a self-lighting fireplace."

"Sure. I'll just go ahead and call the fire department . . . tell them to drop by in about an hour. If it works as well as the re-tractable skylight, we should be up in smoke by then." Cecelie's humor is as wry and cutting as her brother's.

"No, the fireplace actually works," Phoenix insists, adding "really" just in case Cecelie doesn't believe her. Cecelie looks du-bious, but it's hard to tell if she's concerned or only looks that way so that she can watch Phoenix scramble. Rennie does that, too. "There's brandy in the cabinet, and reefer in the box on the book-case, and a decent collection of CDs. All the comforts of home."

"All the comforts of *your* home, maybe. Where are the glasses?" Opening doors on the cabinet, Cecelie pauses by the pictures of herself and Mala in a photo wheel that reminds

Phoenix Bay of a Rolodex. Cecelie flips through a few pictures without comment, then turns back to Phoenix. "Truthfully, I could do without a few of these comforts." She looks pointedly at the skylight and scowls. "Damned thing."

"Oh, you'll get used to life in the fast lane again," Phoenix says, arranging wood in the fireplace. In place of Cecelie and her daughter, the picture file is now open to one of Rennie alone, tanned and obviously happy, taken in Hawaii, probably, judging by the orchid lei hanging around his neck. It's an old picture; Rennie and Carson went to Hawaii for their first anniversary.

"That's what scares me." Sitting cross-legged on the floor, Cecelie sorts through the CDs and pulls out one by Etta James. "How's this? I think I remember her."

"The machine will hold five," Phoenix says absently, as the tinderwood begins to crackle. "Just go ahead and put them on. Whatever you like."

A long moment passes. Cecelie picks up a handful of discs. "I don't know how to do this," she says finally and looks up at Phoenix. No teasing lights snap in her eyes; no joke waiting for the punch line hangs between them. "I don't know any of these groups. I've never even seen one of these machines." She averts her eyes. "I guess I've been gone longer than I like to think."

Jostling Cecelie out of the fog that seems to threaten, Phoenix teases, "Next you'll tell me you've never heard of a self-lighting fireplace or a retractable skylight." She winks and takes the discs from Cecelie's hand: blues and a couple of the women rockers. "See, nothing to it, just a record player with bells and whistles. I'm going to grab the comforter off the bed, okay?"

Cecelie nods and carries the brandy and the glasses and the small box of rolled joints to the table in front of the couch. "At least I know how to do this without fucking up." She lights a match, which she uses to warm the brandy.

How is important to this woman, Phoenix decides: how much, how long, how often. Better *how* than *why; why* can be a dangerous road to travel. "It's simple, Cecelie. The fireplace works more or less like a gas range." Phoenix spreads the goose-down comforter over them. "CD players are done with mirrors or lasers or something. And retractable skylights are probably never going to catch on, so it doesn't really matter." Cecelie scowls, dissatisfied. "Okay, they work sort of like fucked-up garage-door openers." The fire crackles and pops. "But like you said, nothing really important has changed." The education of Cecelie Johnson. She could do worse.

Winking like one of the rhinestones in Jinx's old leather jacket, Venus hangs close, pale against the full moon. *"Daddy, catch me the moon!"* Hank Long would snap his big fist shut. *"It's in here, baby. Look right through there. Quick now before I got to let it go."* And sure enough, the moon would be there, if only for a second. Sleight of hand, although she never did discover the secret. *"How come we can't never keep it, Daddy?"* And he would laugh and grab Phoenix by the wrists, twirling her out and around until the world tilted sideways. *" 'Cause nobody can hold on to the moon, baby."*

Pulling the comforter up around her shoulders, Phoenix leans back into the sofa. The brandy and reefer and the fire that makes shadows dance on the wall keep her warm. She wishes Cecelie would come away from the deck door, where she's watching the moon on the ocean, reflected in a glowing half-light that seems to be generated by the sea itself. All those phosphates, no matter what the detergent manufacturers say. Sometimes off the Florida coast, the ocean glows red. Jinx, who was raised in Florida, swore it was true. Maybe so, maybe so.

"When I was a little girl, my daddy used to catch the moon for me. 'Course he always turned it loose," Phoenix leans back, watching Cecelie watch the night. "It was a good trick. I wish I knew how to do that."

Cecelie turns and smiles. "Maybe you should ask him."

"Too late. He's dead."

"Mine too. Do you miss him?"

Phoenix shakes her head. Hard to miss a stranger. "No, I never really knew him. He ran out on me and Mama when I was seven years old."

"Manny left before I was born. He never thought I was his."

"I know. Rennie told me. He said that's why your dad left him the house. It's not true, is it, I mean about him not being your father?"

Cecelie shakes her head. "No. Mona was faithful to him, in her own way. At least that's what she told me."

"Besides, you'd have to be blind not to see the family resemblance."

"My father saw only what he wanted to see. Men do that, don't they?" Phoenix nods. "When I was little, I used to pray that he'd send Rennie back and pick me. But R.J. was the golden boy. No one ever let him forget it. Or me." She comes back to the couch and slides under the comforter next to Phoenix. "This is nice. So, how is he, other than angry?"

"Why do you think Rennie's angry?"

"Wouldn't you be?"

"I suppose, but mostly it's back and forth. Angry one minute, resigned the next. Then some little thing will happen, like getting a check for one of his porno stories, and he's buoyant. He's like that jar of dimes on the deck, all these emotions jumbled together, and you never know which one you'll get." Phoenix picks up a joint and smoothes the paper. They've been smoking all evening. Wine and reefer and now brandy. So much for good intentions. Two steps forward, one step back. She keeps waiting for the great rush that doesn't seem to come; instead she feels close to the surface. She sighs and strikes the match. "He says if he were straight, he'd call it a midlife crisis."

"So what *does* he call it?" Cecelie's eyes sparkle in the firelight; her hands are rough and busy as she picks at a small callus on her palm.

Phoenix shrugs. "The end of an era."

Cecelie sighs and tilts back her head. Stars seem to hang closer here, by the ocean. "There was a time when my brother could never believe anything bad would ever happen to him because it never had. Now it has. I can't help but wonder if he believes it, even now."

"Oh, he believes it. No room in the trenches for heretics."

"I suppose not." Cecelie turns the glass in her hand, the brown liquid rocking like a quiet sea. The firelight traces gentle shadows, making her look almost innocent. Just the firelight playing tricks. Anyone who builds a career in fieldwork isn't likely to be vulnerable or innocent. And Phoenix can't remember this woman ever being either. "Do you think he blames Carson?"

Phoenix shakes her head, then shrugs. "Maybe for dying." She starts to say "*first*," but the word sticks on her tongue.

"No, I meant . . ."

Phoenix cuts her off. "I *know* what you meant, Cecelie." Her voice is sharp. "No. He can't risk thinking that; nobody can. It'll make you crazy." She's heard of men who have done that, though, picking through the lists of names and faces, asking, always: "Is this the one?" And coming up empty every time. Carson and Rennie met when the epidemic was already working its way through San Francisco and New York. They had to have thought about that, had to have known, two men from the plague cities who found each other. It must have been too late for them, even then. But there are some questions you can't ask even your best friend. "What does it matter? As Rennie says, he gambled and he lost."

"Just like one of Mona's high-roller boyfriends." Cecelie's voice catches so it sounds like a whisper. She exhales sharply, her breath smoky, and turns toward Phoenix, her broad shoulders angled into a shrug, as if she hasn't decided where to fix her eyes. "Is he being published at all?"

"Not much . . . unless you count porn." Phoenix turns, her eyes trailing up Cecelie's chest, pausing a little too long where Cecelie's white shirt stretches taut over her breasts. Cecelie makes no move, if she notices. Hard to say; there are secrets here, too. "He's got a couple of money-making boilerplates." Cecelie shakes her head, confused. "You know, stories where all you change are the names of the characters and the locale. *The Truck Stop Jock* and *Hard-On Harry*, both totally devoid of literary merit, are in the seventh or eighth iteration. I lose track. Harry changes his name a lot, but not much else, especially his massive . . . throbbing . . . member." She lowers her voice to a growl, punctuating the words, then laughs. "When I was a kid, I thought it meant the Lions Club; they were the only members I'd ever heard of. I won't tell you what I thought about organs. But no complaints. Harry and the Jock are almost lucrative enough to keep his ass off welfare. And, there's always the chance that he'll finish his new book and make a million. Meanwhile, I have an offer for a new job as an account executive at an ad agency downtown. Life's good." The bitterness in her own voice surprises Phoenix.

Cecelie raises her eyebrows. "Account *executive?* I'm impressed."

"Don't be. I'm ten years older than anybody should be who takes a job like that." Blue flames lick against a large log. "Not that I've had a lot of better offers lately." Or *any* offers in a long time, she thinks. "I told the partner I'd have to think about it."

"But you're going to take it." Cecelie sounds so sure that Phoenix blinks in surprise.

"How do you know that?"

Cecelie shrugs, then smiles a little. "Because I'm psychic. Because you didn't say no when he offered you the job. Because I would, if I were where you are. I've spent my entire career trying to make sense of the past, but I can't *go* there. Time only allows for movement forward, to believe otherwise is fantasy. So, you'll take it. Different path, maybe, but the same direction."

"I guess this is what they mean by starting over. I always thought I'd have it all together by now, you know, paradise with an ocean view. Well, at least I've got the ocean view. Maybe paradise comes later."

"Maybe." Cecelie stretches, arms back over her head, and sighs. Taking Phoenix Bay's right hand in her own, she turns it palm up. The log pops loudly and shows a red core from deep inside. "Show me your secrets, Phoenix Bay." Cecelie's hand is cool and a little scratchy, like the sand on the beach just before dawn. "My mother put great faith in palmistry. Her favorite reader was Mrs. Fatima, a white Russian who lived in the apartment over ours when I was eleven. We lived there almost a year. Mrs. Fatima would let me stay with her when Mona was gone on weekends. She taught me to read palms. She also told Mona she was destined to be a great star. I guess she wasn't very good." Phoenix titters as Cecelie traces her index finger along the fleshy inside palm. "Ah-ha! I see you've squandered your life on artichokes and easy women."

"There are no such animals as easy women, Cecelie. Some of us are just more negotiable than others, but we're all hard. Life makes damned sure of that. What does it really say?"

Cecelie leans forward and turns Phoenix Bay's palm toward the light from the candles on the table. She smiles a little, glances up at Phoenix, and then focuses on her hand. There is something almost feline in her look. How had Phoenix not noticed that before? "Do you still believe in happy endings?" Phoenix shakes her head no, but feels her face flush, thankful for the dim candlelight. "Maybe you should. Here, look. See how this line goes off and then seems to break and then starts again?" Phoenix squints at the pathways in her hand, expecting to see something more than the usual creases, and she nods because Cecelie obviously expects it. "Well, that's your happy ending." Folding Phoenix's fingers into a loose fist, Cecelie kisses them lightly. Her lips, like her fingers, are slightly cool.

"Is that all?" Phoenix had expected something more concrete.

"For now. You always did want it all too soon, didn't you?" Not so much a question as an observation. Phoenix is surprised that this comment doesn't rankle. Maybe it's the way Cecelie says it, so matter of fact without judgment or recrimination. What had Rennie said about his sister's character? Something. Important. But the smoke and the fire and the stars shining down on them through the skylight make it hard to think clearly, and Cecelie herself, the way the white shirt stretches across her breasts. That, too. They could be back in that awful apartment in New York, with the others out for the night. Just the two of them, the night stretching long the way it was that last night, before they had to grow up.

Melissa Etheridge's rough and raspy rocker's voice wraps around them. There is a woman who understands love and the damage life can do. No innocence there. She just wades into it with her eyes wide open, but wades in all the same. Singers understand what heartache feels like, and love, too. But when they fall, they just pick themselves up and start over. That's where the scars come from. That's why when it finally feels good, it feels so damned good. A relief to know you can feel something at last. "Six months ago, I lost everything," Phoenix says finally. "For a long time, I had it all, or thought I did. And I blew it. I don't know if I loved it too much or not enough, but one day it was gone: the woman I loved, our home, my job. Everything. I showed up here with eight hundred dollars and everything I owned in the back of a used Jeep. This is all that's left and it's probably not enough . . . for me or anyone else."

"It's enough. Trust me." Cecelie's words hang between them. She kisses Phoenix lightly, then leans back, eyes partly closed, her face gone soft, so that she is the girl Phoenix almost loved. Once. Phoenix pushes the ghosts down, as Cecelie stirs, looking at Phoenix for a long moment, staring as if she's trying to find something lost. "My mother was many things: vain, self-absorbed, greedy, insensitive, but she was most of all resilient, tenaciously resilient. I used to think she was steeped in fantasy, and maybe she was, but Mona had absolute faith that no matter what happened, she could start over and the next time would be better than whatever had gone before. It was her universal truth and the only thing of value she left me." Phoenix touches Cecelie's cheek gently. Smooth. So much smoother than her rough hands, smooth as her voice, smooth as the night that has closed around them. "Mona was like these beads, beautiful but always cold." Cecelie unhooks one of her necklaces, heavy with silver and coral, and holds it to Phoenix's throat, and smiles. "I prefer women who are like silver, equally beautiful and easily warmed." The light catches, making the beads glow. Cecelie drops the necklace in Phoenix's hand.

Surprisingly heavy, it moves like sand through her fingers. Holding the necklace up to the light, Phoenix watches the shadows it casts chase across the wall. She is fascinated by the stones, cool to her touch, and the silver that warms in her palm. "Did you dig this up?"

Cecelie exhales a small chuckle. "No, I bought it. Years ago. From a *huaquero.*"

"Oh." Phoenix seems disappointed. "I thought maybe it was something you found."

"We don't get to keep things from the sites, Phoenix, at least those of us with any ethics or who hope to keep working." The idea seems to amuse her, but Phoenix doesn't understand why. "It's bad enough I have this, especially if the *huaquero* was telling the truth when he said it had belonged to a princess."

"Did it?"

"I hope not; those graves are too rare. Not that *huaqueros* are especially choosy. Do you like it?"

Phoenix nods, touching a few of the stones to her lower lip. "How old is it?"

"Five hundred, probably, or maybe seven, although that's less likely."

"Five hundred years old." Phoenix has never touched anything so ancient. What must the woman have been like who wore it first? Was she beautiful? Happy?

"Five hundred A.D., Phoenix." Cecelie corrects, her eyes fixed on Phoenix's face.

Phoenix gasps and the beads fall onto the comforter. "It's ancient! Cecelie, it must have cost a fortune." But Cecelie shakes her head. Old apparently does not always translate to priceless. Picking up the necklace, Phoenix offers it to Cecelie. "It's beautiful. I'd give anything to have something like that."

Cecelie accepts the necklace, shifting its weight hand to hand, as if trying to assess the weight. Her face is quiet; only her hands move. "Would you?" Her voice is edged with cold.

"I meant . . . I mean I wasn't asking for it." Phoenix blushes. Her voice is flustered. What must this woman think?

"Why not?" Cecelie presses. "Why not ask for what you want?"

Phoenix flushes, thankful for the firelight and the cold. Why not indeed? "Because . . ." But she can't tell Cecelie the truth, that she had learned long ago that other women can ask for what they want and get it, but not women like her. Not runners and born losers.

Cecelie's eyes fix on Phoenix. "Here. It's yours. For old times' sake." She holds it up to Phoenix's neck. "Beautiful," is all she says, fastening it gently, then leaning back for a better look. "Maybe the *huaquero* was right; maybe it really did belong to a princess."

Phoenix touches the beads at her throat and smiles, as much from the warmth rising from her belly as the weight of the necklace. "Are you sure?" Her voice is a little hoarse, maybe from the brandy or the smoke or the night air, maybe from Cecelie so close.

"Very sure." Cecelie unbuttons the first two buttons on Phoenix Bay's shirt, and pushes the fabric down and away from her shoulders. "That's better," she says, smiling her feline smile. Phoenix shivers slightly; her eyes fix on Cecelie's. They could let the moment pass, make a small joke, break the spell. But Cecelie's right: Phoenix still wants to believe in happily ever after, at least for this one night. Cecelie leans forward; her fingers touch the necklace, then move on to explore the hollow of Phoenix's throat, the gentle rise of her collarbone. Cecelie's fingers feel like a cat's rough tongue. Easy to imagine these fingers linked so easily in her own, exploring hidden depths of flesh, so accustomed as they are to uncovering secreted treasures. Phoenix trembles.

"Cold?" Cecelie asks. Phoenix shakes her head, as Cecelie pulls her close. No. Not cold. How long has it been since any woman has looked at her this way, with so much want? Not in years, not since she and Jinx were still new, when things were still right. And that was the secret she could never tell, that her deepest fear is no woman would ever want her again, would ever look at her the way Jinx had, the way Cecelie is now. Phoenix needs this blatant want, needs to drown her fears in it. Her eyes catch in Cecelie's, then look away. Her breath falters and her belly drops to a familiar but long-absent throb. When she brings her eyes back, Cecelie's greet her.

"Make me feel real," Phoenix whispers. Through the skylight the night wind rustles. Cecelie leans down and kisses her. But when Phoenix kisses her back, she keeps her eyes open. Beneath the worn cotton shirt and the denim jeans that are frayed and thin, with traces of South America still in the seams, Cecelie's skin is soft. Phoenix, now, is the archaeologist, exploring, exposing what has been hidden away, untouched for too long. Muscles run hard through Cecelie's arms, and thickly through her legs. Phoenix finds each crevice, each fold of skin, each tender curve exciting. Jinx used to call Phoenix's hands magic, the way they could dip and tease and torment and demand, strong and knowing, traveling on instinct. "Your hands are cold," Cecelie whispers, then her breath catches and she doesn't say anything more.

The city lies cool and quiet, the damp sea air magnifying even the smallest sound. Up the street, a security gate clangs shut. Melissa Etheridge lets out the long, low wail of a woman falling, falling in love again. And Cecelie, who prides herself on always being in control, on knowing what she wants and how to get it, sinks into this woman. She's come this far, there's nowhere left to go.

Morning clangs against Cecelie Johnson, who wakes with a start. For a moment, she forgets where she is. Gray light seeps across the bed. Her head throbs. Too much, she thinks. She's struggled with headaches for years, rising from her belly, creeping up along the back of her throat to the epicenter behind her eyes. The woman next to her stirs gently, smiling a little in sleep. The *chaquira* at Phoenix Bay's throat has left small red marks, although those could just as easily be from Cecelie's teeth. Hard to say. Cecelie shivers and pulls the goose-down comforter, the color of cream, around her shoulders.

Mona once had a dress this color, smooth and cool and silky. On nights when her mother was out, Cecelie, still damp and puckered from her bath, would sneak into Mona's room. The dress always hung on the side hook of the closet, wrapped in a clear plastic cleaner's bag that made the satin glow until it looked as if the dress itself were made from the moon. Mona wore that dress to movie openings, premieres, as she always called them. Of course, she wasn't invited to many, but occasionally she managed to wrangle her way in. The dress smelled like Mona: sweet with smoke and Tabu; her mother always kept a big bottle on the vanity table next to her hairbrush with the round bone handle. On nights when she was left alone, Cecelie would take that hairbrush and pull the creamy satin dress around her. She never indulged in dress-up games the way other little girls did; she wanted only to be near the dress. Cecelie was the prisoner of a wicked queen, who made her sleep naked at the foot of her bed; she had to stay there in case the queen wanted her during the night. The bone handle of the hairbrush was cold. The queen's prisoner had to hold it between her

130

legs, the bristles burning the insides of her thighs. By the time
Cecelie rolled onto her belly, the handle was warm. She'd had her
first orgasm with that dress. Then one night, the dress was gone.
Sold, probably; things were always disappearing from the apartment. But it hadn't really mattered; Mona's hairbrush was still
there.

As a child, Cecelie was fascinated by her mother: the way she
guided the powder puff over her breasts, lifting first one, then the
other, dusting them gently, before moving on across her belly, and
finally to between her legs, followed by perfume first on her wrists,
then behind her ears and, on nights she went out, beneath her
bellybutton and between her breasts. Mona Morgan had beautiful
breasts, firm and large, the kind men covet. "My greatest asset,"
she used to tell her daughter, when her daughter still listened to
her. Of all the genes her mother could have passed on—her small,
perfect nose, blond hair, compact frame—the only one she
seemed to manage had produced breasts. Useless for an archaeologist. But one woman's blessing is another's curse, although
Phoenix had not seemed to think so last night. Cecelie slips further under the sheet, wrapping herself close around Phoenix, soft
and smooth and cool, in this bed that smells of flowers and sea air.
She pulls the comforter around them more closely. From the street
below, a truck roars; a stiff morning breeze snaps through the open
skylight; the peacock cries, greeting the day; tears slip from
Cecelie Johnson's eyes.

Paradise comes in many colors and sometimes in the face of a
beautiful woman. Phoenix Bay considers this as she stretches over
Cecelie, sprawling and snoring softly, to see the clock.
Reminiscent of a pie plate, a solid chrome wedge edges its way
around circles of red and purple and green, 1950s jukebox colors.
R.J. had spotted it in the window of a shop in the Castro and
brought it home because he knew it would make Carson smile.
Designed more as an expression of time than for any practical purpose, ten after ten and ten before two are identical, as are several
other possible configurations of time. But then, isn't that always
true? Not a bad gift, one that puts time in its place. Eight some-

thing, Phoenix decides, flopping back against the pillows, careful not to disturb Cecelie.

Saturday. Two days left to decide about the job at the ad agency. Not that she hasn't already decided. Cecelie was right about that last night. Well, she could do worse. But can she do better? Richard James will be pleased. Not that she really cares. Lesbians still make men like Richard James nervous. One of the dyke perks. If he were her student, she would assign a twenty-five-page paper on—what? The witches of *Macbeth*. Perfect. Due first thing Monday morning. She would give him a D+ just for spite. Now, she's going to end up working for him. But today she is free, with nothing to think about but Cecelie.

A pigeon scratches on the roof and a tiny, inquisitive head pokes through the open skylight, followed by a squat neck, the beginnings of a plump breast. "Shoo!" Phoenix hisses under her breath, trying not to waken Cecelie. The bird only tips a little more inside. Phoenix eases out of the bed and picks Cecelie's T-shirt off the floor. "Shoo, I said!" She tosses the T-shirt at the bird who only cocks its head, fixing its beadlike eye on her. The T-shirt floats upward, several feet short, and then opens like a parachute, the kind cartoon characters make from handkerchiefs. "Go 'way! Go!" Waving her arms, Phoenix looks for something more substantial. God, this room is a mess. Clothes litter the floor near the edge of the bed, hastily removed and discarded; on the coffee table, the dregs of last night's brandy; the fireplace lets off the sharp stench of charred logs. One of her shoes at the top of the staircase catches her eye. She pitches it upward, easy, like a juggler with a ball; she doesn't want to actually hit the bird or, worse, lose the shoe through the opening. The shoe angles toward the pigeon, which cocks its blue-gray head curiously.

"Phoenix? What on earth are you doing?" Cecelie, up on her elbows, squints through half-opened eyes.

"A pigeon," Phoenix explains. "I don't want him to come in. It's bad luck to have a bird come into your house."

"What pigeon?" Cecelie rubs her fingers across her forehead, testing the tender skin, then shields her eyes from the insistent morning light.

Phoenix looks up to see that the pigeon, so eager to come in just a moment before, is gone. "Oh," she says blushing, and bending to gather the clothes from the floor. "I guess I scared it off." She holds the clothes over her chest on her way to the closet. Always a little embarrassed by her breasts, smallish and ordinary and now beginning to sag from time and gravity and the weight she's lost in the last year, she hopes to keep the illusion of last night alive for Cecelie a little longer. If, indeed, Cecelie thinks of such things; some women don't.

"So I see." Cecelie sounds irritated as she drops back onto the pillow. "And here I thought the city would be devoid of nature. But no, indeed. We've got peacocks in the backyard, pigeons in the ceiling, and a tiger on your belly. By the way, does it have a name?"

Phoenix drops the clothes into the hamper, and her hands flutter to the tiger. Really no need, Cecelie's eyes are covered by her forearm. She probably thinks it's ugly, Phoenix thinks, standing by the bed, trying to decide what to do. So much a part of her, she forgets how the tattoo must look to someone like Cecelie. "No. It's an untitled piece." Cecelie doesn't laugh. On all fours, Phoenix crawls across the bed toward Cecelie, who moans slightly. Drawing closer, she licks Cecelie's shoulder gently.

"Don't," Cecelie says, never moving her arm from her forehead, then adds as an afterthought, "Please."

Hurt, Phoenix pulls back, shakes her head, and slides off the bed. "I'm sorry . . . I just thought . . ." Cecelie exhales slowly. Jinx used to do that, too, the long, low sloughing off of warm breath, when Phoenix had done something . . . anything . . . to displease her. And she often displeased Jinx, often heard that sigh, especially toward the end.

"I have a headache," Cecelie says finally, from beneath her arm.

"Of course." The oldest excuse in the world. She should have seen it coming. Should've, could've, didn't. Damn. She should have known better.

Cecelie removes her arm and peers at Phoenix. "I get these sometimes—actually, a lot when I travel. The trip up here was . . . tough. I don't suppose you have any codeine? I took the last of mine yesterday."

Phoenix shakes her head. "There's Ibuprofen in the drawer, prescription strength; the doctor gives it to me for cramps. Maybe that would help?"

The white oval tablet looks imposing in her hand. How many? She has no idea, so she shakes out another and then a third, decides against it, and drops one back into the bottle. "You're supposed to take this with food. You want a roll or something so it doesn't rot your stomach?"

"I'll take my chances." Cecelie pops the two pills into her mouth and chews, makes a face, and swallows. Only then does she take the water Phoenix offers. "Works faster," she says, answering the unspoken question. Closing her eyes, she leans back, waiting for the white pills to do their magic. Codeine would be better, but it's hard to come by in the States. She should have thought of that. Bad habits. So many bad habits just waiting to be picked up. Bad habits and weak flesh. If she were religious, she'd call them temptations. As it is, she calls them nothing, just ways to block out the pain, to make her numb, make her forget. "Do you have any reefer up here?" Phoenix, of all people, should understand and if she doesn't . . . well, what's the loss?

Afternoon creeps across the too-bright room. Cecelie opens her eyes, almost surprised that her head is quiet. She's been dreaming or maybe just remembering—hard to tell with these headaches— of the panorama on Phoenix's belly: the tiger, who steps gingerly, one paw on the brown mossy triangle, the other raised, ready to take another step or to pounce; the jungle, finely detailed, with flowering vines down a thigh, but ending abruptly on her backside, as if the artist had suddenly abandoned her canvas. What does it mean, if, indeed, it means anything at all? Cecelie rolls onto her belly. "I don't like to think about her," Phoenix had said, and Cecelie wasn't sure if she meant the tiger or the woman who had spent months, years more likely, putting her there: Jinx, the woman of a thousand needles, who'd built a jungle leaf by painful leaf, calling up blood, mixing it with ink. Even in her absence the beautiful scar remains.

Then there's Phoenix, who purrs when she's stroked, arching

her back, pulling in her leg, just a little more, inviting. Inside, there are rings, gold and caught with beads. Does the tiger protect the rings or are they there as a tether? A pale glint of sun catches in the glass and sends a rainbow across the bed. Cecelie smiles. Secrets. She likes secrets. The rings are troublesome, though. She'll have to learn to work around them or maybe with them, if she's going to keep on sleeping with Phoenix. Is she? She doesn't know. Women can get in the way. Not women, love. Love gets in the way. Like Freddy, the sweetly butch bartender she'd run to when she was first on her own, when she'd imagined there was nowhere else to run; or Monique, the graduate student, with the sadly beautiful eyes; or even passionate, confused Connie, who ran away with the man she met in a bookstore under a sign that said USED POETRY. Ghosts whisk through her mind, quick and naked. None of them had understood that they couldn't give Cecelie what she needs. But what is it she needs? That question has dogged her for years, nipping against her, and still no answer. She's sifted through a couple thousand years of history, and only found more questions.

For Phoenix, the day stretches out long with promises. Make love with Cecelie, run, call the man who can fix the skylight, fuck Cecelie on the living room floor in full view of Mrs. Chin, who won't need her damned binoculars for this, feed Marcel Proust, take Cecelie for a drive down to Pacifica for calamari at that little restaurant on the shore. What *is* the name of that place? Rennie will know; have to remember to ask, if he ever calls back. When Phoenix called this morning, the phone rang fourteen times before a man with a slight wheeze answered. No, Rennie couldn't come to the phone, but he would pass along the message: A stuck skylight? Well, had they tried WD-40? After dinner, she and Cecelie will walk out onto the pier, the one that stretches a full quarter mile out over the ocean, or maybe drive up to Twin Peaks to see the city by night. They can't make love there, though, too many tour buses: "Ladies and gentlemen, to our right, representatives of San Francisco's large lesbian community . . ." How brazen is Cecelie? Too early to tell. Women will do anything at first; their true natures don't come through until later. Or maybe build another fire in the fireplace. Cecelie looks beautiful by firelight.

When Phoenix opens the back door, Marcel Proust fans his magnificent tail for no apparent reason. Maybe just a salute to the sun, or maybe in his loneliness he will court anything. Sad that he has to live here without his harem, she thinks, scattering the feed from the porch. His beady eye fixes on her and he folds his tail so that it once again trails behind him on the ground. As if sensing her disappointment, he struts to the far corner of the yard. Midafternoon and Marcel Proust's impromptu show and Cecelie in the shower are reasons enough to smile.

Drying the last of the dishes, Phoenix feels Cecelie behind her, and leans back into damp arms. Carson's robe, white terry with his blue monogram on the pocket, hangs loose and open, exposing Cecelie's skin, pink from the shower, beads of water in her curly hair, a few overlooked droplets misting her neck, and the wide triangle of black ringlets. Taking Cecelie's hand and tucking it inside her shirt, she whispers, "What would Rennie say?" Cecelie's nails are hard and smooth, oddly cool.

"My brother understands lust." Cecelie nuzzles Phoenix, who leans back a little until her head is between Cecelie's breasts, soft and warm, nothing at all like melons, although people are always likening breasts to fruit. Cecelie has beautiful breasts, which sometimes seem to take on a life of their own. Phoenix gathers them together in her hands, widens her mouth to take in both nipples. Her greedy tongue, hungry, hot and wet with anticipation, leaves traces of lipstick; she feels them go pink and hard between her teeth. Cecelie pulls back, closing her robe, disengaging Phoenix, folding herself back into respectability. Cecelie is temporary, Phoenix reminds herself, the way Jinx was temporary. Seven years, but still temporary; seven long, temporary years that Phoenix had imagined would stretch into eternity. Maybe that's temporary too. Being with Cecelie, learning the scent and feel of her doesn't seem temporary, though. The danger lies in wanting something too much, Phoenix reminds herself. Push the nagging want away. Deadly. Look what happened the last time and the time before that. Why should this be different?

Cecelie is grinding coffee, and Phoenix shouts a little above the roar; such a big noise for a tiny machine. "Peruvian coffee," Phoenix says. "The coffee stores all carry it now." Cecelie sniffs the grounds suspiciously before dumping them into the paper triangle filter. Cute, Phoenix thinks. "So, how's the headache?" she asks, trying to sound more casual than she feels.

"Better. Gone, actually. I guess I just needed some extra sleep. How about you?"

"Never better. Good sex is the ultimate sedative. I think I've found the cure for all the insomniacs in the world; all we need is a good lay."

Cecelie's laugh is warm and rich like the coffee. "And was it?"

"What?" Phoenix is smiling, teasing, determined to make Cecelie ask, relishing the way her eyes have suddenly found something very interesting in the waiting coffee mug, the way her toes curl and uncurl on the chair rung.

"Good," Cecelie all but whispers, raising her eyes to Phoenix.

"Passable, I suppose." Phoenix is still teasing, but immediately regrets the words when Cecelie drops her eyes. She hadn't meant to wound. "Cecelie, I was kidding." Crossing to the table, Phoenix drops to her knees, burying her head in Cecelie's lap, pushing back the folds of terry cloth to taste damp skin, sweet from the shower. "You're wonderful; don't you know that?" Cecelie shrugs and Phoenix realizes the shyness is real, not just an act. "I had my whole day planned—and every other thing to do was make love with you. Would I do that, if you weren't wonderful?" Phoenix unties the belt, pushing it back. She'd planned to take Cecelie into the living room where the sun warms the carpet like sand, but the kitchen will do. Good that Rennie's such a stickler about waxing the floor. She'll have to remember to tell him; she likes to hear Rennie laugh.

The name of the man who can fix the roof is Lucas Walker from Santa Cruz or San Luis Obispo, someplace down there, Rennie said, sounding frustrated or maybe just angry that the roof is open. Phoenix finally made him laugh when he asked when Cecelie had come, and she replied, "Twice last night, then I lost count." Then she'd handed Cecelie the phone.

"He's not coming back until Thursday." Pouring another cup of coffee, Cecelie sniffs it. Satisfied, she sips. "And . . . he's bringing someone with him." She draws out the words, considering this information. "A student, Doug somebody. He says we'll like him."

"Does it really matter if we don't?" Leaning against the open kitchen door, Phoenix watches clouds roll in from the ocean. Not necessarily a sign of rain, but you never know. "Did you call the infamous Mr. Walker?"

Cecelie nods. "Left a message on his machine." Sip, sniff, she carefully sets the coffee mug with the picture of Marilyn Monroe back on the table. "Do you think he's trustworthy?"

"Who? Lucas Walker or Doug?" Phoenix closes the door, which sticks a little at the top. Another thing that needs to be fixed in this house. She's begun to notice the flaws: doors that stick, windows that jam, not to mention that damned skylight, pipes that clang and wheeze, floors that creak. All show and no substance, TaTa Hassee would have said.

"Both. But at the moment, I'm more concerned about Lucas Walker." Cecelie pulls Phoenix down on her lap. "I suppose we'll just have to find something to do until the phone rings."

Phoenix tucks herself against Cecelie; they fit together well. She and Jinx had fit together well, too. And Molly. All the important women in her life. Phoenix cups Cecelie's breasts, tickling them lightly, rousing them as Cecelie snuggles deeper into the warmth, smiling, making little cooing noises. She probably wakes up that way, too, Phoenix thinks. Not like Jinx, groaning and groping blindly, first for her watch and then for her cigarettes. Disgusting habit. You learn a lot about somebody when you wake up with them, although the first few mornings it's hard to tell, everybody on their best behavior. Phoenix hadn't even noticed Jinx's groaning and groping at first, or if she had, thought it cute or endearing; years passed before it rankled.

Cecelie turns and smiles, kissing Phoenix. "You taste good," she says, hugging Phoenix. This is what she misses most; none of the rest of it: the arguments, the distance, life's trivia getting in the way, the lies and then the inevitable scenes that follow. None of that, only this. "There's a couch in Rennie's office. We could wait there for Lucas's call—unless you'd rather go out."

"Oh, I don't think so," says Cecelie, grinning, "We should wait by the phone. After all, we wouldn't want to miss Lucas."

"So, what do you want to do today?" Sliding out of Cecelie's arms, Phoenix turns her back to avoid the sight of temptation lying there, on the leather tuxedo couch that dominates Rennie's office. At this rate, they'll lose what little is left of the afternoon. Cecelie smiles and rolls onto her belly, watching Phoenix pull on Carson's running shorts and a T-shirt so old its lettering is cracked into the soft gray fiber: "U.N.M.," she observes. "What's that for?"

"University of New Mexico. Running gear's upstairs, if you're interested."

Cecelie shakes her head and grins. "Archaeologists make lousy runners. We're afraid we might miss something. Where do you go?" Cecelie stands up, pulling Phoenix close.

"Up the beach, usually. Sure you don't want to come along?" Cecelie makes a face. Well, that's okay, Phoenix decides. She needs time alone to clear her head, try to decide where this thing with Cecelie is going, if it has to go anywhere at all.

"Be impulsive, forget running. Just this once. Stay here. Keep me company." Cecelie looks up at Phoenix like a puppy.

New lovers are good at that, pushing away the outside world. "Tempting," Phoenix answers and giggles, pushing down the throb in her belly, twisting away from Cecelie's hands, which are persistent in their quest for recently hidden places. "But I'm trying to cut back on impulsive acts." She loves the throb of early passion, which always seems to slip away, ultimately, with familiarity.

"Be impulsive." Cecelie nuzzles under the shirt, until Phoenix feels her breath catch, but wills herself to pull on her socks, to find her shoes.

"I can't, Cecelie."

"Why? What's so terrible about being impulsive?" Cecelie is teasing, her voice light.

Exasperated, Phoenix struggles to collect her thoughts, which are tangling under the distraction of Cecelie's insistent tongue. "Because, it is . . . can be . . . for me." Finally, she twists away. How can she make this woman understand that every important decision in her life was made on impulse: where to go to college, which women to love, the kinds of jobs she's had, moving to California, even living here with Rennie. Sometimes she thinks she went crazy on impulse. And it has to stop. Teddy Grayson tells her to make lists: pro and con separated by a long smooth line. But lists are terrifying, too. She's only gotten as far as the line. "My instincts are . . . often misguided." Hard to admit, but true.

When Cecelie smiles, freckles dance on her cheeks. "Well, mine aren't. They say it's time to pick up what we left unfinished in New York. And what do yours say?"

Phoenix blushes, sorry she's led the conversation in this direction, and turns her attention to her laces. "They say . . ." She can feel Cecelie waiting. "They say you're dangerous."

Cecelie chuckles, then muses, as if she likes the idea, "How about that: a dangerous archaeologist. Tell me why I'm dangerous. I've already uncovered your secrets." Her hands have moved up under Carson's T-shirt, under the cotton sports bra, until they tweak the flesh there, already prickly as gooseflesh. "Exposed them," she says, pushing the shirt up, her hot breath against Phoenix's belly. "But maybe they need further study?"

"No."

Cecelie pulls back, and Phoenix, embarrassed at her response, fences. "How do you know I'm not like one of those pieces that falls apart when it's uncovered?"

Cecelie shrugs. "In the first place, that doesn't happen very often." She leans back on the couch, her lips turned up in— what?—boredom maybe or insolence. Rennie does that, too, the same gesture, the same tone, as if there is some common gene or memory between them. "And in the second place, what good is it, if it falls apart the minute it's exposed to light?"

Phoenix dances, back and forth, shifting her weight. "Anyway, I've got to go."

"You're avoiding the issue." Cecelie reaches out to catch Phoenix's hand just as the phone starts to ring. "Ah," she says as

Phoenix picks up the receiver, "Lucas has great timing." She raises her eyebrows when Phoenix hands her the telephone.

"It's for you. Says her name is Gina."

"Shit!" Cecelie takes the phone and drops into Rennie's chair, naked. "Gina! How did you ever find me here? . . . No, I know what I said. I'm just surprised." Phoenix turns, her mouth set, shoulders firm, her back to Cecelie, who forgot to grab her robe before talking to the smoky-voiced woman. Or maybe forgetting the robe was no accident. Maybe she enjoys sitting there, naked, in Rennie's dark and cluttered study, her skin sticking just a little to the brown-leather chair that makes soft sucking noises every time she moves. Flesh against flesh. "Cecelie, this is Gina," the voice had said. Innocent enough, except for Cecelie's reaction, which now seems guilty. "Hang on a second." She covers the receiver with her palm. "Phoenix?" But Phoenix has already disappeared into the darkened hall, closing the door behind her.

The clock over the stove shows twelve minutes have passed, and still the rise and fall of unintelligible voices punctuated by laughter, then those damnable long pauses come from Rennie's office. Fighting the urge to sit outside the door, waiting for it to open, Phoenix tries to decide what to do. She could knock lightly and poke her head inside. "Going running," she could mouth. And Cecelie would smile and wave, blow Phoenix a kiss. Or would she? If she were tough, that's what she would do. But she's not. Tough. *Tough* is more a Jinx kind of word. Tough and moving; tough and gone. Soundlessly, Phoenix slips past the door, down the front steps and out onto the sidewalk.

Phoenix Bay hits the street running. *Too close! Close! Too close!* Her feet churn out a familiar chant, down the beach; past the dykes with the Dalmatian pups; past the surfers in their orange wet suits, designed so the sharks won't mistake them for seals; then up to the Cliff House, where the tour buses belch out streams of tourists; past the stairs down to Musée Méchanique, where the wizard behind the glass booth still waves his magic wand, rolls his glass eyes, and spits out a fortune card for a quarter; on past the ruins of the Sutro Baths, no time to figure out the mystery of the pools today; across to the park, past the statue of Diana, where the witches come and leave roses wedged into cracks in the concrete base; down the path past where the crazy old man's garden used to be and up to the edge, where the ocean and the traces of city spill out a thousand feet below.

Only then does she stop, massaging away kinks and fear, trying to feel and coming up empty, pushing down images of Gina with the smoky voice. Smart, she would have to be smart to interest Cecelie. An archaeology student, perhaps. Cecelie has had affairs with a few, her erratic letters sprinkled with unfamiliar names: "When Lena and I were in Huanchaco . . . " or "Tess insisted we make the trip to Lago Valencia to see the gallos. She wanted to see if the Hoatzin birds really do have claws on their wings. The better to climb into overhangs, you know." Gina would be young, probably, and beautiful. Firm breasts and full lips. Such things aren't supposed to matter, but they do. Of course they do. Why else would there be all those ads in the newspapers looking for tall, thin, curvaceous, vivacious women . . . under thirty? Vivacious. A woman named Gina would be vivacious. With a name like that, how could she not? No crazy grandmother for her. No cracking up in English class. No lover running out on her cursing, "Fuck you! I don't need this!"

Walking back to the house, Phoenix takes the long way through the park, past the arboretum, white and pristine in the late-afternoon sun. Inside the air is like a rain forest, heavy and sweet. She passes the old carousel, housed inside a big barn to protect the antique animals. Any other afternoon, she might stop to ride the tiger, but the line is long, filled with children and anxious young mothers. No room for her here. Haight Street stretches out before her, long past innocence, crowded with tourists and deadheads in their tie-dyes and long hair. For them, it is eternally The Summer of Love. The newspapers crank that up every few years. The children lounging on the street corners look through her; they should be her friends, not the serious women in their tailored suits and severe hair, who hurry toward their overmortgaged Victorians, clutching briefcases even on Saturday afternoon. Those women want no part of her, either.

Doubling back, she trots into the park, picking up speed, following the paths she's memorized. Greenery breaks and she pauses by the duck pond. Mallards and white geese huddle on their tiny island, safe, as they do every weekend. Weekdays, they waddle brazenly along the sidewalk, looking for crumbs and stale popcorn and familiar faces, quacking out their contemptuous chuckles. Here the path angles west, toward the site by the old windmill where gay men cruise. Phoenix mistakenly took that path once, thinking it was a shortcut. Rennie had laughed when she'd told him about how terrified she'd been coming upon one sullen man after another, always alone, eyes always downcast and then the relief that had washed over her when she realized they were all gay, and then the mortification, a moment later, when she finally had understood where she was. "I warned you, Phoenix," he'd said. And it was true, he had, that first night here, but she'd forgotten. "I felt like I should go back and apologize to them for making such a fool of myself," she'd admitted. He'd laughed even harder. She feels that way now. Foolish for running out; foolish for imagining last night could ever be anything more than a reunion between old friends. Foolish. God, it was easier when she was still drinking regularly; everything didn't seem so serious then.

The house is quiet when Phoenix unlocks the door. No sign of Cecelie, but her backpack is still here, its contents spilling across the unmade bed. Phoenix considers repacking it or unpacking it completely. Either would be prying, she decides, and settles for moving the shirts and socks and wrinkled underwear to the leather chair. A small and very heavy envelope falls to the floor with a clunk, spilling its contents: old jewelry, four necklaces and two large but mismatched earrings, and a small dagger in a black-leather sheath. Phoenix traces the sheath with her fingers, then pulls out the knife. A pattern is etched deeply along the handle: hatchets chasing tiny figures.

"A traditional Moche pattern," Cecelie says from behind her.

Phoenix scrambles to put the knife back into its sheath. She hadn't heard Cecelie come in. "I'm sorry. I wasn't prying. I was just straightening up and . . . it fell out of the envelope."

Cecelie picks up the laundry Phoenix had so carefully folded and drops it in a pile next to the chair that she flops into. The chair sighs deeply. "It's okay, Phoenix, you might as well know." She picks up the envelope that Phoenix has laid on the table and arranges each piece on it carefully. "Interesting people, the Mochica." Her voice is so dispassionate, she might be delivering a lecture. "True architects, but with a violent streak. You make a few human sacrifices and there goes your reputation." She chuckles at her small and, to Phoenix, rather unfunny joke. Phoenix winces. "They were amazing artists, though. Here, look at the workmanship on this piece." In her hand is the knife. Phoenix sees nothing amazing about it, but tentatively touches it because, she senses, Cecelie expects it.

"I'm surprised they let you through airport security with a knife."

"Security?" Cecelie's voice rises at Phoenix's naiveté. "For God's sake, Phoenix, what do you think I did—*show* it to them? Besides, Peru is not the States. They've got enough to think about with guerrillas and drug runners to worry about a lousy four-inch knife that couldn't cut butter. No, Phoenix, security is never the problem. Customs is . . . well, another issue. And I personally would hate to be keeping company with some of our more unfortunate countrymen in Castro Castro who may see the States again in this century, but I wouldn't bet on it." Cecelie's thumb and fingers brush in a silent snap and she smiles. "Trafficking artifacts is . . . well . . . not quite as serious as trafficking cocaine, but close enough." Picking at the beads around her own neck, some the color of earth, others brightly colored, much like the ones she gave Phoenix last night, she unties one of the strands. "*Chaquiras*, on the other hand, are considerably less deadly and longer lasting than cocaine. All around, they're a very stable form of contraband." She sounds almost bitter and Phoenix wonders why. Accepting the necklace, Phoenix is surprised at its weight, but more at the intricacy, each bead carefully carved. "These are not all that different from that one you're wearing. I picked them up in the markets when I first went north. You could still find them then. Now, never. Unless you're lucky. I am occasionally very lucky."

Lucky with customs. Lucky with buying beads. And yet

Cecelie doesn't feel lucky. She feels dirty, the way the scavenger tourists should, but never seem to, as they and their hired *huaqueros* dig up graves, not giving a damn about the damage they do, only caring about *chaquiras*. And you can't really blame the *huaqueros*. Poor Indians, who see the graves as their inheritance and if there's a buyer for what they can bring out . . . well, so be it. And there's always a buyer, another tourist hunting souvenirs. Like that damned fool Italian woman who had more money than sense, looking for pity from Luz because all the *huaquero* they'd hired could find was a baby's grave. "Three days out of my vacation," the bitch kept wailing, "and nothing but damned babies!" When Luz had asked—although she could easily enough guess—what had happened to the babies' graves, the tourist had looked at her as if she were mad. "We threw them away, of course; babies don't have *chaquiras.*"

Phoenix touches the necklace gently, then unfastens it, extending it like an offering. "These must belong in a museum or something."

Cecelie shakes her head, refusing to accept the offered necklace. "Honey, you keep it. There are thousands of them in museums already. Besides, what good are they? The site was lost. The *huaqueros* took care of that. And the museums would just catalog them and dump them into storage, along with all the others like them." Picking up the corroded necklace, Cecelie exhales softly, holding it to the light. "But this . . . this is another matter entirely. I'd sell my damned soul to get the site that produced this." Cecelie's eyes shine, almost lustful.

Phoenix examines the blackened metal, trying to make out the pattern. Old, obviously, but valuable? How could the beads, so beautiful and delicate, be virtually worthless and this corroded *thing* be valuable? "What is it?" she asks more out of politeness than curiosity.

"A funerary necklace. Possibly from Moche royalty." There's that voice again. Cecelie is the born lecturer about this stuff, Phoenix thinks, wondering why she never gave up fieldwork to teach in a university. Then Cecelie's voice changes, the languor gone, replaced by something like passion but tinged with anger. "Nothing like El Viejo Señor de Sipán, I'm guessing—but then that's a once-in-several-lifetimes stroke of luck. But it is from an unexcavated tomb, at least according to the *huaquero* who found it. That asshole stumbles on what I've been looking for all my life and this is all that's left." Disgusted, she makes a sour face, her mouth as tight as if she's been sucking on something distasteful. "I asked that bastard . . . hell, I begged him, to take me to the site or at least map it. But all he wanted was to know what the *huacos* are worth. Not that it matters now."

"But he let you have all . . . this." Phoenix holds up an earring. Heavy and large as a saucer from a doll's tea set, she tries it against her ear. Cecelie shakes her head.

"Not there," she corrects. "Like this." Their fingers brush as Cecelie takes the earring, then holds it beneath her nose. She looks a little like Charlie Chaplin. "A nose ornament. A major fashion statement, at least if you were Moche." Carefully laying the ornament on the burled oak coffee table, Cecelie leans back, crossing her legs casually. "Rennie has the most elegant furniture. I'm used to living . . . well, not quite like this." She lights the last of a joint left over from last night and watches the smoke float toward the fireplace. When she turns back, Phoenix is looking at her, expectant. "Phoenix, the *huaquero* didn't *give* it to me." Cecelie's voice is quiet, almost sad. "I lied to him. Told him it was basically worthless, but that I'd run some tests. I thought if he didn't know what he had, he'd take me upriver to the site. But he never did. And without the site . . ." She spreads her hands, palm up. "You've got to understand, I needed to get at that tomb, before the bastard or another just like him stripped it clean."

"But the *huaquero*," Phoenix starts, then pauses, "What does that mean, anyway?"

"Grave robber."

A slight chill runs through Phoenix. Goose walking over your grave, TaTa Hassee always said. "Don't make such a face," Cecelie says. "They're not the good guys, either. They'll take bulldozers to a site when they can. Fortunately, in Peru bulldozers are damned hard to come by. As far as they're concerned, we're the real *huaqueros* because we don't belong there. Of course, our methods are considerably more refined, and our motives are righteous; at least that's what we tell ourselves."

"But he must have trusted you."

Cecelie arches her eyebrows. "Perhaps he did." She inhales deeply, and offers the joint to Phoenix, who shakes her head. "That was his second mistake." She exhales, studies the remains of the joint for a moment, and leans back. The afternoon sun catches the side of her face, leaving the rest in deep shadow.

"What was his first?"

"Greed." Cecelie answers without opening her eyes, without turning toward Phoenix, as if the topic has already lost interest. "The grave was north and far east of where I was working. Near the river. Typical Moche. But in a district the Senderistas control. They aren't known for having a high tolerance for outsiders. He must have gone back in. I guess this wasn't enough for him. And no matter what I said, he wasn't about to tell me where the site was, because then he'd get nothing. The government controls the sites, no matter who finds it. I'm trying to remember when I saw him last. September? August maybe. At any rate, I never saw him after that. So I ended up with *huaquos* and no site and he, I imagine, ended up with his head on a pole." Looking to Cecelie for some assurance that what she's just heard is not true, Phoenix blinks hard, trying to push the image out of her mind. Cecelie nods. "It's not like your world, Phoenix," she says gently. "I can't explain it, really, but . . . Look, if it had worked, it could have been so important; that's what you've got to understand. But it didn't. Besides, you said yourself Rennie needs money. Well, Phoenix, *this* is money."

Unable to contain her curiosity, Phoenix asks, "How much are they worth?" Her only dealings with antiques have been with Mr. Rizzo, the secondhand dealer. And these are way out of his league.

Cecelie shrugs, apparently relieved to have the conversation turn. "Hard to say. I have to clean them up and then find the right collector, but I'd guess enough to buy a happy ending. At least according to the dealer I was talking to, and that was sight unseen. By the way, where were you? I got off the phone and you were just . . . gone."

"Running. You said you didn't want to go." She tries to sound casual, but her mind is still on the dead *huaquero*. How could

Cecelie be so nonchalant about something so horrible? The world has changed them, leaving Cecelie hard and Phoenix terrified and Rennie . . . what? "Besides, when I came back, *you* were out. I wanted to take you down the coast to a place where they have calamari swimming in garlic sauce. I guess it's too late now." She attempts a smile.

"Do you really think so?" Cecelie sounds genuinely disappointed. "Well, maybe tomorrow. Aren't you going to ask where I went?"

To Gina, Phoenix thinks, but she says, "You don't owe me any explanations, Cecelie. You should come and go as you please. I mean, it's not like we're really lovers or anything."

Cecelie's eyes widen, "What is that supposed to mean?"

Phoenix shrugs. "Just that you don't owe me anything. No strings. That's all."

"Is that how you want it?" Cecelie is looking at her oddly. Phoenix nods and tucks her head into Cecelie's lap; her khaki shorts are smooth and warm. "It's better that way." Rising, she kisses Cecelie, whose lips are sticky and slightly sweet. Phoenix pulls back and smiles.

"I went to pick up the rolls," Cecelie says. "The store called and I thought we'd want them for breakfast. I had to try one to make sure it was good. It was."

"But I thought . . ."

"I *know* what you thought, Phoenix, or at least I think I do. Look, I've never been good at games and I don't have many secrets. There are no women waiting in the shadows. Maybe this will work out between us, maybe not, it's too early to tell, but there is one thing you need to know now: I'll never lie to you. That's the only thing I can promise, deal?"

Phoenix nods and lets Cecelie kiss her lightly. Jinx had said much the same thing, once. Love makes liars of us all. Cecelie smiles, content. "Gina specializes in matching artifacts to collectors. She thinks some guy in Japan may be interested, if my luck hasn't run out. Anyway, she'll call me when something happens. Speaking of phone calls, that guy never called back about the skylight, did he?" Phoenix shakes her head. "Well, maybe while we're gone. Do you really think it's too late to go down the coast for calamari? I'm starving."

Night sea air, heavy and damp, pushes into the room. They need to do something about the skylight. Put up plastic with weather-stripping, maybe, the way Villanova did every winter back home. Too late to do anything about it now. Tomorrow. They'll figure it all out tomorrow. They have plenty of time.

Teddy Grayson isn't smiling. She's supposed to be. Smiling. Or at least looking pleased. Long index fingers tap-tap into a peak. *This is the church, this is the steeple.* Savannah wasn't more than sixteen when she taught Phoenix that game. The next year she was gone, run away to Nashville with Croonin' Cliff Conklin. *Open the door and see all the people.* The note she left for Mama said that Cliff was going places. True enough. A man running out on a wife and two kids not yet out of diapers, and taking a high-school senior to Nashville, Tennessee, does appear to be going someplace; if Mama'd had her way, it would've been the state work farm. It took him eight years to marry Savannah, but just two more to leave her, right after his one and, as it would turn out, only record to make the charts was released. It would take Savannah two more tries to hit pay dirt matrimonially speaking, and then only after she'd moved back home, found a new husband and Jesus, in that order. So it goes. She sends Phoenix greeting cards, the kind that come eight to a box, with a picture of a sad-eyed Jesus. The message is always the same: We're praying for you. So that goes, too.

The psychiatrist does not pray for Phoenix, although her tone is the same as Savannah's, sharp and crisp and disapproving. Exasperated. "Phoenix, I want you to tell me again, just so that I can understand, why you believe you're falling in love with a woman you've known less than a month." Only just begun and already the session is going badly. Maybe they should start over, Phoenix thinks. Maybe she forgot something, some important little detail that will erase all those tight puckers on Teddy's lips, uncrinkle the inch or so of skin between her eyebrows, make her unfold her fingers or at least quiet the index fingers. Tap-tap, tap-tap. The thumbs don't get to tap. So much for nonjudgmental listening.

"Fifteen years," Phoenix corrects. That's right, isn't it? Twelve years since that summer in New York, but they'd actually met three years before when Cecelie first came to visit Rennie at Northwestern. Twelve plus three equals fifteen. Phoenix smiles. Teddy doesn't. The masks on the wall leer. "I think it's fate," Phoenix says with less conviction than she planned.

"Fate?" From her tone, Teddy Grayson obviously doesn't believe in fate. At least the fingers are quiet. "Why would you think that?"

Isn't it obvious, Phoenix thinks, but says nothing. Better to circle Teddy Grayson's therapist's trap. One wrong step and she'll tumble inside, then there's no way out except through a maze of trick questions designed to make her see more clearly. She doesn't want to see more clearly; seeing too clearly is what pushed her over the edge last time. She won't go there again. Phoenix struggles to right herself on the couch. Today, she's being the model patient. She folds her hands in her lap and smiles. "It's just that we've been thrown together after all these years. And now here we are." But instead of sounding buoyant, the words float like a sickly balloon across the six feet between patient and doctor. Plop.

"Yes, Phoenix, here we are." There's an almost imperceptible sigh, the tiniest pursing of the lips. "And what are Cecelie's plans? Does she intend to stay in California? Didn't you tell me that her work is in Peru?" Phoenix shrugs and picks at a bit of loose skin on her right thumb. Cecelie wants to go back to Peru; you can see it in her eyes. "It depends on the war."

Teddy Grayson nods; she's obviously aware of the unrest. Phoenix has the unsettling feeling that she is the only person in the world left out of the loop. "But her work is important to her."

Self-satisfied and a little smug, Teddy Grayson presses, "And what about you, Phoenix? Is it important to you?"

"I don't know anything about archaeology."

"I meant your plans." Oh, that. Phoenix shakes her head, studies the mask on the opposite wall. No plans, but no point in belaboring the obvious, no real future and no invitation to Peru, either. Not that Phoenix would know what to do in Peru, even if Cecelie asked. Probably not much need for advertising at archaeological sites. "Well, have you reached an agreement about ending this relationship when she goes back?" An agreement to end a relationship? Well, that would certainly be less bloody than how she and Jinx had finished off each other. Therapists probably actually do that, reach agreements; they're probably even friends later.

A small hangnail on Phoenix's right index finger is begging to be chewed off, but she doesn't dare. Any false move, any wrong step will send Teddy's fingers tapping again. "We haven't really talked about it," she says carefully.

"Where does that leave you, Phoenix?"

With the dangerous truth; that maybe what she has with Cecelie isn't love—but if not love, then what? Compatible neuroses masquerading as love. Phoenix looks at the floor. The therapist rustles in her chair, recrossing her legs, unlocking her face, refolding her hands. The afternoon sun paints the end of the room in shades of white and gold. She picks at the hangnail. A sliver of pain shoots through her. It feels blue. "I'm scared," Phoenix says after what seems like a long time. Her voice is surprisingly cool and bitter. "Scared of loving her, scared of not loving her, scared she won't love me . . . enough. I think we could be good together, not like it was with Jinx, but *really* good. Different. Better, you know?" But of course Teddy Grayson couldn't know. Teddy with her perfect life, perfectly ordered, perfectly executed. Women like Teddy Grayson don't lie awake nights ticking off their losses, their mistakes crowding around them. "But then how much worse could it be, considering Jinx wanted me dead? She actually asked me if I was planning to kill myself, as if I didn't wake up every morning praying for exactly that. I was a cat hanging on a blackboard by its claws. And the woman who was supposed to love me forever wanted me dead. And then one morning, I understood. It wasn't even because she hated me—I think I might have preferred that. No, she was just worried that I might get in the way of her goddamned honeymoon." From the street below, the dreadful sound of metal crashing floats up and through the closed window. A long, forlorn horn wails, a prelude to the inevitable cacophony of horns below, an off-key, out-of-synch chorus that rises in waves. The masks grimace at the sound, but of course it's only the way the light is falling.

"Phoenix, what did you want from Jinx?"

Stupid question. Phoenix steps to the window. A siren draws closer, settles beneath the window, where she watches, the lace curtains pulled back. Ambulance drivers dressed in white sweep up the remains, carry away the victims. Soon the street will be exactly as it was, no trace of mayhem. In another hour, no one will know what happened here. No one except the victims and the people who cleared away the debris. She lets the curtain fall. "To save me."

"Save you?" Teddy seems surprised. "Save you from what?"

"From myself," Phoenix all but whispers. "She was supposed to save me from myself."

"Three-thirty." Greedy as usual, Rennie now has everything from three o'clock covered. Legs drawn up under his chin, he crosses his arms and leans back, satisfied. He likes to win. Phoenix screws up her mouth, studies the board, and puts a dime on two forty-five, ten minutes from now. They're betting on when the retractable skylight will finally close. Lucas, the inventor, Cecelie and Doug, the boy who followed Rennie back from the writers' camp, have been on the roof for almost four hours.

"I don't care who wins, just so they get it done today," Phoenix says. "I'm tired of listening to the wind whistle through the plastic. At first it was romantic, but the last couple of nights some damned pigeon has decided to use it as a hammock. Makes me nervous. A bird in the house means . . ." She pauses and looks at Rennie. "It's just bad luck, or so TaTa Hassee said."

"A wild bird in the house means death," Rennie finishes curtly, adding another dime to the three-thirty box. "I had a superstitious old grandmother, too. You want some of this action?"

Phoenix shakes her head. She wouldn't have described TaTa Hassee that way, but of course it was true. Birds in the house. Crickets on the hearth. Cats and clovers and snakes and a liberal dose of "Save me, Lord Jesus!" She and Cecelie had tacked up the plastic over the open skylight the way Villanova had over the windows back home every fall, windows so loose in their sashes that the wind leaked through, even with the storm windows up. Keeping the warm inside, she always said, although the joke was on her; there was rarely any warmth in that house, and not enough plastic in the world to change that.

"How long did it take Lucas last time?" Lucas had taken nearly two weeks to call back, and the better part of another to actually arrive. Rennie shrugs. He either doesn't know, doesn't remember, or just doesn't give a damn. A stiff breeze ruffles the legs of his trousers. The Eugene O'Neill look, he calls it. Dressed in baggy putty-colored trousers, a white shirt with a blood-red bow tie under an argyle sweater vest, he looks either like O'Neill in his prime or a character in a Fitzgerald novel. How thin Rennie's become. Carson's gold watch dangles as loosely on his wrist as a bracelet. Polishing his round glasses, he looks up, smiling. He is a beautiful man.

Adjusting his glasses, his eyes fix on a pair of pigeons marching in time along the edge of Mrs. Chin's roof. One, neck puffed, chest full, head bob-bopping, struts behind another in a kind of courtship walk. "How do you know when pigeons do it?" Rennie squints behind the thick glasses he wears most of the time now that the contacts have started to bother his eyes.

"Do what?" Phoenix is listening to the banter on the roof. Maybe two forty-five isn't such a bad bet after all.

"You know: IT; sex; the big pigeon bang. I watch them and can never figure it out."

"Oh, that." Phoenix glances at Mrs. Chin's roof and shrugs. "Don't know. Maybe they don't, maybe it's all a show and they reproduce by parthenogenesis or something." That was very big with lesbians a few years back. Of course, like a lot of good ideas, it didn't work very well. "Supposedly there are lesbian sea gulls. Maybe there are lesbian pigeons."

153

"Oh, well now, Phoenix, that just doesn't make any sense at all. I mean how would that even work? What sane bird would want a beak up her butt?"

"Maybe it doesn't have anything to do with sex; maybe it's something else. You'd still be gay, wouldn't you, even without sex?"

"Highly unlikely. But you girls do things differently, or so I've heard, except for you, Phoenix Bay, you and Jinx probably did it right to the end." Not true, of course, but almost comforting to know the image they'd crafted so carefully remains intact, even now.

"You're right. That's how I knew it was over. First we stopped talking, *then* we stopped fucking." Phoenix turns to watch the pigeons, wondering why the one being pursued simply doesn't lift its wings and fly.

"What's so unusual about that?" His voice sounds bittersweet, but he smiles. "Sometimes there's not a whole lot left to say. Sometimes it's as if you've known someone your whole life and you don't have to say anything at all." She wonders if he means Doug, the itinerant dope grower, sometimes poet and parttime chef, who apparently had nothing better to do than drive to California with a man who, to his mind at least, looks like Eugene O'Neill and might, if Doug plays his cards right, make him famous. Phoenix has progressed from a casual distaste for the boy to avid dislike: how he so obviously hangs on Rennie's every word, how he unobtrusively begs for invitations to the parties that Rennie is no longer interested in attending, how he maneuvers conversations around to his slim and shallow poems that could have been written by a teenager. But then Doug, with his dirtyblond hair and chiseled good looks, seems little more than precocious teenager.

"You don't . . . care about Doug too much, do you? I mean, it's so soon, Rennie."

"Who's to say?" He smiles benignly and Phoenix is unsure whether he means the comment about caring or it being too soon. "After all, I'm on a very condensed timetable. Besides, how long did it take for you to fall in love with Cecelie?"

"I don't know that I am in love with Cecelie."

"Oh?" Rennie's left eyebrow cocks; he's the only person Phoenix has ever known who can actually do that, one eyebrow at a time. "Too bad. She's in love with you. I believe she calls it *soroche.*"

"That's altitude sickness, R.J."

He lifts one shoulder, a sort of half-shrug, and grins. "Well, you have to admit the symptoms *are* remarkably similar." He's never actually seen his sister in love, if that's what this is. She and Phoenix seem determined to call it anything but love. "Anyway, as the adage goes, Love is blind."

"Not to mention deaf and stupid. I believe that is your line." She starts to add "crazy," but the flash of Cecelie sleeping stops her. Cecelie isn't the one who's nuts, Phoenix reminds herself; she may not even be the one who's afraid of love. If only love weren't so seductive, with that throbbing, out-of-control feeling of being washed clean by another person, or if only that part could last forever. Instead it comes in waves: falling in love, then the inevitable destructive slide when it ends, a deadly downward spiral, not so different from madness. Every night with Cecelie, she's less sure she'll be able to avoid it. Some subjects are too dangerous even to think about. "Will you have any new tapes for me to work on this weekend?" All Rennie brought back from camp were two tapes, mostly filled with meandering thoughts, and he hasn't done much since camp . . . or since Doug. Six of one, half a dozen of the other.

He shakes his head. "I'm blocked."

"You're not blocked, you're distracted." She's guessing but from his look, she's hit the truth. "And what's worse, I think you like being distracted. Is he at least that good in bed?"

Rennie seems to consider this for a moment, then looks at Phoenix and smiles. "Unfortunately, no. But his other attributes make up for it. He's plotting to woo Mrs. Chin with sweet rolls. We've got to do something; this morning she threatened to call the humane society."

Mrs. Chin's calls have increased lately to two, sometimes three a day. "She just hates peacocks, what can I tell you? Maybe we *should* take the damned thing to the zoo." Phoenix has grown to dislike the bird, too, his loud and plaintive cries sound too much like a woman in pain. Some things are better left unheard. "Or we could eat him."

"*Eat* Marcel Proust?" Rennie's voice escalates in campy horror. "That truly is sick, Phoenix, although it wouldn't be a bad title for a short story. Speaking of . . . Doug has some ideas about a new ending for 'The Truck Stop Jock Does Vegas.' He thinks it could lead to a sequel."

"Just what the literary world is waiting for." Sarcasm, she decides, is a rare and wonderful talent. "Shall I alert the Pulitzer committee or should we just wait and surprise them?"

"Oh, hell, Phoenix, he's only trying to help out."

"With what? The Jock going to Vegas? Who cares, Rennie? Who cares if he goes into outer space and fucks aliens?" She's not sure if she means the Jock or Doug, which at the moment would be fine with her, too.

"I don't know why you're being so difficult." Rennie has obviously decided to ignore her pique. "I'm supposed to be the temperamental artiste in this family." Rennie tips his head back to get the sun's full benefit. "Besides, Doug has potential."

"To do what? Ride on your coattails? That's why he's here, you know." She's sorry as soon as the words are said. Rennie has been happy with Doug here. Maybe he does hope that some of Rennie's fame, however much is still left, will rub off. And what would that really hurt if it did? Unless he breaks Rennie's heart, or worse, sends him back to the place where he was when Carson was dying: lost and alone and terrified. What difference does it make if the boy has about as much talent as that puffed-up pigeon, if he makes Rennie feel alive? "I'm sorry," she says, reaching out and stroking Rennie's forearm lightly. "I just don't want to see you get hurt."

"I'm a big boy. And I don't need my little mamas to protect me." Phoenix winces. Little mamas? Is that what he thinks of her and Cecelie? In one slow and yet still nearly fluid movement, he rises from the deck. He and Cecelie share an elegant grace that would have better suited dancers. He bends, bracing his hands on his knees. "Damned arthritis. I feel like I'm a thousand years old. They should warn you about this."

They, of course, are his doctors, mostly despised, often discounted, and generally considered personally responsible for his every ache. He still blames them for Carson's death. If only they'd known what it was sooner, even though at the time there was nothing: no drugs, no treatment, no cure. A newsletter clipping over his desk promises more: *Experimental PML Treatment Results Good.* In the margin, Rennie's note: "Too little, too late." "Do you have any Ibuprofen up here?"

"In the nightstand." The same prescription Phoenix has for menstrual cramps is what the doctors have prescribed for Rennie's arthritis. Sisters under the skin. "But don't take them without eating; it'll fuck up your stomach. There are Cokes in the refrigerator and cheese and crackers." Bless Carson for thinking to install that small convenience up here. Rennie comes back to the deck and eases onto the chair next to her, putting a small pile of Oreo cookies between them. Oreo cookies will upset his stomach and the Coke, which might settle it, apparently didn't appeal to him. He twists the cap off a bottle of Calistoga water. "What about your innards, R.J.? Playing kind of fast and loose aren't you?"

"Innards?" He draws out the word. "I do love your folksy phrases, Phoenix." He chuckles and lifts the bottle. "Cookie?" He drops a pair into her hand.

"Aren't you afraid they'll make you sick?"

"I'll take my chances." So much like Cecelie. "Besides, I'm already sick, and damned tired of hearing about the state of my innards, as you so colorfully call them." He twists off the top of the cookie and licks out the white cream. Little rituals. "Carson loved these things. Whenever we went to Mexico, he'd buy up a couple dozen of those minipacks with, I don't know, a half-dozen cookies in them. The humidity made the big packages soft or soggy or something. That time Cecelie brought Mala up, he turned the kid into an Oreo junkie. Drove C.C. nuts. She couldn't find them anywhere in Peru. Carson even tried mailing them once, but they never made it through customs. Even when he was in the hospital, before those last few weeks, he kept reminding me that we had to get Oreo cookies for Mala when she came. Sometimes I like to think they're maybe out there somewhere, Carson and Mala, eating Oreos. At least I hope so. Any number of angels would probably want to take care of a kid, but frankly I'm not sure how many of our friends made it to paradise. I like to think he has someone to play with and Mala has someone to look out for her."

"Cecelie never talks about her." Phoenix nibbles around the edge of the cookie, careful not to touch the center, saving the best for last. Cecelie's almost religious silence about her daughter has been so complete that, except for Rennie's few comments, Phoenix could forget the child had ever existed. If it weren't for the *chaquira* Cecelie never removes, which Phoenix suspects more than she knows has something to do with Mala, the child is as unreal as a shadow on a movie screen.

"I'm not surprised." Rennie leans back. "You have to understand that to our mother, the past was irrelevant. No matter what, you never looked back. The best, as the song says, was yet to come. Cecelie's great irony is that she spends her life in the past and yet refuses to acknowledge her own." He drains the last of the Calistoga water. "How much longer until you lose, Phoenix?"

"Seven minutes until three o'clock. It's all yours after that."

He grins. "Good. You lose and I'm rich. I'm saving up for a Ferrari. How much do you suppose this bottle is worth?" He turns and winks at Phoenix, then tips his head back at the sound coming from the roof. "Break time!" Rennie shouts toward the ladder, "Come on down!" He sounds like the host on one of Gran Cicero's television game shows, calling contestants out of the audience; sometimes she would sit on the edge of her footstool, twitching, as if she expected to be called next. First Doug, followed by Cecelie, and finally Lucas himself drops from the ladder onto the deck. Of the three, only Cecelie acknowledges Phoenix, and brushes a light kiss near the top of her head.

"I stink," she says, drawing back, when Phoenix tries to pull her closer. "It's hot up there." Wiping her face with her shirttail, she leans back against the railing. "Luke thinks it's ready to roll." So Rennie may not win, after all.

Lucas Walker strides across the room to the control panel. Large and burly, he reminds Phoenix of the men from home: big-shouldered, broad-backed, with huge hands and a full red beard that makes him always look as if he's smiling, even when he's not. But he's smiling now, as the motor deep in the wall engages and the skylight moves forward, without a creak or a groan. "Yes!" he booms, fist up, as if the home team had just scored the winning touchdown. "I knew you could do it, baby." He's talking to the skylight, Phoenix realizes, amused by this big man's naiveté.

"Smooth as fucking silk." Lucas Walker's voice bounds across the picnic table in the backyard, where they're having a late lunch. "Now your problem, as I was telling Don here . . ."

"Doug."

"Sorry. Doug. As I was telling Doug here, your problem is corrosion. You see it all the time by the ocean. Now, I got it worked out on the A-18, that's my new model. I just put a couple dozen of those babies in a housing development on Maui—that's where I was when you called; or did I say that already?" Cecelie and Doug nod; Phoenix and Rennie look at him blankly. Obviously Hawaii was a major topic on the roof. "Now, to be honest, I don't expect so much as a whimper from them. That's because one night I was sleeping and all of a sudden it hit me. Sleeves." Phoenix and Cecelie exchange amused looks. Doug looks bored. Only Rennie appears interested.

"Sleeves," echoes Rennie.

"Damned right! Sleeves. Woke me up from a sound sleep. Right then, I knew my troubles was over." Lucas sinks his big, white teeth into the side of his third turkey sandwich. A few crumbs catch on his mustache and bounce up and down while he chews. Marcel Proust draws close to Lucas and fans his tail. "Now, that's one damned fine bird." Lucas tears off a bit of bread and tosses it toward the peacock. "Wouldn't mind one of them myself. Where'd you say you got him?" The bird, rarely known to eat table scraps, shamelessly pecks at the crumb.

"Carson brought him down from the Humboldt County project." Rennie's eyes are fixed on Lucas, or maybe fascinated by the crumbs in his beard that keep moving up and down.

"That a fact? Whatever happened to that project? I approached Carson about putting Light Walkers in up there, but I never could convince him they'd be a selling point. He thought it was too far north. But, like I always say, you never know what'll tickle somebody's fancy."

"The company still owns the land, but the project is on hold." Absently, Rennie pokes at his untouched potato salad with his fork.

"Damned shame about Carson. Couldn't believe it when I heard. He was one of my first customers. That A-14 of yours is the very first Light Walker installed in San Francisco. Bet you didn't know that." He turns to Cecelie and grins, his voice confidential, "See, the A-14 was really number thirteen out of the chute, but my partner said nobody'd buy something that had a bad-luck number attached to it. They'd think it would never work right. What do you think?"

"I think that explains a lot," Cecelie says.

Lucas seems to consider this, then goes back to chewing for a moment. "So that makes the A-18, the new model I was telling you about, really number seventeen. Go figure. Now, I could put one of them in for you, but I got to tell you, Rennie, she'll cost you. I'd give you a deal, because of Carson and all, but I'd still have to make up my costs. You understand?"

"The one we have is fine, Lucas. We hardly ever need it out here by the ocean." Phoenix notices he doesn't mention that the development company owns this house.

"I know what you mean." Lucas nods. The look is the same one that Midwestern farmers wear when they survey their crops in spring, weighing advantage to reality. "Now on Maui, it gets so damned hot, they're grateful to have the Light Walker. Especially at night. Never seen so many happy people in my life. I told my partner, I think we ought to relocate."

"Especially now that you've discovered sleeves," says Doug, his eyes glint, cruel and amused. He's the bright boy tormenting the playground dullard.

"Damned right," says Lucas, missing or ignoring the sarcasm. "Why there's whole sections of this country sweltering. It truly would be a kindness to give them a chance at the Light Walker. You get what you give, as I always tell my partner."

"Tell me, Lucas, who is your partner?" Phoenix pushes the bowl of potato salad across the table and watches as Lucas, sinking the spoon into the salad, comes up with a small mountain that drops onto his plate. Plop.

"M.M. and I," says Lucas, taking a mouthful. Confused, Phoenix shakes her head. "Me, Myself, and I," Lucas says, between chews. "The only bad idea he ever came up with was the name. And that's a story in itself." Lucas looks around the table, waiting for a sign of encouragement to go on with what he obviously considers to be a fascinating anecdote. Phoenix paints a subtle smile on her face. She likes to hear him talk; he reminds her of a world she left behind a long time ago. He grins and wipes his mouth with a napkin, freeing the crumbs. "See, it was supposed to be Luke's *Sky* Walker." Midswallow, Doug chokes on his beer and coughs, until Rennie thumps his back. "It was a natural, because of my last name being Walker and my first being Lucas and it being a skylight. Had the truck painted in what you might call an outerspace theme. Next thing I know, I get a letter from Mr. George Lucas's lawyers, saying they're going to sue me. For using my own name. Can you believe it? Didn't seem right. Not at all." Lucas shakes his head sadly.

"Why?" asks Cecelie.

"Cecelie, for God's sake—Luke *Skywalker?*" Doug chokes out the words. Cecelie shakes her head. *"Star Wars?"* He prompts, starting to laugh. Cecelie shrugs, still confused. Lucas looks wounded.

"Luke Skywalker is a famous movie character, Cecelie," Phoenix whispers.

"My sister has been out of the country for several years, Lucas."

"Oh," is all Lucas Walker says. "So I called it the Light Walker." He abruptly pulls back from the table. Doug's response must have hurt, and he, still chuckling, hasn't even noticed. "Well, I got to be going; it's a long drive back down the coast. Thanks for everything, Rennie. You change your mind about the upgrade, you let me know. And if ever want to sell that bird, I'd give you a fair price." He shoots Doug a cold look as he climbs the stairs to the house.

After Rennie and Lucas have disappeared into the house, Phoenix turns to Doug. "Was that really necessary? To humiliate him?" Her voice is low and cold.

"What did I do?" the boy whines, widening his eyes, trying to suck her in. "Luke's *Sky* Walker? What did he expect?" Cecelie eyes him coldly and Doug senses he's lost an ally. "Well, I, for one, think it's damned funny, even if you ladies—oops, I mean *women*—don't. Now, I think I'll go see if Rennie needs anything." As Doug retreats, Phoenix is struck by how sparse he is: the way the skin seems to pull too tightly across his high cheekbones, his light hair, the thin shoulders, and long arms which end in the hands of a pianist or of a poet. Doug would like that, being thought of as resembling a poet.

"What do you really think of our young friend, there?" Phoenix asks.

Cecelie pauses, considering. "That he's not as young as he seems."

"Yes, but is he as dangerous as he seems?"

Cecelie sinks back down into a chair. Her skin, pale from the thin sun, glows. "I hope not. And I'm not sure he's dangerous. Rennie likes having him here, and that's important. Maybe we're just . . . jealous."

"Maybe," Phoenix agrees, although she is unconvinced. Maybe Cecelie is right, maybe they are jealous, but not just of Doug. They are jealous more of the untended minutes that seem to be sliding away. Phoenix is struck that Doug knows Rennie in ways she and even Cecelie never will and that saddens her. In another week, maybe two, Doug will go back to wherever he's from, taking his poems and a little part of Rennie. She won't be able to stop him and doesn't know if she would even if she could. She tears a bit of crust from her almost-untouched sandwich and tosses it toward Marcel Proust, who eyes her suspiciously and struts away, tail dragging regally behind.

11

Cecelie Johnson's right nipple is alert. "Looking lonely to me," Phoenix says wrapping her lips around it, leaving traces of Odyssey Red lipstick.

"Don't you ever get tired of that?" Cecelie holds her lover's tangle of hair, in case the answer is yes. No one has ever before paid this much attention to her body, which she considers strong but not sexy.

Surfacing, Phoenix leans back, rearranging the disheveled bits of black lace and pink ribbons clinging to her midriff, her breasts swaying slightly, pale and sweetly eager to be noticed. Cecelie smiles. Every night, Phoenix produces from a box in the back of the closet some new fluff of fantasy: lace and satin and leather and silk. "You want me to stop? We could always do something else."

Endlessly creative in their love making, Phoenix's ideas have taken them to lonely stretches of beach in the late afternoon ("Not here, Phoenix; what if somebody comes?" "Oh, I imagine *some* body will."); furtive and breathless, to a tangle of damp grass and brush off the narrow paths that wind between the two old windmills in the park (the gay men cruising there had politely averted their eyes, amused); to the last row of a theater, which had promised On Stage, Live Lesbians ("Better than dead ones," Phoenix had observed) but had delivered a pair of straight women, one waggling an admittedly very long tongue in the general vicinity of the other; and then last weekend, to the lesbian sex club where Phoenix had jumped up when a woman with spiked hair and a chain connecting a pair of rings through her nose with one in her right eyebrow had announced a tattoo contest (amazingly, the tiger had lost, but not before a half dozen women had petted it—one offering to feed it raw meat; Phoenix only laughed).

Unwatched, the television cranks out a stream of sports shows, one of the many luxuries in this house: like the electric pencil sharpener, the microwave oven, Carson's CD player, R.J.'s laptop computer, endless rivers of hot water, soft toilet paper, flour you don't have to sift twice, ice cubes that the freezer creates on its own, five different kinds of soda pop, and Phoenix, a dangerous luxury in herself. Aliens, all waiting to be appreciated just for their very existence. Or perhaps she is the alien. On the screen, a pickup truck, looking like a toy on huge tires, rolls over a row of cars. A rotund-voiced announcer wails, "Monsters on the rampage! Like nothing you've ever seen!"

"Well, now, I wouldn't be takin' any bets on that," Phoenix shoots back at the screen, her voice tinged with the worst of her country upbringing. Sometimes, when she's excited or very tired, the past seeps through, slow and thick, only to have her snatch back the twang as soon as she notices. Other times, like these, she dredges it up purposely for a laugh.

"Have you ever been to anything like that?"

"Oh, hell, yes." Leaning back on her haunches, she stretches for the remote control at the far end of the bed. "Williamson County was a regular cultural oasis. Stock car races every Saturday night, unless one of the really tony events was in town, like a mud sling. And, of course, we can't forget hitching rides to the county dump to watch the boys shoot rats—providing nothing else was in season. And you California girls thought you had it good." To outsiders, Phoenix Bay was raised in the American dream: a land showing a peaceful, provincial face of uncomplicated people and simple desires far outside the reach of city horrors; of unlocked doors and ice cream socials and band concerts in the park; of Main Street and Sunday morning church services in the red shadows cast by a stained-glass Jesus; of sweat and hard work and harder regrets. It was, in truth, a land with unmentioned but never-forgotten secrets and nowhere, ever, to run or to hide; a place where there is no forgiveness, only tolerance and long memories and fear.

Untangling herself from Cecelie, Phoenix shifts to the foot of the bed, where she sits cross-legged, aiming the remote control at the television, channel surfing. She settles on MTV, where a woman dressed in a fuchsia pink body suit is flying around the world. "I always hated it there. Mama says it gets in your blood so you have to go back. Of course, they don't want me back. Good thing. I'm a city girl now." Phoenix Bay has spent her entire adult life in cities, partly because she's a lesbian, mostly because she imagines cities afford more hiding places, more tolerance. Easier to disappear in a place where fear fogs the night, where tension and tempers crack and cackle like sputtering neon. Easier to find forgiveness.

164

Cecelie stretches out long on the bed, and settles her head in Phoenix's lap. The setting sun paints the room in shades of gold, and the colors make her heart quicken. Her eyes ride the edge of the sky, an outlaw watching the horizon. Here, we're all outlaws, she decides, and refugees and merry widows. That's what the thing Phoenix has on is called. Cecelie knows this without being told. Mona used to wear those, too: black lace and tiny ribbons, but red, never pink. Fingering the lace, tasting the skin inside Phoenix's open thighs, sweet and golden, the word *wicked* flashes across Cecelie's mind. "Wicked child," that's what Mona had called her the night she found Cecelie crouched inside the closet, the door open no more than a crack, watching her mother and . . . who? Mickey? Silver Eddy? Or one of the nameless shadow men, who arrived late at night and were always gone by morning? It wasn't the first time she'd watched, heard her mother laughing, always laughing at first, followed by the inevitable sob and crash of sighs; it would be the last time she was so careless, edging against the door to better see her mother (never the man— hairy and hard, sharp edges and paunch exposed like the underbelly of a dying fish), soft and beautiful in the streetlight shadows, streaks of neon turning her pale flesh pink, then blue, then pink again. "What the hell are you doing? How dare you spy on me?" And the man laughing, his voice following Cecelie's shame all the way into the living room, where she slept on the roll-away bed. Her bedroom's walls were an old-fashioned dressing screen, a prop from "Bonanza." Mona had played a saloon girl in a couple of episodes, not even a speaking part. They don't just give away props to bit players. Who had Mona fucked to get it? The prop man? The assistant to the assistant director? That screen was one of her mother's proudest possessions and now Cecelie can't remember what happened to it. But she remembers Mona's breasts that night, pale and full, how the lace ruffles tickled when she leaned over Cecelie: "If you ever do anything like this to me again, you'll pay."

The far end of Carson's captain's-quarters room is painted in green shadows from the television, which cranks out a series of silent black-and-white images. Stretching up from the bed, Phoenix pads noiselessly and naked across the room to the chair, leans across Cecelie's back, nuzzles her neck. On the screen a woman with too-blond hair extends a cigarette waiting for a light. The woman's dress drapes low across deep cleavage. "You can turn up the sound," Phoenix says. Cecelie doesn't answer, but doesn't object when Phoenix settles on the floor between her legs. Resting her cheek against Cecelie's left knee, Phoenix reaches for the remote control.

"Don't bother, I know the story." Cecelie drops her hand, petting Phoenix's hair.

"So, how does it end?" Stroking Cecelie's thigh, her nails make little trails through soft flesh, softer hair. A night breeze stirs against the curtains, like ghosts sighing.

"She keeps selling herself to the highest bidder, but he's always married or a jerk or a gambler—she especially likes gamblers. Some of them try to fuck her little girl, but even she won't put up with that. She takes everything else, though. She thinks she's tough, but she's really just stupid. Everybody knows the truth but her: Nobody wants her and all she has left are dreams that are never going to come true. The end."

"What happens to the little girl?" Phoenix watches the woman on the screen back herself into a corner, then drop to her knees while a man—ominous, you can tell by the hat—levels a revolver toward her beautiful chest. Her mouth forms the word *No*. Too late; the gun recoils. Wide eyes plead with the camera. She crumples.

"The little girl? Why, nothing. Nothing happens to her at all." The camera zooms in closer to the body, until the frame is filled with the folds of her dress, white satin probably, but hard to tell; nobody has bothered to colorize this film. In a moment the credits will begin. Cecelie reaches for the remote control, but not before her mother's name rolls into the top of the screen. "Mona took me to see this movie twenty-seven times. My job was to sit on the bench across from the popcorn stand, while she hung around the lobby, waiting for somebody to recognize her. Sometimes they did. If not, I was supposed to run up while there were people around and say, 'Look! It's Mona Morgan!' She used to coach me on how to say it; 'A little more lilt in your *Look* she'd say." Cecelie inhales slowly. "I found this in with Rennie's other tapes." She sounds more curious than angry, although with Cecelie it's sometimes difficult to tell. Jinx did that too, hiding behind her eyes. "He taped it off some late show. So, Mona made it to video after all. She'd be pleased." The VCR whirs anxiously, a high-pitched whine.

Pulling on one of Carson's robes, loose and long, Phoenix pads out onto the deck. Here at the shore, the stars seem to hang closer, clear and crisp and never-ending: Venus, Mars, and there, the Big Dipper, huge and easily defined. Back home on summer nights, Phoenix would sometimes take her sleeping bag onto the porch, where she would fall asleep trying to count the stars. Every night she had to start over; it never occurred to her that the task itself was impossible. Instead, she felt like a failure, night after night, falling asleep before she was done.

"A kiss for your thoughts." Cecelie snuggles close. In the reflection from the door, they look a little like grossly dissimilar Siamese twins.

"What happened to a penny?"

"No pockets." Cecelie nuzzles Phoenix's neck. "So what are you thinking about?"

"Nothing . . . just counting stars." From here a few fires dot the beach like stationary fireflies—college kids and surfers playing out the night, waiting for dawn. Phoenix sees them sometimes when she runs, yellow wetsuits gleaming against the waves. The moon reflects against the water, painting the beach in a soft, eerie light, some nights bright enough to cast shadows, forcing the night walkers to avert their eyes; privacy is precious at the edge of an angry city.

"You should see the stars at Tres Cruces." Cecelie leans back, the way a child might. "Sometimes they're so close you think you could reach out and grab one. And in the spring, there's this fantastic sunrise that goes on for hours. Last year I took Mala up. Blew us both away. And Rennie was all the time thinking she was deprived because I never took her to Disneyland. I guess he thinks I was a pretty lousy mother. Maybe he's right."

Phoenix reaches out and squeezes Cecelie's hand. "I'm sure you were a fine mother. You did more for her than . . ." She starts to say more than anybody else would. Maybe just more than Phoenix herself would do, taking in the daughter of a guerrilla when Pikimachay became too violent and the child's father was sent to jail. Mala's mother wanted to save her daughter from the violence.

"I wanted Nayla to come north with us," Cecelie says, although Phoenix hasn't asked. "But she wouldn't. Couldn't. I suppose she had her reasons. I heard later that the village she'd gone to had disappeared and then Carlos was killed in prison. I never told Mala about her parents. I thought . . . when she was older, I would. The way things were, it seemed the less she knew, the less anyone knew, the safer she would be. Her father was brave and brilliant. I would have told her that, and her mother was a fighter. They loved her. We all loved her." Cecelie pulls the comforter around her and looks out into the night. From this distance, the fires on the beach could just as easily be burning in the street outside La Fortaleza. Ayacucho was no longer safe. The next morning, Nayla would go into the countryside, to her grandmother's village. She could continue her husband's work there, until he could join her, until they could send for Mala, who would be safe in the north with Cecelie. That night they had stayed together at the Santa Rosa, the only hotel with hot water in town. Mala had laughed with a toddler's glee at having two women as her own private audience while her mother bathed her in the sink. The next morning on their way to the airport, Nayla had sung Quechua lullabies. Mala, her black eyes shining with the thought of adventure, kept struggling to free herself from her mother's hold. At the airstrip, the soldiers had stared curiously, but hadn't stopped them. "Wave bye-bye," Cecelie had said in English because English made Mala giggle uncontrollably, as if Cecelie were making up nonsense rhymes. "Bye-bye?" the baby had repeated, trying out the strange sounds. Cecelie started to jog across the runway, when a glaring soldier, not much older than a boy, raised his rifle. Walk, never run. Cecelie slowed and walked slowly. At the steps leading into the plane, she'd turned back to wave. "God go with you," she'd called to the woman standing at the gate. Nayla made no sign that she'd heard.

"Phoenix, we need to talk." Cecelie wipes her hands carefully, pushing down each cuticle. Satisfied, she folds the towel and raises herself up onto the kitchen counter, and smiles. "There's something I need to tell you."

Phoenix's throat catches. Those words always portend disaster: Daddy leaving; Molly moving to another room; and Jinx, the night she had come home, wearing her intentions in her eyes. So, Cecelie has made her decision. She won't be staying. She'll go back this week or the next or the one after. Her work is waiting in Peru, and Rennie is stable. Will she say, "This doesn't mean I don't care about you" or "We can still be friends, of course"? Of course. The way Phoenix and Jinx are friends. The way Jinx still cares about her, when she bothers to think of her at all. "So, talk," Phoenix says slowly, grateful the catch in her throat doesn't betray itself in her voice.

"I need to go to Hawaii." Cecelie ducks her head a little to the side.

"What?" Phoenix asks, as if she hasn't heard right.

"Hawaii. I need to go there. And I . . . thought maybe the travel agency account . . . well, maybe you could get me a cheap flight. I hate to ask, but Gina needs me to come there."

Pushing down the jealousy that surfaces whenever Cecelie mentions Gina, with the smoky voice and the late-night telephone calls, Phoenix nods. "Why not? They've offered them to damned near everybody at the agency. Want some company?"

"Sorry, babe, not this time." Blinking hard, Phoenix turns away. Cecelie will go to Hawaii and then what is there to stop her from going on to Peru? Nothing. Nothing at all. And even if the war keeps her from going back there, nothing will stop her from leaving. Still, for a woman running off to paradise Cecelie doesn't look happy. But, then, neither had Jinx the night she'd run away. Guilt. Phoenix brings that out in women. "We'll go together next time," Cecelie says.

169

Phoenix exhales, and attempts a smile. Never let them see tears. "Sure," she says, "next time. So tell me about Gina—I mean, have you known her a long time?"

Cecelie looks at her oddly, as if she's trying to decide where this conversation will lead or how much to tell. "A long time? Yes, I suppose so. There's not all that much to tell. You might find her interesting. She's very, well, worldly, I guess." Worldly. Yes, she would be. "I don't know exactly how long I'll be gone," Cecelie is saying, "It depends on what happens." Cecelie is rubbing her forehead the same way Rennie does when he worries: back and forth, thumb massaging the spot above the bridge of his nose. He does that most often lately when the conversation turns to money. All those years with Carson lulled him into complacency. "If you can't get the tickets, there are always Carson's frequent flier coupons. If I can convince Rennie it's for a good cause." She sounds doubtful. "There are two Japanese collectors interested in the *huacos*. But I have to go there; that way if anything goes wrong, it's all on me. Gina's shrewd."

"In her business, it's probably essential." So, Cecelie has found a buyer for the jewelry. And Phoenix had imagined Cecelie was—what? not joking, but not exactly serious about the pieces being worth anything, certainly about them being dangerous. Those blackened pieces of contraband seem benign, like the marijuana plants. Hard to think of any of it as contraband. But as Doug says, "Contraband is a necessary commodity." Doug once spent nine months in a county jail for growing dope in a barn; his partner never even went to trial. "Shit happens," Doug says. He and the ex-partner are still friends.

"I'll be glad to get them out of here. Having them makes me feel dirty," Cecelie admits, though Phoenix hasn't asked. "Maybe I should turn them in, take my chances. I could say they were passed to me here in the States. They might believe that."

"That's crazy, Cecelie. They'd never believe that. Besides, what good would that do anybody?" The money from the house in Mexico won't last much longer, already spent on Rennie's medicine and doctor bills. And who knows how much worse it will get? They hear him throwing up in the early morning and prowling the house at night. Afternoons he spends on the couch in his office, dictating into his tape recorder and napping fitfully. Evenings Doug reads him pages edited the day before and takes down Rennie's changes. Sometimes they argue. Doug isn't afraid to argue with Rennie, isn't afraid that a difference of opinion will kill him. No real history there. He isn't afraid of losing Rennie the way she and Cecelie are.

"I just wish there were another way to do it. You know?"

Phoenix nods and buries her head in Cecelie's shoulder. She smells like coffee and peppermint soap. "Just do what you've got to do, Cecelie. That's all any of us can manage."

Morning rattles the city awake for another Sunday, and Phoenix Bay opens her eyes, finally. She's been awake for hours, her eyes firmly, defiantly closed, as if the appearance of sleep would be enough to entice the real thing. The clock radio is playing one of Tracy Chapman's songs about futile love. There should be some comfort in knowing even the rich and famous ones can't get it right all the time, either.

In sleep, Cecelie turns toward her, and Phoenix stiffens. They have been sleeping together for a moon cycle, an anniversary of sorts, but nobody says I love you. Phoenix Bay wants it to matter less than it does. Love is dangerous, too dangerous to think about now, when there's already so much to think about. In two weeks, Cecelie is going to Hawaii, without any indication of when she'll be back—or even if she'll be back, although Cecelie says otherwise. Either way, Phoenix will stay here with Rennie, unless he tosses her out in favor of Doug. No chance of that, Rennie assures her. At least for now, she thinks.

So far her fledgling career in advertising consists of two clients: The Sunspert Specialists and an art gallery. That campaign is going badly. The gallery's manager is afraid to make a decision and the owner is on an extended medical leave. In this city men who take extended leaves of absence rarely return. At least The Sunspert Specialists are easy, dependable, like the job. She is the go-between for the clients and the creative department. Back and forth. A translator in the language of want. Snuggling close to Cecelie, Phoenix closes her eyes, just for a moment, she promises herself, then she'll get up and go running with Doug.

Phoenix awakens with a start to the sound of Rennie's "Rise and shine, ladies!" coming up the stairs, followed by the warm smell of bread baking. Cecelie groans and curls her pillow under her chin the way a child might cuddle a teddy bear and falls back asleep. No anxiety there. Phoenix turns back to her own side of the bed, careful not to wake Cecelie, who likes making love early in the morning. No games, no excitement, just warm and soft and easy. Love being easy could take some getting used to, Phoenix decides, sticking first one leg, then the other out from beneath the covers. Chilly, but not altogether uncomfortable.

"Good morning, darling. Did I wake you?" Rennie is smiling as she stumbles into the kitchen. Since Doug's arrival, he's been almost giddy in the mornings. Shaking her head, she looks at Rennie and smiles sleepily. "Here, have a sweet roll. Doug's secret recipe. He's next door wooing Mrs. Chin. She just loves Doug's buns."

"I'm glad he's good for something."

"What brought on such a fine humor and so early in the morning? Did my sister keep her legs crossed last night, or worse, her hands to herself?"

"Hardly." Settling next to Rennie at the tiny table, she pokes at one of Doug's sweet rolls. Cinnamon and crusts of sugar frosting stick to her fingers. Hard to imagine Doug as a pastry chef, everything about him is so spare. "I was having the strangest dream— something about being back home. I guess smelling the rolls baking brought it out." She picks up the sweet roll, still warm; the goo settles thickly on the back of her tongue.

"It happens. The past lurks odiously close to the surface." Rennie grins. "However, these are guaranteed to sweeten even the most dour in the morning. Look at me."

Phoenix sniffs the roll suspiciously. "And no wonder. Rennie, these things are full of pot. Where'd Doug learn to bake? The Alice B. Toklas school of culinary arts? I think these things are making you balmy."

"Oh, I hope so. Those and the joy of love in bloom. That's the title of some old torch song, I believe. Sex, cinnamon rolls, and a secret garden. What more could a man need? By the way, Doug thinks we'll be ready to harvest in a couple more weeks. Life is good."

"We aren't going to be ready to harvest for another month at least. Speaking of, where did Doug get the stash for these rolls?"

"For God's sake, Phoenix, he brought it with him. So you can relax—it's not yours." Exasperated, he pushes the newspaper toward her. "Here, read. Cheer yourself up. There's even half a column about Cecelie's war in Peru. I'm saving it for her."

"How intriguing, my own war," Cecelie says from the doorway. "Cinnamon rolls?"

"Fresh from the oven, courtesy of our pastry chef in residence. Phoenix and I were just discussing the recipe." Cecelie accepts Rennie's dry lips on her cheek, before picking up the paper.

"How are you supposed to tell anything from this?" Cecelie is trying to read the tiny map, no larger than a stamp, next to the article. She rattles the paper, as if more news will shake loose.

Phoenix swallows the sweet roll slowly, feels it catch. Something always catches when Cecelie mentions Peru. "It's probably not too bad or the story would be larger," she offers, although she knows that isn't true. Poor South American countries rarely merit more than a mention on the international news pages.

"I think we should listen to Phoenix." Cecelie looks skeptically at her brother. "Besides, my darling sister, everything works out the way it's supposed to, just not the way you necessarily think it should. Coffee?" Rennie winks at Phoenix, who manages a smile against Cecelie's scowl. "Okay, I promise, we'll watch the *noticias* this evening." Rennie seems to find his sister's frustration amusing. "Cecelie is the only person I know who would take a war personally. I've waited years to get her back to the States, provide her with all the comforts of home, even a playmate, and now that she's here, where it's safe and—thanks to Luke the Sky Walker— even warm, all she's interested in is war." He ruffles Cecelie's hair. "What *are* we going to do with you? Must big brother send you to your room . . . with Phoenix, of course, to teach you a lesson?" Phoenix blushes and averts her eyes.

173

"Love me for what I am, I guess," Cecelie says grudgingly, as the phone starts to ring. "I'll get it. It's probably Gina."

"Cecelie's going to Hawaii, Rennie. She probably told you."

"To sell the *huacos?* Yeah." Rennie is reading the editorial page. He starts with the front page and methodically works his way through. "I offered her Carson's mileage coupons, but she said the trip was already taken care of." He sounds relieved.

"She feels guilty about selling the *huacos."* Phoenix picks at the sweet roll, wishing Doug would come back so they could go running. At least he's good for that.

"I don't know why this time should be different," Rennie observes. "Look, here's an article about the experiments on the next space mission. Seems they're taking seeds into outer space. Now isn't that just a grand idea?" His voice is sarcastic. "Space gardening while we're dropping dead on earth. Our tax dollars at work."

"Do you mean this isn't the first time she's sold artifacts?"

Lowering the paper, he looks at Phoenix oddly. "Of course not. Our dear mother taught her to do what has to be done to, shall we say, grease the wheels of life."

"Oh." Phoenix is trying to decide if she's disappointed or just surprised.

"Mornin', fellow time travelers!" Doug clatters through the door, already dressed to go running. "Mrs. Chin is in love." He plops down at the table and brushes a curl of hair out of Rennie's eyes. "Better," he says, smiling.

"Good for her. Is she going to shut up about Marcel Proust?"

Doug reaches across Rennie for the newspaper, going straight for the comic pages. "Oh, who knows. I think she likes complaining. So, Phoenix, beach or park this morning?"

Phoenix shrugs. "You pick."

"Phoenix isn't quite awake and she's being very grouchy because Cecelie is running away to Hawaii without her."

"No shit? Off to catch some rays, blow some Maui-Wowie, and hang with the beach babes, huh? No offense, Phoenix. But it sounds good to me. California's cold as piss in summer."

Phoenix winces at the bizarre metaphor. "It's a business trip," she says guardedly.

"To sell the *huacos*," Rennie explains, "and Cecelie is suffering from a case of ethics."

"Yeah?" Doug sounds surprised. "But she's just, like, the middleman, right?" Doug leans over Rennie, scanning the sports section or pretending to, but his eyes are on Phoenix. "Look at it this way, she like *found* the stuff, right? Well, okay, she didn't exactly *find* it, but close enough. And now some rich Japanese dude wants it 'cause he gets his rocks off by having some dead guy's necklace, right? So, who's it hurt? Not the grave robber who found it—who knows what happened to him? Besides, it was his own fault. Greed makes people a little nuts. Believe me, I know that one. And not the dead guy. He's been dead for—what?—a thousand years? For sure, he doesn't know the difference. The Japanese guy's is going to get his fix no matter who supplies it. Seems to me that if Cecelie doesn't go for it, the only people who'll be fucked are the ones sitting right here. Now, am I right or am I right?" Doug sits back in his chair, satisfied. The eternal illogic of a dope grower. "Let's go to the park, sweetcakes, then cut back along the beach. Best of both worlds."

Exiting the park, Phoenix and Doug cut up to the levee that runs along the highway fronting the beach and pace themselves against the morning foot traffic. A popular spot, gray-haired walkers and casual cyclists compete for space with the runners. From here, they can see the house. Rennie says he likes living here because the ocean makes him feel as if there are still possibilities. Looking out across the sea, Phoenix knows what he means. Rennie's life has been filled with possibilities and promises. Sometimes he still seems to be the beautiful boy, running across the quad at Northwestern: "They're going to publish my book, Phoenix. Do you know what this means? Come on, buy a drink for a soon-to-be-famous author." If they had known what was waiting for them, what would they have done differently?

Doug crosses the highway to the low cement wall that attempts to hold the sand in its place, and stretches out his legs, long and sinewy. This morning the breeze is calm and the sun clear. A pair of surfers paddle out to greet the day. Two years ago,

175

one of them might have been Carson. Phoenix pulls up next to Doug, who raises one leg onto the wall, stretching. "Cramp?" she asks. As serious about running as he is casual about everything else in life, Doug rarely stops before they're back at the house.

Doug shakes his head. "Just thought you should know the score," he says, squinting at Phoenix. The sun exposes the lines etched into his face, around his eyes. Laugh lines. Or maybe not. Maybe just age. How old is Doug? He seems very young, but here in this light, Phoenix isn't so sure. "I know you don't want to hear this, and for sure you don't want to hear it from me, but I'm going to tell you anyway. R.J.'s not doing so good. I mean, he's getting sicker, you know?" Phoenix nods, although she doesn't know. "He made me promise not to tell you girls, said you'd fuss over him." Doug grins at that word: *fuss.* Definitely Rennie's word. "He's got this low-grade fever—he says it's nothing to worry about, but . . . I don't know. He lies to me, too." Phoenix considers the possibility that Rennie lies to them all about his health. "I just thought you should know." Doug shrugs, as if he's said all there is to say.

An ancient dog plods patiently along the sand, looking contemptuously at the younger dogs romping in the surf. "Maybe he needs to have his medication changed," Phoenix finally offers.

"To what?" Doug sounds cynical, almost amused.

She fights the urge to slap him. "I . . . well, I don't know . . . something else."

"There *isn't* anything else, Phoenix. You know that. We've got what I can score on the underground. And that carload of pills from the clinic doctors. He's trying to figure out what to do. Maybe he'd like to check out that doctor in Switzerland. See, that's why Cecelie selling her stash is the right thing to do. Next to this, Cecelie's fucking ethics don't mean shit."

"She says she's going to sell them." Phoenix snaps, without meaning to. He's right. Rennie needs cash. No insurance, even if he had any, would cover trips to some doctor in Europe. No point in thinking about that now. "We've got the crop; it's doing okay." But Phoenix knows it won't bring enough. Doug knows it, too.

"Cash from those *huacos* is what he needs," Doug says.

In a way he's right. Why shouldn't she sell them? Who will it

176

hurt, really? And how important are artifacts or archaeologists and codes of honor, compared to Rennie? That's all that matters and it all costs money. Doctors in Switzerland. *Curanderos* in Peru. All the miracles are elsewhere, doing what American medicine will not or cannot. "We should start back," Phoenix says. "They'll wonder what's become of us."

"You want to go running at sunrise tomorrow?" he asks, suddenly changing the subject. Doug doesn't yet understand how uneventful sunrises here are: endless shades of gray lightening into blue to match the sea, unlike Hawaii, the land of eternal sunrises and sunsets. All that drama and beauty in one place is hard to imagine. It must look like hope. "I've never seen the sun rise over the water. Probably makes a difference in the whole rest of the day." She shrugs. Maybe that's what it takes.

Monday morning and the fog has stretched across the Great Highway and up onto the deck, shrouding the day. Rennie perches on the bed next to Phoenix and touches her cheek lightly. Shaking her head, she opens her eyes slowly, then sits up suddenly, shivering, her eyes wide. "Rennie! What's wrong? Are you okay?" She tries to hide the panic in her voice.

He smiles softly. "It's okay, Phoenix. I'm fine. But you have a phone call." She slips a little closer to Cecelie to make room on the bed for him. Dressed in trousers and barefoot, his shirt hangs open, as if he'd just pulled on his clothes to answer the phone.

Jostled awake, Cecelie pulls herself up in bed. "Rennie? God, what time is it?" She peers at the clock, then remembers to tug the sheet up over her naked breasts.

"A little after five-thirty," he says, handing Phoenix the phone. "I didn't want to wake you, but I thought I should. It's Phoenix's sister."

"Savannah?" Phoenix groans and covers her eyes. "Why did you tell her I'm here?" So like Savannah to call and ruin a perfectly good morning. "She'll just love this. Me in bed with a faggot and a dyke." Phoenix takes the phone off hold. "Savannah, are you nuts? It's not even six o'clock in the morning."

"Phoenix? Is that you?" Her sister always asks the obvious.

The connection is fuzzy, like waves washing through the lines, sending Savannah's voice loud, then soft again.

"Of course it's me. You woke the whole damned house up." This is all the fault of the phone company and their crazy cheap-rate hours.

"Well, Phoenix, I waited as long as seemed prudent." *Prudent*. A new word for Savannah; must be something she's picked up hobnobbing with all those other university wives, although it's hard to think of Floyd, a man who's spent the last twenty-five years teaching farm boys how to raise hogs, as a professor. In the background, Phoenix can hear Savannah's stupid little dogs, "ankle-snappers" Villanova always calls them, Punkin and—what's the other one's name? Something equally insipid—yapping in the background. "Floyd! Put Punkin and Dunkin up, I can barely hear Phoenix. We have a terrible connection." Yes, Dunkin, that's it. Stupid name for a dog, but then these aren't exactly like real dogs.

"You woke me up at the crack of dawn to listen to dogs barking?" Phoenix slips her unoccupied left hand under the sheet and into the crevice between Cecelie's thighs, warming her fingers. "Why don't you get Floyd one of those pot-bellied pigs; they don't bark and when you get tired of it, you can invite the neighbors over for a barbecue."

"You're shameless," mouths Rennie, slipping off the bed. "Don't forget to bring the phone back downstairs when you're done." Cecelie squirms and Phoenix laughs.

"Phoenix, just what is so funny? Why are you laughing? This is quite serious."

Damn! Even after all this time Savannah still makes her feel like a guilty child. Phoenix slips her fingers out from between Cecelie's legs. "I'm sorry, Savannah; I wasn't laughing at you."

"Well, I apologize for waking you, but . . ." Savannah's words are lost to the wave that is washing her voice the two thousand miles toward California.

"Savannah, for God's sake, hang up and call the operator. Tell them we have a lousy connection." Phoenix is shouting when the line suddenly clears.

"Oh, honey, I can't. This is just too important." Honey? When has Savannah ever called her anything other than Phoenix? "It's Mama. Floyd wanted me to call you right after it happened Friday night, but Mama said no. Then after last night. I was going to call then, but Floyd said, 'Phoenix needs her sleep. Nothing can be done until morning anyway.' That's what he told me. Bad enough we didn't get a minute's rest ourselves, no point in burdening you." Savannah's voice has climbed nearly an octave higher, the way it does when she's upset: high and fast and tangled.

"Savannah, what's wrong?" Phoenix sits up, pulling the sheet around her tightly.

"Well, Phoenix, honey, Mama's still with us, thank the Lord Jesus. I know I should've called right off. Floyd said I should, but everything here has just been so muddled since Friday night. Of course, it was really Saturday morning. It's her heart again, but this time . . . well, Doctor Leonard says only so much can be done, not like before, when he wanted her to have the surgery last February. Oh, you'll like him Phoenix, he's just the nicest man. But you know how stubborn she is. And then in June . . . well, she never would listen to me. Then Friday, she was out in her garden all day. I told her it was too much for her in this heat, but would she listen to me? That night, Mrs. Pengrove— Do you remember her? Well, she still lives next door, if you can believe that. She saw Mama's lights were on, so she called over there. And when she didn't get no answer, she went right ahead and called the paramedics. Thank the good Lord, Tollie's gallbladder was acting up and she was in the bathroom looking out her window. When Floyd and I got to the hospital, Mama was sitting up and looking not all that bad. I wanted to call you right then, but she's the one said not to bother. I didn't feel right about that, I can tell you, but you know how she is. And I'm not one to go against anybody's wishes, you know that. But then last night she had another attack and . . . honey, it doesn't look good. Phoenix, are you still there?"

Take a deep breath. Concentrate. Don't take bad news lying down or naked, and no matter what, never let them see you cry. "Yes, Savannah, I'm still here. Why didn't you tell me about this before now?"

"Well, Phoenix, I just got done telling you. Fact is, if I didn't live close, I probably wouldn't know either. 'It's not like you're a trained nurse.' If she's said that to me once, she's said it a hundred times. Makes me feel just terrible. Floyd kept tellin' me you had a right to know. 'Lay your burden down,' that's what he told me."

"Savannah, let me get this straight—my mother had a heart attack in February, another one in June, and a third one on Friday night . . ."

"Saturday morning, actually."

Not bothering to acknowledge the correction, Phoenix doesn't even pause. "And nobody bothered to tell me? She's been in the hospital since Friday night and you wait until Monday to call me? What the fuck is the matter with you? Goddamn it, Savannah!" Cecelie tries to pull Phoenix close, only to be shrugged off. Hurt, Cecelie slips out of bed, wrapping Carson's robe around her as she goes, and settles into the leather chair.

"Phoenix, I'll thank you not to take the Lord's name in vain. I only did what Mama wanted and what I thought was best for you." On the defensive now, Savannah's voice has grown haughty. She plays the elder sister role well on the phone. "Mama was doing well enough until this bad attack. Besides, in February you were . . . well, to be honest, Phoenix, you were . . . well . . . so nervous."

"You mean nuts, don't you, Savannah?"

"No, of course not, honey. You were never . . . I mean, not like *her.*" Savannah's voice drops to a whisper at the allusion to their grandmother. "You weren't . . . like *that,* were you?"

"No, Savannah, I was not."

"You see." Her sister's voice has brightened. "I told Mama it wasn't anything like that. I said you just needed a little change of scene. But she thought we couldn't risk upsetting you. I mean, with you so far away from home and all."

"Then *you* should have called me, Savannah. I could have done something." Phoenix's throat begins to ache. Hard. So hard not to cry. "Savannah, what exactly are they doing for Mama? What about that doctor, what's his name?"

"Leonard. Doctor Leonard. Oh, you'll like him, Phoenix."

"So you keep saying."

Savannah ignores this. "He's a fine man—awful young, but he seems so sincere. He's a heart specialist. And a good doctor, too; everybody says so. Even Mama likes him, as much as she likes any doctor. You know how she is."

Phoenix considers that she doesn't know how her mother is at all anymore. They've become strangers separated by blood and distance and the past. "This doctor, he'll do a bypass now or something? Or send her to St. Louis? Surely they have heart specialists there who can take care of this." Villanova will be fine, a little trip to St. Louis or even Memphis, a few hours in surgery and it will all be over.

Through the waves on the phone, Phoenix Bay hears her sister exhale. "Honey, it's gone too far. Doctor Leonard says we need to be prepared to expect the worst. That's why I'm calling. I think . . . well, I think you'd better come home. Floyd already called Mitsy. Now that she's divorced, she's a travel agent. She managed to get you on TWA Flight 300 to St. Louis, where you'll connect to Flight 7352 to Marion. Are you writing this down? Well, it doesn't matter, they'll give you an itinerary at the airport. The plane leaves at ten-ten from San Francisco. Mitsy calls it SFO. Isn't that just the cutest thing? You go to the TWA ticket counter there. Mitsy has taken care of everything. Floyd will pick you up at the airport."

Phoenix shakes her head slightly, trying to remember if she knows anyone named Mitsy. "What airport?"

"Oh, for heaven's sake, Phoenix, the Marion airport, of course. Are you paying attention? You'll change planes in St. Louis. Maybe you should write this down. There's only the two flights today and the late one doesn't get in until nearly nine, so we got you on the early one. You need to be here, with your people as soon as you can. Besides, I don't like Floyd to be out driving after dark." Savannah's voice is slow and careful, as if she's explaining a complex equation to a stupid child.

"It's too soon, Savannah. I'm not ready."

Savannah exhales again, exasperated. "Well, Phoenix, you'll just have to *get* ready. You have more than four hours, how long can it take you to pack a bag?"

"I mean . . . I'm . . . not ready, Savannah. Are you?"

"For heaven's sake, Phoenix, I don't have to get ready. I'm already here. Now, I really don't have time for this. Floyd is waiting to take me back to the hospital. We just came back here so I could call you and take care of the babies. There are so many rules for that intensive care: five-minute visits only on the hour. And if you miss your hour, they make you wait until the next one. Too many rules, if you ask me, considering the circumstances."

Phoenix is starting to float away. She used to beg Jinx to hold her when it happened, sure that one day she would float off and never be able to find her way back. She won't ask Cecelie to hold her, though. "What circumstances?"

"Why, you coming all the way from California, of course, and Mama so bad and all, it seems they could bend the rules. What would it hurt?"

Phoenix hasn't floated in a long time, months maybe. She'd floated the night Jinx left. When she stopped floating, she'd started to scream. She doesn't remember when she stopped screaming. Now, she's floating and crying, but quietly, so Savannah can't hear. "And Phoenix, bring something decent to wear. After all, this isn't San Francisco."

"No," Phoenix agrees, "I didn't think it was."

"Phoenix, are you sure you're okay? You sound, well, strange."

Phoenix smiles a little. Floating isn't so bad once you get the hang of it, almost pleasant. "I'm fine. It's just the connection. Is Mama conscious?"

"She was when I left; why? Is there something you'd like me to tell her for you?" Savannah is fishing, waiting for the inevitable confession of love, perhaps.

"Yeah, tell her no regrets."

"What? What is that supposed to mean?"

"Nothing, Savannah. I'll see you when I get there."

Phoenix switches off the phone and closes her eyes. Cecelie settles on the bed, touches her cheek lightly. If she stays here long enough, the plane will leave without her. Savannah will call again and Rennie can lie, tell her Phoenix has run away to Mauritius. Cecelie will make ceviche tonight and the four of them will sit on the deck, watching the sunset, laughing, making bets on when the fog will come in. Doug will win; he always does. All she has to do is sit here long enough, and nothing will happen.

12 Scrambling through the St. Louis airport for what seems like miles, Phoenix Bay finally arrives, panting and frazzled at the gate with the tiny prop commuter planes. Oppressive humidity that makes the air feel damp, even inside the terminal, has caught her unprepared. A young man with the worst case of acne she's ever seen, reading a crumpled copy of *Road and Track*, looks at her coldly as she sinks into the seat next to him, the only empty one in the room, which serves as the holding area for a half dozen gates, maybe more. She has the uneasy sensation they are all awaiting dispatch to hell. Behind the desk at the gate where her plane is supposed to be is a large sign with the word *Delayed* next to her flight number.

"Have they said when we'll be leaving?"

Road and Track glances at her and shrugs. "Twenty minutes." She wonders if it's a guess or if he has some inside airline information. There is no one behind the desk to ask. Fighting down the urge to walk back to the main terminal, to find the next flight back to San Francisco, she surveys the other passengers. Across from her, a toddler squirms on a young woman's lap, reaching up baby hands for a red-and-white Coke cup. The woman slurps loudly, then sets the cup on the floor. The baby wails. Phoenix rummages through her pockets, looking for one of the tissues the attendant on the last flight gave her. She'd started crying on the St. Louis approach; she'd done so well before that. It was the engine's sudden clutch, the sensation of brakes being applied, that had started the tears. She wills herself not to cry. "No tears, no regrets," TaTa Hassee would say. Phoenix can't remember ever seeing any of the women in her family cry. No tears, but lots of regrets. Or maybe not.

"No Regrets." Phoenix Bay's mother loved that song, played it a dozen times a day on an old phonograph left behind by Savannah when she'd run away with Croonin' Cliff Conklin. He'd promised to buy her a hi-fi console, but never did; they would have heard if he had. "Phoenix, baby, listen to this song." Ice rattled in Villanova's pint mason jar, half-full with a mixture of iced tea heavy with sugar and bourbon. Who recorded that song? She remembers the chanteuse, with hair like a cone of cotton candy and Cleopatra eyes, leaning forward so that her pale, round breasts threatened to tip out of the album cover, and how she could draw out that one word, *no,* bouncing it like a soap bubble. The name, she's forgotten; she remembers everything else. Swaying back and forth in the porch swing under the honeysuckle, TaTa Hassee would sit, the dowager queen of Carbon Street, Phoenix on the steps just beyond her feet. Through Villanova's bedroom window, which opened onto the porch roof, the record player cranked out the same four songs every night, over and over because Villanova had set the little black arrow to *replay.* It wasn't the only record she owned, just the only one Mama seemed to want to hear. She had worn out her Peggy Lee, who asked is that all there is the way no other woman could, before or since. Sometimes, Villanova would take the glass and roll it across her forehead, then down her neck, little beads of cool water mixing with sweat slipping down inside her dress, while TaTa fanned herself with one of Villanova's *True Confessions* magazines. Just inside the screen door, Gran Cicero, perched on the green-vinyl hassock, hands locked between open knees, rocked back and forth in front of the television, a greenish halo cast around her.

That year was a summer of dreams. The Kennedys had turned Washington into Camelot. Cliff was cutting a demo record in Nashville. Vietnam was still just a faraway place and Korea an ugly memory. And Hank Long was coming home: *Passing through for the kid's birthday. See you, H. Long.* On his picture postcard an armadillo wearing a ten-gallon hat and a balloon over its head the way cartoon characters do, saying, *Howdy, Pardner!* It was postmarked Tulsa, Oklahoma. "No Regrets" slunk through thick night air.

Phoenix had spent most of that morning gathering wild strawberries from along the old railroad tracks, because wild strawberries were her father's favorite. "Wild strawberries for a wild man," he would say, swinging her high over his head, although she was much too big for him to swing anymore; she hoped he wouldn't be disappointed. She'd dressed carefully in her yellow sundress, the one TaTa Hassee had helped her make for the 4-H show the month before; she'd won a red ribbon. Red was her favorite color, it didn't matter that it meant second best. And she was wearing the genuine turquoise ring, shaped like a Phoenix bird, that Savannah had sent all the way from Nashville; she hardly ever came where she now called "up north" anymore, preferring to let the U.S. Postal Service do her bidding.

"When Daddy comes, we'll have strawberry ice cream and my birthday cake," Phoenix reminded her mother and great-grandmother. She had worked Hank Long's name into every other sentence most of the day. The two women exchanged a glance Phoenix wasn't supposed to see, and TaTa Hassee said, as she always did, "That'll be right nice, Sis." TaTa called all her female descendants Sis; it saved keeping track of all those names of all those cities she would never visit. "Now you just keep on turnin' that ice-cream crank, elsewise it won't set up right." Up and down the block, children in white cotton nightgowns that glowed against the darkness chased fireflies, celebrating their capture with delighted shrieks. They would put them into jars with holes in the lids and a few sad blades of grass inside. The fireflies were always dead in the morning. The yards began to empty one by one as mothers called their children home. And the fireflies, seeming to sense their reprieve, filled the darkened yards, tails winking like little yellow stars.

It was late by the time Villanova emerged from the house with the birthday cake that was decorated with wild strawberries spelling out the number 10. Eight matching red candles and two pink ones crowded toward the center and one side. Part of the other side was missing, as if someone had reached in and pulled free a handful. Looking down on the wreckage, Phoenix started to cry. "What happened to my cake?"

"Stop that whinin'!" Villanova, walking carefully as if she were on a sheet of ice instead of her own front porch, balanced the cake on a metal TV tray, which swayed a little under the weight. "Your grandmother got hungry. She couldn't wait."

"Damned nut," TaTa Hassee said, as she often did about her only living daughter.

"Oh, hell, what difference does it make?" Villanova snapped, digging in her pocket for her Zippo lighter. "It all tastes the same."

"But it's my *birthday* cake! And I was savin' it for when Daddy comes. Now *she's* gone and ruined it. When Daddy comes . . ." Phoenix heard the slap coming before she felt it. No regrets, no surprises, either.

"Why do you always act like this?" Her mother was angry, her face flushed, her hands trembling. "When're you ever going to learn?"

Phoenix crawled into the swing, pushing close to her great-grandmother, who smelled like ammonia and sugar, an old-woman smell. TaTa pushed her toward the far end of the swing. "You're too big for that, Sis, and even if you wasn't, it's too danged hot." Phoenix stepped out of the swing, careful not to jar her great-grandmother, and hunkered sullenly on the concrete porch steps, knees drawn up under her chin, until she sensed her mother watching. She dropped her knees and sat up straight, knees together, the way Mama was always after her to do.

"That's my good girl," Villanova said, leaning over her daughter, offering her engraved Zippo lighter that glowed like a small square moon. "Now, birthday girl, go on and blow out them candles, then give Mama a big birthday kiss." Her mother's cheek was damp and a little salty under Phoenix's lips; she smelled of dusting powder and bourbon. "That's my sweet girl. You taste like strawberries. You been pickin' the strawberries out of the cream? See, Mama knows everything you do. Lordy, it's a hot night."

The screen door creaked as Gran Cicero lumbered, stiff and bearlike, onto the porch, lured by the promise of food. "Set yourself down here in the porch swing, Mama." Villanova moved to the stairs next to Phoenix and sat, looking out into the thick night. "I swear, the good Lord sure must've been thinking of hell when He made Williamson County."

Joining a line of glassy-eyed passengers parading like trained ducks, Phoenix follows them down a staircase, out of the terminal, and onto the tarmac, then up into the cabin of an airplane small enough to be truly terrifying. "The streetcar I take to work every-day is bigger than this," she says to the man in the seat ahead of her. If she's going to die in this tiny contraption, she at least wants to be on a first-name basis with the other passengers. But the man next to him turns, his eyes cold, "Don't talk to the prisoner, ma'am." Then, remembering his manners, "Please." Prisoner transport for the federal penitentiary. At first glance, it's hard to tell the prisoners from the guards; they all wear cheap suits and grim faces. The tiny airplane rumbles, then buzzes, and finally be-gins to sway and bounce down the runway. Usually, she loves the exhilaration of takeoff, that slow and steady rush of power, enough to shrug off earth's constraints. But here the rush is gone, replaced by an irritating sensation of struggle against the wind. For the next forty minutes she will watch flat fields and orchards unfold into a crazy-quilt pattern of green and brown. She will not cry.

Egypt stretches slow and lazy under an early-evening sun. Phoenix Bay has come home, and she is struck by the realization that she doesn't belong, has never belonged, here in this angry land with its untamed storms and tempered secrets. California, where the weather so rarely changes that people are allowed to, is easier. Here, the people only wait.

Waiting in the Marion airport for her half sister's third hus-band Floyd, she watches the runway, hoping for another plane to approach the cracked concrete ribbon that abruptly ends in weeds. PRAIRIE GRASS, the sign next to the big window tells her. Big Jim Thompson, the governor who'd had his eye on the White House until Ronald Reagan sold him out, tried to turn back the clock by having schoolchildren plant prairie grasses along the highways, an attempt to make the state look as it had when the first settlers crossed through. Those who'd come up from the hills of Tennessee, following the coal, weren't just passing through, though; they had stayed for the rich black soil and didn't move on, at least not easily. They did not court the future, had little use for the past, and only tolerated the present. So far as Phoenix knows, it has always been so, just as this land between the Mississippi and Ohio rivers has always been called Egypt. When Cecelie heard that, she'd asked why. But Phoenix couldn't remember those fifth-grade history lessons delivered by women with tissue-paper–crinkled skin, members of the Daughters of the American Revolution.

Mama could have joined the Daughters of the American Revolution. A long-forgotten ancestor had actually had the misfortune to freeze to death at Valley Forge. Aunt Nan had paid a woman in Carbondale eight hundred dollars to find that out. Eight hundred dollars and Phoenix was wearing shoes that made her toes curl. Eight hundred dollars and the living room in the house on Carbon Street couldn't have been more than fifty degrees in January. Aunt Nantucket said Mama should join the DAR and TaTa Hassee and Savannah, too, if she ever came back from Nashville and stopped disgracing the family. She didn't mention Gran Cicero; they must have had a rule about letting in mad-women. Mama had laughed until she'd had to dab at her eyes with the hem of her brown sweater. Don't think about that now. Think about anything but Mama.

Floyd is twenty-six minutes late. All that rushing for this. Cecelie packing, while Phoenix went running with Doug. Rennie had routed the boy out of bed to go with her because neither he nor Cecelie trusted Phoenix to come back. Running, she told them, was the only thing that would keep her from screaming. Nothing could stop her from floating. The trip to the airport had been frantic, too. Cecelie had insisted on getting there too early—apparently the only things that operate on time in Peru are planes. Ironic for a country in which punctuality is suspect. Cecelie often kept Phoenix waiting in cafes and outside movie theater. "If you wanted me there on time, why didn't you say '*a la hora inglesa?*' " she'd asked, nearly indignant." Every important engagement has become *a la hora inglesa*. Phoenix glances at the clock, plate-sized with huge black numerals, the kind relegated to public places. Floyd is now officially on Peru time.

Almost night and still hot. Wearing Carson's leathers was a bad idea. Well, nothing to be done about that now. If she goes into the ladies' room to change, she might miss Floyd, and she doesn't know what Cecelie has packed. Besides, it has to get cooler eventually. Or she'll get used to being hot. The prisoner and his two guards are long gone, even though they'd deplaned a good twenty minutes after everyone else. Phoenix had stared when they'd passed, willing the prisoner to look at her. But they had disappeared through the waiting room, into the heat of the afternoon, without a glance. Now, the waiting room is empty, except for a dozen orange plastic chairs and, at the far end, a rent-a-car counter with no one behind it. She could rent a car, if she still had a credit card, or more than the forty-seven dollars she'd stuffed into her pocket.

Well, this was Savannah's idea, let her and Floyd pay for it, the least they owe her since that fiasco three years ago in San Francisco. Served them right. They nearly scared Jinx to death: Savannah outside the door hollering, "I'm coming, Phoenix! Floyd, where's the damned key? Hold on, Sissy, I'm coming!" until Jinx had finally opened the door. What was she supposed to do, leave them out in the hall, banging on the door and hollering like they were being mugged or Phoenix was being murdered? Instead, they'd ruined a perfectly good scene. They should have gone to *Beach Blanket Babylon* like they were supposed to. Jinx had spent seventy bucks to get them tickets to the most popular show in San Francisco, and Savannah didn't want to go because she thought it was like those beach-blanket movies of the '60s. And Floyd had wanted to get up early to go to the Maritime Museum, as if the damned ships were going anywhere. For a man who'd spent his entire life landlocked and raising hogs, he was inordinately fond of ships, or maybe he was just hoping Savannah would fall in the bay and be swept out to sea. Savannah never did learn to swim. Not Phoenix, though. From the time she was old enough to run away for the afternoon without anyone noticing, she and her buddy David would go out to the strip-mine lakes, drink warm beer stolen from his uncle's fishing cooler, and swim until past dark. Poor Mama always thought those late nights with David meant something. Or maybe she just wanted them to. When Jinx had found his picture in that old photo album, she'd laughed. "Your mom wanted you to marry a faggot?" Jinx had a beautiful laugh. Mama might have liked Jinx. Savannah had hated her, especially after that awful night.

Savannah had pretended not to notice the garter belt that had somehow gotten caught in the hemline of Phoenix's red silk kimono and was trailing after her. "We didn't expect you back so soon," Phoenix said, daring Savannah to ask. Once Savannah got religion, she couldn't stand for anyone to have a really good time. Poor Floyd pretended not to notice, but it was harder to tell with him; maybe he really didn't notice. He was rooting through a shopping bag, one of those plastic things with a picture of the Golden Gate Bridge on both sides, which only the tourists carry, until he found what he was looking for: a pair of placemats shaped like the Golden Gate Bridge. He had a dozen: two for Phoenix, two for Jinx, and the rest to take home to his daughters. That accomplished, though, he'd seemed unsure what to do with himself, so he stood by the window, looking down at the street, his hands stuffed in his pockets. Phoenix had pulled herself off the couch to go turn down the stereo when she finally noticed the garter-belt tail. Not much to be said about that or the one black stocking that had crumpled around her left ankle or its mate next to Savannah's feet, which were so primly attached to the floor. "So, Floyd, how was Alcatraz?"

The newspaper racks promise the *St. Louis Post Dispatch,* the *Southern Illinoisan,* and the *Marion Daily Republican* for a quarter, seventy-five cents on Sunday. All are empty. A large sign with a picture of a Kodachrome lake with water as blue as the sky and a dozen geese in flight assures Phoenix Bay that she is at the hub of paradise, with 14,362 residents as of the last census, the largest man-made lake in the state, forty churches, eleven motels, and, in the fall, ninety thousand ducks, a hundred thousand geese, and several thousand hunters. The sign doesn't mention the federal penitentiary, the new Alcatraz, tucked away in the national forest. It does assure her the airport is equipped with two runways, each long enough to handle Air Force One; she doubts the need for that, unless the penitentiary people know something about the presidency that she doesn't. She knows more about hunters and geese.

That first long winter after Hank Long left and Savannah ran away, Villanova took Phoenix and drove the eighteen miles out to Eli Baylor's hunting club, which wasn't really a club at all, just an old, falling-down house trailer on the edge of his cornfield where he'd dug a dozen goose pits—foxholes lined in concrete. "Three women and the girl," Villanova told Eli, who smoothed his hair back under his cap, considering the offer.

"Picking house is hard work," he said, cupping his hands around a kitchen match while he lit a cigarette and inhaled deeply. He snuffed out the match between his thumb and forefinger. The November wind was already crisp and the light from the old trailer gave his skin a strangely yellow cast against the dusk. Eli might have been made of leather, he was so weather-beaten. "Ain't no job for a white woman," he said at last, the cigarette riding on his lower lip. Phoenix was fascinated at how the cigarette never fell even while he talked. "Ain't never had no white woman in the picking house," he repeated slowly and a little more loudly, in case Villanova was hard of hearing or simply daft.

"Three women and the girl," Villanova replied, "every night for the season." Eli shrugged and walked back to the trailer. The door squealed when he pulled it closed.

Every night for more than two months, those Bayless women had cleaned geese in the front half of Eli's barn for the hunters who came every fall down from Chicago and up from New Orleans. Men with heavily lined faces and large hands, soft from their desk jobs, drove fancy cars and wore hunting clothes from L.L. Bean and Eddie Bauer. Rich men in drag as hunters. The locals in their mended khaki, stiff from mud and sweat, and their soft worn flannel shirts, laughed at the weekend hunters who brought the dead geese to the picking house, where Villanova and the other women sat, legs spread wide, a goose dangling. "Phoenix, get all the pin feathers. Do I have to tell you again?"

The picking house was dark and heavy with the smell of smoke and old blood. And Eli was right, those Bayless women were the only white women there. Black women with fast and sure hands, which never seemed to bleed like Mama's, outpaced Villanova and Phoenix, and of course Gran Cicero and TaTa Hassee, who were too slow to be of any real help but quiet enough not to be much bother. Not that it mattered. They were paid by the goose, not by the hour.

"Goose grease," the women told Villanova, looking at her ruined hands. "Vaseline won't do no good." But Villanova wouldn't listen and no matter how she slicked her hands with Vaseline, they always bled and the other women exchanged knowing glances: *White women don't know enough to work the picking houses . . . Ain't it the truth.* The other women sang and told stories in a rich and rolling cadence as they worked. But they never included Gran Cicero or TaTa Hassee or even Villanova. The girls, no older than Phoenix, snickered whenever Villanova scolded about pin feathers. They never had to be reminded; they never missed any. And Phoenix, her stomach churning from the smell of entrails and singed feathers, from the steam rising off vats of boiling water and the kerosene heaters, envied those girls who smiled and sang along with their mothers.

Some Saturday nights Eli would send Villanova out on a delivery to one of the motels where the hunters were staying. Those nights he always drove Phoenix and TaTa Hassee and Gran Cicero, who wasn't so crazy she couldn't be convinced to chop off the head of a goose or gut it out, back to town. He never did that for the other women's families or trusted them to make deliveries. Phoenix was proud of that, even though it meant the other girls at the picking house would snicker more the next night. "Your mama will be along directly," he would tell Phoenix. He never spoke to Gran Cicero. Then, to TaTa Hassee, "She said for y'all not to wait supper." Phoenix would watch the taillights from Eli's green Ford station wagon, with the one red door and the goose painted on the hood, until the night swallowed them. And she would sit on the front steps, the cold seeping into her cotton pants, waiting until TaTa Hassee called, "Sis, get on in here, afore you catch your death." Mama was never home by the time Phoenix went to bed. Sometimes near dawn, Phoenix would awake to the sound of music coming from her mother's bedroom. The door had a big, old-fashioned keyhole large enough to look through, and if she knelt just so, angling her head to the right to avoid the knob, she could see Villanova sitting on the edge of her bed in her nightgown, smoking, looking at nothing, listening to Peggy Lee.

Some women get new dresses for Easter; for Villanova it was during goose season. For years after they'd stopped working at the picking house, she would still disappear some cold Saturday nights. By the end of January, there was always a new blue dress or two or three, matching leather pumps, even a handbag. Twice there was a hat. Always, there were gloves.

Settling into one of the orange plastic chairs, which grabs onto her damp leather pants with a determined sucking sound, Phoenix drapes her left leg over the armrest. A woman in high heels and a very full skirt scurries past toward the car rental booth. Mama used to have a dress like that, a long time ago. Large breasts sway under the red sundress. Her hair is caught by a red bow in a jaunty ponytail. Smiling, she waves at a point beyond Phoenix's head, where the lone ticket agent waits, bored as a cemetery caretaker. Phoenix turns, expecting to see the man smile and wave back; he only stares sullenly at the magazine before him. His loss. Phoenix turns back, watching, as the woman swoops past, a red bird in flight. Mama used to wear red in summer, too. But Mama hardly ever smiles.

A chill runs through Phoenix, although the air inside the lobby is heavy and warm despite the air-conditioning. She could call her sister; but she forgot to pack her address book. She wouldn't know where to call, anyway: Savannah's house or Mama's? Or the hospital? Which one? Savannah didn't say, not that there are many choices. She considers calling Cecelie, but can't decide what to say: "I'm stuck in the Marion airport"; but then what? Besides, she'd promised to call after she's seen Villanova. She wants to call Jinx. She's wanted to talk to Jinx all

day, to bury herself in the familiar voice: "What's wrong, baby?"
But now Jinx calls another woman "baby." Or doesn't. Either way,
the husky voice wouldn't be for her. No comfort there.

Through the airport's plate-glass doors, Phoenix Bay watches
her mother—only young, not much older than Phoenix—walking
carefully across the parking lot, her elbow supported by Santa
Claus, if Santa Claus wore polyester golf shirts and plaid slacks.
She should get up, run across the checkerboard tile, smooth and
slippery as glass. Do little girls ever skate here in their sock feet?
Do little girls still do that? Her chest hurts. Too hard to breathe
this refrigerated air. Her heart pounds. Maybe TaTa Hassee was
wrong, maybe it wasn't weak minds and strong hearts, maybe it's
the other way around. The glass doors grind open, then shut again,
easy yet definite, like the footsteps on the checkerboard floor.
Phoenix pushes her palms flat into the leather that covers her
knees, hard. A fist is buried in her. Jinx used to make her feel like
this: split apart, then growing back together again, but this time
it's wrong, as if the tissue is knitting in rough knots. Time clutches
in one long, horrible moment. And she knows, even before her sister says, "Phoenix, baby, I'm so sorry."

For nearly as long as she can remember, Phoenix Bay has approached religion as a sort of cosmic flea market. God has what
you need but is a wily barterer. The eternal problem is how to
drive a bargain with the unbargainable, but that never stopped her
from trying when there was nothing else left. All the way across
the country, she had tried to find the right bauble to tempt God,
only to come up short. Now, He's let her mother die while she was
sitting in an airport waiting room.

The tiny chapel where Savannah has told Phoenix to wait
while she and Floyd attend to the "arrangements," as her sister so
neatly calls them, is in an interior room of the mortuary. Eight
padded pews face an altar where electric flames flicker at the tips
of a dozen plastic candles. On a large stained-glass window,
lighted so that it is always early morning, Mary sits, draped in a
blue robe covered with dogwood blossoms; at her feet the baby
Jesus plays. But the artist wasn't especially gifted with faces: The

eyes are too large and the mouths too small, so the holy mother and her child stare, slightly aghast, into the depths of the chapel. In the background an organ plays "What a Friend We Have in Jesus," which melds into "I Come to the Garden Alone." The tape whirs. Closing her eyes, Phoenix tries to pray, but has forgotten how. She stretches out, full-length in one of the pews. From this angle, she can see only the face of the mother.

Few nights have entangled her as this one. Three, maybe four. The night Jinx left, of course. Molly sleeping with another woman, for the first time. The night Daddy left. Maybe one or two others in between. Nights when the darkness expands and the adrenaline pumps, but there's nowhere to run. She'd run away from Molly, but it hadn't helped. And the night Jinx left, she'd gone to the beach, where even the cold couldn't touch her. She'd tried to run away the night Daddy left, but her mother was waiting by the front door, on the couch in the dark, as if she'd known Phoenix would try to escape. Catching Phoenix by the waist, Villanova had pulled her down into her lap, and rocked her until morning. When the first shafts of light showed pink and pale, her mother had pushed her away, saying, "That's enough. No tears, no regrets." She handed Phoenix her lunch in its usual paper bag and attached a handwritten note: *Phoenix is a Bayless from now on.* Phoenix had folded the note into squares so tiny the school secretary had sniffed when she unfolded it, sniffed again when she read it. Phoenix couldn't meet the woman's eyes. Outside on the playground she could hear the children calling to each other in their morning games. It was winter. It was not snowing.

Phoenix slips out the side door of the mortuary into the parking lot where Floyd's white Cadillac cools and opens her suitcase, looking for her running shoes and sweats. Using one of the huge doors like a screen, she pulls off Carson's leathers, then checks the backdoor for signs of her sister or Floyd. Nothing yet. They'll be a long time. Something about picking out a casket. "Hardwood or bronze-tone?" Savannah kept asking Phoenix on the way here, as if she actually expected an answer. "Well, Phoenix, you must have some preference." Phoenix's preference is to be anywhere but here, in a mortuary parking lot, the white gravel shining in the last traces of sunlight. Her preference is to run away and never look back.

Phoenix Bay is a runner, even when she doesn't run, even when the mirror showed her fat and bloated from all those late nights in the bars, even when her legs ached from sitting too long, and the years had turned her muscles to a fine yellow mush. She was a runner in high school—not great, but determined. Then one day, she simply stopped. Now she can't remember why.

Her legs pump under her. The moon hangs low and pleased in the east, competing for attention with a fat, pink setting sun. Finally the air is starting to cool. She'd forgotten the terrible heat that is summer here, how it hovers, so thick you can see it rising from the asphalt in wet waves. But not this evening, the evening of the day her mother died.

A pair of eyes—how old? fourteen? fifteen, maybe? hard to tell, she's known so few boys and then she was young herself—lounge lazy and bored with the end of the day in a lumpy yard by one of the houses she passes, watching her, a middle-aged stranger. Not middle-aged, she reminds herself, and not really a stranger. But to them, she is: a stranger and old, too old to be running, as old as their mothers, whom they have never thought of as young, as runners. One of the boys pushes himself off the grass, in the easy move of long-legged youth, then hits the pavement beside her. No yellow mush there. "Where you runnin' to, lady?"

"Nowhere," she pants. Pants. She's not yet gone a full mile and already her breath is short, her skin slick with wet. "Just running." She glances at her new running companion, his pace slowed to accommodate her, too slow for a boy so young with legs so long; she knows that. What does he want? She is a city woman used to the pleas of strangers: "Quarter? Spare change? God bless you." His friend, shorter and less muscular, is jogging to catch up like a determined puppy. It occurs to her they are brothers, older and younger.

"Where she goin'?" the younger one asks, his voice tinged with the faint remnants of a drawl, brought to this county by its Tennessee settlers more than a hundred years ago. He pronounces *going* like *gwan*.

"She say nowhere," his brother, if he is the brother, answers. They are still running, drawing curious stares from drivers of the few passing cars and trucks. Two brown teenaged boys and a pink middle-aged stranger. What a sight we must be, she thinks. One of the cars honks; she doesn't look up, doesn't slacken her pace, merely lifts her middle finger in the direction of the sound, a silent salute. The boys laugh.

"Why she runnin' if she ain't goin' nowhere?" The younger one, for his own reasons, addresses the other boy instead of Phoenix directly.

"Don' know," the boy on her right answers. Then, to Phoenix, "Why you runnin'? Ain't you got no car?"

"For . . . the . . . exercise . . ." The words come in hot puffs.

"Humph!" snorts the older boy. "She ain't got no car." Ahead of them is a tall grassy space, part of a large yard, green with deep evening shadows. Phoenix pulls off the sidewalk, leans against a tree, waiting for her aching sides to calm. No wonder everyone over sixteen passes through the streets in air-conditioned cars with the windows rolled tight.

"You're a runner," she says to the older boy, more statement than question.

He grins, a wide, lopsided grin that takes over his face. "Yes ma'am, in spring. In winter, I'm center." Ma'am. Everyone here will call her that. The quaint custom that seems as oppressive as the air itself.

"He fast," volunteers the younger boy, the first time he's spoken to her directly.

"I can tell. And you? Do you play basketball, too?"

"No'm." He shakes his head, then drops it to his chest, suddenly shamed. Phoenix has crossed some line, some hidden barrier.

"He special." The older boy's voice is low, almost confiding. The younger one looks at the ground, his right foot suddenly and deeply interested in a clump of weeds, the white leather of his shoes streaked with green, as if he's often confronted with weeds demanding attention. Special? She starts to agree and then realizes the older boy means special education. Of course. No basketball for the dummies. No track or football, either. Some things never change. The boy who thinks *special* is as much a slur as a polite euphemism shrugs, his toe working the weed.

"You could be a sports trainer for your brother," she says. No protests. So, she was right. "In California, where I live, rich people pay for that."

"Shit," says the older boy, drawing out the word, disbelieving. "Don't nobody pay somebody else to make 'em run."

"Sure they do. Run and lift weights. Every movie star has his own sports trainer. You could practice on him." She nods toward the younger boy, who's raised his eyes, still skeptical of this white stranger who knows his shame.

"The Terminator got one?"

"Arnold Schwarzenegger? I suppose so; I never thought about it."

"You really from California?" The older boy's eyes are narrowing, looking for some telltale sign. She wonders what that might be. She nods. The flush has left her face. It's time to finish her run, then go back to the mortuary and Savannah, who's probably already in the parking lot pacing, her mouth puckered into a scowl.

"You know Captain EO?" the younger boy asks.

"The Michael Jackson exhibit at Disneyland?" The boy nods eagerly. "I know of it. It's in Southern California. I live in San Francisco."

"Shit," says the older boy again, nudging his brother and nodding toward the direction in which they'd come.

"We got to go," the younger boy offers, smiling at Phoenix.

"We be walkin' back," his brother says, pointedly. Phoenix laughs.

"Good luck! Maybe I'll see you again."

The older boy grunts. The younger turns and waves, still smiling at the thought of California and Captain EO and Disneyland and the Terminator, until his brother cuffs him on the back of the head.

"What you do that for?" the younger boy protests.

"Stop lookin' at her. She ain't nothin'. Dummy, she don't know Captain EO and that mean she ain't never been to Disneyland, which mean she don't live in California. She just some crazy white woman passin' through. She don't even belong here."

Savannah Bayless Conklin Tompkins Watson perches primly on the edge of a gilt French provincial chair outside the office of Simons and Sons Mortuary, waiting for her husband, who is inside with Frank Simons, waiting, too, for her sister to come back from wherever she's run off to this time. They were always waiting for Phoenix, or at least Mama was. Even today, she'd hung on after that last attack, as if Savannah didn't know why—she was waiting for Phoenix to walk through the door, all smiles or sullenness, you can never anticipate which. Phoenix would have made it, too, if not for that delay in St. Louis. Serves her right. Serves them both right.

When Mama was pregnant with Phoenix, Savannah would sit at her feet, rubbing her mother's swollen ankles, praying for a girl, striking childish bargains with God. That was before all those tests were invented to take the mystery out of childbirth. Time was, and not that long ago, you had to wait months before you even knew if what you suspected was true—no boxes on the drugstore shelves to buy, no bottles to pee in, no little strips to change color. Now you know when there's time enough to do something about it or nothing at all. Not like that time in Nashville with Cliff. Savannah hadn't known early enough, that was the problem; had put off knowing, week after week, until there was no more doubt, even without the test. Her skirts wouldn't zip. When Cliff finally noticed, he threatened to send her back to Villanova. He already had a family and there wasn't room for another, he'd made that clear from the start.

But it had died, probably sensing her fear or the fact that nobody wanted it and what lay ahead. It died while she was alone, her shift at the Copper Kettle over. Cliff was out. He was always out, singing in the bars or trying to get gigs, or just out. The woman across the hall had heard her crying. "God, oh God! Somebody help me." Savannah was sure she was dying. The woman—her name started with a *J*, Savannah remembers that much—was a nurse; at least she wore a white uniform and worked at a hospital. She went out early every afternoon and came home late at night, like Savannah. They would nod to each other in the hall, neighbors exchanging pleasantries. By the time Cliff got home, she was already back from the hospital. They would have kept her longer if she'd had insurance. Instead they'd just scraped and scraped, the sound rising up through her until it stuck in her throat, threatening to choke her. They'd sent her home with a box of sanitary napkins, long and thick. (Even now, when she sees them, she thinks of all that blood.) She was too tired to cry.

She never knew of course, but always thought it would be a boy. Five years later, Cliff made her go to New York, where abortion was newly legal. There was no room in a singer's life for babies. The operation was nothing, he'd said, she could be home that night. And she was. Even after Cliff left her for the last time and she married Tony, the sweet-faced butcher, there were no babies. Her body seemed to sense she didn't have a talent for them; at least it never tried to give her more. The irony was that Tony had wanted a child so badly he'd divorced her for a woman who was undeniably fertile. And Savannah settled on dogs. You can't do as much damage to a dog. They're more resilient than all those fragile babies who turn out wrong because of something you said or did, or didn't say or do, at some crucial moment that you didn't even recognize as crucial. That must have been what happened to Phoenix. Gran Cicero, too. That's where it had all started.

Now there was a crazy old woman. Hateful, too, in a sneaky sort of way. Not a tear was shed when she finally died. Mama should have left her in the mental institution, where she belonged. Just like Mama to do exactly as she pleased, never mind who got hurt in the process. No wonder Hank left. Villanova never even asked him about Gran Cicero moving in, just came dragging her home that Christmas Eve; let him decide what he'd do. And he had. Men aren't as strong as women, no doubt about that.

At least Floyd is a better man than Phoenix's father; a good man, a good Christian man who needed a wife. A good Christian wife. Not to raise children—his were all grown and launched into their solid lives by the time he met Savannah—but to keep order in his life. Sometimes, when she sees him standing in the kitchen—her kitchen, the one she decorated herself using *Better Homes & Gardens* as a guide, with the matching almond appliances bought new and with cash, and her collection of pigs dressed in their cute little clothes—and the light catches him just right, it seems there's a halo around his sweet bald head. Silly to think of him that way, as an angel, her personal ticket to salvation, but she does. Sometimes.

He hadn't asked about her past. At first, she'd assumed he thought she had none, at least none as damning as hers was. Once, after Brother John's Wednesday night lesson, which had focused on cleansing the spirit with the truth of the Word, she'd been overcome by a fit of confession. Floyd had listened quietly, the way he must when one of his students talks to him, saying nothing, the tips of his fingers touching. "Whatever you're going to say, Van, well, I can't see where it has anything to do with us." He'd closed his eyes for a moment and then went back to reading his paper. She knew then that he had heard the rumors and gossip—small towns have long memories—and that it didn't matter, at least not to him. That night she started to forget, too, and to become the woman Floyd saw when he looked at her, the woman she always imagined she could be. She closed off the memories, the way she'd closed the doors on all those apartments she'd left—sometimes with Cliff or Tony, sometimes alone—firmly and without looking back, and threw herself into being Floyd's wife. It was a fair exchange, better than she deserved.

Dropping into the chair next to Savannah, her hair dripping and her skin still pink and damp from the run, Phoenix eyes her sister cautiously. "Where's Floyd?"

"Inside with Franklin, finishing up."

Taking the tail of her gray T-shirt, which is dark with sweat, Phoenix wipes her forehead. "It's still hot as hell out there. Met a couple of the locals. They called me a crazy old woman, who's just passing through. Pretty astute, I'd say." Phoenix chuckles. Savannah glowers.

They have so little in common. Ten years older than Phoenix, Savannah remembers her best as a toddler, round and pink and aggravating. The woman next to her rankles. "I'm sorry you didn't have a chance to say your good-byes to Mama before the Lord took her, Phoenix. Right to the end, she fretted about you, being in California all alone."

Phoenix screws up her mouth. "I'm *not* alone, Savannah."

Ignoring her remark, Savannah dabs at dry eyes with a lace-edged handkerchief. "I told her a thousand times that whenever you decided to come on home Floyd would take care of it, no questions asked. But you know how she always was." Their mother is barely dead and already Savannah has moved her into the far-distant past. Phoenix reminds herself she is no better; long ago she had reduced Villanova to little more than a shadow. Still, her sister's comment about Floyd paying her way grates. One more addition to Savannah's litany of Phoenix's failures. Savannah daintily blows her nose, smiles, and reaches for her sister's left hand, which Phoenix abruptly pulls back, pretending an urgent need to neaten her hair.

"I'll pay Floyd back for the plane tickets, I told you that." Guilt creeps in like fog, all this talk about money and obligation. She's never been good at either, and likely not to get better. This will hang between them for a long time, the way that night with Jinx has always hung between them, and before that Cliff. "I'll work out a payment schedule or something."

"Phoenix, don't be silly. I know how hard things have been for you. We are just so glad to do it for you." Savannah draws out her words, reaches across to squeeze Phoenix's fingers, and this time catches them unaware. "You're my baby sister. That's what sisters are for."

"Is it? I always wondered."

"Aren't you just the funniest girl?"

"So you say." Phoenix reclaims her hand and studies a small nick in her thumbnail.

"Why, it just seems like yesterday when you'd get yourself all doodied up. You were just the cutest little thing, got up in my dresses and high heels, parading in front of the mirror like a little princess. You couldn't of been more'n four years old."

Phoenix looks at her sister sideways. "You hated it."

"Why, Phoenix, I never. I always said you'd make a great actress."

Phoenix flushes, then smiles. "I wanted to be Lucille Ball. Make people laugh. I thought that would be the greatest thing in the world, next to singing the blues. That was my first choice."

"Well, our family never did have a voice for singing more than in church. And who would want to be Lucille Ball? She was so, well, unattractive, I always thought. I suppose she was happy as any of those people, but her last television shows were rather pathetic, don't you think? Of course, with her kind of money, what difference does it make? Those people must just sit home and count their money. Speaking of money, Phoenix, we need to chat about Mama's estate."

"What estate? A six-room frame house and a used Ford in the garage is not an estate."

"Well, Phoenix, of course it is." Savannah is twisting her hankie like a woman wringing out wash. "I know it's not much compared to California, but there are still decisions to be made."

"It doesn't matter, Savannah." Phoenix crosses, then uncrosses her legs, shifts in her chair. She wishes Floyd would come back. "Do whatever you think is best."

"You seem so different than when Floyd and I were out in California." Savannah looks at her sister closely, the way children examine strange and exotic bugs. The brindle hair is short now and tangled, but certainly more fashionably cut. Her lips look as if she's been sucking on cherries, dark but not unappealing. But there is a calmness in her eyes, which don't dart away as they always had from the time she was a child. "Phoenix, look at me when I talk to you"; somebody was always having to remind her of that. Now, she refuses to look away. Perhaps it's that man she's living with. All these years and finally there is a man in Phoenix's life. Well, better than that horrible woman Jinx. She never told Mama about how Phoenix was living in San Francisco, not that she didn't have the opportunity, Mama pressing for every detail after they'd come back. Instead, Savannah had turned herself into a common liar. Phoenix wouldn't understand that. Everything was always easy for her: the youngest, the smartest, the prettiest. All the advantages. Phoenix wasn't Mama's shame.

Phoenix never knew what it was to look into the face of every man in Williamson County hoping to find a clue. Did that one smile at Mama a little too long? Did his eyes linger on Savannah with a faint glimmer of recognition? She remembers Mama smelling of roses one afternoon, her skirt wide and bright with painted-on flowers, almost singing. "Savannah, honey, this here's your daddy." He was tall, she remembers that. Big as a mountain. She remembers holding on to Mama's skirt, stiff with its starched petticoat. Mama laughing, pulling her free, pushing her toward the man called Daddy, who lifted Savannah up high, high as the ceiling. Laughing. Holding her so high the room spun below. But the face is blank, like a man standing with his back to the sun, a silhouette without a name. Years later she had tried to probe the depths of her mother's past. "Who is he?" Mama had always turned her back. "What does it matter, Savannah? It has nothing to do with you." Then, "Mama, it has everything to do with me. He's my father. You owe me." And her mother, with those cold, level eyes, "I don't owe you one goddamned thing."

Even during these last awful months, with Villanova sick and Phoenix no help, even these last days in the hospital, when there was nothing left to gain or lose, Villanova closed out Savannah. "Please, Mama, I need to know." Villanova had patted her daughter's hand and smiled as if all the venom between them was gone, and no reason to talk about it anymore.

"What does it matter, Savannah? It was so long ago. Besides, he's gone now. I'm sure of that." Mama had drifted then, from the morphine or from Savannah herself. And then it was too late.

By the time Phoenix had arrived, late as always, vague and irresponsible and unresponsive, Villanova was dead and Phoenix didn't even cry. Tough. That's what she is, just like that awful woman she was living with in San Francisco, Jinx, the one who reminded Savannah of an angry boy, although she didn't really have the features or the shape of a boy. It was more her bearing, the set of her jaw, the way she was always leaning against the doorway or the wall, as if she couldn't be bothered to stand upright. When she and Floyd were out for that convention three years ago—or was it four? Time twists the older you get—they saw girls with green hair pasted into points like a rooster's crown, rings in their noses, sometimes even their eyebrows, sitting in doorways just waiting, watching. Men in dresses, not even bothering to try to look like women, just in dresses, beards and all. No one turned to stare. And Phoenix, dressed like she belonged in a carnival sideshow, with her hair tangled as if she never took a comb to it, was wearing a skirt too short for a woman with big legs. Not that Savannah's own legs are any better, but at least she has the good sense not to show them. And all those chains clank-clanking. Chains and rhinestones and dimestore beads dangling. No wonder that school fired her. Then she shows up here all in black leather; what could she have been thinking? Well, thank the good Lord Mama didn't have to see this. Savannah never would have heard the end of it. And without knowing why, she begins to cry.

The house of Phoenix Bay's childhood is doused in the cheap perfume old houses wear of families who have lived there a long time, their sweat and perfume and bad breath and fried-fish dinners so deeply embedded in the walls that no amount of new wallpaper or paint could ever cover entirely. The walls smell of ghosts and speak in whispers disguised as creaks and moans and sometimes a wheeze or a crack, as if time has been pressed here like a bridal rose in a family Bible.

Whenever her mother wallpapered a room, which was often, Phoenix would marvel at the history left on the bare plaster walls by the previous inhabitants. Notes, often written in pencil and meticulously dated, were recorded on the bare plaster next to newspaper patches dating back as far as 1927, although the house, at least parts of it, is actually much older. Through these notes Phoenix Bay explored the past. She left notes of her own sometimes, and a poem once, although Villanova discouraged such things. Phoenix imagined she was leaving her mark for the future. Then the summer she turned eleven, there was a real reason for a note: a grease-fire in the kitchen. She picked her spot carefully, next to the detail by J. Stone, 1921, which acknowledged the door between the kitchen and dining room had been widened to accommodate a wheelchair. Whose wheelchair? Villanova had shrugged, wiping an escaped curl back from her forehead, streaking her brow with the white paste, then went back to slathering a long strip of wallpaper covered in flowers. Floral medley.

At one time, Villanova had actually owned one-hundred-eighty-seven rolls of floral medley, a jarring combination of rainbow flowers, even brown and green, colors unseen in nature, tinged with streaks of gold and orange, as if the sunset had caught a mutant garden at its peak. A special deal, she had explained, only fifteen cents on the dollar because the Holiday Inn had turned the order back, doubtless fearing the garish display would disturb the sleep of the traveling salesmen and goose hunters who stayed there. "As if all cats aren't gray in the dark." Gray cats would have been preferable, TaTa Hassee said, and even Gran Cicero had nodded. "The Holiday Inn uses only the highest-quality wall coverings in its rooms." Villanova had been reading *Holiday Decorating Codes and Guidelines* while the general manager was on the phone. She considered herself, if not especially blessed or lucky, incredibly shrewd to have found such a bargain.

In more than thirty years she never managed to use up all that paper. Floral medley had given Phoenix an appreciation for stark white walls that did not threaten to close in, burying the residents in flowers of varied and indeterminate breed. Phoenix always suspected the floral medley didn't help Cicero's already confused mental state, although who could really say? Once in college, Phoenix had gone on a field trip to a state hospital, the same type that Cicero had been in, although not the same hospital. She was struck by how green everything was: green walls, green ceilings, green vinyl furniture, and fluorescent lights casting a green sheen on the patients. Maybe Gran Cicero thought all that green had finally given birth to Mama's flowered walls. Now, sitting in her mother's kitchen, surrounded by floral medley, Phoenix Bay is surprised at how little the house has changed. She keeps expecting to hear the drone of the black-and-white console TV from the next room, Gran Cicero inches from the screen, muttering, muttering, "Goddamn it. Shit. To hell. Gonna call the sheriff on you people," at the start of each commercial. Phoenix misses Gran Cicero the way you might a malevolent ghost, pleased at its absence, but nostalgic too. They'd rarely exchanged even so much as greetings, certainly never anything resembling conversation—Gran Cicero conversed only with TV game-show hosts—but she was a fixture, like the leaking roof that sent tears across the ceiling after a storm. No wonder that first her father, then her sister, and finally Phoenix herself had run full-tilt into the world. Every last one of them was running from, Phoenix reminds herself, not like the winners who run to.

Savannah is pacing, her voice rattling high and anxious through the kitchen. Phoenix winces. Nervous, she decides. And why not? Savannah has never lost a mother before, either. They don't know what to do, what comes next. Savannah settles nervously in one of the yellow, vinyl-and-chrome kitchen chairs. "Of course, the whole house needs to be repainted or wallpapered, whatever we like. We'll ask the decorator." Savannah's long, hot-pink fingernails drum softly against their mother's starched tablecloth, where perky yellow daisies loop cheerfully across white cotton. Phoenix closes her eyes and catches a glimpse of Villanova with her iron, the steam rising, the cloth hissing, the room smelling warm and thick. Her sister's fingernails switch to a snare drum staccato on the table's metal edge. Phoenix wonders if her sister plans to change her nail polish for the funeral. Something dark and sober, like burgundy, but never black, like the girls on Haight Street wear. Phoenix wishes she had brought a bottle of it with her. That would be a nice tribute. Savannah lights a cigarette, then, as if thinking better of it, snubs it out and begins rummaging through her purse for a small notebook where she's written *Kitchen.* Probably a page marked *Living Room,* too, but what about the bedrooms? Are they *Bedroom One, Two,* and *Three,* or *Mama's Room, Gran Cicero's, Phoenix's?*

"The decorator?" Phoenix has a hard time imagining any decorator interested in a house with so little personality.

"You know Gayla Martin from my church circle? Well, of course you wouldn't, but anyway, her sister took the whole sequence of decorator courses through the extension college and works at the Sears store in their custom-decor department. She's very talented. Did my whole living room." Savannah cocks her head and smiles. "Now it will cost initially, but in the end it'll be worth it. Of course, real estate here is nothing at all like it is in California, as you can imagine."

"I can imagine." Phoenix is peeling an orange, watching the tiny spray of juice and oil fizz into a fine mist that covers her fingers. She licks the slightly bitter oil; it reminds her a little of

Cecelie, who always leaks bitters from her nipples when she comes. She smiles at her sister, just in case Savannah thinks she's not paying attention.

"It's all a trade-off, or so Lonnie says." This last sounds a little triumphant and Phoenix can't imagine why.

"Lonnie?" Phoenix doesn't know anyone named Lonnie.

"Floyd's son. You know, the real estate agent. He says we're just lucky that Mama decided to go with siding ten years ago; otherwise we'd be facing the exterior, too. You remember how this house never would hold paint."

Phoenix remembers no such thing. The exterior of the house was always just there, an indelible part of the landscape of her childhood. What she remembers clearly is the elm tree that seemed to anchor the front yard. Wide and cool, ancient as TaTa Hassee. But now there is only a flat patch of too-green sod, rimmed in white rock, planted with marigolds. Phoenix buried her best goldfish under that tree, and the tiny green turtle, and the chameleon she bought for a dime at the county fair. There, too, were the baby rabbits, killed but not eaten, by Mister Whiskers, TaTa Hassee's cat. And the charm bracelet her father gave her the night he told her he was leaving and this time not coming back. The bracelet was a tiny music box, no bigger than a matchbook, with a pink poodle painted on it. When you wound the key, it played "Daddy's Little Girl," or at least the first stanza. "This here'll remind you of your old dad and how much he loves his girl." "How much, Daddy?" "This much, baby," then stretching his arms wide he'd pulled her close. Jinx had called her that, too: "baby." And Savannah, just this evening. She doesn't trust people who call her "baby." The music box was still playing when she'd covered it over. "What happened to the tree?" she asks her sister.

"What tree?"

"The big one, out there. What happened to it?" It seems important to know.

"Oh, that." Savannah looks up and spreads her hands, examining each nail carefully. Even her diamonds have lost their shimmer in this pale, yellow light. God, has this kitchen always been so dark? "I don't really know. I suppose Dutch elm disease or something. Or maybe the tornado a few years back. At least we don't have to worry about it messing up the roof when it storms. That happens with those old trees. They come down just like that." She snaps her fingers decisively. "What a mess. The insurance company calls it an act of God, and there you are stuck with a dead tree through the roof." Savannah pours more coffee, takes a sip, and smiles. "Now, mind you, while I don't know exactly what this house is worth, Lonnie says his educated guess is probably not more than thirty. I know that sounds like nothing to you, but this isn't California."

The way Savannah feels it necessary to keep reminding her of the obvious amuses Phoenix. "No, Savannah, this certainly is *not* California." Coughing, she spits a piece of orange into her hand: spent white skin with bits of flesh bleeding through. Her tongue toys with one of the small seeds, perfect, smooth, like a tiny, disconnected clitoris. Wiping her mouth, she is trying not to smile. Her sister shoots her an ugly look.

"Of course, Floyd and I are willing to settle for less. We want you to be happy; that's all that matters." Phoenix looks skeptical. "I was telling Floyd that now with him semiretired and Mama . . . well, gone . . . that there's not a reason in the world why we can't go to Arizona for the whole winter instead of just January. Now, Floyd would be content to move down there lock, stock, and barrel, but I say November through April is escape enough for me." Phoenix, who is trying to imagine how Scottsdale, Arizona, could be an escape from anything, detects the slightly superior tone women weave into their speech when they talk about husbands. "And the babies just love it." The babies. Of course. Savannah's silly little dogs. Not ordinary poodles, she was quick to point out when Phoenix had made that blunder on their way here, peek-a-poos, a special cross-breed. "Peek-a-boo, baby. Daddy's here, now he's gone." Her father's big hands block out the light, blinding her for a moment. Phoenix Bay feels as if she's going to throw up.

"Does Mama have any schnapps?" Villanova gave up bourbon when she found religion, but there was always a bottle of schnapps. Cough syrup, she said.

"We were under the impression you'd quit drinking, Phoenix." Savannah's voice is as sharp as her glance.

"Yeah, well, I did . . . mostly. " Phoenix shrugs, caught.

"After all you've been through. Now, wasn't that enough? It certainly was for Floyd's oldest boy, Earl. He hit bottom and in a big way, I can tell you. Lost everything, his job, even his wife." Savannah drags out the last word for emphasis.

"Yeah, me too. Only mine left because I went nuts, not because I got drunk." Phoenix can't resist. She shoots a wicked grin toward her sister. Bottom is like paradise, it comes in a lot of different colors, but it almost always wears the face of a woman. Savannah looks so wounded, Phoenix is almost sorry. But then, Savannah never would admit her sister is queer. "Just thought that a shot might, you know, drown a few of the ghosts." Her sister looks at Phoenix oddly. "I only meant that being back here is hard, Savannah."

"Well, of course it is." Patronizing, Savannah's voice is softening, now that victory is assured. "But you're just so much better now. I was saying that very thing to Floyd just this evening after you went running off. I told him 'our Phoenix is her old self.' " She beams, then lowers her voice to a confidential whisper. "And I never for a minute believed you were really crazy. I mean, not like, well . . . *her.* " She means Gran Cicero.

Phoenix inhales and scowls. "I was depressed, Savannah, not stark-raving mad."

"We all get that way every once in a while. You know what I do? I take the babies out for a nice little drive into the forest or over to the lake. Oh, they just love that. And next thing I know, I've snapped right out of it. You should try that some time."

"Too bad I didn't think of that, Savannah. I could've saved a bundle on psychiatrist's bills. As it was, I just concentrated on new ways to do myself in."

"Oh." Her sister's hand trembles as she reaches for the coffee pot. "Well, of course you'd never really do anything like that, Phoenix." She doesn't raise her eyes as she pours.

Phoenix catches her sister's wrist. "You really don't remember, do you?"

Savannah's hands flutter; her eyes refuse to meet Phoenix's. "There's nothing to remember, Phoenix. Here, have some decaf."

Savannah pushes the sugar bowl across the table. "Put lots of sugar in it. That'll help."

"That's for junkies, Savannah. And it probably doesn't work for them, either." Phoenix reaches for one of Savannah's cigarettes. This is the first time she's ever smoked openly in her mother's house. All those Bayless women were clandestine smokers: TaTa Hassee hiding in the bathroom, smoke billowing out into the hall whenever she opened the door; poor old Gran Cicero, sneaking off to the attic—a minor miracle that she didn't burn down the house; Villanova disappearing to her bedroom porch every night after supper. Phoenix snubs out the cigarette. Who is she to challenge ghosts? "The problems I have are a little less, shall we say, physical. You say I'm not like her—well, you're wrong. I'm more like her than you or Mama could ever bring yourselves to admit. You two couldn't have it any other way. And you need me the way Mama needed Gran Cicero. But tell me, Savannah, what does a martyr do when it's over?"

"Phoenix, really, the way you talk. Why, if I didn't know you better . . ."

"Savannah," Phoenix begins, then stops, exasperated. But what is there left to lose? "How can you know me? You left when I was seven years old. So, I'd say you've missed damned near thirty years. Not great years, mind you, but a few were memorable. Like the time I tried to strangle myself when Daddy missed my birthday. Mama never told you about that, did she? You know why? She never noticed. You don't know me at all; neither did she."

Savannah's hands flutter, sweeping away imaginary lint. "Well, Phoenix, maybe that's true, what you say . . . about me. But not about Mama. It just broke her heart that you never came home. Not even for her mother's funeral. You don't know how that hurt her."

"Gran Cicero's funeral? That was years ago." Phoenix glares. She is the headlight; Savannah, the doe. "Besides, what difference could it have made? She never even knew who we were. Do you know who she thought Mama was? The landlady. That's all we ever were to her."

Savannah exhales slowly, exasperated. Just like Mama. "Well, Phoenix, some things are just better left forgotten. That's what Floyd always says. And what good does it do to dredge all this up? What's important, now that you've come home to us, is to decide what's best for you. Honey, we want you home, here with us." Home? The word sounds dry. A limp breeze rubs leaves against the screen. A large June bug slams its stupid, slow-moving body into the porch light, a bare, dim bulb. Savannah's hands sweep-sweep. "Floyd and I have talked it over. We'd sell our share of Mama's house to you for fifteen thousand, interest free, payable over twelve years. No banks or mortgages, nothing like that, just family. It's a very good offer, Floyd says." Phoenix blinks. Is it possible her sister really thinks she wants this house, with its ghosts and floral medley wallpaper, the yellow crushed-velvet sofa, the brass floor lamp with its tattered silk shade, the moaning pipes and cranky furnace that gurgles late into the night? "That would include the furnishings," Savannah continues. "Of course, there are a few things I'd like . . . for sentimental reasons, you understand." The hard edge is back in her sister's voice.

"No. No-no-no-no." Reciting the word as if it were a mantra, Phoenix shakes her head, trying to clear it. But like a needle stuck on a scratched record, she can't seem to stop. Her fingers grip the edge of the table. She'd run from this house and the crazy women in it, this town with its prying eyes, this whole judgmental world with its ruined land and soured people. Nothing will suck her back, not this sister she hardly knows, certainly not this house. She will not build a shrine to a past she doesn't want to remember, and can't forget.

"Well, Phoenix, I certainly think I'm entitled to a few things." Indignant at the imagined affront, Savannah's mouth is working like a fish. Mama used to do that, too, just like she used to precede every indictment against Phoenix with one word: *Well.* "It's only fair, Floyd says." When Savannah whines, she sounds not altogether unlike her damned peek-a-poos at feeding time.

"Savannah, please, I don't need this." The kitchen is closing in around her. Sweat runs down her face like tears, or maybe mixed with tears, she can no longer tell; it feels the same. She's been sweating ever since she got off the plane, and now this. "Like I told you at the funeral home, you figure it out." She lowers her face into her open hands.

"Well, Phoenix, I just don't know what to say. All we're trying to do is help you out and this is the thanks we get." Savannah's pained little smile seems stuck to her teeth. "All right, Phoenix. We don't have to decide anything this instant, while you're still so upset about Mama." Savannah is using her simpering voice now, the one she uses on Floyd and, likely, those dogs. "I was thinking, though, that tomorrow before the visitation maybe you would want to do a little shopping. There's the cutest boutique at the mall. You could take Mama's car and go on over in the morning to find a little something. My treat, of course." Savannah smiles too brightly, and pats Phoenix's hand.

"I have clothes, Savannah."

"I mean for . . . well, what were you planning for the funeral?" Savannah almost whispers.

"The funeral?" How odd; Phoenix had almost forgotten. "I don't know. Does it really matter?" Her head throbs. Her sister shifts in focus.

Savannah has turned dour, as if the humidity has rusted her face closed. "Well, Phoenix, of course it does. I thought it would be nice if we knew what each other was wearing. I have the sweetest little black eyelet that I got on sale. Not that black does a thing for me. You'll see, once you get past forty, it looks like you're going to a funeral." Realizing what she's said, Savannah hics, a nervous, girlish noise.

"So why'd you buy it?"

"Because . . . well, they were having the Fourth of July sale, and . . . you just never know." Savannah's guilt shows in her hands, the way they flutter, tucking back imaginary wisps of hair.

Phoenix nods absently, before she comprehends. "You bought a dress for Mama's funeral before she was even dead?" Or before you called me, Phoenix thinks.

"You don't have to use that tone of voice, Phoenix. And it is a perfectly lovely dress. The shop has the latest things. Très. That's what it's called. Like in *très chic*. Their clothes come from New York *and* California."

"You went shopping for a funeral dress and my mama wasn't even dead?"

"Phoenix, really, it wasn't like that. But now I'm grateful I found it. I wouldn't want to have to rush around at the last minute. It was on sale." This she offers lamely.

"Oh. Well, that does make all the difference."

Savannah sniffs. "Well, think what you will. I have an account there. You just go on over in the morning and tell Yvonne, she's the owner, that you're my sister and she'll fix you up. Not the same exact dress, of course, but something compatible would be nice."

"Don't you think we're a little old for the sister look?" Phoenix likes the sound of evil on her tongue, how it rolls off like a heat-seeking missile, locates the target, and explodes, somewhere deep in her sister's brain. She smiles sweetly, watching Savannah take the hit.

"Well, fine then. Just don't wear anything . . ." Savannah pauses.

"Dykey?"

Her sister exhales and looks at the ceiling. Phoenix looks, too. Nothing there except streaks of brown in the shiny yellow paint, where the roof had cried last spring. "I wasn't going to say that, but since you brought it up, what you had on at the airport was, well, mannish."

"I should hope so, the clothes belonged to a man."

"What man? That man you live with?"

"No. And I don't live with Rennie, I explained all that."

Savannah starts to say something, but the sound of a car pulling in next to the house followed by the hollow crunching of boots on gravel stops her. They both look up in expectation as Floyd comes through the door, his round face painted in greeting. "How are my girls getting on?"

"Fine, Floyd," Savannah answers automatically.

He chuckles. "Well, that's just fine. Just real fine. Have you had a chance to tell Phoenix the good news, Pumpkin?"

"She said she'd think on it," Savannah lies.

"Quite a deal compared to what real estate goes for in the Sunshine State, wouldn't you say, Phoenix? What's a shack like this worth out there? Half a mil?"

"Give or take," Phoenix answers. Floyd lets out a long, low whistle, shaking his head slowly in appreciation. "But you know what they say: Location is everything." She likes Floyd. All this isn't his fault.

"I wish you two wouldn't refer to Mama's house as a shack." Savannah gathers her purse, pats her hair, preparing to leave.

"Just a figure of speech, Pumpkin. Phoenix knows what I mean, don't you? When we were in Frisco, why I remember telling that to your friend . . . what was her name?"

"Jinx."

"That's right. Nice girl. You two still living in that place near the little park?"

"No, Floyd, they aren't friends anymore," Savannah interjects. "I told you that. Phoenix is living with a man now."

Floyd locks his hands across his round belly, considering this new bit of information, although Savannah is probably right, she likely did tell him. "Is that so?"

"He's an old friend, Floyd, who happens to be a man. He has AIDS." She adds this last to test the water. Best to know exactly what you're up against.

Floyd shakes his head, more sympathetic than surprised. "Terrible thing. You remember that Davis boy last year, Pumpkin? He didn't last too long, poor fella. He lived in California, too. San Diego, I believe. Maybe you knew him?" Phoenix shakes her head. "His folks wanted him at home. Damned shame and such nice people, too." Who, Phoenix wonders, the Davises or their dying son? Floyd has a tendency to talk more to himself than to anyone in the room, a running commentary in which anyone can join at any time.

"I was just saying, when you came in, how pleased we are to have her home." Savannah steps toward the door, apparently hoping Floyd will follow. "We've just been so worried—haven't we, Floyd?—out there all alone and none too well herself."

Floyd's broad face takes on a solemn look. "Oh," he says, shifting his weight from one foot to the other. He's never felt comfortable in his mother-in-law's house, although he could never quite put his finger on why, just as he's never been quite comfortable the way his wife talks to her sister. She should just leave well enough alone, but she never does. Why would she dredge it all up again? Still, he feels obliged to say something, so he offers, "We sure are glad to have you here, honey, and that's the truth. Just too bad about your mama, is all."

"Not that it wasn't expected," Savannah says, nodding.

"No, indeed," agrees Floyd.

"It wasn't expected by me."

"Well, Phoenix, Mama and I didn't see any reason to burden you."

"Savannah always did want to take care of me," Phoenix tells Floyd.

"That's what big sisters are for," Savannah says, smiling all the while.

With Savannah gone back to her coordinated almond kitchen and all those little ceramic pigs with their painted-on grins, looking far happier than any real creature could, Phoenix is left to poke through the drawers and closets of her mother's house. Now her house, hers and Savannah's. She has the sensation she is doing something wrong, as if any second her mother will appear. But the drawers yield their secrets in silence.

TaTa Hassee's room is empty except for a dresser and the bed, its mattress stripped bare, exposing a wide stain. Phoenix opens the drawers on the old dresser. Empty. Even with its chipped veneer and cloudy mirror, it would sell for six hundred dollars in San Francisco. They'll be lucky to give it away here. This part of the world is saturated with the past, unlike California, where everything is new and crisp.

Across the hall is Gran Cicero's room, smaller and with only the one window: Plexiglas nailed shut, the only Plexiglas window in the house, maybe in the neighborhood or the entire town, for all Phoenix knows. It had been her room, sweet and cozy, before Gran Cicero's unwelcome arrival. "But *why* do I have to sleep with Savannah, Mama?" "Because your grandmother needs this room." "I hate her, Mama. I hate her and I don't want her here." She can still feel her mother's hand against her cheek, her fingers digging into her shoulder, shaking her. "Don't ever let me hear you say that again! Do you hear me? Never!" No mirror in this room, just a painted bureau, five drawers, each empty. Gran Cicero couldn't be trusted with hangers or hooks or glass. Even after she'd gone blind from cataracts, she could still find the television, her link to the outside world. All that was left to her were game shows with the glittery hostesses she could no longer see and hosts who smile too much and kiss housewives from Anaheim and office managers from Fresno. Will California never run out of game-show contestants?

When the plague was still new, gay men were amusing themselves getting on the game shows. Any distraction would do. She knew a man who won a new car, a pair of diamond earrings, and a trip to Australia, all expenses paid, just because he was good at puzzles. The car was sold to pay the taxes on the prizes, his mother got the earrings, and he and his lover ran off to Australia and never came back. But then the fascination with game shows had ended. There was too much to do, too many real puzzles to try to solve.

Phoenix Bay opens the door to her mother's room slowly, as if Villanova were sleeping there. Slippers of moonlight pad across the floor. Her mother's housecoat, pink chenille with blue flowers, hangs on the back of the open closet door. The room is smaller than Phoenix remembers, shabby, although it never was elegant, and furnished with only the necessities: a bureau, its veneer uncracked but slightly wrinkled; the headboard of the bed rising in curlicues that always reminded her of the shape of a woman's backside. Phoenix tries the narrow door to the little porch. Stuck. She leans into it until it gives finally. A listless breeze moves into the room, blending with the scent of her mother. Without turning on the light, Phoenix lies back on the bed. She is fully dressed. It seems indecent to sleep naked in her mother's bed. Turning her face toward the open door, the moon turns wavy through her tears.

Phoenix Bay awakens with a start. The clock next to the bed registers eight-seventeen and twenty-seven seconds. Thank God for digitals, otherwise you'd be left wondering about all those lost seconds. It takes a moment to get her bearings, even longer to remember that her mother isn't in the kitchen downstairs. Her old gray sweater with the missing third button would be draped over the doorknob. As she bends to get the milk from the refrigerator, her work jeans with wide pockets and white stitching would stretch taut. TaTa Hassee and Gran Cicero would be at the kitchen table, motionless as ancient statues, waiting for breakfast. The old women, like Phoenix, started every day with cornflakes limp in skim milk, chocolate sandwich cookies, and grumbling. But this morning the house hugs its silent ghosts.

"We're your people, honey, we love you." Savannah's parting words last night click against the morning. "We want you home, where you belong." Never mind what Phoenix wants, where she belongs. Outside the front door, instead of the morning newspaper she finds a quart of strawberries and a fudge cake, brown goo sticking to the plastic wrap. A bee hovers hopefully, fat and yellow and treacherous. Bees don't grow so fat in California, or if they do, she's never seen one. In the kitchen she runs hot tap water over a spoonful of Folger's coffee crystals; Villanova never could make a decent cup of coffee. Instant coffee and fudge cake and strawberries for breakfast. Well, she's had worse. From the living room, a cheap imitation grandfather's clock chimes nine times, slightly off key. Obviously no musicians in this family. Eight hours to kill before the wake and then another full day until the funeral. Savannah probably told the mortician to stretch it out, in case Phoenix has any plans of an early escape. The phone rings, splitting the silence. Following the sound into the living room, Phoenix stands over the jangling phone. She drops into the Barcolounger, one leg draped over the arm. On the seventeenth ring, she finally picks up.

"Well, thank goodness. I was about to give up."

"Who is this?" Phoenix asks, although she knows perfectly well.

"Darling, it's Van." Savannah calls herself that now. Before Floyd, it was Vanna. What's next: Va? Or maybe just V. And then one day Savannah will disappear altogether. Just like Mama. "What took you so long to answer?"

Licking a bit of icing off her right thumb, Phoenix picks a lie, "I couldn't find the phone."

"Well, Phoenix, it's where it's always been." When did Savannah start sounding like Mama, that same exasperation whenever Phoenix steps over some invisible line?

"Well, Savannah, it's different now. It's yellow." But the words don't have any sting. Apologies never do. "How's Floyd?" She's hoping to catch her sister off guard.

"Floyd? Why, he's fine, of course. It's you I'm calling about. How *are* you?"

"I found a fudge cake and strawberries on the porch this morning. Not bad."

"How nice. Who left them?"

"Don't know. TaTa Hassee's cakes were better, though. This one attracts bees."

"Bees?"

"And the instant coffee's terrible. I sent Mama a coffee grinder for her birthday and signed her up for one of those companies that sends a different kind of coffee bean every month. But I can't find it anywhere." Right now at home, Cecelie would be making coffee from dark beans, slick with oil, ground fine in their neat little coffee grinder that buzzes when she pushes down the top. A happy sound. "Did Mama really drink this instant shit?"

"Don't say *shit*, Phoenix. Have you found something nice to wear? I called Yvonne at home last night. She runs Très. I told her to put anything you'd like on my account."

"Anything I'd like?" Phoenix doubts there is anything at Très to like.

"Well, within reason, of course. Fortunately, black is in this summer."

She pours the coffee onto a scraggly philodendron. "My, that *is* fortunate."

"Don't be snide. Besides, who can't use another little black dress?"

Me, Phoenix wants to say, but settles on another lie, "I already have something, actually." She wonders where she'll find anything even remotely suitable for her mother's funeral, and what difference it would make if she doesn't. These people already think the worst. Nothing she can do would change that. And Cecelie was no help, packing Carson's white linen suit, now hopelessly wrinkled, a black bustier, stockings and a pair of stilettos that pinch Phoenix's toes. But no dress. Well, what did she expect? Fashion isn't Cecelie's strong point. Maybe there's something in Villanova's closet. Anything sounds better than Yvonne and Très.

Savannah sighs. Phoenix imagines her sister sitting in her kitchen surrounded by ceramic pigs, drinking coffee from a pig-shaped mug, slipping bits of toast and bacon to Dunkin and Punkin, the lap dogs. Savannah's lap has always been better suited to dogs than to children. "Well, Phoenix, whatever you say. I just want to make you feel at home. By the way, what have you decided about the house?" Savannah's voice is brittle. Phoenix is definitely another one of those burdens Savannah would like to lay down.

"I told you last night, I don't want it."

"Well, Phoenix, I do wish you'd reconsider."

"I have reconsidered. I've re-reconsidered. It's generous of you . . . and Floyd," she includes him because her sister probably expects it. "But I'm going home day after tomorrow." Day after tomorrow suddenly seems very far away.

"Oh, can't you stay a while longer?" Savannah's voice is high-pitched and wheedling.

"Say, Savannah, I really would like to chat, but somebody's at the door. Maybe it's another cake; you know how the neighbors are." The door hangs silent.

Her sister brightens. "Of course, darling. Give my best to . . . well, to whoever's there. Mama had so many friends, everybody loved her." Phoenix wonders when this surge of popularity might have occurred. "Now don't forget, we'll pick you up at five. And, Phoenix . . ."

"Savannah, I've *really* got to go." She hangs up, smiling, wondering what else her sister wanted to say. They'd covered the basics: the house, her clothes; all that was left was pretending to be respectable. Phoenix bypasses her mother's closet and negotiates the attic ladder down from the ceiling trap at the end of the hall. The attic is so hot that the dusty air threatens to singe her lungs. How could she have stood to come up here, so close to the roof, the bare plank boards hot to the touch? And yet for years, this was her hiding place. She was Cinderella in her mother's green chiffon party dress with the ruffled ballerina-length skirt and one ripped sleeve, the fabric fragile and stiff with dust. "I used to love that dress," Villanova told her once, her eyes shining. "There was a boy who said it made me look like a princess. Well, ain't I some kind of princess now?" What boy? Did he tear the sleeve? But the dress is gone.

Years later, Phoenix had turned to exploring her own flesh here. Tying dimestore scarves to her wrists, pink nylon tickling her hard little breasts, she was one of the wicked naked women in the magazines she'd found mixed in with Mr. Willetts's back issues of *Outdoor Life* left in the alley for the Boy Scouts paper drive. Wicked women had huge breasts and dirty feet and lounged on unmade beds; their hands roamed in as-yet-unspeakable places. You knew they were wicked because they were smiling. No real woman was ever so desirable or so wicked.

The old wardrobe smells of mothballs and cedar. In it she finds a black suit, fashionable again: a long neat skirt, with a deep slit up the back, and an almost elegant jacket encrusted with shiny braiding swirling over wide lapels. Stripping off her clothes, Phoenix tries on the skirt, a little tight through the thighs, but otherwise fine . . . more than fine with the black bustier and heels. Standing on her toes, she turns in front of the window, catching a dusty reflection. All her life she's checked her reflection in front of windows; mirrors make her nervous. Just like Villanova. The window looks out on her favorite view in the world. If she had this house, she'd sleep here in the attic and look down on the backyard and out onto the roofs of the houses marching toward the center of town. There's a swing set where Mr. Willetts of the dirty magazines used to live. Children. She could adopt a little girl or maybe even have a baby. Lesbians do that all the time now. And get a job teaching high school English. She'd plant a vegetable garden in the back; find somebody who could tell her what to do about the mess of the grape arbor. Cecelie could teach at the university. They never had much of an archaeology department, but that would be a challenge, wouldn't it?

A screen door opens, then bangs loosely on its hinges; gravel in the driveway scrunches softly. Phoenix slips into the shadows.

An angular woman, with gray hair and a determined gait, and carrying a brown casserole dish, marches toward the back door. Tollie Pengrove. Phoenix smiles. Mama always said Tollie was tougher than she looked. Now she even looks tough. Setting the dish on the top steps, Tollie wipes her hands on the skirt of her brown-flowered housedress and knocks. Phoenix stops breathing, as if Tollie might hear. The doorknob jiggles. Satisfied that no one is home, Tollie ambles toward the garden. Villanova spent one entire Saturday turning up that hard soil with a spade, until her hands bled. The next day, she bought a yellow rose bush. Every year, she bought another. Fascinated, Phoenix watches as the woman pulls off the best roses with her bare hands.

Shadows paint the yard in crisp shades of green, so Phoenix does not at first notice the vase, the cheap green-glass kind that florists buy by the gross. Villanova always kept a few in the garage to hold screws and mismatched bolts and slightly rusted nails. Cramming half the roses into the vase, Tollie sits on the steps scribbling something on a white card. Without looking back, she clambers off the stoop and strolls back across the yard toward her house, the casserole balanced on one hand and more than a dozen of Villanova's yellow roses in the other.

Phoenix slips down the stairs and opens the door. Tollie has penciled, "A gift from God's garden in your hour of sorrow" beneath a complicated verse about Jesus. It occurs to Phoenix that if she had stayed here, she never would have thought she was crazy.

 14

The river, thick, green, and unforgiving, glints against her memory. Dragonflies dance along the surface; silver-blue needle bodies shine like crystals in the sun. Closing her eyes, she can hear their wings buzzing, buzzing, the way they did the morning TaTa Hassee handed her over to Brother Larry on the banks of the river. "M-i-double s-i-double s-i-double p-i." She could say it faster than any of the others in Mrs. Wilson's second-grade class. Except for David. He was on the shore with the rest of them that morning, watching as Brother Larry, his black suit soaked to the knees, carried Phoenix into water until it lapped at his waist, until it reached up to soak the hem of her white organdy dress. Did he speak to her? He must have, but the words melted in the sun and were washed away by the water as he pushed her under. Three times. Curious snakes swam close. Dragonflies sang. Each time she came up screaming, her eyes focused on Brother Larry's beard, huge and black, and glinting with beads of water; his eyes, luminous with the reflections of clouds in the clear high-summer sky, focused on Heaven.

When it was over, her great-grandmother's calloused hand closed around Phoenix's wrist, pulling her along the sticky mud bank, until she was forced to dance on her toes just to keep up. David was on the path ahead of them, swatting at mosquitoes, walking close to his daddy. Through the young willows along the bank, the car roofs glinted black in the sun. Wild foxtail prickled Phoenix's damp bare legs, catching in her ruined anklets, turned gray from the filthy water, thick with slime. TaTa, head forward like an old camel, never paused, never looked back. "Stop drag-gin' your feet, Sis. There ain't no place at Heaven's table for lag-gards." Bees, attracted by the dampness and her child's sweetness, crawled along her bare arms that were rubbed raw by the wet organdy. She wanted to cry, for the ruined dress, for the torn lace on the anklets, for her mother. Instead, she'd started shivering—so hard her teeth chattered. Her great-grandmother didn't notice. "Now you been saved, you don't never have to fear death, no more." Phoenix didn't feel saved; she felt ashamed.

David Starwell is the only purely good memory from her child-hood. A dreamer, he thought his name was prophetic; promised that as soon as he was old enough, he was going to run away to New York or maybe even Hollywood and become a star. He actu-ally did run away to New York his sophomore year in college, and even became an actor of sorts. But fame was elusive and he settled for dating one of the actors on "All My Children" or maybe it was "Days of Our Lives"; his letters were a little unclear. He used to send her playbills, with little notes scribbled inside. The last one came around Christmas three or four years ago. David was cast as Older Man I. None of the characters had names; it was that kind of play. And when Phoenix tried to write to him months later—they had that kind of relationship—her letter had come back with a yellow, computerized sticker from the Post Office, letting her know he was gone, leaving no forwarding address. She doesn't like to think about what that means. Instead, she thinks about how it was when they were kids. They mattered then, the way kids do who have only each other.

The town would have said she had her mama and great-grand-mama—nobody ever mentioned Gran Cicero—and after his daddy was killed, David still had his uncle, the Major. Everything about the Major was big and very bright. His hair was yellow and streaked with silver, and when he smiled, his whole face would light up like a Christmas tree. His shirts were so white they seemed to glow. The Major said it was good for business—he sold washing machines, and dryers and refrigerators and stoves—in a store called Major Appliances. David said it was a play on words and was supposed to be funny. Phoenix never understood why. The Major kept three things on his desk in the back of the store: the purple heart he'd won in Korea, his high school football picture, and a Plexiglas paperweight in which a gold-plated key to his white Cadillac convertible appeared to be floating inside. That was supposed to be funny, too.

The Major's best friend was the clock repairman Earl Hicks—nearly everybody called him Poor Earl, even though he had more money than God. They shared the same building with two storefronts; on the left was Major Appliances, and on the right, Hickory Dickory Clocks. Backyard neighbors as well, they had taken down the fences, making one large, seamless garden. Summer nights, Poor Earl and the Major would sit in white wrought-iron garden chairs, smoking pipes, listening to the St. Louis Cards game on the radio, while Phoenix and David acted out plays in the side yard. Some nights, women—those looking for husbands and those eager to shed the ones they had—would stroll by the Major's house, pausing at the corner, sniffing the air like cats, stooping to straighten a seam, and hoping that the Major would look up, call out an invitation to join him for iced tea on the patio. He never did.

Dressed in a dead woman's black gabardine suit with shiny black buttons the shape of toenails, Phoenix Bay sits on the edge of the porch swing, motionless, waiting for a breeze. Swinging would be nice, but every movement, no matter how small, sends an arthritic groan from the old chains and dislodges flakes of paint like dead gray skin. Hot. Too damned hot to be dressed in black gabardine in the middle of the day. It would be cool at the river. But Savannah told her to be ready and waiting. Ready to stand in the chapel at Simons and Sons, making small talk with strangers, with her dead mother not six feet away in a bronze-tone casket. (Savannah had finally decided on bronze tone because she thought Villanova would keep better, for God's sake.) There are some things she will not do.

Quick as a thief, she backs her mother's Ford Fairlane out of the garage, the gas gauge hovering just below the half-full mark, and cruises past the business district. Major Appliances is still there. Wonder who's running it now? She'd heard the Major died a few years ago. Hickory Dickory Clocks is gone, though, replaced by a frozen-yogurt shop. If she hurries, she'll be able to see the sun set over the river in Grand Tower, sit on the mud bank, and eat catfish from Moe's—real catfish from the river, not those pitiful things from city supermarkets, raised in artificial ponds, never once knowing the taste of mud on their whiskers—and hushpuppies, with coleslaw so sweet the cream lies thick as love on your tongue, all served up on a thin white paper plate with ruffled edges.

Moe's is still there, the same long building with fading clapboards, each nearly a foot wide, reflecting the early-evening sun onto the white-gravel parking lot. The paper plates are gone, replaced by Styrofoam, but the catfish is the same, like the sunset along the river, slow and streaked with gold against the water, Missouri on the opposite shore, old trees as thick and green as anything she's ever dreamed of and loved and missed without realizing it. A dragonfly, quick and blue, dances against the mud bank where a pair of boys fish, not once looking at the barefoot stranger in a long black skirt and satin bustier glowing like a black moon under her open jacket.

Walking slowly back to the Fairlane, carrying her shoes in her right hand, Phoenix Bay considers her options. Savannah is probably having a fit. Poor Floyd. If she really pushes it, she could still make it back in time to put in an appearance at the wake. If she doesn't, Savannah will make sure Phoenix hears about it until the day *she* dies. The old car trembles as it approaches sixty, then sixty-five, finally seventy. Windows down, radio on, she could be sixteen again running off to—where? Anywhere away from that hated house and those Bayless women. Or running away to a new life on a farm in southern Oregon with Molly. She almost got it right there: her life, loving Molly, until winter closed in around the house and she was sure spring would never come to that unforgiving land. She'd stayed until she could stand it no longer and then one afternoon floated away, down the gravel road and into the cab of a semi hauling broccoli to New York. Funny, she can't remember the trucker's name, just the dog's, Shannon, a woolly half-sheepdog, that spent the next three thousand miles leaning across Phoenix's lap, trying to hang his head out the window. She suspects the trucker was gay; at least he didn't make a pass at her or expect her to give him head, the way she'd heard truck drivers do when they pick up lone women. And he didn't mention his family or even look up at the waitresses at the truck stops where he ordered her hamburgers that were often called "big rigs with a side"; the side always turned out to be coleslaw. When he dropped her off in front of Rennie's apartment in New York, she still had the hundred and thirty-three dollars she'd started with and Molly's onyx necklace.

An irritating red glow flashes at her from the dashboard, flickers twice, then comes alive in earnest. Shit. Five hundred yards ahead, a battered Texaco sign groans under a lank breeze. A cinder-block building, painted yellow, seems to glow from the light of a red-neon sign: GAS - SERVICE - GAS. A clapboard house, painted the same yellow, sits at the far end of the driveway. Pulling in under the sign, steam pouring from beneath the Ford's hood,

Phoenix kills the ignition and slumps onto the steering wheel, her face in her arms.

"You want I should crack that for you? She'll cool down faster, if you know what I mean. Then I'll take a look see. Probably your thermostat." The voice is slow and rusty. Phoenix has fallen in love over less than a voice like this. Opening her eyes, she turns to look at the woman behind the voice. Tall, but not exceedingly so, and solid—muscular but well padded, too. A badge over her left breast tells Phoenix she is about to meet Little Fritzy.

"So," says Phoenix, smiling her best smile, "this must be my lucky day."

Phoenix has spent the last forty minutes sitting on the hood of Little Fritzy's rebuilt 1981 Trans Am, drinking lukewarm Coke from a bottle and watching Little Fritzy, or specifically Little Fritzy's ass. The rest of her is obscured by the hood of Villanova's car. Sliding off the Trans Am, Phoenix picks up her shoes; the pavement is finally cool. "It's a 1974," Phoenix volunteers, mostly in an attempt at conversation. No reply. "It's my mother's. She always drives brown cars." Or maybe they only seemed brown, maybe they'd started out some other color and had turned to rust like the chains on the porch swing.

Little Fritzy pulls herself out from beneath the hood and looks at Phoenix oddly. "You say something?"

"Phoenix. I said, my name's Phoenix."

"Oh," says the woman, who automatically extends her grubby right hand, then looks down as if reconsidering, wipes her hand on the leg of her jeans, and grins. "Little Fritzy. Glad to meet you, Phoenix. After that city in Arizona or that bird that sets itself on fire?"

"The city in Arizona. It's a family thing." Phoenix doesn't see the point in mentioning that the city is named for the mythological bird.

"Yeah?" Little Fritzy brightens. "Me too. My old man was Fritz. He wanted a boy. 'Stead, he got me. 'Course I didn't turn out so little, if you know what I mean." The Ford's hood clangs shut. A lone pair of headlights splits the night. Little Fritzy holds her hand out, displaying the ruined thermostat. "You want this?" Phoenix shakes her head, extends the half-full Coke bottle. Counter offerings. Little Fritzy takes it and in one long gulp finishes off the contents, then looks at Phoenix. "You're not from around here, are you? I mean, that car is for sure—what'd you say it was, your mama's?"

So Little Fritzy isn't quite as deaf under the hood as she likes to let on. "I used to be. From around here. A long time ago. Now I live in San Francisco. I'm just back here . . . on family business. How much did you say I owe you?"

Pursing her lips and moving them side to side, a gesture Phoenix suddenly finds inexplicably endearing, Little Fritzy appears to be considering the price. "Seventeen and fifty. So what's it like? Living in San Francisco, I mean?"

"It's okay. Good. Better than here, I guess." Little Fritzy nods. "At least for me." Then, feeling like the traitor she is, Phoenix adds, "But this is home."

Little Fritzy snorts softly. "Hey, it's okay, you don't have to apologize to me. Nothing much ever happens here—not compared to what I hear about San Francisco—except for pool. You shoot pool?" Phoenix nods. "Well, you want to come with me? It's past closing time anyhow. But you'll have to wear your shoes." She looks pointedly at Phoenix's feet and grins.

"They pinch," Phoenix admits.

"Yeah, they look it. That's a pair of come-fuck-me-pumps if I ever saw 'em. Look, I got a pair of sandals in the car; you want to wear 'em, they're yours."

Two o'clock in the morning and Phoenix is in Little Fritzy's kitchen, watching her make breakfast with the skill of a short-order cook, which she once was until Fritz retired to Florida. "It's security, you know what I mean?" All night she's been saying that: "You know what I mean?" Most of the time Phoenix has had no idea, but nodded anyway. Little Fritzy, it turns out, is a passable cook, with a voracious appetite. Picking at the eggs and sausage links that look like fingers lined up along the top of her plate,

Phoenix is suddenly aware that she is tired, so tired that she shivers. Little Fritzy notices and smiles, comes around the side of the table, wraps her arms around Phoenix's shoulders, and leans in close. Too close. "Cold?" Phoenix closes her eyes and leans her head back into Little Fritzy's chest. Soft and smelling of grease and Lysol. But when Little Fritzy bends to kiss her, Phoenix pulls away. "What's-a-matter? You can trust me, you know what I mean?"

But Phoenix Bay doesn't trust anyone, especially strangers who shoot lousy pool and who look on her with knowing self-righteousness. She wants gratitude, wants to make this woman scream and call out her name, just because she can. She inhales, turns, and pulls Little Fritzy's face down to meet her own. "I know *exactly* what you mean."

In bed, Little Fritzy turned out to be one of those grunting women. Grunting and gritty and sour under Phoenix's tongue. By the time dawn finally showed itself in the cluttered bedroom, Phoenix Bay was sure. She hates Little Fritzy, how she awakened with a grunt, smiling, trying to pull Phoenix back; and how her eyes looked, like a sad puppy, watching Phoenix dress.

"Leave your number, hon. I get to Frisco, I'll look you up. You know what I mean?"

Phoenix does indeed know what she means. Smiling, she quickly jots a number on a gritty scratchpad by the red plastic telephone. The pencil is dull. Not that it matters. Little Fritzy will never make it to California and even if she does, the number is for the Sanchez Street flat. Blowing Little Fritzy a kiss, Phoenix closes the door quietly behind her, pulls the skirt of her mother's suit up around the tops of her thighs and begins to run across the wide lawn toward the gas station and the Ford. The grass pricks her feet like needles. Phoenix Bay bites her lower lip hard, to keep from crying.

The phone is ringing when she walks through the door of her mother's house. The sound follows her up the stairs, rattles against her as she changes into running clothes, pushes her back down the steps and out the screen door, chases her onto the street. She can still hear it ringing as she passes Tollie Pengrove's house. If it's still ringing when she comes back—if she comes back—she'll rip it out of the wall by its roots.

But the phone is silent when she turns up the driveway and stops short at the sight of Savannah's car. Phoenix stretches, then walks slowly up the porch steps and through the front door. Savannah, red with fury, is sitting on the couch, like a prim yet enraged bird. "I don't need this, Phoenix." Her voice is so low it's frightening. Phoenix looks at her sister, closely for the first time since she's come back. Without makeup, Savannah looks old. Tired. A pang of pity courses up, but Phoenix says nothing. As if she hasn't heard, she starts up the stairs, peeling off her T-shirt as she goes. Following her into the bathroom, Savannah sits down hard on the toilet seat. "Phoenix, what could you have been thinking? I've never been so humiliated in my life. I didn't know what to do. Where were you last night?"

"Out." Phoenix is groggy and as hung over as if she'd been drinking all night. The wages of bad sex.

"And exactly what is that supposed to mean?" Phoenix notices that when her sister is angry, she looks a little like a fish, mouth pursed, eyes bulging.

"It means out. It means I went for a drive and the thermostat blew on the way back. And it got late. A friend on the other side of Carbondale put me up."

"I don't believe you." Her sister's voice is cold, colder than Little Fritzy's lips.

Phoenix raises her hands in mock surrender. "Fine. Believe whatever you'd like, Savannah. Now, would you hand me that towel or are you planning on getting in the shower with me?" Peeling off the damp running shorts, Phoenix angles her ass in the general direction of her sister's face. Savannah gasps.

"What the hell is that?" She means the tattoo.

"Don't say hell, Savannah. God will get you for swearing."

"Well, Phoenix, I suppose *that's* what you were doing last night?"

Under her breath, Phoenix chuckles. So like Savannah to think that years of work could be accomplished in one night.

Lesbian magic. "Don't be silly, Savannah. No one around here's that good." Phoenix steps into the shower and pulls the curtain. Under the showerhead she opens her mouth, lets the spray clear away the last taste of Little Fritzy. Here it's easy to block out her sister's words. Steam rises, thick and clean. When she finally steps out of the shower, she finds a note Savannah taped to the mirror: *Be ready by three.*

Three o'clock. Phoenix paces, checks her watch. Five after in fact, and no sign yet of Floyd's white Cadillac. Her heel catches on a splintered plank on the porch and as she reaches down to free it, a black limousine pulls into the driveway. From behind the wheel, a very dainty and elegantly dressed man emerges and opens the side door, where Savannah and Floyd are already seated. "Show time?" Phoenix asks. He nods. Taking her elbow, he guides her toward the car.

Balancing on the edge of a gilt chair in the special little room inside the mortuary, Phoenix Bay sighs. No one has spoken to her, the family pariah. At least there's that to be grateful for and the fact that Savannah didn't recognize Mama's suit. But from the cut and fabric, Phoenix guesses it was something her mother had worn about the time Savannah was born. Every time Phoenix moves, the jacket releases a scent of mothballs and Avon cologne.

"What's that perfume?" Savannah picks up her purse and sits gingerly.

Phoenix says the first thing that pops into her mind, "Escape."

"The new Calvin Klein?" Savannah wrinkles her nose. "I never thought it would smell like that. Maybe it's gone bad. How long have you had it?"

"Not long. I tried to wash it off, but you know perfume." Lies, all lies, and Savannah believing every word. Phoenix squirms. Her feet hurt, although not as much as they will once she leaves this too-cool funeral home. A crisp sixty-five degrees from the feel of it. Must have something to do with keeping the flowers and the bodies fresh. She eases her left foot out of the shoe, which she dangles from her toes. Carlotta Washington, an art teacher she once worked with, used to do that. Drove the students nuts. Phoenix always thought it was incredibly sexy.

A pale, overstuffed version of her mother in a black silk dress leans against Phoenix. "Aunt Nan, so good of you to come," she says automatically, wincing a little as her mother's elder sister pulls Phoenix's face into her bosom, which smells of expensive flowers. No mothballs and Avon for Aunt Nan.

"Well, Phoenix, honey, where else would we be? I'm just so sorry you couldn't get here until this morning." So that's what Savannah had told the family: delayed flights or business emergency? Nantucket whispers with fruity breath, "She's with God now."

"I hope so," Phoenix tells her aunt, who looks slightly alarmed. "I remember how every Sunday, when Mama was getting ready for church, she'd say, 'One morning I'll wake up and the devil'll be looking right at me. And he'll say, 'I knew you could make it, Villanova.' " Her aunt's eyes are considerably wider than Phoenix remembers. But her grip, as she digs into Phoenix's shoulder, is undeniably strong for a woman nearing seventy. Mama used to do that, too, whenever she wanted Phoenix to shut up. Aunt Nan is looking over Phoenix's head at Savannah for clues. The one big advantage of being the outcast, you can get away with just about anything.

Finally, Aunt Nan says, "Well, Phoenix, we all know there was only one Villanova." Phoenix's mother used to say that too, her face flushed from bourbon and pride. Phoenix never bothered to point out that there was also only one Nantucket, too. Mama always wanted to have a picture of herself taken next to the sign at the Villanova, Pennsylvania, city limits. A family custom of sorts. Aunt Nan had one. In fact, there isn't much Aunt Nan doesn't have. Now, she has cornered Savannah in the aisle, whispering. Phoenix leans back into the chair, surprisingly uncomfortable for something so well-cushioned, and closes her eyes. Hard to hold on, here in this cold room, so full of familiar strangers. Maybe she should open her eyes, but it all seems like too much effort. She feels thick and heavy and slow, as if the world were playing on a 33 RPM record and she is sinking. Quicksand. Maybe if David hadn't fought that time, he would have known to tell her this is what it feels like.

If nobody makes her go into that little chapel beyond the curtain, she'll be fine. Listening to the organist butcher Bach, she wishes they would play the tape she'd heard that first night. Something about Jesus. Villanova always liked songs about Jesus. Or maybe that was TaTa Hassee. So hard to remember. Phoenix Bay feels a hand brush her shoulder. "Miz Bayless?" Opening her eyes slowly, she looks up and into the face of Ichabod Crain. In her eighth-grade reader there was a large drawing of this same narrow face with its long pointed chin, the huge crooked nose between tiny eyes wild with fright. These eyes, though, are clear and almost kind. "I'm Brother John. Sister Savannah has told me so much about you. Phoenix, isn't it? Such a lovely name." Brother John is from Savannah's church, a nondenominational, fundamentalist sect that meets in a prefab barn of a building with blue siding and a large cross painted on each side. Savannah pointed it out on their way here from the airport. "Is there anything you'd like me to include in the service, a special prayer, perhaps a hymn?" She takes his extended hand, soft as a baby's, and rises from her seat. All six feet of her thanks to the shoes. Many men are inhibited by tall women, but this one doesn't flinch.

Aware of Savannah's suspicious eyes, she whispers. "I don't think 'No Regrets' would be appropriate. Does the organist know 'Is That All There Is'?"

"Is that a Protestant hymn?"

Savannah rolls her eyes and climbs gracelessly over Floyd to wedge herself between her heathen sister and this man of God. "What we decided on earlier will be just fine, Brother John," she says, adding, "My sister is from San Francisco," as if that explains everything.

"Oh, the city of Saint Francis, one of my favorites." Phoenix isn't sure if he means the saint or the city, not that it matters. His smile is genuine. She smiles back and lets Savannah lead her to the seat next to Floyd. Brother John disappears beyond the curtain. Strains of 'I Come to the Garden Alone' begin. Phoenix wonders if Tollie Pengrove considers that to be a sign.

Brother John reads the particulars of the life of Villanova

Bayless. The words sound faintly biblical, but then some ministers make everything sound holy. Beside her, Savannah sniffs loudly and squeezes Phoenix's hand too hard, pushing Villanova's wedding ring, a thin band of yellow gold, into her flesh. Phoenix found the ring in a satin-covered cigar box, the pink ribbons faded almost white. Phoenix and every other third grader in Miss Jullian's class had made one of those boxes. A wonder her mother kept it all these years; Villanova Bayless was not a sentimental woman. Phoenix tucked the little box into her suitcase. It's the only thing of her mother's she wants. If Savannah recognized the ring, she hasn't said anything. But she didn't recognize the suit, so maybe she's forgotten the ring, too. Floyd clears his throat, dabs at his eyes, then blows his nose loudly.

"To everything there is a season," Brother John says, probably quoting the Bible, not Bob Dylan. *Die-lan,* Villanova always insisted, the accent hard on the first syllable; Phoenix never was able to convince her otherwise. Villanova could be incredibly bullheaded, like that whole thing with Savannah's father; why couldn't she at least give Savannah that? Instead, she had died with that secret intact. So many secrets. In the satin-covered box there was a picture of a Villanova, young, her mouth pursed, eyes cast upward, trying hard to look like a movie star. Phoenix had sought some trace of her mother in that pretty girl's face, only to come up empty.

As the organist begins to play again, Savannah leans close, so close Phoenix can smell her breath: mints and tobacco. "We'll just wait here until the others have gone, then we'll have a few minutes alone with Mama." Phoenix shakes her head no. But when Brother John extends his right arm to her—his left is already occupied by Savannah—she takes it because she can't think of anything else to do and walks with him into the little chapel where the mother of God is smiling.

The chapel looks just as it did that first night: artificial sunlight streaks through the stained-glass window, an eternal morning; recorded organ music plays softly, never a false note, never a missed beat, only the occasional hiss in the background. The real organist has gone, leaving perfection in her wake. Except for a few stragglers in the back, and the line of family forming behind Phoenix and Floyd, the chapel is empty. The front door opens. Children's laughter. Aunt Nan's grandchildren, bored in their polished shoes and ruffled dresses and bow ties, are chasing each other through the parking lot. A little girl shrieks at some indignity and Phoenix hears one of the boys send up a tinny howl, "Pa, I never!" before the door closes again. Refrigerated air whispers cold against her neck. Even the rose petals tremble. So many roses, enough to put a dozen summers of Mama's garden to shame, and white gladioli and purple iris. The flowers match the colors of the stained glass in the window. A stranger looking in would think Villanova Bayless was the most beloved and loving woman in Williamson County, exactly Savannah's intention. Villanova had no real friends, at least not the kind who would send dozens of perfect red roses. A spray nearly as large as the casket itself drapes gracefully. *Beloved Mother* is spelled out in gilt letters on a long, white satin ribbon. At the end of horse races, the winners wear blankets of roses, too. Mama might have liked that, to be a winner; but she never even tried. One of the roses is fading, its head bowed but still sweet, too sweet, as red roses so often are. Mama likes yellow roses, not red. Why didn't Savannah know that? Why didn't she ask? But this is Savannah's show, paid for with her rich husband's money. Even Villanova is cast in the supporting role. And Phoenix is just a bit player trying to remember her lines, following directions. Then Mama won't be ashamed. Of her.

Balanced on her toes in too-tight shoes with heels too high, her skirt stretched across her thighs, she is a Barbie doll with small breasts, being marched through a world she doesn't like. Floyd's hands, one beefy paw on either side of her waist, guiding her forward. Take six steps or eight or ten, hard to judge, and she'll be there at the head of the casket. She could do that, if she weren't floating, if her legs hadn't lost all feeling, if her shoes, those damnable shoes, hadn't tightened around her toes. She doesn't remember these shoes. Where on earth did Cecelie find them? Four lethal inches of heel with a perfectly pointed toe. Such shoes are designed to be worn when you're on your back. Then she remembers: Jinx bringing them home, smiling. "Want some of this, baby?" Forgetting where she is, Phoenix Bay grins, then recoils, horrified. She is smiling at her own mother's funeral.

"You doing okay there, kiddo?" Floyd sometimes calls Savannah that, too. Still, the way he uses the casual endearment, the way his hands rest so fatherly on the small of her back rankles. She doesn't belong here in this artificial cold, in a shaft of artificial sunlight angled to fall across her and her dead mother's face. Behind Floyd, Aunt Nan, Uncle Horace, and Cousin Suwanee shift their weight, as if an untalented choreographer had coached them and these are the only steps they can remember. Phoenix needs to lie down before she floats away entirely, but the euphoria is already rising. She has to remember to tell Teddy Grayson it feels like nitrous oxide. Phoenix smiles from the pure wonder of it. Floating. And then the unthinkable happens. The heel of her right shoe snags a thread in the carpet, pitching her off-balance, toward the casket, where there is nothing to break her fall except that blanket of red roses. Floyd's beefy hands, hands that are used to wrestling hogs—large and generally willful animals—reach out to steady her and lock around what would have been her shoulders if she were barefoot or if he were taller.

"Oh, for God's sake, Floyd, let her go!" Savannah's voice is a good octave higher than normal, rising above the organ music and the whispers from the back of the room. And Floyd, who has never, in anyone's memory, defied his wife or touched breasts that he wasn't married to, lets go. Slumping to the floor, Phoenix huddles next to the casket, like a frightened child, her mouth frozen into a grinning gash. Choking noises, more animal than human, begin to echo through the chapel. In the background the tape plays "I Know That My Redeemer Liveth."

"Dear Lord," says Brother John.

"What the hell?" The first words spoken by Uncle Horace since he's arrived boom through the chapel only to be lost in the inevitable buzz that swirls like a comforting fog around Phoenix. She has become what they all expected: Villanova Bayless's crazy, queer daughter in her ridiculous shoes and strange clothes, sprawled on a dais of Astroturf, skirt hiked up exposing black lace garters and stockings and green vines with purple orchids etched into the tender pale skin there. Howling.

"Phoenix?" A hand touches her shoulder gently, then smoothes her hair back from her face. She recoils, then looks up, confused. "It's me," the voice prompts, waiting for recognition that doesn't come. "David. Here, let me help you up." David? Wiping her eyes with the back of her hand, Phoenix looks into his face, suspicious. "Would you like to go outside?" Then the fog lifts, and she smiles. Older, of course, and not as handsome as she remembers, but still David. David of the quicksand. David of the warm beer on the old dock out by the lake on summer afternoons. Her first and only real friend here.

Questions twirl like small cyclones through her mind, but the words don't follow. "You're losing your hair," she says at last.

He grins, gently pulling her upright. "But I'm making up for it around my middle." Phoenix stares. "That's a joke." She smiles, tentatively, while Savannah, her face white with rage, leans toward David as if Phoenix weren't even there.

"Get her out of here." Savannah's voice is low and tinged with hate. "I don't want her anywhere near the cemetery. I don't care what you do with her, but get her the hell out of here." Savannah no longer cares what Brother John thinks. What can he do, anyway? Throw her out of the church? But he won't; she's not the one who's crazy. Three members of the Ladies' Church League have formed a tight knot by the door. Savannah sees their secret smiles. All those years spent trying to make everything perfect, to make them forget she's Villanova Bayless's bastard daughter who ran off to Nashville with a married man before she even graduated high school, were for nothing. Wasn't she always the first to volunteer for the shifts none of the other Hospital Sunshine Girls wanted? Didn't she run the church rummage sales, as thankless a task as there ever was, and never once did she claim the best donations for herself first, the way the others do? All that and for what? To have Phoenix humiliate her. Savannah sinks into one of the gilt chairs while the rest of the family files past the casket. Mama always told her, "The harder you try, the less you get." Never once has she been disappointed.

As David leads Phoenix Bay down the aisle of the little chapel, she looks over her shoulder at the scene behind them. From this distance, the woman in the casket doesn't look like her mother so much as like a snapshot she saw once a very long time ago. She doesn't know if that makes her feel bad or just empty. At the chapel door, Phoenix balances one hand on David's shoulder and slips out of the offending shoes. "You ready?" His voice is smooth and practiced, as if he were in one of his beloved plays and this just another opening night. She nods as he pushes open the door and the afternoon sun streams over them like halos. Shielding her eyes from the glare, Phoenix steps into the sun, her head high, carrying her shoes. Gravel, hot as a devil's pincers, sends a thousand needles into her soles. Her stockings will be ruined. Better that, though, than to stop and put those shoes back on under all those veiled but vigilant eyes. If Villanova taught her nothing else, it was to hold her head high and never let the bastards see you cry. Not a one—not Nantucket's grandchildren or the women from the Ladies' Church League or even Tollie Pengrove, the rose thief—looks up as Phoenix passes.

Without asking, David turns the white Cadillac convertible onto the lake road, just like old times. Still and quiet, the lake is thick with algae. She peels off her ruined stockings and pushes Villanova's skirt up her thighs, so that a few of the vines that trail there can peek at the sun, and plunges her feet into the murky water. A stranger happening by might mistake them for lovers: Phoenix's freckled shoulders bare, the black satin and lace bustier elevating her breasts into fine, fleshy mounds; David's shirt open, sleeves rolled up. She imagines they are beautiful together, here in sunlight filtered by leaves.

But David hasn't aged well. Small-town softness has eroded his beauty, left him just another middle-aged man running an appliance store. The same red and green neon still burns in the window, he says; surely she saw it when she was downtown. "I haven't been downtown," she lies, letting her feet trail in the warm soupy water. He looks wounded and she is surprised how much it pleases her. Nothing much has changed at Major Appliances, he tells her. Every Christmas, Santa still pushes his elves back into the washing machines, while Mrs. Claus pours in the soap, over and over again. "The Major had that made special. There's not another one like it, probably in the world." That, Phoenix has no trouble believing. What she's never understood is why anyone would want such a gruesome scene. David rearranges himself, crossing his legs. His feet are too white, like the soft underbelly of a frog, and his suit legs pull a little too tightly. Too much beer and no exercise. Still, he looks healthy, unlike Rennie, who is so thin that his elegant new clothes, the ones he thinks make him look like Eugene O'Neill, hang on him the way they might on a mannequin.

"So are you going to tell me?"

"Tell you what, Phoenix?"

"Why I never heard from you? Why you never told me you'd come home."

David uncrosses his legs and buries his forehead between his hands as if his head is suddenly too heavy to support. "I'm sorry. I thought about writing, I really did, but I always thought it would be to send you my new address. Back in New York or maybe L.A. You know that the Major died." Phoenix nods; her mother's few letters were often filled with details of the dead and dying. "Colon cancer. It takes a long time to die from colon cancer." Colon cancer must be a great indignity for a proud man. "When I first came back to help him out with the store, I said it would be for six months, then it was a year. Then one month, I think it was May, I forgot to send the check to the storage company in New York. I just forgot. After the Major died, I knew it was too late. How could I go back if I couldn't remember who I used to be? Here it's easier."

Easier? What can be easy about being here? A dragonfly darts close to her bare shoulder, hovers, then scoots away. Phoenix raises her left foot, dripping green from the algae. A large circle is left where the foot used to be, until the water covers up its loss. She studies the circle. "I thought you were dead." Only then does she look into his face. No death there.

"I'm sorry to disappoint you."

"No," she says, taking his right hand, surprised at its softness.

What did she expect from an appliance salesman? "It's just . . . you learn to expect it, or at least I do. But it's good you're okay. Great, really. Somebody has to get out of this alive."

"Cowards do." He brushes what's left of his hair with the palm of his hand.

"You're not a coward, David, just because you're lucky." Her toes have trapped a bit of green slime, giving the appearance of rotting flesh.

"I came back because it was easier. That's cowardice, Phoenix." His voice is resigned.

"What happened? When we got out, we swore we'd never come back." She doesn't look at David; instead she watches a dragonfly skip across the water by the dock. "We said if we could get far enough away . . . and never look back . . . that this place, none of them . . . could ever hurt us again. Were we wrong?"

"We were kids, Phoenix." David touches her shoulder, where the sun has painted a leaf in shadow. He is surprised at how hard and muscled she is. He draws his hand away. "You were always the tough one, and you wanted so much more than the rest of us."

Us? She can't remember David ever tying himself to the same people they'd scorned. But he's right, they were children then, and desperate, or at least she was, to escape. "Not too many people would agree with you after today, about me being tough, I mean."

David smiles. The same salesman's look of sympathetic pleasure that the Major wore. "They'll forget. And even if they don't, they'll pretend it never happened. Selective memory is our best defense here. It's easier than facing the truth and certainly safer." Safe? Easy? She doesn't understand. "When he was sick, the Major had all the mirrors taken out of the house, as if that would make a difference. I haven't put them back up. I probably won't. It's too hard to see what's there." David sets the empty bottle back into its cardboard case, running his index finger around the rim of the last full bottle. "Anyway, as the man says, home is the place where they have to take you in."

"Robert Frost."

"What about him?"

"He's the one who said: 'Home is the place where, when you

240

have to go there /They have to take you in.' " With a stocking, Phoenix dabs at the green between her toes. "Savannah wants to sell me Mama's house and have me move back."

"Will you?"

Phoenix shakes her head. "No. I hate it here. All my failures rise up to greet me. Besides, as anonymous said, It's a smart woman who knows when it's gettin' on towards time to go." Struggling to her feet, Phoenix pads toward the car, leaving damp imprints on the gray boards of the old fishing dock. On the drive back, she leans her head back against the deep leather seat, watching the trees arc overhead, blotting out the night sky. The wind slaps her, snaps under David's open shirtsleeves. He drives with one arm angled across the seat. "Remember when we were kids, David, and we cut our fingers and swore to always tell each other the truth?" The glow of the dashboard shadows his face pale.

"Blood secret. You said we couldn't be blood brothers because you're a girl. So?"

"So tell me your secret."

His eyes never leave the road, and he smiles slowly. "Okay. I'm in love with my golf partner's ass and I took three strokes off on my last scorecard."

"No, David, something serious, something you've never told anybody else."

They're at a stop sign, where the county blacktop intersects with the highway back to town. He turns to look at her. Pretty, he thinks, but alien, too, the way the women in New York were. Hard edged and brutal with honesty. He takes a deep breath. "Okay. When I was still in New York, there was this man I used to see around the bars. We'd tried out for some of the same commercials, but he always got the jobs. You know the type: big, blond, ruggedly handsome, could have any man he wanted. Only he never wanted me. I heard he moved out to the Coast for a sitcom. Then one afternoon I saw him. It was horrible, Phoenix, how he looked. I didn't even recognize him at first and then, when he recognized me, I looked away. I just . . . turned away and pretended I didn't see him. A few weeks later, the Major called and I came home. Your turn."

She is silent as he turns onto the highway. The streets of her childhood shuffle together along lines of small frame houses marching in place, windows glowing, yards dark and thick with shadows. Streetlights ape stars. Children dance under ancient trees, one last game before bed. She must take it all in, must not forget. "I won't be coming back here again," she says at last as David pulls into the driveway at Villanova's darkened house. The others must be at Savannah's. Tomorrow they will come to pick the house clean, but it won't matter, Phoenix Bay will be on her way back to San Francisco. Home.

"I figured as much. Is that your deep, dark secret?" Phoenix Bay shakes her head, then takes a handkerchief from David. She hadn't even realized she was crying. He walks with her across the yard. Tufts of grass and hardy weeds peek through the cracks in the base of the porch steps. She sits on the edge of the steps, the way her mother used to. The swing creaks, as a huge yellow tomcat jumps down and stalks across the porch, indignant at the intrusion. David stands on the stoop. They have run out of words. He kisses her lightly on the forehead. "Take care of yourself, Miss Phoenix Tornado Bayless." She nods, attempts a smile. "Toledo," she corrects. "Phoenix Toledo Bayless."

"I know," he says, ruffling her hair. "I didn't forget."

"You'd better go. I still have to call San Francisco tonight." She watches the red taillights of the Major's car until it turns the corner, watches the few surviving fireflies dance their evening dance. Tears plop onto her hands. Inside, the telephone rings. The melody of a familiar song pitches through the night. If she closes her eyes, she can almost see them, those Bayless women, here on the porch. She wiggles her fingers, urging the cat closer. "My mother is dead," Phoenix whispers, trying out the words. "I didn't love her enough." The cat settles onto the step next to her, purring.

15

Rennie Johnson rises through a morphine sea toward the light. Air bubbles break the surface. Pop. And pop again. His lungs hurt. Too fast, he'd gone too deep and come up too fast. Manny is always warning him about that: diving too deep. But it pleases Manny, too, you can see it in his eyes. Proud. His son is finally a man. The only manly thing Rennie can do: dive too deep.

He breaks through the surface. Bright, white light, the way the sun always is in Mexico in August. In another week Manny will send him away to school, to a place where there is no sea, only mountains and horses. His father loves horses. The school has promised to turn this boy who dives too deep into a man. A real man, his father said, laughing. Manny leans out over the railing, laughing; his mouth stretches wide over large and very white teeth, waving Rennie aboard. One of his women bends forward across the railing, smiling, her golden breasts beaded with sweat or maybe from the surf. And hungry. His father's women always look hungry.

Rennie Johnson opens his eyes slowly. His back aches. Someone has thought to prop him on his side so he can see the sun, or maybe that isn't why. He vaguely remembers voices coming and going, hands under his armpits, his knees, the light changing to dark, then back again. But it all seemed so very far away at the time. The room is green and cool and eerily quiet; golden afternoon light runs across the tiled floor. Rennie smiles and lets his eyes drop closed. So hard to focus. The sun is too bright. Trying newfound muscles, he stretches, attempting to rearrange himself in a straightjacket of pillows. The moan surprises him, escaping before the morphine takes over again, urging him back down.

Someone has rearranged him again. The pillows gone, he's on his back. Opening his eyes, he waits for them to focus. Night now, or early morning. The window is dark. In a chair near the corner of the room, Phoenix sleeps, Carson's jacket draped over her like a blanket, his straw hat on the floor by her bare feet. Poor Phoenix, always wearing somebody else's clothes. He should give her Carson's credit card, send her off to Macy's, or wherever dykes shop, to buy something for herself. He still has one credit card that hasn't been cut off. Yet. He's used them up, one at a time, until now there's almost nothing left.

The answering machine is filled with messages from irritable women begging him to call them back about the unpaid bills. He picked up once for Miss Marshall, who'd sounded especially coy. "What do you plan to do about your bill, Mr. Cole?" "This isn't Mr. Cole, this is Mr. Johnson." "Well, Mr. Johnson, when might I speak with Mr. Cole?" "Probably never." "Do you have a number where we might reach him?" "No, and if I did, it would be very long distance." "Now, Mister . . . Johnson is it? . . . there's no point in being evasive. You must be aware that we will locate Mr. Cole." He'd smiled at her naiveté. "Please let me know when you do, Miss Marshall." He didn't wait for her reply, simply flicked the phone switch to "off" and lowered the antenna. Poor Miss Marshall with her eight-dollar-an-hour job of dunning deadbeats for money they don't have and aren't likely to get. What a lousy way to make a living. Well, maybe she has a lover that makes up for it, someone who gets her through 'til morning. He could use that now.

That's what Doug is supposed to be for, although he's not much good at comfort. And who can blame him? He didn't know it would be like this. Had Rennie led him on, as prim old women might say, because he needed . . . what? Someone to see him the way he might have been. There are easier confessions to make. It isn't fair, being forced into the role of widow and celibate all in the course of one hateful and hated afternoon. And then to be offered, miracle of miracles, a reprieve. You aren't repugnant or grotesque or beyond redemption. In the eyes of another man, you see what you were and what you can be again. Or might be. Doug is his link to wholeness, the one thing that makes him believe he is still absolutely and completely alive.

Maybe women don't need that. They don't seem to. Not that they operate on some higher moral ground—his amoral mother certainly disproved that—but they carry some deeper, primal understanding. They're tough, not scared off easily by life's gore and guts. Probably from all that birth and death and blood they have to contend with. Over and over, month by month for decades, sloughing off blood until they aren't afraid anymore, not even of the Big One. They may not like it, but they aren't scared, not the way he is, not the way Carson was: fear churning against your belly until there's nothing left but bile and blank terror. No wonder Phoenix is here instead of Doug.

The door opens and Phoenix stirs in the chair, forcing herself awake maybe, to exchange whispers with a nurse. Another woman. So many damned women clustering around him these last few days. Whispering women. You come into the world surrounded by them and apparently go out the same way. If that, indeed, is what's happening. Hard to say. He's never died before; how are you supposed to know? Carson was no help. If he knew, and there wasn't much he did know by then, he'd died with his secret. Maybe George, that man everyone calls an angel, will come and say when it's time, the way he had with Carson. And if he doesn't come, what does that mean? There must be some sign, some signal, some inner-knowing. Isn't that part of the deal? To know? He's not ready. He knows that. Even if what's left isn't much, he's still not ready for it to be over. Not yet. But when are you ever ready? Are you? Ever ready?

"So, you're awake." The nurse bends close, pushing away the sheet, pulling back the cotton gown that covers his chest. The stethoscope is cold and smooth, like a bit of polished marble. He studies her profile: plump cheeks, good skin, no pockmarks, a nice nose, wide eyes, the all-American girl next door. She probably grew up playing softball on a grass lot somewhere in Iowa. When did she know she was queer? Or did she always know, the way he's always known? "So, how do you feel?" Her breath smells sweet, like candy canes.

He tries his voice. "Sore. My lungs. Hurt." There. The voice works, but talking burns. She nods and wraps the blood-pressure cuff around his limp right arm. Blood pressure. Temperature. Pulse. Vital signs. He remembers that from somewhere or maybe it's something else he's always known. Vital. From the Latin *vitalis*. Manny used Vitalis to tame his wild hair. As a boy, Rennie used to sit on the floor in the bathroom after his father had gone out, smelling the air. In the bathhouses of his youth, he used to sniff out that scent like a rutting animal, following the senselessly erotic odor of Vitalis on the necks of a few men, older or more brown or more cheaply lived than the men he surrounded himself with during the day. Darkness disguised them all. He expects the nurse to say something, some word of encouragement. Instead, she fiddles with the bag hung by his bed. "Your sister is here, Rennie."

"Where?" he asks the nurse's back, before catching Phoenix's anxious eyes. Don't blow this, her expression says as she shakes her head slightly.

The nurse turns, still smiling, "I'm sorry, Rennie, what did you say?"

He shakes his head. Nothing, nothing at all.

Balancing on the edge of the bed, once the nurse is gone, Phoenix confesses, "I had to tell them I'm your sister so they'd let me sign the papers. I'm a good liar . . . remember?" Yes, of course, he remembers. Phoenix angles a straw to his mouth. The water is almost warm.

"Ice?" The word feels soft.

She shakes her head. "They aren't into it. Cold spots or something. I've been worried about you. By the way, you've lost some days in here, buddy. It's Monday." Rennie nods and closes his eyes. Buddy. Odd that she would use Carson's pet name for him now, when she never has before. How childish it sounds on her lips, almost artificial. For the first time he notices music playing softly, somewhere near his head. Chopin. Not Phoenix's taste at all; she likes the women rockers. But he and Phoenix have never had the same taste in much of anything. Amazing that they've been friends all these years. No, more than friends; she is his sister as much as is Cecelie. He certainly knows her as well and has, these last few years, seen her more frequently. He can tell no one, but he loves her as much.

"Cecelie will be here this afternoon." Phoenix climbs onto the bed next to him, pulling close. Before Cecelie . . . and Doug . . . she used to slip into bed with him sometimes. She was warm and soft and smelled of soap. She was always gone by morning—she didn't sleep much then—and he was always sorry to wake up and find her gone. She touches his hair. Her fingers smell sour, like stale cigarettes and something he can't quite place. She picks up a washcloth, cool, and dabs at his forehead, then around his eyes, kisses him lightly. Her lips are soft, like bird feathers. Moving the cloth down, under his chin, across his throat, she talks, her voice smooth and warm as breath. "Cecelie didn't leave a number, so I had to wait for her to call. When she heard you were in the hospital and she couldn't get a flight, she threw a fit. It didn't help. Everybody was trying to leave at the same time. The post–Labor Day crush, I suppose." No point in mentioning the hurricane that had left Phoenix cold and trembling in front of the television, listening for every scrap of news from the islands. First, that it was coming. Inevitable, the newscasters said. Inevitable force. And then reports that the islands were locked down, waiting. And she'd waited, too, here with Rennie, through all those terrible hours when she didn't know what would happen next to either of them, willing him to live, willing the storm to move on, to leave Cecelie for her. And then the news that the storms had left apparently all of Oahu virtually untouched. When Cecelie had finally gotten through to the house, she was frantic. Doug had been the one to tell her that Rennie was in the hospital with pneumonia. The boy's last good deed. "Cecelie saw a wholphin," she says at last. "Half-dolphin, half-whale. Pretty strange, huh?"

Rennie nods. Cecelie throwing a fit? Hard to imagine. Maybe Mona hadn't beaten the life out of her, as he's so long suspected. Phoenix runs the washcloth across his chin. He feels it catch. Scratchy. The same people who have been moving him must not have been shaving him. Maybe he'll grow a beard again. He could do that. He forces his mind to focus. "Doug?"

"Back at the house." The lie sticks, but it's easier than the truth: that Doug is gone and, if he's smart, never coming back. "I think he's afraid of hospitals; but who isn't? Close your eyes and I'll wipe the sleep out of them. Do you remember being a kid and believing you could go blind if you didn't do that?"

Rennie nods and dutifully closes his eyes. He wishes she would bring some of the good washcloths from the house, the Egyptian cotton ones he'd got for Carson. Maybe she should call

Doug, now that he's awake, have him bring them over when he comes. If he comes. He should come. Surely, he isn't so scary now that he's awake. That poor puppy of a man. Still afraid of hospitals. Not hospitals, of course, but the people in them. He'll never grow up; maybe that was what had first attracted Rennie to him, all that youthful exuberance. Is that what Carson had seen in him those early days in Mexico? Not likely. Rennie was never as unformed as Doug. He wants to tell Phoenix not to worry, that everything will be fine, but he needs to listen to this passage from Chopin for just a moment or two longer. Just another moment.

She folds the washcloth and carefully rearranges on the covers over his feet all the magic she could muster: a bouquet of Marcel Proust's discarded tailfeathers, the ampoule from Cecelie's *brujo*, Rennie's favorite fountain pen, all held together with one of Carson's silk ties. She wanted to keep it on Rennie's chest—better, she thought, for the pneumonia—but the nurses said no; feathers, even from a blessed peacock, are bad for the lungs. She compromises by keeping them at the end of the bed, out of sight, under a light blanket. Once, when she'd returned to the room, someone had changed Rennie's bed and left the charm in her chair. Did they laugh at her silly attempts at magic? Probably not, she decides. Most of the nurses are lesbians and most lesbians believe in magic. There isn't magic enough in the world to change the events of this last week, to undo Doug's damage. Poor Rennie, too sick to hear the truth. Poor Phoenix, too terrified to tell him.

There will be time enough for that later, when Rennie's stronger or when she is. Then she can explain how she should have seen the possibility of flight in Doug's eyes after he found Rennie: how his hands had kept pushing back that lank of hair; how he wouldn't or couldn't look at her—or worse, Rennie; how he'd disappeared as soon as the paramedics had arrived; how when she'd come back from the hospital the next day, the grow-room door was open. She'd stood in that empty room and cried for Rennie and for herself, and for her stolen past. She deserved better; they both did. At least Doug had cleaned up the bathroom; he probably thought that was some compensation for taking off with thirteen years of her life. Was Doug still boy enough to believe one would cancel out the other? Or did he think they owed him and the plants were some sort of trade? Betrayal. What else is there to call it? Maybe he'd sensed her distrust all along, and that made taking the plants easier. Bastard. She can't forgive him for that. She should've seen it coming, but hadn't; she can't forgive herself. Still, in a funny way, she understands Doug, not that it lets her hate him any less. The first night at the hospital, hadn't her own instincts told her to run? Run like the rabbit she is, run the way Doug had, the way Rennie himself had during Carson's last weeks? But she hadn't. Run. Instead, she'd slept in a hard green-vinyl chair, her head sometimes on Rennie's bed. Mostly, she just watched. Matching her breath to his, willing him to live.

San Francisco International Airport lounges like a long and lazy lizard on the city's haunches. The beauty that San Francisco is known for is not here, in this exposed wasteland of barren, brown hills and mudflats and concrete freeways. Arriving forty minutes early for a plane that will turn out to be an hour late, Phoenix steps up to a mirror in the women's room, attempting to smudge out the circles under her eyes. Once, when she was first in love with Jinx and she'd flown for hours to see her, they couldn't wait to get further than this room, cramming themselves into one of the orange stalls, Phoenix opening her shirt, pulling Jinx against her. When they finally emerged, they'd laughed at the averted eyes, the tight mouths of the women behind the mirrors. Stepping into one of the stalls, she is amazed at how small it seems now. Small and dirty.

Tired and drawn, Phoenix drops into a black vinyl chair, very modern, at the gate where Cecelie is supposed to make her appearance and picks up part of an abandoned newspaper: HURRICANE INIKI TAKES TOLL—THOUSANDS HOMELESS. She has no patience with the news, and even the half-finished crossword puzzle, left behind by a passenger or another impatient lover perhaps, irritates her; some key words are wrong. Easy words, too. What kind of an idiot did this? She starts to wad up the paper, then thinks better of it because there is nothing else to read. She unfolds it, trying to smooth out the wrinkles, to undo the damage, to start again. She is suddenly embarrassed to be alone, waiting by this deserted gate at the end of the terminal.

Panels from the Names Project Quilt sway over the electric sidewalk. Colors like small, almost forgotten rainbows spell out Midwestern names. This section seems to be from Iowa, but no, there's Wisconsin, too, and Missouri. No hurricanes there, but tornadoes and one mother of a faultline. Last year, Savannah had called to say that Phoenix should buy earthquake insurance; everyone in Illinois was snapping it up, preparing for the big one that some earthquake pundit had predicted. "It's inevitable," her sister kept saying, while Phoenix laughed.

Beautiful men smile down on Phoenix from pictures sewn into the cloth, sometimes a shirt or a belt or a scrap of poem is stitched there, too. She doesn't recognize the names, not that it matters. Much. The first time she saw the quilt, when it was still mostly a San Francisco phenomenon, she had known some of the names. But that was a long time ago, when the epidemic was still new, before she met it on a first-name basis, before she began to live with it. That first time, she'd looked at the names curiously, searching the panels, looking for answers. Now she understands: There are no answers, just one name bordered by the next and the one after, into neat rectangles. Semi-permanent reminders. Cloth, after all, rots with time, leaving . . . what? Dust. If she were up there, what would her rectangle be? A peacock? A book of Anne Sexton poetry? A tiger prowling a symmetric jungle? And who would care enough, would miss her enough, to do that? Certainly not Jinx, likely not Cecelie, maybe Savannah—although the shame would be too much for her—not even poor Rennie, already so battered himself. Before Cecelie came, before he dragged Doug home like a pup, she'd asked Rennie why he didn't go out more. "Nobody's around," he'd said. And she, smiling, not yet understanding, had asked, "Have they all left for the summer already?" He'd looked at her for a long moment: "No, Phoenix, I think they're all dead."

Head thrown back, squinting, a few unintended tears leak out. Cecelie finds Phoenix staring up at Madison, Wisconsin, trying to make out the features in the face of a high school graduation photograph. Someone has sewn a silver crown over the picture. What does that mean? It seems important to know, but there is no one to ask. "How is he?" Cecelie means Rennie, but Phoenix, not understanding, shakes her head, then turns, clinging to Cecelie as if she were the only real thing left in the world. They will remember this moment, the names swaying above them in an artificial breeze, the late-day sun stretching through the tall windows. They will remember it as the first time they cried together.

Caught in the inevitable afternoon traffic on Highway 101, Phoenix curses while Cecelie drones on about Hawaii and the hurricane. Even natural disaster is a topic safer than Rennie. Prospects of the storm kept away Gina's buyers. "I ended up having to put the *huacos* in a safe-deposit box." Cecelie pulls a key from her pocket. Flat, with huge teeth, the key looks remarkably like an enlarged version of those that came with the one-year diaries TaTa Hassee gave Phoenix every Christmas. Phoenix never seemed to find anything to say after January 3. "But the trip wasn't a total waste. I saw Fred Wong. Do you remember him?" Apparently Cecelie is determined to send the conversation in any direction but toward Rennie. A wild-eyed man in the lane next to them leans on his horn and shakes his fist at a delivery truck. Phoenix grimaces. Cecelie shrugs. "I guess you wouldn't. We were in graduate school together. He's been at the University of Hawaii . . . well, practically forever. His field is ancient China. He's the only one in his family who's ever been there. His father's the dry-cleaning king of Van Nuys—he actually calls himself that. Very assimilated. Fourth generation. Anyway, I was at Fred's place when the storm warnings started and helped him board up. Turns out he's afraid of heights, so I ended up on the roof. He did the windows."

Cecelie is so matter-of-fact that it takes a moment for the obvious question to form. "Why were you on the roof?"

"Hmmm?" Cecelie is rummaging through her pack; she looks up and smiles. "Oh. He has a Light Walker. Only his works. Turns out he knows Lucas, too. Anyway, I ended up staying out there. Fred thought it would be safer than in the city. Flying glass, you know."

One advantage of a Jeep is how you ride above traffic. Phoenix looks down on the man in the next car; he's driving barefoot. At least he's not jerking off, she's had the experience of looking down into more than one sports car to see that. The barefoot man leans into his horn, and Phoenix, for no particular reason, honks too, setting off a cacophony of frustration that sounds for a second like geese. Ignoring the commotion, Cecelie goes back to rummaging. After so many years of living out of a backpack, she is well-organized. She scowls at not being able to instantly find what she wants. "Anyway, Fred's off to China for two years. His field experience is nonexistent, so that's why he was surprised about being invited. He's part of a cultural exchange program." Phoenix likes the idea of exchanging culture: a symphony for two ballet troupes; a Picasso for two rock bands. The combinations are endless. Interesting to think of it extending to archaeologists. Well, why not, all that past just waiting to be unearthed. "It's quite an honor," Cecelie explains. "University professors from all over the world are going."

"Too bad you're not a university professor," Phoenix is trying to sound less sarcastic than she feels. Cecelie shakes her head, which means . . . what? Either she doesn't want to go to China, which is unlikely, or she wasn't invited. Cecelie never wanted to teach, not that she hasn't had offers. It's what you do when you get too old or too lazy for the field, she says. At least she's honest, Phoenix reminds herself. Important, considering that most of her previous lovers have lacked that particular trait.

Cecelie closes the pack. "I brought you this." She holds up a tiny, wizened figure. "Fred gave it to me. He's trying to bribe me to take his job while he's gone. He thinks I'm safe and won't try to steal it. You didn't want one of those orchid leis, did you?"

"No, but I wouldn't object to being laid in orchids." She turns to Cecelie and winks. Cecelie smiles, pleased.

"It's really beautiful there, Phoenix. Not like Peru, of course, or even Mexico, but I can understand why Rennie loves it." Her voice trails. She turns the little figure over in her hand. "From Fred's house, you can see the Chinaman's Hat."

"Sounds appropriately racist."

"It's a big rock."

"I *know* it's a big rock, Cecelie. I am not totally unfamiliar with the world."

Cecelie chooses to ignore the obvious dig. "The first morning

I was there, before the storm warnings came up, I waded out to watch the sunrise. But I stayed too long and fell asleep and ended up having to swim back. I got one hell of a sunburn." She rolls up her sleeve, displaying a brown arm, no trace of pink left, then shrugs. "I tan fast. I was riding out the storm in aloe gel, and Fred was making lists of what to take to China. He's trying to figure out how to have a case of Charmin shipped in twice a year. Turns out he has hemorrhoids. Can you believe that? Universities really make you soft." She's laughing at poor Fred's poor asshole. "He asked me what we did in Peru. I told him we didn't worry about toilet paper. I can't wait to tell Luz about that. Anthropologists always love that shit. By the way, have you seen this?" Cecelie produces a newspaper folded to a far-back page and points to a small article, very small thanks to the hurricane: PERU'S TOP REBEL LEADER CAPTURED.

"Cecelie, please. I can't read and drive at the same time."

"Oh. Anyway, it calls Guzman's arrest the capture of the century. Says that the countryside is turning against the Senderistas. Do you suppose that's true?" And the whole of what she is saying rushes through Phoenix like an electrical shock: She's going back. Maybe not today or next week or even next month, but she will go. She's leaving me. Cecelie stuffs the newspaper between the seats. "It probably won't make any difference at all. They're very organized. Very smart, you know." Her voice is almost flat. What does that mean? Hills crowded with pink and green and yellow boxes perilously close together form a mosaic. The first and only time Savannah had seen this, she'd asked, "What if there's a fire? What would they do?" as if she were secretly hoping one of the houses would burst into flames so she could witness the answer. "It's certainly something to think about," Cecelie says.

"Yes, something for you to think about," Phoenix says. The effort of trying to mask her terror has sharpened her words. Holding Cecelie would be like trying to trap mercury. Still, these last couple of months have made Phoenix hope. And that is the danger. Hope leaves you too open. She knows better. Forgetting is when she gets into trouble.

"So, what do you think?" Cecelie's eyes hide behind dark

glasses, probably a meager attempt to tame the light. Cecelie must have one of her post-flight headaches.

"It's your ass and your career—do whatever you like. You always do anyway." Phoenix's voice is brittle and harsh.

If Cecelie is surprised, it doesn't show. "Why are you being like this?"

The space inside the Jeep has become close, the air tense and too warm. "How would you like me to be, Cecelie? You tell me maybe you're going to Hawaii or then again, maybe not, maybe it'll be back to Peru. What would you like me to say? No, I tell you what, you write out the words and I'll say them, just like a script in one of your mother's movies. You want me to say go back to Peru? Okay, I can do that. You want me to tell you to take Fred's job? Well, I can do that, too. What I can't do is stand at the airport and wave good-bye and pretend that it's fine with me for you to go running off to God knows where, never mind about me . . . or Rennie. But you've got to tell me what you want from me, because honest to God, Cecelie, I just don't know anymore." Phoenix gasps, attempting to hide her tears, but her voice has already betrayed her.

Reaching across the seat, Cecelie lays her hand lightly on Phoenix's forearm, but before she can say anything they've pulled through the brick gates and up to the front of the hospital, all glass and concrete tacked onto an aging compound. "Phoenix, please, I want you to understand . . . to try to understand . . ."

Phoenix shakes her head. "No offense, Cecelie, but I'm too damned tired to even try. While you were off dreaming of digs in Timbuktu, I was here. With Rennie. All day, all night, for the last five fucking days. While Doug was running off with my plants and you were sunning yourself on some damned rock, I was up there. I'm tired and I can't do it anymore. It's your turn . . . that is, unless you have to run off again." She didn't mean to say that and regrets the words the moment she sees Cecelie's lips purse. Tears, the ultimate sign of weakness, escape. Shamed, Phoenix leans against the steering wheel, refusing to look at Cecelie. She will hate me, now, Phoenix thinks. Women like Cecelie . . . like Jinx . . . never cry.

Cecelie inhales, making a long, almost cool sound. "I'm sorry about your plants, Phoenix; I told you that on the phone. If I had known Rennie was getting sick, I never would have gone to Hawaii. You should know that." Her voice is tight, but not angry. Phoenix would rather have rage, tears, anything other than this quiet, cold. "I don't know what you want from me, either. I got back as soon as I could. I'm sorry it wasn't sooner, but nothing can be done about it now."

Phoenix wipes her eyes with her sleeve, the way a child would. "I'm sorry," she says, unsure if she's apologizing or lying. She breathes deeply. There is no easy way to say this. "Cecelie, you need to know, before you go up, he's . . . well, he probably looks worse than you expect. Just so you're prepared." A car pulls up; the driver waits patiently. No honking allowed in a hospital zone. "There's someone behind me; you'd better go. Oh, and one more thing—they think I'm his sister; you'll have to be somebody else."

Cecelie's eyes are unreadable behind the glasses, but she nods as she unlatches the door. "Fine. I'll call . . . if there's any change. Otherwise, I'll just plan to spend the night here." Pushing down the tears, swallowing hard, Phoenix turns her face away quickly so Cecelie won't see. She waits for a long minute, watching Cecelie pass through the sliding glass doors, hoping she'll turn and wave. She doesn't. Finally, Phoenix pulls away from the curb.

Sighing loudly, the ocean slams into the shore with a boom that rocks through the peaceful evening as Phoenix turns onto the Great Highway. Pushing open the front door, she steps over two days' worth of mail, then, thinking better of it, turns and picks it up. Offerings to a lonely house: a couple of official-looking envelopes, one from the U.S. Bankruptcy Court addressed to Rennie, a postcard of an Hawaiian sunrise addressed to all of them from Cecelie, and the usual assortment of advertisements for everything from rug shampooing to lost kids—nothing that can't wait, at least until she's had a bath and some sleep. Padding down the hallway toward the bathroom, Phoenix notices the flashing lights on the answering machine. She flips it on to listen while the tub fills: two calls from Hawaii; one from George, who doesn't sound like an angel—but who knows what an angel actually sounds like?; then Rennie's editor in New York saying he's received the outline and the initial chapters and wants to talk. What outline? What chapters? She should call, tell him Rennie's in the hospital, but it's too late to do that today. Four banks are trying to collect on past-due credit card bills and Mr. Cole must respond to their messages immediately. For some reason, this makes her smile. Three messages are from an operator in the Philippines who is trying to reach a family Phoenix has never heard of; obviously a wrong number. Then, as Phoenix is peeling off her underwear, Jinx's voice fills the hallway: "I didn't know if I should call, but I've been thinking about you, how you're doing. I'd really like it if you would call me back, Phoenix." Then Jinx reciting ten digits; she not only abandoned her old life, but her old area code as well. Four perky beeps announce the end of the messages.

Trembling, Phoenix lowers herself into the steaming water, leans back, closes her eyes, and drapes a washcloth over her face. Too much. The last few days have been too much, and now Jinx. Why couldn't that, at least, be ended? Why can't just one fucking thing in her life end without shadows dogging her? Beneath the hot water, the background of the tiger's jungle turns bright pink. Like Phoenix these past months, the tiger and her jungle have shrunk, grown loose and angular. Maybe if she stays in the water long enough, it will disappear altogether. Or she will. Damn Jinx. Why now, with Rennie in the hospital, and she and Cecelie so close to—what?—whatever it is they have to decide eventually. Why does her heart start pounding at the sound of a few words on a machine? Sputtering, she comes up for air as the phone begins to ring, once, twice; on the third ring the machine picks up. The familiar voice makes her breath quicken. "I was hoping you'd be home now, but I guess not. I just wanted to say I've been missing you and to tell you that I'm sorry about how we left things. I guess I just wanted you to know. Maybe now isn't the right time to say this, but I've been thinking about it a lot. Since I left." The machine is silent for a long moment, as if the caller is considering her options or gathering her courage, or both. "Phoenix, I really do love you. Maybe you don't believe that. But it's true. This is really complicated, but we'll figure something out. You don't have to call me back, I just wanted you to know." Another long pause, then, "Please call me, baby."

Phoenix sighs and closes her eyes. This is what she's been waiting for. It should feel different. Better. More real. But she's too tired to think about it. Pushing her head under the water, she waits for the comforting roar. Nothing can touch her now. She will stay like this for a very long time.

16

Heavy dusk covers the windows, shading the room, when Phoenix Bay finally opens her eyes. Carson's neon clock registers ten minutes past eight, the most she's slept in days. Stretching diagonally across the bed, she sighs deeply and reaches for the phone. Her belly throbs. Nerves. The phone in Rennie's hospital room rings, once, twice, three times. No answer. Nothing unusual about that really. Cecelie is either out—Rennie won't answer the phone when he's alone, she knows that—or maybe they've taken him off for more tests. Rolling off the bed, she stretches and goes to the glass door that leads onto the back deck. Damp sea air rushes against her, like an invitation. She smiles. Of all the things she loves about this house, she loves most how it hangs so close to the sea you can taste salt on your lips, feel it in your hair. She can't imagine being this happy anywhere else. No sign of Marcel Proust and she can't remember if she heard his evening calls, he's so much a part of the day-to-day sounds, but he was gone this afternoon when she got home. In the past few weeks, he's been gone more frequently, only to show up unexpectedly, fanning his tail, cocking his head, an apology maybe, or just a bid for attention. One day, will he be like Doug, gone for good? If he's not back tomorrow, she'll call . . . who? The animal control people, probably. Or the police. But who knows if peacocks are even legal in San Francisco? More legal than marijuana plants, that's for damned sure.

She drops back down on the bed and dials another number, feels her breath catch when the ringing stops, the receiver lifted, that inevitable moment before hello, before you know for sure you're talking to a machine: "Hi! This is Jinx. Me and Perry are off looking for the perfect orgasm. If we find it, we'll let you know. So, you know what to do. And if you don't, you've definitely got the wrong number." Perry and me? Didn't Jinx learn anything from all those years of living with an English teacher? She should say something, but what? As she tries to decide, the machine disconnects and a stranger's voice answers, "Hello?" Phoenix hesitates, trying to find the words, and exhales sharply. "Who is this? I can hear you breathing!" She switches the phone off quickly, soundlessly lowers the antenna, as if the night were witness. She has been reduced to this: the obscene caller, the heavy breather, the jilted lover dialing furtively in hopes of hearing the voice that will never be for her again.

Darkness comes too fast, now that summer is fading. The shortening of the days is almost painful, like a window shade being slowly pulled down. She used to imagine going to Copenhagen or Oslo or even farther north to chase the daylight. The midnight sun. But when night comes, finally, it's long and desperate. Where would she go then? Where does the sun shine all the time? The phone is ringing, purring really. So like Rennie to have a discreet telephone. She turns it on and before she can speak, a voice she loves, soft and familiar, whispers, "It's me. I thought maybe you'd tried to call. I heard the phone, but couldn't get there in time."

Phoenix whispers too, even though there's no reason; the house is empty, no one to overhear, no one to disturb. "I got your message. I just wanted to tell you that. And I'm sorry, really sorry." She pauses, toys with the antenna. "Look, there's something I need to know."

"What?" So easy to imagine the woman on the other end of the phone, so casually beautiful. She wants to crawl inside this woman, stay there, safe and warm.

"About what you said on the message. Did you mean that?"

"I always mean what I say."

"Will you say it again?"

"I love you, Phoenix. Is that what you wanted to hear?"

Phoenix smiles. "I love you, too." She's surprised at how easily the words come; she'd imagined it would be harder. "Maybe I always have, even with everything that happened. I guess I never stopped loving you." She can't finish; there is nothing more she needs to say.

"I know."

"Cecelie?"

"Hmm?"

"Nothing. Just that. I'll see you soon." Phoenix switches the phone off, lowers its antenna. On her way out, she hits the rewind on the answering machine. The past erases itself so easily. Funny, she always imagined it would be harder.

Arriving at the offices of Brenner McKee and James just after dawn, Phoenix Bay inserts her key into the lock and is surprised to find the door already open, the lights in Dylan Brenner's office on. "Morning," she calls, passing the large, windowed office, where the senior partner sits in front of his computer. Dylan turns, smiles, and, incredibly, waves her in. She hesitates, sure she's misunderstood, and takes a tentative step toward the door. He smiles.

"Coffee?" he asks, taking a glass mug from a neat pyramid arrangement on the walnut credenza behind his desk. She nods, easing herself inside the door as Dylan picks up a chrome-plated carafe. "Cream? Sugar?"

"Black is fine." Maybe he's one of these men who only pretends to enjoy the stark quiet of offices before the day begins, but secretly hates to be alone. "What brings you in so early?"

"No rest for the wicked." He nods toward one of the two leather armchairs opposite his desk: high-tech, like the rest of the office. "Sit, please." Dylan Brenner is elegant, the way only older men seem to be: silverhaired, solid, deeply tanned, as if he spends his life on a golf course, although he's rumored to be a workaholic. He must have a tanning booth at home. He leans back in his chair and smiles, showing sparkling, even teeth. "And you're here because . . ."

"I need to get caught up," she admits. "I've fallen behind . . .

a little . . . with my mother dying and now my friend in the hospital." No point in letting him think she's lazy or slow or both. "I guess I didn't realize advertising moved so fast."

He laughs as if this is an original thought. "And how is Rennie?" Phoenix looks at Dylan for a long moment, confused. She's seen this man three, maybe four times in the two months she's worked here, and those encounters had been brief, all business. "Rennie Johnson, the writer, is your sick friend, if I'm not mistaken?"

She nods, nervous under Dylan Brenner's unflinching gaze. "Better," she says, her voice guarded. "But he's still in the hospital. How do you know Rennie?"

Dylan Brenner eases his chair forward, folds his hands on the desk and smiles, but something about his look, too smooth, too perfect, seems unreal. "Oh, only by reputation. But I knew Carson Cole. Very well." Brenner pauses, as if considering what to say next. Finally he offers, "He designed my house." He leans back in his chair, waiting, Phoenix decides, but for what?

"I'm surprised Rennie never mentioned it . . . after I started working here."

If Brenner is surprised, it doesn't show. "Oh. Well, he may not know. That was all a very long time ago. And Carson and I . . . well, let's just say we didn't part on the best of terms. You understand." Of course she understands or thinks she does. This man and Carson were—what? lovers, friends? certainly more than architect and client—important to each other. Lovers, she decides, although she can't say why. Maybe because of that comment about how they'd parted. Only lovers and fools leave things that way. And Carson Cole was no fool; she suspects this man isn't, either. "We managed a sort of reconciliation before Carson passed away last winter," he continues, although she hadn't dared ask. "I went to see him in the hospital, just after Thanksgiving. We have a few mutual friends who felt it was time to . . . mend fences, I suppose is the best way of putting it. The day I was there was one of his better days, or so I was told. Even so, I found it tragic. We talked or at least I talked and he listened. For a change." Dylan Brenner smiles at this obviously personal joke. "Carson was always a great talker, I'm sorry he lost that so soon. But the point of the story is, he was concerned about Rennie, what would become of him."

"I thought you said he couldn't talk?"

Dylan Brenner waves his right hand, almost dismissively. A gold Rolex chain link catches the light. The watch is the same style as the one Rennie wears. Carson's watch. "The greatest concepts demand the fewest words, Phoenix. I learned that when I was a very young copy writer. I promised Carson I would do what I could for Rennie, even though I wasn't sure how. And then you showed up here. I didn't realize it would be quite so simple."

Skeptical, she looks at him, trying to assess his intent. "But how did you know that Rennie and I are friends?" She sets the cup on the floor.

"Oh, I didn't. At least not at first. Then one afternoon Richard came in here with one of his insufferable complaints. Richard is convinced he's a genius. He's not, of course, but he'll never believe it. He was ranting about the temp agency sending him an out-of-work English teacher who edited gay porn in her spare time. That intrigued me, a woman editing gay porn. So I asked around and Marty in the Art Department filled me in. And here you are." He is smiling.

Phoenix nods and picks up the cup. The coffee is unpalatably cool. So that's how she came to be here, nothing to do with her great gift for advertising. And that's why there were never any questions about all the time she's missed. Dylan Brenner is just paying off a debt. The old boys' network. Well, why not? What was he supposed to do—drop an anonymous check in the mail? And what is she supposed to do now? Flounce out of the agency, hurt and indignant? No, this is the real world, as Richard's stupid campaign slogan says. "What about Marina?" She needs to know if the woman whose office she's claimed so easily was pushed out as smoothly as she was taken in.

"Oh, she's doing fine," Dylan Brenner says, smiling, misunderstanding the question. "Unfortunately, motherhood seems to agree with her. She's brilliant, you know. I'd give anything to have her back." Phoenix feels as if she's been punched, and it must show in her face, because he adds almost too quickly, "Of course, your work is certainly adequate, Phoenix." Certainly adequate? But not great. Not brilliant, like Marina's. Just adequate. So-so. Well, what had she expected? To discover great creative genius after all these years? One more delusion. The truth is, she needs this job, and the elegant man on the other side of the desk needs her to have it. "Do you have any idea when Rennie will be getting out of the hospital?"

She shakes her head, still flustered by Dylan Brenner's strange confession. Why did he tell her? What does he want? Men like Dylan don't divulge secrets without reason. "Probably in a few weeks." Her voice is guarded. "Cecelie came back last night. His sister," she explains in case he didn't know that, too. Hard to tell how much he knows about her, about them all. "She was in Hawaii . . . on business," she adds quickly, so he won't think they're the kind of family that jets off to paradise on a whim. "The travel agency account gave me a deal on the tickets." But, of course, he would know that. He probably had arranged it, just as he'd arranged all the rest. If he expects her to be grateful, she isn't; she feels used and a little dirty. "I won't have to spend so much time at the hospital now that Cecelie's back. I can get caught up. Marina had some accounts in her file Richard wants me to take a look at."

"Fine." He obviously is less interested in her work than in her life. "This is Rennie's first bout with pneumocystis?" He is hungry for details, she realizes, some shred that will connect him with Carson. She nods. "Then he'll probably do fine. It's the second and third that are so rough. I lost my lover to that two years ago. You may have heard."

She hadn't, but she nods. "I'm sorry. It must be terribly hard." Apparently the rumor mill that gave Richard James the crucial bit of information about her, Rennie and the Truck Stop Jock and Harry with his indefatigable hard-on doesn't work in both directions. What would have happened if she hadn't told Marty about Rennie, hadn't traded a few harmless jokes? Where would she be? Probably not here drinking coffee with Dylan Brenner and trying to stay on Richard James's good side, if he has a good side. No wonder he dislikes her.

"Well, off to work." She raises the empty coffee cup and smiles. No wonder her work is only adequate, if that's the best she can come up with, she decides. Rising from the chair, she pauses; he raises his eyes, questioningly. "I really do appreciate this opportunity, Dylan. I want you to know that. I'll do the best I can for you."

He waves his hand in a dismissive gesture. "I know you will, Phoenix. Just promise that you'll let me know if there's anything I can do. If Rennie needs anything . . ."

"We're okay, Dylan, really. We're doing just fine." Too bad she doesn't believe it, she thinks, as she closes the door to his office, leaving him alone. Wait until Cecelie hears about this.

"What's this?" Sorting through the stack of mail that's been collecting for weeks, Cecelie holds up a government-brown envelope.

"Don't know, don't care," Phoenix says, brushing Cecelie's left ear with her lips. Then reaching inside Cecelie's white shirt, she balances a perfect breast in her left hand, weighing it. Cecelie makes little purring noises. "It came when Rennie was first in the hospital. I guess I just forgot about it." She starts to say "open it," but Cecelie is already running her finger under the flap. Phoenix kisses her lightly and goes back into the kitchen.

Today is Rennie's first day home and everything has to be perfect. On the dining room table the last of the summer roses send out a determined fragrance, as if that alone will be enough to stave off the inevitable long nights of fall; a bottle of Pernod is on the buffet, a homecoming gift from his editor in New York. He and Rennie have had seemingly endless long-distance conversations about Pernod—Rennie insisting it was what O'Neill drank in his final days, the editor saying it sounds more like Hemingway or maybe Fitzgerald. But Rennie, still in his O'Neill phase, refuses to be swayed. The editor sent it as either a joke or a concession. A pale consommé simmers on the stove, warming the kitchen, like love. Phoenix rubs sage and garlic into the breast of a fat chicken, organically fed, according to the wan young dyke at the health-food store around the corner. Sage because TaTa Hassee always prepared chickens that way; garlic because it's good for immune systems, although it would probably take considerably more than what she's using. She adds another clove for good measure.

"Phoenix, I think you should look at this." Cecelie is at the kitchen door, frowning. "It's from the bankruptcy court."

"Wait a minute, my hands are messy." Cecelie holds the paper in Phoenix's line of vision. Why is it so easy to read over some stranger's shoulder on the subway and so difficult when there's a paper being held in front of your face? Phoenix reads slowly, then starts again. Craig Cole and Cole Development are filing bankruptcy. Phoenix raises her eyebrows. "So?"

"Phoenix," Cecelie sounds exasperated, "Craig is Carson's brother." As if that explains anything. Phoenix shrugs. Why should Cecelie care what Carson's brother does or doesn't do? Neither of them have ever met the man. "For God's sake, Phoenix, don't you get it?" Her voice rises, and she sounds, Phoenix realizes, close to panic. "Cole Development *owns* this house."

Shit. How could she have forgotten? Rennie had told her that, the whole tangled mess of Carson's will, with the stipulation that Rennie was to live here "in perpetuity." Apparently forever doesn't last as long as Carson had envisioned. Wiping her hands on the front of her jeans, Phoenix sinks into a chair and looks at the paper more carefully. There has to be something they can do. Some loophole. Aren't there always loopholes? "Maybe it's not as bad as it seems," she finally offers, but Cecelie looks skeptical. A telephone number next to an attorney's name followed by an admonishment to not contact anyone directly connected with Cole Development is midway down the sheet. "Call them," she says, handing the paper back to Cecelie. "You call this attorney. I'm going to the hospital to pick up Rennie."

"Phoenix . . . don't say anything about this." Cecelie looks as if she's about to cry. "Until we have to." There's a lot Rennie doesn't know, the least of which is Doug's disappearance and the stolen plants. What difference can one more lie possibly make? Omission, she corrects herself, one more kindly omission.

Cecelie Johnson slumps onto the couch, rubbing her fingers across her forehead, as if she might somehow push away the pain.

In the hospital, Rennie was always wanting her to massage his forehead, but it didn't help him anymore than it's helping her now. Soon he and Phoenix will be back. Home. And what can she do but tell them what the lawyer said? Carson's brother has lost it all: this house, the company, everything . . . in a jojoba bean farm scheme. What the hell are jojoba beans, she'd asked the attorney, who hadn't laughed. There was that to be thankful for. He hadn't said he was sorry, either; he could have at least offered some condolence, some crumb; instead he'd cautioned her not to contact Carson's brother. She'll definitely want to contact her own attorney, he told her, adding, "confidentially, don't expect too much." Carson's will reduced them to tenants—no, worse than tenants, poor relations living rent-free in a house that no one really owns.

She's felt this before, the emptiness that starts in your throat and works its way down. When Mala died, but even before: when Mona announced they were moving, again; that Cecelie would be changing schools, again. She should have known this was too good to last, that Mona Morgan's fat, homely, stupid daughter would never find a place where she really belonged. The bankruptcy process should take three months, four at the most, according to the attorney. When she was a kid, three months was a lifetime, but now, months are only whispers. Three months, four at the most. That will take them up to Christmas. Then what? Rennie is fond of a story about how last Christmas, while he was walking in the rain, a well-dressed drunk had pushed money into Rennie's empty coffee cup, when all he'd asked for was the time. Now she understands why he relishes that story; he imagines he's escaped that fate, that Carson is still taking care of everything. He imagines it will go on, as the will said, in perpetuity. Only now, their house built of tax dodges is tumbling down around them.

Hearing the front door, Cecelie paints on a smile, one of the few good things her mother ever taught her: Smile no matter what. Stepping into the hallway, she opens her arms, kisses her brother lightly. "Welcome home!"

Rennie took the news about Doug leaving without emotion. Maybe he had guessed, all those weeks in the hospital and not one word from the man. He'd cried, though, when Phoenix told him about the plants. "I'm so sorry," he kept saying, as if it were his fault, "I wish I could make it up to you." And no matter how hard Phoenix tried to convince him that it really wasn't the end, that she could start over, he still looked tragic. His tears had frightened Cecelie more than the news from the lawyer about the house; she'd never seen her brother cry, never before had felt him to be fragile. There would be time enough later, she and Phoenix agreed, to tell him about the house. To decide what to do.

The weeks in the hospital have turned Rennie into a gray and fragile old man. His hands tremble. His skin seems translucent, slightly blue from the veins running beneath the surface. He's lost weight, not the way some AIDS patients do, leaving them looking like prisoners of war, but enough so that his shirt cuffs gape. He rolls his sleeves up on his forearms, an attempt at looking jaunty. "I've lost three weeks, I need to get back in the saddle." He attempts a grin. Rennie's hatred of horses is an old and tired joke. He picks at the mashed potatoes, pushing them under the chicken, the way a child tries to hide uneaten food. "Manny used to say when a horse throws you, you need to climb back on. He was never smart enough to figure out that if you hadn't been on the damned thing in the first place, you would never have been thrown." Phoenix and Cecelie try to smile, but the expressions feel false. Surely Rennie must see, but if he does, it doesn't show. "I'm thinking about an epic: The Truck Stop Jock Meets Harry's Hard-on. What do you think?" He's teasing Phoenix and she smiles. Rennie is superstitious about discussing new work, *real* work, as he calls it, as if the pornography is something else. Maybe it is.

"When can we see it?" Cecelie ignores his little joke or perhaps misunderstands. Hard to tell with her. Rennie smiles, genuinely pleased. It's rare for her to show an interest in his work or much of anything else that has happened in the last five hundred years. Recent history to Cecelie. He once told her he was going to do a story just for her called "Hard-On Pizarro and the Temple of Doom." Even Cecelie had to laugh, although she hadn't understood the Temple of Doom part. He'd rented her the Indiana Jones movies. She'd laughed until Marcel Proust shrieked.

Rennie runs his hand through his hair, which has grown fashionably long while he's been sick. "I hope to have something soon. I have a deadline. I think it's too tight." He always says that about deadlines. "And I will live to see it finished. That's a promise." So determined and assured, he sounds exactly like the old Rennie. "But I definitely won't make it, if I don't get to work."

"And you won't be able to work if you don't take a nap." Phoenix is surprised to hear her mother in her voice. She flushes, embarrassed, but the others don't seem to notice.

"I'd like to play a round of the game first," he says, rising slowly, his hands braced flat on the table. The game: betting on the sunset, betting on the fog, betting on when Marcel Proust will make his evening call. If they were better gamblers, they could win a fortune in Reno or Vegas, but Doug won most often. And before him, Jinx. And Carson, of course. Doesn't say much for winners, Phoenix decides, following Cecelie and Rennie upstairs.

"What shall we bet on?" she asks. It's too early for either the sunset or, from the looks of the horizon, the fog.

"How about how long until I fall asleep? In the hospital I had my after-lunch nap, which preceded my before-supper nap. I was worse than a damned cat. Eat, sleep, and shit." He eases into the chaise, apparently more interested in the company and in the almost-painfully bright sun, than in actually playing. "Give me three-fifty and four o'clock. I feel a nap coming on," he says, as Phoenix opens the jar of dimes. At least Doug had left them this. Small miracles.

"So, Rennie, I met one of your fans the other day," Phoenix says, arranging the dimes. Rennie could be a wealthy gentleman crossing on the Queen Mary, the way he sits so casually, straw hat and round glasses, head tilted back toward the sun.

"I used to have a fair number of those, as I recall. Anybody I know?"

"Dylan Brenner." She watches Rennie's face carefully, looking for some sign of recognition. None comes. "You know, the senior partner where I work."

He raises his glasses, looks down at her, and smiles briefly. "I'm flattered."

"You don't know him?"

Rennie considers this for a moment. "I don't think so, but . . . you know, you meet a lot of people. Remind me and I'll give you an autographed copy of—what do you think he'd like?" Phoenix shrugs. "Well, I'll just pick something. Score some points for you. Maybe he'll give you a raise." He rearranges his glasses and settles back, hands folded across his chest; the Rolex band glints in the afternoon sun.

"I doubt that."

"His loss."

"Rennie." Cecelie jostles his leg and extends the jar.

"Oh, my turn. Sorry. I'll just ride with Phoenix. Is that legal?" All summer they've been making up rules as they've gone along. When it's your game, you can do that.

"Where'd this board come from, Rennie?" Phoenix is picking at a black square that is starting to chip from the weather.

"Carson designed it, you know that."

"Yes, but," she looks at Rennie, who has closed his eyes and pulled the hat down over his face. Whoever has naptime called in the next fifteen minutes will win. She checks the board. Cecelie. "I mean, was it here when you moved in?"

"Hmm? No. I don't think so. He wanted to learn chess, but never could get the hang of it. No patience."

"I'm surprised. He always seemed so calm." She is fishing, very gently, hoping Rennie won't notice. "You know, I've always wondered what he did . . . before you two met, I mean."

Rennie opens his eyes and looks at her suspiciously. Or is she only imagining that? "The same thing he did after we met. He was an architect. Why the sudden interest?" Rennie is growing irritable, but she needs to know—what? If what Dylan Brenner says is true.

"Just curious," she lies. So much easier than the truth. "I never knew much about his past, and when I was cleaning out his closets I ran across some of his college T-shirts and I just . . . wondered. You know."

Rennie nods, then smiles. "If you mean the University of New Mexico, one of his nephews sent them as a joke. Carson went to USC. In fact before he moved up here, he was doing pretty well in Southern California during the land-development heyday. Then he and Craig decided this was the new promised land: Vallejo, Vacaville, Richmond, all of our more exotic environs."

"Vallejo? Doesn't seem like Carson. Did he live there?"

"God no," says Rennie, raising his hat and winking at Phoenix. "Carson had taste. Before he got this place he lived in Marin County. Tiburon. Never, my darling, in Vallejo." He lowers his hat, still amused, apparently, at the thought of Carson in a traditional suburb. "And so ends the story of the early life of Carson Cole, because unless you can read that cryptic code he called shorthand in his files, that's all there is to know."

"Doesn't that bother you?" Phoenix asks, surprised at Rennie's cavalier attitude toward the past. Cecelie, curled next to Rennie on the blanket, shoots Phoenix a warning look.

"No, Phoenix, it does not. I've always found my own past to be only remotely interesting and everyone else's to be absolutely boring. My sister here is the only person I know who actually gives a serious damn about what anyone was doing before this actual moment. I knew all that I needed to about Carson. Nothing else matters." He checks his watch. "It's almost three-thirty. Time for my after-game nap." Stiffly, he rises from the chair, adjusts his sweater, and waits a moment before taking a step, as if his legs might betray him. Finally, he smiles. "Cecelie, you win. Next time I'll ride with you."

Once Rennie is settled on the couch in his office, with the door closed and the fan running, Cecelie recounts her conversation with the attorney. "Three or four months," Phoenix repeats slowly, as if saying the words might change their meaning, make them less ominous. Neither dares say the obvious: Rennie might not be alive in three or four months, or he could be so sick he couldn't or shouldn't move. "Cecelie, I think we should try to buy it. This house is all he has left of Carson."

They are sitting on the deck, the doors open to listen for any sound from Rennie's. Cecelie sighs and looks out toward the sea.

"This house, or to be specific, what's in it, is all he has left, period, Phoenix. So how the hell are we supposed to buy it? It's worth more than two hundred thousand dollars."

"What?" Phoenix has never considered property this close to the ocean to be valuable. Carson lived here because he liked to surf, not because of property values. "It can't be."

"Well, I'm afraid it is. I went through Carson's files while you were gone. We can't even afford the insurance on it, not to mention taxes. The company took care of all that."

"I thought Rennie said Carson's shorthand is impossible to understand."

"This isn't in shorthand, it's in contracts. Even if we could raise the down payment, how could we ever pay the mortgage, that is if we could even find a bank crazy enough to finance us?"

"What bank *wouldn't* want us?" Phoenix tries to sound more perky than she feels. "A sickly porn writer, a crazy English teacher, and an archaeologist in residence? Why, there's not a bank in the country that wouldn't want that kind of credit risk. Look at how many call us now." It's a bad joke, but Cecelie finally smiles, a tiny attempt, but a smile just the same. Encouraged, Phoenix adds, "Well, maybe Dylan Brenner can do something, pull some strings."

Cecelie looks doubtful. "You heard Rennie. He no more knows Dylan Brenner than the man in the moon. And once Dylan has massaged his conscience over Carson dying or whatever it is that brought on his surge of benevolence, he won't give a damn what happens to us."

Cecelie is right, of course. Except for that strange early-morning conversation, Phoenix hasn't even seen Dylan, except in passing. Besides, giving her a job is one thing, asking him to buy the house is out of the question. "What about the *huacos?* You always said they're worth a lot."

"Not that much." Cecelie's voice is tired and low. "And they're only worth something if Gina can find a buyer."

"I thought that was a sure thing?"

"Not anymore. Something about the economy in Japan going sour."

"You mean Richard James is wrong? God doesn't like them best?"

"Phoenix, be serious."

"I *am* being serious, Cecelie. What do you want me to do, wrap myself in sackcloth and keen?" Phoenix stands and leans out over the railing. A trio of surfers in their orange wetsuits paddle out to meet the waves. "I figure so long as I'm not out there at three o'clock in the morning, praying to die and trying to figure out the best way to open my own arms, I'm not as bad off as I've been." She turns toward Cecelie. "I don't know about you, but for me this isn't bottom. It's one hell of a detour, but it's not bottom."

"A detour?" Cecelie finally says, shaking her head, "Phoenix Bay, you amaze me. So tell me, what are we going to do?" Cecelie spreads a newspaper out in front of her and splits a melon, large and round as a harvest moon. Seeds spill out and she begins to peel the skin, yellow and smooth. Rind and seeds and bits of flesh drown out the front page of the newspaper by the chaise: INIKI VICTIMS START PAINFUL REBUILDING PROCESS.

"We've got three months, right? Maybe four?" Phoenix drops to her knees next to Cecelie. "A lot can happen in three months. Look at us. We fell in love in less."

"Not counting a dozen or more years in-between?"

"So it had a long fuse." Phoenix reaches behind her for the jar of dimes. She lays three out. "Six o'clock."

"There won't be any fog tonight," Cecelie protests.

"Then we'll bet on the sunset." Phoenix takes a wedge of the yellow melon, sweet and sticky, the texture of flesh on her tongue. "I'll take six o'clock and six-thirty." Insistent, she adds another dime. "Your turn."

Cecelie begins to scoop a few dimes from the jar, then pauses. "Why do we keep playing this game, Phoenix?" Without waiting for an answer, she lays a pair of dimes on six-fifteen. Her tongue darts out, catlike, to catch a dribble of melon.

Phoenix covers Cecelie's hand with her own. The calluses of the digs have softened and all but disappeared. Only a few scars remain. She picks up the hand and kisses each finger lightly, licking off the melon juice. "Because, Cecelie, it's the only game in town."

17

Something is wrong. Looking up from his desk, Rennie Johnson surveys the room, searching out the offending picture askew, the file mislaid, the memento fallen. Seeing nothing, he turns back to his work. Probably just his imagination, he tells himself, and then he sees it. The file cabinet's second drawer is ajar, because it must be lifted ever so slightly when it is closed to compensate for the faulty track. Carson knew that. No one else would. And now it has been closed wrong. So.

Pursing his lips, he studies the evidence, trying to decide what to make of it, then pulls open the drawer. Nothing of value here that would have interested Doug, who claimed more than Phoenix knows: a few nearly valueless pieces of jewelry, including a cheap tiger's-eye ring, given to Rennie by his first lover; a genuine first edition of *The Grapes of Wrath* with a forged Steinbeck autograph—well, he'll find out about that soon enough; and the portable television and VCR machine from the guest room. Nothing that matters. The drawer holds Carson's files, contracts mostly, related to this house and Cole Development. He pulls out the one that seems to be standing a little high, "Disposition of Great Highway Property," and balances it on the edge of his desk, flipping through the pages, neatly caught at the top by clips. Carson was an organized man. Nothing out of the ordinary, nothing missing. Satisfied, he turns to replace the file when his left hand begins to tremble. One of the side effects of the drugs, the doctors assured him when it first happened in the hospital. He feels like a palsied old woman, trembling hands, dancing without music. The file tumbles, pulling a page loose. Scowling, he bends stiffly—another side effect of yet another drug—and picks it up, reading the terse, formal paragraphs as he sinks into the leather chair, which exhales softly under his weight.

So, it's come to this. Not that he's surprised. Craig always was a fool. But jojoba beans? He knew there was trouble even before Carson died, but there was no way by then to untangle the house. Carson's brain was already twisting, his thoughts roaming, the simplest of decisions—when to eat, where to shit—were left to Rennie and then, finally, to the nurses. Carson had thought he was so smart, making the house one of the company's assets. Maybe he was. Or maybe they both were stupid. The clause was in the will because, although neither of them said so, Rennie was the one who was supposed to die first. A legal dodge gone awry. Not that there's a damned thing to be done about any of that now—unless . . . Flipping through the Rolodex, Rennie finds the number he wants, lights a cigarette, and dials quickly. A gruff and sleepy voice answers on the fifth ring.

"Rennie? It's two-thirty in the morning. What the hell do you want?" Jerry Kiwata clears his throat loudly and coughs twice. Through the phone lines Rennie hears the unmistakable sound of a cigarette being lighted. He smiles. An attorney with bad sinuses who's addicted to cigarettes seems like a bizarre combination; but at this hour, many things seem bizarre. "Are you okay?"

"More or less. I just got out of the hospital, if that's what you're asking. And it's only eleven-thirty here. Jerry, I need some legal advice. Is your meter running?"

"Can't it wait?" Jerry sounds miffed. He would forgive a late-night plea for help, Rennie knows this—he'd called often when Carson was dying, talking until morning made the desk lamp unnecessary, until the ashtrays overflowed on both sides of the country. Is this so different? Maybe it was his comment about Jerry's meter running. Over the years, he and Jerry have settled into the comfort zone of long-ago lovers who managed to become and remain friends, even with a continent separating them. Jerry never could shake New York, saying California is too unformed for his taste.

"No. If I don't get some answers, I won't get any sleep."

"Okay, shoot." Jerry sniffs loudly. "Sorry."

"What would you say if I told you the house, our house here in

San Francisco, is owned by Cole Development and that in Carson's will there's a clause that I can live here, tax free, in perpetuity?" His words are slow, in contrast to his breathing, which matches his racing heart.

"What would I say? I'd say I'm not a tax attorney, but it sounds shaky as hell. The IRS has been coming down hard on those kinds of deals in the last few years. But aside from that, if anything at all were to go wrong with that company you'd be in deep shit. So, why are you asking?"

Rennie swallows hard. "Then what would you say if I told you Cole Development filed for bankruptcy a month ago?" The other end of the phone is silent for a long moment. "Jerry?"

"Yeah, I'm still here." Jerry exhales noisily and coughs once. "Look, Rennie, I don't know much about California law, but I think you'd better get an attorney out there, a smart one. I can make some calls in the morning, get you some names. But you want my initial take on this?"

"What are friends for?"

"You've got a big problem, buddy, unless you can come up with a way to buy the place outright. Even then, . . . I don't know." Jerry sniffs again, lights another cigarette, and exhales softly into the receiver. "Like I said, the tax boys aren't looking kindly on these kinds of deals. And you could be setting yourself up for some tax liabilities linked to Carson's estate. If you don't mind my asking, what are your assets?"

"As we speak? Practically nonexistent. There's Carson's Rolex, one functioning credit card, and about thirty-seven hundred dollars left from selling my dad's house last summer. I frittered the rest away on doctors and tossing a few bones to the bill collectors to keep them quiet."

"What kind of bill collectors are we talking, Rennie?"

"For Carson's credit cards. They kept us going while he was in the hospital."

"You notified them right after he died, didn't you?"

Rennie wonders how much to admit. Rubs his thumb across his forehead. He's suddenly very tired and Jerry seems small and very far away. "I did," he lies. Lying comes more easily than the truth that he's been using the credit cards of a dead man for nearly a year, even signed up for two more when the offers came in the mail nearly a month after Carson's death.

"So, just write to them again. Send a copy of the death certificate if you have to. Problem solved."

"Right, Jerry. I will. I'll just write to them again." Every time a car passes on the street below, the room comes alive with shadows, chasing each other like kittens. His eyes droop. "I . . . I'm really tired, Jer. Sometimes it happens like this, I just get really tired . . . all of a sudden. If you call me tomorrow with those names, we can talk more then. Right now, I can't."

"It's okay, Rennie, you don't have to explain. Get some rest. We'll talk tomorrow. And Rennie? It's going to be okay, one way or the other. I'll take care of everything, buddy."

Rennie nods as the phone goes dead on the other end. One way or the other, whatever the hell that means. What is it Phoenix says? Something about things working out the way they're supposed to, just not the way you necessarily *think* they're supposed to at the time. Optimistic fatalism. Pulling a blanket over his long legs, he curls into the couch. He should go to bed, but the bedroom suddenly seems very far away. It's quiet here. Safe. Nothing bad has ever happened to him in this room. Until tonight, he reminds himself, as he starts to fall asleep, and maybe Jerry's right, maybe this isn't as bad as it seems.

The hospital changed Rennie. Always restless, fueled by an energy that gave every word, every motion a sense of importance, he has become nearly static with fear perhaps, or grief. Wit has given way to cruelty, hope to fatalism, and tolerance to stifled rage. And there is nothing he can do to change any of it.

It started, Phoenix and Cecelie would later agree, the morning after he talked to Jerry Kiwata. "Why didn't you tell me? What the hell were you two thinking?" He was in the midst of his medication ritual—place a pill on the back of the tongue, followed by a sip of orange juice and a grimace. He goes through this routine seven times, four times a day. Place, sip, grimace. He hates pills.

Hates that they remind him so frequently of what he would rather forget. Hates how Cecelie and Phoenix watch, anxious and aware, as if he were the willful child and they the adults. Always there. Mothers prompting: Take your vitamins before you leave the house. If only these were vitamin pills, then maybe he wouldn't mind so much.

"We were only trying to help. We didn't want to upset you on your first day home. Besides, you found out almost as soon as we did." Cecelie, trying to be pleasant, takes a few sweet rolls from the microwave. With Doug gone, they're back to the Armenian sisters' fare.

"We were going to tell you," Phoenix offers. "I thought maybe Dylan Brenner might know somebody who could help. Do you think Carson knew about the jojoba beans?"

Rennie considers this, raises his eyebrows as if it were a possibility. "He might have. I don't really know. We had a deal; I didn't design houses, he didn't write. Even if he did know, what possible difference could it make?"

"I looked them up in the encyclopedia." Taking one of the rolls, Cecelie sniffs it before spreading butter along the top, where it forms little puddles in the ridges. "The beans produce a valuable wax." She takes a bite, then licks butter from her index finger.

"Apparently not too valuable," Rennie says between pills.

Each time he swallows and makes a face, Cecelie does the same. Sympathy pains, Phoenix decides. "At least we're not the only ones." Cecelie settles into the place next to her brother, and sets one of the rolls in front of him. "Here, put some butter on it. You're too skinny."

"And you're too fat." When Cecelie laughs at this, he glares. "Do you think I'm kidding?"

"No," she says patiently, the smile fading, but only a little, "I think you're a pain in the ass. Anyway, some dentists in Arizona lost a bundle, too. That's what the lawyer's secretary told me."

"Oh, well, now that *is* comforting." Phoenix wonders if he means the dentists losing money or Cecelie talking to the secretary.

"Why were you talking to the secretary?" she finally asks.

"Because talking to the secretary is free." Cecelie pulls a bit of the roll off, sniffs it carefully, and for no reason Phoenix can determine, sets it aside. "Besides, the lawyer said we need our own attorney and hung up on me."

"We have our own attorney. I called Jerry last night." Rennie picks at the sweet roll, hating how they taste after orange juice. Whatever happened to the luxury of a black-coffee breakfast at eleven, after working all night? Well, that was before.

"Yes, but we didn't know you'd do that. Anyway, he told you how to fight this, didn't he?" Phoenix sounds too hopeful, looks to eager, he thinks, fighting the urge to slap her.

"Fight with what?" He's tired. Of talking. Of listening. Tired. And it's not yet eight o'clock in the morning. "The company owns this house and the company has gone belly up thanks to Craig and his fucking jojoba beans. The end." Ignoring Cecelie's offered sweet roll, he sips coffee and turns to Phoenix determined to punish her for that crack about fighting back. "Tell me, Phoenix, as an advertising executive, don't you think they could have come up with a better name than jojoba? How would you like to come up with an ad campaign for something that sounds like Santa Claus with gas? Or would even that be too creative for you?"

Phoenix, who has been putting beans in the coffee grinder, blanches as she pushes down the top of the machine, letting it run in spurts. Its irritating whine jerks through the kitchen over and over. Any sound is preferable to the bite in Rennie's voice. "That wasn't necessary, Rennie," she says at last.

"Nothing is necessary, Phoenix," he says, coolly. She doesn't have to see his face to know he's smiling, a strange half smile that sometimes reminds her of a weasel. One had lived in the tree outside her window back home, when she was a child. Sometimes at night, she would look out to see it there, eyes gleaming, lips pulled back in what might have been a grin, if such creatures could grin. If she had stuck out her hand, the animal would have attacked. But if she'd told anyone—TaTa Hassee or Mama—they would have shot it. She'd spent most of that year imagining she was its protector. And it knew, she imagined, and was secretly grateful. Still, she never dared stick her hand out that window. "Well,

Rennie, I'm surprised. I didn't think you'd take the news so well."
Sarcasm has always been her first defense.

"How exactly would you like me to take it, Phoenix? Up the
ass, maybe? Chain myself to the front door? Or the ultimate
masochistic statement: Hang myself in the basement—and don't
think I haven't thought about it. Or maybe bite the real estate appraiser. It's not the most efficient way of transmittal, but who
knows, I might get lucky."

"Rennie!" Cecelie has finally had enough. "This is Craig's
fault, not hers. He's the one who got involved in the damned
beans. And no, we didn't tell you the second we found out, because you are sick. If trying to protect you from bad news is a
crime, then we're guilty. But if you want to yell at someone, yell at
Craig. You've got his number. Call him. Tell him he's an asshole.
Tell him what his damned beans cost you. But leave Phoenix
alone. She has nothing to do with any of this. We're just trying to
help you out."

"You want to help me out, my dear, eternally absent sister?
Then stay the fuck out of my business." Phoenix gasps. Stretching
stiffly, Rennie locks his hands behind his head, Carson's watch
sliding loosely up his forearm. Closing his eyes, he exhales shal-
lowly. The room is silent. Finally, he lowers his arms. Rising
slowly from the table, he turns and leans close to Cecelie, his
voice low, confiding. "You really don't get it, do you? All I want is
to be left alone. Maybe the two of you should think about that."

Not until his office door closes do Phoenix and Cecelie dare to
look at each other. Hadn't he asked them to come here? To stay
with him? To help him fight the ghosts? Hadn't he said he needed
them? "He doesn't mean it," Phoenix says at last, suddenly afraid.

"Oh, he means it." Cecelie sounds worn. "It's not what he really wants, I suspect; but he does mean it." Phoenix is amazed at
Cecelie's calm, watches as she sniffs her sweet roll again. Where
did she ever learn such a habit? Maybe from all those years of living without adequate refrigeration. Finally she looks at Phoenix
and smiles. If the look is meant to be reassuring, it isn't. "This is
how he gets . . . when he's scared. You get scared, you run. Some
of us just run in different ways. But we all run. It's what we do,
Phoenix, it's what we are. I remember when he was eleven or

twelve, the doctors thought he had leukemia. He didn't—it was anemia—but it took weeks, maybe months for them to figure out what it was. One day at the clinic, he overheard the doctors talking to Manny. That night, he ran away. Into the jungle. It took days to find him. Mona even went down there. Of course she made my dad pay for it. Do you know what he said when they finally found him? 'If I'm going to die, it's going to be my way.' Twelve years old. He was scared then and he's scared now. And he's still running. I'll talk to him. We'll figure something out. Now, go, or you'll be late for work."

Phoenix shakes her head. "We need to settle this."

"And so we will, just not this instant. Some things have to get a lot worse before they get better. Give it time." Cecelie's voice is calm. Her comprehension of time is rooted in what she calls "the blink." The blink is all of them, this house, this moment, even this decade on the continuum of time; in a moment it will be gone, as if it never happened at all. But of course that's crazy, Phoenix reminds herself, what's happening now is all that matters. Phoenix considers pointing out that they don't have the luxury of time, that Craig has stolen that. But she doesn't argue with Cecelie, either.

The warm days of San Francisco's second summer are gone. Indian summer it used to be called. No longer. When did that change? He can't remember noticing, just one morning there was the TV weatherman talking about second summer. Cool dampness drapes the city in gray, like chiffon, every morning. Rennie shivers. His eyes droop, although he slept last night for hours. He's tired of being cold. Tired of waking up alone and afraid. Tired of waiting for the inevitable in the shape of a microbe, too small to be seen by the naked eye, but oh so deadly. Warming his hands on his favorite coffee mug, the one with the picture of Shakespeare on one side and the words *Appearing Nightly* on the other, he waits for sounds of life from the girls' room. The mug was a birthday gift from Phoenix. She remembered how he used to write and drink coffee most of the night, a habit developed in college. He'd done it for so many years, he eventually reached the point where coffee didn't interfere with his sleep. Then he would finally crawl into bed just before dawn, about the time Carson was getting up. The memory makes him smile. Carson used to say that when they retired, he'd make Rennie into a day person.

Pulling one of the dead judge's cashmere sweaters closely, Rennie notices a small moth hole on the left sleeve below the elbow. Amazing that the moths don't get into more of these, he thinks, pouring another cup of coffee. The judge spent his whole life in Oregon, except for six years in school "back East." Where back East? Columbia, like Jerry Kiwata? Yale? Harvard? Northwestern, maybe? What would the judge think if he knew the end his clothes had come to? Would he even care? Not likely. No need of a wardrobe, even a cashmere one, where the judge is. Where he's going. At four o'clock this morning, he was watching Phoenix's faith healer on TV. When the reverend told him to put his hand on the screen and be healed, Rennie had actually considered it. Maybe tomorrow. But do you have to send the money in first? He should remember to ask Phoenix. The faith healer talks a lot about love offerings. Too bad he means only money. He talks about hell, too. Burning in the eternal fires of damnation. At least it would be warm there. But hell probably isn't fire and brimstone; it's probably ice and glaciers, like the South Pole. Nothing for thousands of miles except intolerable cold. He wants to live where he would never be cold again.

Phoenix interrupts his thoughts by rattling down the stairs. Seeing him, she mumbles a hurried greeting before skirting to the far side of the kitchen. She's a little afraid of him since their episode day before yesterday. He has to remember to be nicer to her. But sometimes she irritates him with all her pharmaceutical buoyancy. Prozac. Happy pills. Certainly took them long enough to kick in. "God, I'm going to be late again." She gulps the coffee that must be too hot, judging from her surprised look.

"Tell King Richard that the streetcar broke down again, he'll believe that." Rennie has never met Richard James, but Phoenix's descriptions have been so unflattering, he's decided to dislike the man on general principle.

"Can't," she says, rummaging for her purse, keys and, finally, shoes. Phoenix can never seem to keep track of her shoes. There always seems to be a pair tucked under the sofa or forgotten under the table or abandoned by the door, and God knows where upstairs. "That's the excuse I used last Friday." She retrieves her shoes from a spot behind the back door and clatters out.

Rennie smiles. At least she's entertaining. Sometimes. Better than when she first came, each of them skirting ghosts, going through the motions of life. Now only one of them has to pretend. He inhales slowly, testing his lungs. Every morning he tries to breathe more deeply, the way the respiratory therapist showed him. She even gave him a tube with an orange ball inside to practice on. Every morning, he's supposed to make the ball bounce more. Today it seems a little higher. He's supposed to be pleased, not supposed to know that it's all a game; even if his lungs get better, there are all those other organs to worry about. He's been meaning to check an anatomy book out of the library, to find out what could go when and how. He likes to be prepared. That was the problem with Carson: They didn't know what to expect. If they'd known, it would have been better. Wouldn't it? He doesn't know. His thoughts have been taking strange turns lately and that frightens him most of all, how they career out of control only to settle on some inconsequential detail of the past, while the present rolls on untended. And he can tell no one.

His sister, always slow and bleary in the morning, brings him the newspaper, still damp and cold from the stairs. He looks forward to its morning dose of mayhem and destruction. There's something comforting about the world falling apart. Wordlessly, she drops it on the table next to his right elbow. She is still angry with him. Phoenix afraid, Cecelie angry. Fuck 'em. He will not play the role of the eternally grateful, ever complacent dying man. He is too damned angry for that.

"Phoenix was late again this morning." It is all he can think of to say and good morning seems contradictory. There is nothing good about this morning: gray and cold, and promising nothing better for the rest of the day. "She'll never change, you know that, don't you?"

"I'm counting on it." Cecelie drops into the chair next to him and props her feet up on Phoenix's chair. She sniffs, then sips the coffee. "So," she says. He looks up, waiting. Instead, she runs her fingers through her hair. Is it more gray than when she first arrived or is that only his imagination? His own has grown unattractively thin, thanks to the onslaught of drugs. After a long moment she asks, "Did you call any of those attorneys Jerry recommended?" Her voice is terse, as if she already knows the answer.

He shakes his head, wishing for a cigarette. They hate it when he smokes, so he no longer smokes in front of them; instead he hides in his office like a guilty teenager. "I'm letting Jerry handle it. He got the fax you sent, made some calls." Cecelie cocks her head, as if this bit of information surprises her. She apparently thought he had done nothing at all. Rennie exhales slowly, evenly, slightly pleased that there is no whistle coming from his lungs this morning. "He thinks . . ." His brain stumbles. What? He shakes his head and begins again. "Jerry thinks . . ." Tears well in his eyes. He can't remember. Panicked, he looks at his sister, who is nodding expectantly. "I don't remember his exact words," he finally says, his voice defensive, "but it comes down to the fact that we don't have a snowball's chance in hell." He finishes in a rush, looks into his coffee cup; his lower lip trembles.

If Cecelie is surprised, it doesn't show. "Then what do you want to do?"

"Well, we could implement Plan B." When they were kids, he used to develop long and intricate schemes in which he would escape from whatever boarding school Manny had stashed him in that year, somehow make it to L.A., and he and Cecelie would run away together. His favorite took them to London, where they'd cross the channel to Paris and live on the Left Bank as bohemians. It seemed infinitely preferable to riding horses in Colorado or New Mexico or Arizona, his father's three favorite locations. It certainly had to be better than living with Mona. But his best plans were always foiled by money or specifically the lack of it, although he'd got as far as L.A. more than once, only to have his mother ship him back to wherever he'd run from. "We could run away and find paradise with an ocean view. Watch the sun rise over the sea."

She smiles. His sister is beautiful in her own way. No wonder

Phoenix loves her. He's selfishly pleased that he's never had to share her with another man. Sharing her with a woman is different. He would be jealous of a man. "Sounds good, but I was thinking more short-term," she says. "Rennie, an attorney called yesterday afternoon. The court is sending a real estate appraiser by today. I thought we could go out. Have lunch downtown maybe."

Yes, he would like that. Going out. But not downtown, with all those gray buildings and deep shadows and frantic, overdressed people rushing, always rushing. "You decide," he says, resigned, "but not downtown. Let's go someplace sunny, someplace warm, like home."

Men draped in rainbows harmonize under the persistent percussion of passing traffic on a sunstreaked street. From the open-air markets, the sickeningly sweet smell of too-ripe fruit swells. Women haggle over melons and squash.

A tiny, rounded woman holding a very large melon jostles into Cecelie. *"Perdón."*

"De nada." No problem. A boy pushes against her legs, cassette tapes fanned like a hand of playing cards.

"Markahuasi." The boy nods toward the singers and down at his tapes. Fiesta music of the Andes swirls. *"Di mi pueblo."* The musicians are a long way from home.

"¿Cuánto cuesta?"

The boy puffs out his chest, *"Diez dolárs."*

Cecelie scowls, shakes her head, *"Cuesta demasiado,"* and turns away.

The boy bounds in front of her, still grinning, "Okay, okay," he says, grinning. *"Ocho."*

Cecelie smiles. Peeling the bills from those threaded under her belt buckle, an old habit, she hands them over.

"Gracias, señora," says the boy, with a deep, affected bow. Cecelie laughs and hands him another bill. "Cowabunga, dude!" He winks at her. An older version of the boy, one of the members of the band, nods to Cecelie as she steps inside a darkened cantina, where she left her brother twenty minutes earlier. Blinking

twice, letting her eyes adjust to the darkness, she sees Rennie at a rear booth.

Seeing her, he waves. "I thought you got lost." He sounds a little accusing.

"I told you I had to send a fax. You're the one who wanted to wait here." But Rennie isn't listening to her; from the way his head cocks, she suspects he's concentrating on the music from the street.

A ceiling fan turns slowly, mixing light and fresh air and warm spices from the kitchen. *Ajo* and *picante de parillada* she recognizes, and something else, slightly familiar. *"Cabrito,"* the plump and serious owner tells Cecelie when she asks. Goat. She wrinkles her nose and shakes her head.

"Traigame un plato de pescado ahumado, por favor."

The plump man wipes his hands on the gray towel at his waist, his idea of an apron, and turns to Rennie, who is studying his hands. *"¿Qué le traigo, señor?"*

Rennie shrugs. Cecelie scowls. *"Dos,"* she says. Satisfied, the man retreats toward the kitchen.

Her brother smiles at last, but only a little. "Smoked fish." He sounds disappointed. "I like *paella* better."

"Why didn't you order for yourself, then?"

He shrugs. The door opens and, for a second, the music becomes clear and loud. He frowns, then leans across the table and whispers, "Cecelie, something's happening to me. Those singers, I can't understand them. I've been sitting here listening and sometimes I know what they're saying, but then . . ." He spreads his long fingers on the table between them. He's afraid, Cecelie realizes with a start. She's said the words, told them to Phoenix over and over, but never until this moment has she understood. He must think that what happened to Carson is happening to him. First, you forget a few words, then a few more and then . . . He rarely talks about those last months with Carson, what it was like, what he went through.

"Rennie, it's Quechua." She reaches across the table, covering his hands. So alike, their hands. "Not Spanish. There's no reason you'd understand." Relief comes in shades across his face.

"Their song is about the sunrise on the mountains welcoming a new and bountiful day." On the wall behind him is the large, requisite aerial view of Machu Picchu and next to that, a series of pictures of a village she doesn't recognize.

Cocking his head toward the door, he asks, "Why would they leave to come here?" To sing on a crowded street in a strange and dirty city, he means.

"We all do what we have to. Maybe they thought things would be better here, maybe they are. Look, Rennie, you know that I'm not good at beating around the bush, and I've never been very accomplished at tact, so I'll come to the point. The fax was about a job offer." He raises his eyebrows, frowns a little, studies his fingers, and finally nods. He does not look at her. "I'm going to take the teaching appointment in Hawaii. And unless you've gotten a better offer in the last hour, I suggest that you come, too."

For a long moment he says nothing. Finally, he reaches into his shirt pocket, takes out a cigarette, and in one smooth move lights it and extinguishes the match. "What I love about Mexican restaurants is that they still let you smoke."

"This is Peruvian, you know that. And you shouldn't smoke."

Ignoring her comment, he leans back and blows a series of double smoke rings. "Manny taught me to do that," he says at last. "What would he think of us? Do you ever wonder?"

"No." Cecelie's voice is cold, her answer quick.

"I do. Lately. I thought about him a lot in the hospital. How he was the quintessential tourist. How that's what he passed on to us, the sense of belonging nowhere. *Decian que no servia para nada.*" Rennie's voice trails, he smiles, snubs out the cigarette.

"Who said Manny was good for nothing?"

"What? Oh, I don't know. Mostly the servants, I guess, the people he paid to take care of me when I was down there. He couldn't be bothered." Cecelie winces at the venom in her brother's voice, but there's nothing she can say, she knew her father so little. "When I met Carson, I thought . . . I *believed* that I had finally found a place where I could belong. A home. And that nothing could take it away from me. I truly never imagined losing it all

285

to jojoba beans. But if you're doing this all for me, it really isn't necessary. I'll get by. I always have."

"Would you believe me if I told you that I'm doing it for myself?"

"No."

She leans back, stretching out her long legs, looks up at the ceiling. "Well, you're wrong. I'm tired of running, too, Rennie. I'm tired of waking up alone. I just don't want to do it anymore. It's a two-year appointment, but a good offer. Fred says the dean is impressed with my field experience. He thinks it will enhance the curriculum. God, do people still talk like that? I've been away from the universities so long, I can't remember."

Nervous, the words come more rapidly. She wants Rennie to look at her, to smile, to send her some sign that she's made the right decision. "Fred's renting me his house while he's in China."

Pulling out the Polaroid pictures Fred took while she was there, she pushes them across the table. A small but respectable house appears to be trapped in a sea of foliage: a large living room with tiled floors, and a bank of windows showing more green, one huge bedroom with a ceiling fan and French doors that open onto a deck, and finally a smaller bedroom, more windows, more green. In the last picture, a huge skylight glints in the sun. "What do you think?" she asks, although she can see he's pleased.

"Is that a Light Walker on the roof?" Rennie asks at last.

"An A-18. Lucas installed it himself."

"He's everywhere, isn't he?" Smiling, Rennie returns the pictures. "What can I say other than it's damned near perfect. Too bad about the Light Walker, though."

"Then you'll come?"

"Do I have a choice?"

"There's always a choice."

Her brother leans forward, elbows on the table, and looks at Cecelie closely. "A wise and talented man once said: 'In these, our plague years, what we would do is too often incompatible with what we must do.' "

"Who said that?"

"I did. It's the opening line of my new book. Do you like it?"

She nods. "It's beautiful, Rennie. Really."

He smiles a little and nods. "Would you like to hear the last line?"

"Of course."

"Ruege por nosotros." Pray for us.

18

The day before Thanksgiving and the stores are long since dressed for Christmas. Obscene, really, when you think about it, these weeks that grow longer as the days themselves shrivel into nothingness and The City dresses itself in tiny, twinkling lights as if those could ever be enough to push back the night. Phoenix Bay sits alone in her office, watching the second hand of the wall clock tick away what's left of the day. Four o'clock, Dylan Brenner had promised, when she'd asked for a meeting. But four had turned into five before he even got back from his client meeting. Now it's nearly six-fifteen, and he's still on the telephone. By stretching across her desk, she can see the lights on the receptionist's phone; his is still red. Damn. She exhales sharply and drops back into her chair to wait. She'd promised Cecelie she'd be home early. "A surprise," Cecelie told her, being mysterious. There have been enough surprises in the past month to last Phoenix Bay a lifetime.

First, the whole fiasco with the house, then Cecelie and Rennie deciding they were cold and the cure would be to move to Hawaii. Hawaii, for God's sake. He and Carson had always planned to retire there, but . . . Well, why not Hawaii? But what will she do in Hawaii? Keep house for them like a poor relation? No, she has to find a job. "Tell Dylan Brenner what's going on" was Cecelie's solution. "He must know somebody in Hawaii." And when Phoenix had begun to protest that she couldn't leave San Francisco, that nobody actually *lives* in Hawaii, Cecelie had silenced her with two words: "Why not?" Why not, indeed. Finally, her phone rings, a pleasant dingdong, apparently designed not to interrupt the creative process.

"Phoenix? Glad you're still here. What was it you wanted to see me about?"

As she takes the chair across from him, Dylan Brenner is smiling, but she's learned that doesn't necessarily mean he's happy or even content. The smile is an automatic expression, the result of years spent in advertising. "So, Phoenix, hope my little delay didn't put a crimp in any travel plans?" She shakes her head. Ironic that he would mention travel. "I'm heading up to Tahoe in the morning. Snow's in the forecast, you know." She didn't know; doesn't ski and isn't one of those Californians who is compelled to "visit" snow, as they say here. Midwestern winters cured her of that. He smiles expectantly.

She inhales slowly. This would be easier if she could come to him with an award-winning portfolio or years of experience, or just about anything. Never good at asking for favors, she crosses her legs and launches her rehearsed speech. "I . . . well, you asked me to keep you posted . . . about Rennie, I mean. What's going on with him and all." It had sounded better in her office, but Dylan Brenner's smile never falters, so she presses on. "We're going to Hawaii. Moving there . . . And I thought maybe you might know someone there, an agency I could work for, or something." She finishes feebly and finds she's staring at his perfect, white teeth. God, this man must spend a fortune on dentists.

Shifting slightly in his chair, his smile breaks for the first time. "Phoenix, tell me something, and please be honest. What do you think about this business?"

What is there to think? She stumbled into this job, thanks to him, and stayed because it was easy. Obviously, not the right answer. "I like it, of course." She pauses, then smiles, hoping to look convincing.

He nods, considering. "But are you passionate about it?"

Passionate? Phoenix hasn't been passionate about a job since, well, since before she came to California. She used to be passionate about teaching, when the students were more eager, when you could see the light in their eyes. Students who didn't trust the world, but who wanted to. Those were passionate days, and those days are long gone. "I guess I've found it difficult, lately, to be passionate about jobs," she admits.

"That's too bad, because I am. I love this, all of it. Loving what I do has been my beacon." Dylan Brenner folds his manicured hands on top of his immaculate desk. Cufflinks, in the shape of gold nuggets, tap the glass lightly. "It gives me strength. I would hate to lose it, but I would hate more never to have known it."

She looks at him, confused. What is he saying? That he won't help her because she lacks passion? And what does that mean, anyway? "I appreciate that, Dylan, I really do, but . . ." He waves her silent.

"Phoenix, you've got to understand, people come to me once a week, sometimes more, asking me to help them go here, transfer there, put in a good word for them. And I don't mind, that's the way the game is played. And I ask every one of them the same question I'm asking you: If this were the last thing in your life you could do, would you?"

She could lie, she thinks, tell him that she loves advertising, that she can't imagine doing anything else. Lies would let her have it all: Cecelie, Rennie, their paradise with an ocean view. But the words stick. "Dylan, I don't just *want* to go to Hawaii," she says at last, alarmed at the rise in her voice, "I *have* to. We need this." She waits, motionless, watching his fingers peak, the way Teddy Grayson's do when she's listening closely, when she's about to drop a bomb. This is the church . . . Gray eyes, the color of the ocean at dawn and just as chilling, lock on hers. Funny, she never noticed his eyes before. No wonder Carson left him—if Carson did leave him—who could love a man with eyes so cold, with a smile so practiced? And then she understands, all his talk about help was just that—words. He's built an empire on words.

"Phoenix, I'm not saying there's nothing I can do, but I can't recommend you to an agency. Tell me, why did you leave teaching?" He's starting to smile again. Automatic pilot.

Startled by his question, she inhales sharply. She's seen how the truth can erode the most well-meaning smile, can cloud even the kindest eyes. Nobody wants to hear how her life fell apart, piece by piece, how carefully she had put it back together, how fragile it still feels. She can't tell Dylan Brenner that, so she says, "It just didn't work out. I needed a change."

He is a chess player considering his next crucial move. Finally, he nods. "One of the advantages, some might say disadvantages, of having been around the business community for as long as I have, is that you're occasionally invited to sit on boards of directors for certain organizations, some worthy, others probably less so." He leans back in his chair, locking his hands in front of his chest. The index fingers tap-tap a silent cadence.

"That's nice, Dylan, but I . . ."

"Bear with me, Phoenix." He smiles, and this time she is sure it is genuine. "One of the boards I've sat on for several years now, seventeen, maybe eighteen, is for a children's academy on Oahu. It's very beautiful there. Peaceful. And these are children who need a great deal of peace in their lives because they've known so little. It was started late in World War II by a religious order to help children afflicted by the war, those who had lost their parents or who were so devastated by the fighting that . . . well, that they would never be able to function normally in society. You're much too young to know anything about that time, of course, but the fighting in the Pacific Theater was very difficult for many children; most people don't realize that. My older sister was with our father at Pearl Harbor during the attack. Alice was seven years old at the time. Our father was a lieutenant commander in the Navy who had been stationed in Hawaii for some years; we lost him in the fighting two months later. The combination of events, the air raid, our father's death, the war itself I suppose, affected my sister deeply. For years, Alice didn't speak. She trusted no one. It was as if she had created her own world, stepped inside, closed the gate, and then couldn't find her way back out. Our mother, against the advice of her family, took my sister to the academy. We weren't Catholic, you see, and to them that was tantamount to blasphemy. Alice lived there for many years, it became her home. My sister will never be like other women; over the years, I've come to accept that. But she paints, she reads, she even has one or two trusted friends. And me, of course. We lost our mother some years ago. I credit the fact of her recovery, however limited it may seem to others, to the academy. Naturally, when I was asked to sit on the board, I agreed."

Phoenix cocks her head, trying to understand why Dylan Brenner is telling her this. "It sounds like a wonderful place."

He brightens. "Yes," he agrees. "As a teacher you would find it interesting. Of course, the religious order turned it over more than twenty years ago, so that it is now a nonprofit in its own right. And the children there now suffer less from the effects of war— although there was certainly that during Vietnam—than from the effects of life. But you're right, it is a wonderful place, Phoenix. And it is kind of you to listen to my reminiscences, but there was a point to the story. If you are considering going back to teaching, the headmistress of the academy is a close personal friend. She is a strong woman. A woman of some influence. I think you would like her. More important, though, I think it is a place where you might become passionate about your work." He leans forward. "If you would like, I'll call her after the holiday."

Fear should stop her from accepting. She hasn't forgotten her slide into nothingness, all those eyes on her. She could walk out and never look back. But she wants this. It's her ticket back to part of herself. "I would like that very much, Dylan. Very much. And thank you." He nods, satisfied, but this time Dylan Brenner doesn't smile.

Rennie Johnson catches his reflection in the back window that overlooks the garden. His own face is replaced by a woman's. She waves and smiles. Smiling real estate agents, armed with clip- boards and fountain pens, have been marching through the house all week. They make him nervous. The glass darkens, leaving only his reflection. He averts his eyes. The man he was crouches in shadows; the man he has become waits. He is time's prisoner. Mirrors reflect a truth he finds repugnant. Who could ever love this? Again. He stoops to pick up a peacock's tail feather. He's gathered a respectable number of them this afternoon. Odd how Marcel Proust can lose so many and still emerge magnificent. The woman from the window, too thin and too buoyant, he decides, emerges from the kitchen and calls to him. "I'll be leaving now, Mr. Johnson. I'll let myself out." He doesn't look her way. "I said, I'll be leaving now." She probably thinks her hard edges and brittle smile make her beautiful to men; she is wrong. Rennie finally relents and raises his right hand without turning toward her. He hates it when they come here and he's alone. No, he hates it that they come here at all. Damn Carson for putting this house in the company's name. He should have known something like this could happen. But how could he? How could any of them have foreseen the economy going so sour for so long? But jojoba beans? Even that dundering fool Craig should have been bright enough to see through that.

Cecelie promises that everything will be all right, now that she and Phoenix have finagled teaching jobs. And they still have the necklace and nose rings and God knows what else locked up in a safe-deposit box, waiting for a buyer. The "right" buyer according to Gina, as if there could be a wrong buyer.

Stooping over the last survivor of a few determined but never very successful rose bushes, he wields a pair of clippers like a half-mad surgeon. "Need some help?" He squints toward Cecelie's voice, then beckons her toward him absently. The flowers he planted on a whim the first year he moved to this house are not much more than rangy weeds now. A landscape architect friend drew up plans for this yard, once, pastels showing each planting. Too enthusiastic, though, Rennie had planted roses before the plans were finished, and then he'd lost interest. Now, most of the roses are dead and the plans are in the file cabinet. "Just cleaning up. Do you think I should leave the garden plans here for the next owners? They were designed for this yard, you know. And it's not easy to find the right combination of plants so close to the ocean." Roses are not the right plants, he knows that. He turns back to the rose bush, studying its withered stalk and the single dried-out bloom forgotten on the end. He snips it off. The leaves are gray and limp. How late is too late to cut back a rose bush? That sort of thing must be in a book somewhere. In paradise, roses grow to the size of plates and orchids hang from trees. He wonders if it will feel like home. "Hawaii must be one hell of a place to grow things," he says. "Maybe my dick will grow, or Phoenix Bay's tits, but God help us if yours take a growing spurt." He chuckles and his sister scowls. "I think I'll leave the plans. No point in wasting them. By the way, Phoenix's Mr. Rizzo called. He's coming by tomorrow morning to make a bid. Can you be here?"

"Sure." Cecelie picks up the bouquet of Marcel Proust's feathers, fanning them. "I'm sorry we have to do this." She looks almost as if she's going to cry.

Rennie slumps onto the bottom step and wipes his brow with the back of his forearm. "Don't, Cecelie," he says, surprised at how breathless he sounds. His lungs are stronger, now; the little ball fairly shoots to the top of the tube every morning, but the gardening has left him drained. They've agreed to sell almost everything, which means everything of Carson's and, to a lesser extent, his. Phoenix says it's best to start fresh, not that she came with anything much. And Cecelie has owned damned little that she couldn't carry on her back. So that leaves him. He doesn't know if he has the energy to start fresh, whatever that means—but he's willing to try.

Cecelie pulls Carson's fisherman's sweater tight around her, hugging herself against the inevitable December dampness. She'll be happier in Hawaii, he thinks, where she can go back to her khaki shorts. The students will think she's a real Indiana Jones. And Phoenix, now that she's going to be teaching again, needed something besides Carson's suits. So Rennie had taken the last of Carson's credit cards to Union Square and come home with three dresses: flowered, with low necklines and wide skirts, suitable for walking along Hawaiian beaches, the salesclerk assured him. Phoenix is a beautiful woman, settled and strong. No wonder his sister wants to run away with her to paradise. "Anyway, I'm glad you can be here when Mr. Rizzo comes. If I'm left alone with one more clipboard-carrying stranger, I'll become an ax murderer." In truth, he's almost eager to meet the junkman, who got everything Phoenix owned for eight hundred bucks. Of course, Phoenix told Mr. Rizzo she was moving to Mauritius, and thought he believed her. Who the hell ever heard of moving to Mauritius? No, Mr.

Rizzo just knew desperation when it looked him in the eye. Won't Mr. Rizzo be surprised to meet him? Rennie smiles; he drives a much harder bargain.

Sometimes there's nowhere left to go but up. Leaning into the California Street hill, Phoenix Bay's lungs contract and then grab. All these months of hiking this hill, and she still can't make it to the top without wheezing. A cable car clangs past; tourists hang from the steps and bars imagining that they look like natives, as if the natives have nothing to do but ride cable cars and take pictures of each other. She still owes Cecelie a cable car ride by moonlight. "Next week," Phoenix kept saying, and the next thing they knew summer was gone and then fall. Now night constricts around the feeble winter light. Streetlamps flicker on, faint and yellow. Chinatown glows and jangles around her, as she turns to look down at the street below. She's come a long way. Phoenix turns and starts to climb again, there's still a long way to go.

A lot can happen in three months. Phoenix Bay reminds herself of that every morning, tying the laces on her battered running shoes, now showing the wear of the sands of time, or just sand, as Cecelie, ever the pragmatist, reminds her. The television ads promised considerably more than the shoes have delivered; by now she should be able to skip to the top, all the time smiling like a *Sports Illustrated* model. Nearly a full year of climbing this hill, waiting for it to get easier. No, easy. When does it get easy?

In a boutique window near the crest of Nob Hill, tiny blue lights blink and twinkle in leafless silver trees that shine over a sweet-faced angel with wings made of peacock feathers, which ruffle in an artificial breeze. Marcel Proust. Carried off to live with Lucas Walker down on the coast. Maybe he'll be happy there. Lucas promised to find a hen, even to send pictures if they produce chicks. "Not if Marcel takes after his namesake," Rennie said, and Lucas, as always, had looked a little baffled, but laughed anyway. The angel opens and closes a banner: THE SEASON OF MIRACLES. Who couldn't use a few of those right now?

On the corner a little girl, eight or maybe not quite, tap dances to thin music from an old man's harmonica. Cracked patent-leather shoes clack-clack against the pavement. "Sell it, honey," the old man says between breaths, and the child smiles, extending her arms, twirling until her plaid dress, a little too tight in the waist and short in the skirt, but stiff from starch and a hot iron, shows dimpled thighs. The old man plays blues harp, the old-timey kind that still filters out onto the streets from back-street bars on summer nights. Not much Christmas music you can tap dance to. The child twirls and curtsies as Phoenix claps and drops a folded pair of bills into a coffee tin. Phoenix nods to the man with the harmonica, who has already retrieved the bills, leaving a nest of pennies and dimes, and tucked them into his shirt pocket. The child dimples, as the man with the harmonica starts to play again. Showtime.

Teddy Grayson watches the street from her window, the form of her last patient approaching, walking more quickly up the incline than most would even try. It wouldn't surprise her to look out one evening and see Phoenix actually running all the way to the top. Such a strangely metaphoric objective, but so much about this patient is metaphoric. A colleague once, years ago, was a proponent of something he called "reality-check therapy." A hidden camera filmed the patients during their sessions and then, weeks or months later, he would play the film back to them. The results, for the most part, were disastrous: patients recoiling in horror at what they saw on the screen. He'd left the profession in disgrace. But what of those who had seen, truly seen, what he was trying to show them? Were they cured? What would Phoenix see if she could let herself look? Failure or triumph: a woman who has come so far, or one who believes she hasn't yet come far enough, can, perhaps, never come far enough? What does she see in the mirror? What does anyone? The psychiatrist closes the lace curtain.

Phoenix Bay perches on the edge of the psychiatrist's couch. All these months of coming here, the end should be more momentous, she thinks, her left knee jiggling. But endings seldom are. "I've come to say good-bye, but I guess you already know that," she begins even before Teddy is fully settled in her chair. The psychiatrist nods, almost smiles. She'll miss this patient, difficult as she's sometimes been. If they had met under different circumstances, would they have become friends? Probably not, the psychiatrist decides, still . . . "When I first came here, I remember telling you that I didn't know how to do this. I still don't. You want total honesty? That's what this is supposed to be about, right? Well, to tell you the truth, I'm relieved that I don't have to . . . do this anymore. That was Jinx's exit line, I probably told you how she said: 'I don't want to do this anymore.' And then she walked out without looking back. At least one of us landed on her feet without stumbling. Too bad it wasn't me. But some girls have all the luck, I guess. Some girls don't let life touch them at all. Maybe that's why they're lucky. I wouldn't know. All I know is she can't hurt me anymore; maybe nobody can ever hurt me that much again. I've tried to figure out if she pitched me off the edge of the world or if I just slipped. I honestly don't know; either way, it doesn't matter. I forgive her. Maybe one of these days, I'll even forgive myself.

"I thought about calling her. You know, to tell her we're moving to Hawaii tomorrow, but I don't think I will. I don't owe her that. She might think so, but I don't. Maybe I'll send a postcard when we get there, one of a naked woman running along a black-sand beach. She'd probably like that. Not that it really matters what she likes or doesn't. In a way, though, I owe her some things: She taught me what love is, or at least what it's not. She taught me to take my time, next time. That's why Cecelie had to say 'I love you' first—I couldn't risk that. Again. You see, love tears you apart; I knew that even before I could walk. That's one advantage of growing up with a country-music soundtrack playing in your mind, you learn early on that what gets you through the night ain't necessarily worth a good goddamn in the mornin' light. That's not original, it's a line from one of Cliff's songs that Savannah used to sing. He had another one about three o'clock in the morning, but I don't remember how it went. Something about waking up with nothing but an empty whiskey bottle and a couple of wet cigarettes.

"I know what that's like. Some mornings, I could feel the knife at my throat. Not a real knife, just my own fear so sharp. And then one night . . . I didn't. I woke up and it was six o'clock in the morning and Cecelie was there and Marcel Proust was singing and the room was already light. And I wasn't scared. I was scared all the time with Jinx. Scared she wouldn't come home, scared she would, scared she'd leave, more scared that she'd stay and we'd destroy each other. We damned near did. I guess you'd know that better than almost anyone. You and Carson.

"I used to tell him my secrets. Before he got sick, he'd say, 'Your secrets are safe with me.' I believed him. He made me promise to take care of Rennie. I never told anyone that before. I guess he made a lot of people promise that. Me. Dylan Brenner. Cecelie, that time when they were all down in Mexico together. Even his brother, Craig. Of course, that didn't work out too well— the jojoba beans and all. But even Craig tried. Last week Rennie got an envelope delivered by Federal Express with twenty-three hundred dollar bills inside. No note, just twenty-three hundred bucks held together with a jumbo paper clip and Craig's business card. He didn't have to do it; he could have cut Rennie loose and not looked back. We all could have, I suppose. Except Carson made us promise. Not that he had to, you understand. We would have done it anyway. And Rennie took care of us, too. He didn't have to do it, either, but he did.

"Rennie and Cecelie are the only home I know. You have to belong somewhere and we belong to each other now.

"Dylan Brenner told me you have to be passionate about what you do, and then he arranged for me to be a teacher again. Only this time, the students are lost instead of the teacher. I guess he thinks I'll fit in. Either he knows about . . . all this . . . or I'm not as good an actress as I thought. Maybe it shows, that I've seen what bottom looks like, and that I know how to find the way back.

"I guess it's like my daddy used to tell me: Winners run at, losers run from. I never understood what he meant until recently. Losers run scared. I've been running scared all my life. Until now. Maybe he'd be proud of me. I don't know. I don't think he ever bothered to really know me.

"All those people who've been telling me how tough I am are right. I am tough. It's like calluses; you rub a place raw long enough, and pretty soon it's tough. And then one day, you know that you aren't the same anymore. And it's okay, because you made it through to morning.

"Oh, I almost forgot, I brought you something." Between her fingers is a red silk cord, bought for fifty cents in Chinatown, and from it dangles a large, carved bead. Teddy Grayson looks at her curiously. "It's a *chaquira*, a bead, from the necklace Cecelie gave me last summer. The string broke and before she fixed it, I saved this one bead out. I was going to put it on a cunt ring, you know, so that once Cecelie left me she'd still be there, like Molly and Jinx. Only, it was getting a little crowded down there, so I figured what the hell? Anyway, I took out the rings last night. Cecelie never liked them much. She doesn't mind the tiger, though. Good thing, I don't think I can get rid of that. You know, the rings are smaller than I remembered, certainly smaller than they sometimes felt. I think I'll keep them to remind me of where I've been. Cecelie says one day we'll go to Peru, see where the *chaquira* came from. I'd like that. I've never traveled, really. Amazing, isn't it? I've lived all over the country, but I've never really traveled. Just followed women around, waiting for them to love me. This time I'm not following. We're going together. I guess that's what you'd call progress. Or love.

"So, that's about it. I know I've already paid for my fifty-minute hour, but there's not much more to say. If we were friends, I'd promise to write. But I guess that's not part of the deal, is it?" The psychiatrist shakes her head gently. "No, I didn't think so. I will promise you this: I'll never forget you and when you look at the bead or see some woman trying to run up this damned hill, you'll remember, too. I know you're probably not supposed to, professional distancing or something, but you will."

Teddy Grayson stands and extends her right hand. "Goodbye, Phoenix. And good luck in Hawaii." After the door closes, she hangs the *chaquira* on her desk lamp. She switches on the light, watches the large bead chase shadows on the wall. She smiles. Phoenix Bay is right, she will remember.

From the plane's tiny window, Phoenix watches the ocean break through, silvery against the dawn. Down there, somewhere, on a cargo ship the Jeep is creeping toward Hawaii. Maybe she'll get to take it fishing after all. Hank Long would be pleased.

Folding up yesterday afternoon's *Examiner*, her eyes glance at the headline: TORRENTIAL RAINS HIT SAN FRANCISCO. Unseasonable, according to the report, although there's nothing really unseasonal about rain in December, just unexpected after eight years of drought. On their way to the airport, Rennie had insisted that the taxi driver wait while he ran back inside the house. "Forgot something," he'd said. He was gone only a minute, but long enough to return to the cab soaked and chilled, and as far as she could tell, empty-handed. Not that there was anything left in the house by then. Mr. Rizzo had taken the last of the furniture that morning and Carson's urn was safely packed in Rennie's carry-on bag. They'd arrived at the airport only to be told the plane was delayed more than an hour because of the rain. One hour, then two. While Phoenix and Cecelie paced, Rennie sat, shivering, his feet propped on his bags, reading the paper, apparently delighting in the local weather forecasts of a long, wet, and very dreary Christmas week. Maybe he was glad to be escaping, too. By the time they left San Francisco, it was past midnight.

Across the aisle, he's stretched out on the bank of empty seats, snoring softly. One arm drapes across his forehead, his hand dangles against the carpeting. Carson's gold Rolex shines. Rennie is a beautiful man, no longer the angry young rebel, but still beautiful. Cecelie stirs, the airplane's descent rousing her. She smiles at Phoenix. "Still no regrets?"

No regrets? Phoenix closes her eyes against the sunrise that the plane seems trying to outrun. For a moment, her mother dances across her mind, a porch swing creaks, ice tinkles against the side of a mason jar, and then as the light catches up with them, again, the vision fades. "Not a one," Phoenix says, climbing over Cecelie to stretch. "I'll wake Prince Charming."

Stroking a lock of dark curls off Rennie's forehead, she smiles as he opens his eyes, still blurry from the Valium. "Rennie, you've got to see this sunrise." Crossing the aisle, he kneels on the seat the way a child might, pressing his face close to the window. He turns back from the window and grins, as the sea blushes pink and an orange sun skims the horizon. "Beautiful," he says, watching until the plane turns, blocking their view.

A flight attendant, obviously tired and a little disheveled from the long Christmas Eve flight to Honolulu, passes through the aisles with a large, blue trash bag. Taking what is now yesterday's newspaper, Phoenix starts to hand it over, when Rennie's hand catches her wrist. "Let's keep it. For old time's sake."

Phoenix looks at him skeptically. Rennie is not a sentimental man. "What on earth for?"

Ignoring her, he beams at the woman with the trash bag. "I was just wondering, do you know how much rain fell in San Francisco last night?" The flight attendant smiles her bored, courtesy smile and disappears to find out. Rennie squirms out of the seat to take down the carry-on bag and tucks the newspaper inside, then turns to Phoenix. "Did I tell you that Lucas is going to be on the big island for the next month? I gave him our address, asked him to drop by for New Year's. You don't mind, do you?" In a moment the attendant returns with the weather report: Nearly an inch of rain fell overnight, with more predicted today. "Looks like it'll be a wet Christmas in San Francisco, sir. But the weather's been perfect in Honolulu. You've picked the right time to get away." Rennie nods.

"You know, Lucas always told me that the real problem with those early Light Walkers is that you can never get them closed when they're wet. A rather serious design defect, wouldn't you say?" Rennie stretches his arms back over his head and grins. Phoenix's eyes widen. How long was Rennie in the house? Two minutes, three at the most. Long enough to throw the switch to open the Light Walker. Long enough to pull Lucas's number off the control panel.

"Rennie, you didn't!" Phoenix jostles his shoulder.

Rennie winks. "You know, Phoenix, it's going to be a beautiful day in paradise. I can't say I'll miss all that rain and fog in San Francisco. Of course, we'll have to make up a new game. Hurricanes, maybe, or tidal waves? Or maybe I'll take up surfing. Or golf. What do you think?"

Before Phoenix can answer, Cecelie slips into the seat next to them. Amazingly, her head isn't throbbing. The sunlight catches her cheek, turning it warm and golden. "Perfect, isn't it?" She means the sunrise, the ocean, the outline of the island.

"Damned near," Rennie agrees, taking his sister's hand, "damned near."